The Scandalous Life of Nancy Randolph

Also by Kate Braithwaite

THE
SCANDALOUS LIFE
OF
NANCY
RANDOLPH

KATE BRAITHWAITE

LUME BOOKS
A JOFFE BOOKS COMPANY

LUME BOOKS
A JOFFE BOOKS COMPANY

Lume Books, London

A Joffe Books Company

www.lumebooks.co.uk

First published in Great Britain in 2024 by Lume Books

We love to hear from our readers!
Please email any feedback you have to: feedback@joffebooks.com

ISBN: 978-1-83901-574-8

This one is for you, Chris
I really think so.

Character List

- Mae
- Phebe

James, a footman

The Randolph/Tucker family in Williamsburg

St George Tucker

Lelia Tucker, his second wife

St George Tucker's stepsons, through his marriage to Frances Bland, the widow of John Randolph of Matoax:

- Richard Randolph, known as Dick
- Theodorick Randolph, known as Theo
- John Randolph of Roanoke, known as Jack

Fanny Tucker, one of several half-siblings to Dick, Theo and Jack, the daughter of St George Tucker and Frances Bland

The family at Bizarre

John St George Randolph, known as Saint, son of Dick and Judy Randolph

Theodorick Tudor Randolph, son of Dick and Judy Randolph

Anna Dudley, a cousin

Enslaved people at Bizarre

Sarah Elliot

Ben Elliot, Sarah's husband, and their children:

- Billy
- Lottie
- Sally

Syphax

Rachel, the overseer's woman

Sundry other characters

David Meade Randolph, husband to Molly Randolph

Randy and Mary Harrison of Glentivar, friends of Dick and
   Judy Randolph

Patsy Randolph, daughter of Thomas Jefferson, wife of Tom
   Randolph

Aunt Page, a busybody

Maria Peyton, friend of Judy Randolph and Fanny Tucker

John Brockenhurst, second husband of Gabriella Harvie

John Marshall, a lawyer

Patrick Henry, a lawyer

Gouverneur Morris, a statesman

Gouverneur Morris, his son

Mrs Pollock, a gentlewoman

Jane Pollock, her daughter

Part One

Part One

Phebe

She'd live out her days on the Tuckahoe Plantation, that's what the girl believed—until God, or Mr. Randolph, had other ideas. That's when she learned she belonged to people, not to a place. That's when Old Cilla made her promise to make the best of whatever came her way. It was the way the world worked—unkind, or sometimes plain cruel, especially for the women. A girl like her? She'd never have no say in what happened.

But there wasn't much Phebe didn't see.

What went on with Miss Nancy—at Bizarre, at Glentivar—had the whole state of Virginia talking—Whites and Blacks, rich folks and poor. Only Phebe saw what unfolded between her mistress and those three brothers. Only she knew their secrets. And their lies.

Couple of times, Miss Nancy's sister moved as if she might ask. Nothing more than a leaning in, a parting of lips—but Phebe, trained from birth to observe and anticipate, she saw it. Miss Judy kept silent though, and for the longest time, it seemed the truth would not come out.

Except the scandal never did leave Miss Nancy. It lingered, like the stink from a skunk.

None of them had the life they expected.

Chapter One

Tuckahoe, Virginia. March 1789

Death brought the family home to Tuckahoe.

Carriages swept up the lengthy driveway, and the plantation house echoed with the knock of hard heels, the thud of trunks and the opening and closing of doors. New scents filled the hallways. Rosemary and lavender, musk, cloves and bayberry.

Nancy, allotted a stool at the foot of Mother's bed, reached out and gripped her older sister Judy's hand. They were close in age, sixteen and fourteen—old enough to watch their mother leave them. Father sat by Mother's pillow, head bowed, a bead of sweat sliding from his temple. Opposite him, her oldest sisters, Molly and Lizzie, watched Mother intently, their eyes shifting from face to chest. Nancy turned to Judy, but her eyes were closed, and her lips moved in prayer. Nancy didn't want to pray. She wanted to send her stool flying and run from the room.

The heat from the fire, combined with the warm breath and

bodies of so many family members, made her skin itch. She counted five jugs of narcissi. They were Mother's favorite, but in the claustrophobic heat, their yellow jauntiness turned her stomach. William's silent weeping didn't help. She glanced at Father, saw his jaw tighten with disgust at her brother's weakness. William was nearly twenty. A man. Never man enough for Father though. Tom, a year older, didn't cry but kept clenching and unclenching his hands. Nancy lifted her chin to gaze at a thin gap in the window drapes. The bones of her neck shifted and settled. She willed her mind to be as empty as the blue sky outside. If only she could pray as Judy could.

Of the children still at home, Judy was the sensible one. Where her sister sought approval and tried to do everything right, Nancy questioned and tested. Warned not to touch a hot kettle one day, Judy clasped her hands behind her back and nodded while Nancy sucked on the burn on her forefinger for a week. Everyone agreed on it. Judy was more obedient. Better. Less prone to hiding behind the smokehouse reading novels.

Nancy forced herself to look at the woman in the bed. Anne Cary Randolph had grown thin these last few months. Her collarbones were hollowed out, the ropey muscles in her neck protruded. Sharp lines creased her cheeks and dragged at the corners of a mouth unable to smile through the pain. Her eyes were closed. Mother had green eyes with a dark rim, eyes that could silence a room, discipline a slave, chastise a child or warn a husband but also glow with warm approval. Those eyes.

More silence. Puffs of air and supplication escaped Judy's lips. Lizzie leaned in. They waited, like drops of rain quivering on a pane of glass.

"She's gone," Molly said.

That night, in their bedroom, Nancy and Judy scratched their names and the date—March 16, 1789—on the windowpane before curling up in each other's arms, tears on their pillow and in each other's hair.

The women of the family spent the first days sewing mourning clothes and to-ing and fro-ing between the kitchen and the storehouse. It would not do, Lizzie said, to let Old Cilla think grief distracted the family from plantation business. Molly and Lizzie cleaned their mother's body and laid her out in the parlor, sending Nancy and Judy scuttling for pitchers of water, towels, combs, rosemary leaves and tansy. More family and neighbors visited. In the gloom cast by dark walnut paneling, turned mirrors, and pulled drapes, Mother's face seemed to belong to someone else. Her high forehead, thin nose and cheeks turned porcelain white.

"Is she cold?" Nancy's ten-year-old brother, John, found his answer in the force of Father's hand across the back of his head. After that, they all stayed quiet.

"Naturally, your father will remarry," Aunt Page declared as the family walked back to the house after Mother's interment. She spoke to Molly, but plenty loud enough for Nancy to hear. "With my sister in the ground, the older girls must look to the future."

The Tuckahoe Plantation, one of Virginia's finest, sprawled over twenty-five-thousand acres of land dedicated to tobacco and wheat, worked by more than two hundred slaves. Aunt Page, their mother's youngest sister, was a frequent visitor. She was younger even than Molly, and by far the most approachable of Nancy's many aunts and uncles.

"Why would he remarry?" Nancy pulled her gaze from the bare fields waiting for tobacco seedlings and saw the older women exchange glances. "It's not a stupid question; Patsy's father has not."

"Apart from the obvious reasons? Or are you too young to comprehend me?"

"I'm not ignorant!"

"If you say so."

Nancy pulled up short, her hands on her hips.

"Please use the brains God gave you," her aunt said. "Think of the plantation. What happens now? Who looks after the slaves? Who takes the key for the storehouse? Who cares for the sick and knows when to call the doctor? Who runs the dairy? Tends the vegetable garden? The smokehouse?"

Nancy rolled her eyes—Mother had never set foot in the vegetable garden—but her expression only set Molly off.

"Our aunt is right. Who makes sure the chickens and the pigs are fed? Who checks the chimneys are swept and the glasses clean? Who salts the meat and dips the candles? Who counts the linens and orders the clothing for the five of you still at home? Every plantation needs a mistress. Tuckahoe is no different."

"What do you say, Judy?" Nancy looked over her shoulder, but her sister was gazing down the line of mourners trailing back to the house across ground still hard from a deep, late winter frost.

"What do I think about what?" Judy's cheeks were blotched in pink. Grief brought out the angles in her face, particularly the high cheekbones and short straight nose all the Randolph daughters shared.

"Oh, nothing. Or nothing to worry about now. You know, you'll need a cold compress before you meet him."

"Nancy! I don't think of such matters at a time like this."

"If you say so. Take my advice though. There's no question your Dick Randolph is the tallest and most handsome of Mr. Tucker's stepsons."

8

It seemed the whole of Richmond had turned out for the funeral, and others had traveled from as far away as Williamsburg and Charlottesville. Mother had been the oldest of nine siblings, and Virginia was full of families that had intermarried in the century since their forebears had sailed to the New World from England. Carys, Randolphs, Pages, Blands—a tapestry of cousins with familiar names indicative of lineage and privilege. Molly and Lizzie were hard-pressed to find places for their guests to sleep, even in a house as large as Tuckahoe, and Father shared his room along with everyone else. That night, the Randolph children gave up their beds and lay down on mattresses, cloaks, and blankets. They slept in chairs and under tables, wherever a scrap of space could be claimed. But before rest, there was hospitality. Their slaves laid out the dining room with pork with pease pudding, roasted woodcock and mutton ragout. The men gathered there first, with the womenfolk keeping to the parlor, but as the rum and brandy began to flow, the younger crowd relaxed and mingled in the Great Hall, while older men grumbled about the price of tobacco, and married women discussed their children.

Judy told herself not to seek out Dick Randolph, even as she scanned each room for his curling brown hair and wide smile. She thought of his letters, tied in red ribbon and locked in a wooden box beneath her bed. The key hung on a chain around her neck, keeping them safe from Nancy's prying eyes.

She felt him before she saw him. Dick touched her arm, his breath warmed her ear. "I'm so sorry for your loss, Miss Randolph."

"Thank you." She offered her hand and for a moment, thought he might raise it to his lips.

"We all wished to convey our condolences." Dick gestured toward his younger brothers. "The loss of our own mother last year is still hard to bear, especially for Jack."

"It must be. Now, I begin to know what you have been through. I worry for all my younger siblings."

"They're too young to be without a mother. You know, my father died when I was five. I barely remember him, and Theo and Jack not at all."

"It will be the same for Harriet and Jenny. John and Jane will remember her, but—oh, I don't know how we will go on." Her voice broke. She took the handkerchief Dick handed her and pressed it to her face, struggling for composure.

"Dear God, I have made you upset! That wasn't my intention! Please." He gripped her elbow. "Let's step outside for a moment. The fresh air will help."

"Where do things stand with those two?" Aunt Page asked as Judy and Dick Randolph slipped out through the west door. "They must have met less frequently since Mr. Tucker moved the family to Williamsburg."

Nancy nodded. When Dick's mother was alive, the family—comprising her three sons with John Randolph, and another five children from her remarriage to Mr. Tucker—had lived at Matoax, a large plantation south of Richmond. Dick Randolph had ridden to Tuckahoe regularly. Coming to see Tom and William, he'd claimed.

"Mr. Tucker has his eye on them." Aunt Page tipped her head toward a tall, hawk-nosed man with sandy hair swept back from his high forehead, standing at a nearby window.

"You know he wrote to Mother?" In the fall, after the move to Williamsburg, Dick had declared himself to Judy and requested an interview with Father. Judy shared little, but their mother never shied away from expressing her opinions about her daughters' duties and marriage prospects. "She replied immediately."

"Not favorably, I imagine."

"No. She said Judy was too young. But Dick was allowed to write. She had to show Father her replies."

"Your mother was sixteen when she married your father. Only seventeen when Molly was born. She was adamant Molly didn't marry until she was eighteen at least." They both glanced at Molly's husband, David Meade Randolph. Nancy had been known to imitate his braying laugh, although never in front of his wife. "And then she tried to make Lizzie wait until she was twenty but … well, let's just say your sister was determined."

Determined. That was one word for it. Their brothers had taken great pleasure in teasing Nancy and Judy about how Lizzie ensured her marriage took place.

"She receives letters from Dick Randolph then?" Aunt Page continued. "And responds?"

"I believe so, but don't ask me for details. She's so secretive and dull about it. She barely lets me mention his name. If I was as lucky as she, I'd never stop talking about it."

"That I can believe."

Nancy shrugged this off. "I wonder what will happen between them. Now Mother is gone."

But Aunt Page bustled off without bothering to reply, and Nancy took a last glance outside. Judy and Dick Randolph were so disappointing. They remained within clear sight, sitting on a bench with space for at least two people to fit between them. It wasn't the time or place for anything more, but she longed to see some token of their romance—their fingers touching, their heads leaning in. How else were they supposed to tell each other they were drowning in love?

"I'm sorry to be here in such sad circumstances, Miss Nancy." Mr. Tucker, Dick's stepfather, offered her his arm. "You were brave today, as I hear you have been every day since your mother's passing. I cannot mend your pain, but its point will blunt in time."

"Will it? Is it strange of me to hope it will not? The idea of *not* hurting at this loss seems even worse than living with it."

"There are as many ways to grieve as there are mourners." He patted her hand. "One day at a time."

They spoke for a few moments of Williamsburg before Nancy excused herself to see how her little sisters fared. Her face grew warm as she approached Dick's younger brothers standing by the arch to the south hallway. Long-limbed and awkward-looking, Jack Randolph was a year older than her—a pale, thin youth with a small, girlish mouth and a dimple on his chin. Theo, the middle brother, was shorter, thickset, with a heavy jaw. More handsome than Jack, although nothing like as attractive as Dick, Theo pushed a hand through his dark hair as Nancy passed. Did their eyes follow her? Then the sound of Jenny crying reached her. She swooped down to where the little girl grumbled by the sitting-room fireplace, took her in her arms and murmured a favorite lullaby. All thought of the Randolph brothers vanished in concern for her motherless sibling.

In the following weeks, Nancy and Judy spoke of their mother often. Without her, the house was altered. Mother was never one for outward affection, but they missed her presence, from her critical eye upon their clothes and hair, to her many rules and precepts. Nancy longed to think of other things and push the hurt and strangeness into a corner, but reminders were everywhere.

It was soon obvious that Old Cilla managed the household well enough for Molly and Lizzie to return to their own homes. With their absence, the girls' days lacked structure. They felt it, like a loosening of stays or of hair unpinned.

Spring turned to summer. Dick Randolph became a frequent visitor.

Chapter Two

Judy found the late-August heat oppressive. When the family dined in the winter, sharp gusts of cold air assaulted them whenever the slaves brought in a new dish. On summer nights like this, those chill days could not come fast enough.

Tom was away at Monticello visiting the Jeffersons, but William, Dick, Judy and Nancy were at the table, squinting in the candlelight, while Father brooded at its head. A neighbor, Colonel Harvie, had joined them with his daughter, Gabriella, a girl Judy's age. Having guests made her more than usually self-conscious about Dick. Everything he did was magnified as if she were as responsible for his words as she was for her own.

"And so, I'm back, staying at Matoax for the next few months," he explained. "Although my stepfather, Mr. Tucker, doesn't believe our future is in the land, I'm sorry to say."

"Tucker's a good man," said Father. "But when all's said and done, he's a lawyer and not a Randolph. Not born to the land as we are. We are family. Only distant cousins, yes, but descended from the same

Warwickshire Randolphs, and we have stewarded Virginia honorably for over one hundred years. The land has made us who we are."

William cleared his throat. "Tobacco isn't the crop it was though, Father. I heard—"

"Don't speak on subjects you know nothing about."

William's face crumpled, and he pushed the meat on his plate with his fork.

"What do you say, William? Shall we bag some rabbit tomorrow?" asked Dick. "We could be up at dawn and show Tom we can do just as well without him. When does he come back from Monticello and charming the sophisticated Miss Patsy?"

Nancy giggled, but Judy frowned. To support William was one thing; to promote gossip about Tom in front of the Harvies was quite another. "He should be back tomorrow," she said. "Mr. Jefferson has taken an interest in Tom. It's an honor to the family."

"The Randolph family doesn't need honors from anyone." Father wiped his thin lips on his napkin. "I've a great deal of respect for Thomas Jefferson, but he's our equal, not our better. Remember, he spent his youth here. Learned his letters in the same schoolhouse where you and your siblings learned yours. Our families have looked out for each other for generations. Tom would be a good and fitting match for Patsy Jefferson, if he likes the look of her. It's time for some weddings in the family, I think. You can't live here at Tuckahoe all your days."

Judy saw Dick's fist clench on his fork. Father's approval of their match was obvious, but Mr. Tucker remained to be convinced.

A few weeks later, Dick arrived at Tuckahoe unexpectedly. He threw himself from his horse and stormed into the house, calling Judy's name. She ignored Nancy's raised eyebrows and rushed downstairs, flush with thankfulness that Father was not at home.

"What's happened? What's wrong?"

"It's exactly as I feared." He paced the hallway. "Tucker received your father's permission but will write and request we delay."

"Delay? Why?"

"Oh, because I am not steady enough. I lack purpose. I'm uncertain of my future plans."

"But that's not true!" She longed to grasp his hands.

"He wants to know how I'll support my wife and, in due course, our family. As if Matoax were nothing. As if I'm incapable of running a plantation. As if everyone must be a lawyer just because he is."

"How ridiculous!" She caught his arm. "And so terribly unfair."

He stilled, and his gaze fell on her lips. Judy's eyes widened as he pulled her to him and clamped his lips on hers.

She registered pain—the crushing of her lips against her teeth—then shock at the force of his tongue in her mouth. She stiffened, thought to pull away, but Dick drew back first. He was on the verge of tears. Real tears.

That changed everything. She pushed her lips to his. Again, Dick pulled back, a question in his eyes. She knew what he asked, and it might be wrong, but suddenly, it didn't feel wrong. How could it be wrong when they were promised to each other? Father approved of Dick, and Dick needed her. Besides, it had worked for Lizzie.

"Wait here," she whispered.

Nancy was where she'd left her, sitting by the window with her nose in a book.

"I need your help. We—Dick and I—we need your help."

"Why? What's happened?"

"We've had a disappointment. We must be alone together and

16

uninterrupted. You understand, don't you? You know we love each other."

"Of course I do. You belong together."

"Oh, thank you for saying so!" She pulled Nancy to her and kissed her cheek. "I'm going to take him to the river. To our quiet spot. I need you to stand lookout for us. Say you'll do it. We mustn't be disturbed."

Nancy tied on her bonnet and followed her sister and Dick Randolph outside. Dick smiled and held the door for her, so normal and composed that had she not seen the color in Judy's cheeks or heard the urgency in her voice, she might have thought nothing unusual was afoot. They walked unhurriedly, but with purpose, avoiding the kitchen house and Plantation Street, turning instead to the fields and the path to the river. A group of slave children returning from the fields came toward them. One boy limped along behind while the others hurried past with their eyes on the ground. Dick stopped him.

"Where are you hurt?"

"Just my ankle, sir. It ain't nothing."

"Make sure you show it to your mama. And mind she takes you up to the house to see Miss Judy here if it's not better by morning." He patted the boy on the head, and they walked on.

"That was kind," Nancy murmured. "You will be a good master."

"I intend to be more than that. Judy knows. We will free our slaves." He stopped and looked back. They were beyond the view of anyone at the house. "Walk a little behind us, Nancy."

Heat rose in her face as they moved ahead. Dick tucked Judy's arm through his. Heads bent together, they spoke in whispers. They paused beside a wheel of exposed roots of a bitternut hickory pulled from the ground in a recent storm. Nancy thought of speaking, but what could be said? She turned her back and stared up the path back to the house.

Time slowed. She heard them stride out across the grass to the riverbank, but soon they were out of earshot, and other noises pricked her consciousness. A breeze rustled the leaves of a nearby line of trees. Birds called. She watched thin curls of pale clouds drift across the sky. What were they doing? It wasn't her concern. But suspicion made her lightheaded. Judy was such a good girl, such a determinedly good girl. Wasn't she?

Nancy had to know. She grabbed her skirts and stepped off the path. She navigated the long grass, moisture seeping through her shoes and stockings. Where the grass met a broad swathe of buttonbush covered in white pincushion flowers, she hesitated. She should go back and wait. She should leave them in peace down there, on that soft bank behind the buttonbush, with just space enough for two people to lie together.

Instead, she found a break in the bushes and pushed her way inside. She stepped warily, knowing the ground fell away on the other side, where rocks and broken earth made a wall above the riverbank. She pushed through the foliage until she saw them. Already, Judy lay on her back with her hips tilted up and her boots hooked around Dick Randolph's naked back. Her sister's eyes were closed, her eyebrows knitted in concentration—or discomfort—impossible to say which. Nancy turned her eyes on Dick—on his shoulder blades, on the dark hair on his thighs. She watched his muscles contract. And then he gasped and moaned.

Nancy bit her lip and stumbled backward. She waited, holding her breath until, hearing nothing, she judged it safe to creep away through the shrubs. Back in the pasture, she grabbed her skirts up above her knees and ran in great bounds through the grass to where they had left her. Everything was as it had been. Nothing was the same. She struggled for breath and composure, knowing if she saw anyone, she'd be unable to nod, far less speak. When at last Judy and Dick reappeared, Nancy set off toward the house, too fast for them to catch her. She couldn't bear to see their faces. She feared her own face would tell them what she'd seen. The image of Judy's boots and Dick Randolph's naked skin danced in her eyes, impossible to blink out of sight.

In the safety of the room she shared with Judy, Nancy pulled a shawl of her mother's from a chair. Wrapping herself in it, she lay on the bed with her back to the door and sobbed. Judy. Her good sister, Judy. This was all because Mother was gone. Memories of her—her eyes, her face, her voice—produced another wave of salty tears.

But she couldn't cry forever. The pillow grew cold beneath her cheek. Nancy opened her eyes and felt the weight of her damp lashes. Her nose was blocked, and her lips stung. Heroines in novels always benefited from tears, but crying for too long only made her head ache, and besides, the last thing she wanted to display now was a blotched and puffy face. She dragged her sleeve across her eyes and sat up. The bed creaked, but she heard another noise. A shuffling sound. From below.

Nancy dropped to the floor at once.

"Phebe!"

Jenny's nursemaid lay curled under the bed with her fist in her mouth.

"What on earth are you doing? What has happened?" The younger girl did nothing but shake, so she wriggled her way under the bed and rubbed her shoulder. "You must tell me. Let me help you."

19

Phebe, one of Old Cilla's granddaughters, was two years younger than Nancy, her thin face as familiar as her own in the looking glass. Years ago, Cilla had nursed Molly and Lizzie. Then Phebe's mother, Sal, had cared for Tom, William, Judy and Nancy. In the nursery, Sal's daughters, Mae and Phebe, felt like part of the family. Now, Cilla ran the house, Sal managed the laundry and Mae was nursemaid to Jane and John while Phebe tended to little Jenny.

"I must go," Phebe said after Nancy coaxed her out from under the bed. "I shouldn't be here. I only came in for a moment. I heard you on the stairs and tried to hide. I'll go now." She edged to the door, her eyes sliding away.

"Not until you tell me what has happened. Has someone upset you? Tell me who."

"No one knows. I promised not to say." Her face crumpled. "It's Mae."

Phebe's sister was expecting a child. Nancy had seen her the day before, walking down Plantation Street with her hand on her back, and marveled that the woman's long thin legs could support the swell of her belly. "She had the baby?"

"It died, Miss Nancy." Tears spilled down Phebe's cheeks. "Came out blue with the cord around its neck. And then Mae just bled away from us. Mama and I watched it. Tried everything. But she's gone." Her shoulders shook with the effort of speaking. Nancy drew her down to perch on the bed. The younger girl's frame was narrow, her body stiff to the touch.

"Hush. Take your time. I'm so sorry to hear about Mae."

"I'm sorry too, Miss Nancy. I don't want to be no trouble."

Nancy reached under her pillow and pulled out a handkerchief. "Take this. Sit as long as you need. I'll go and see Cilla. Has my father been told?"

20

Phebe shook her head. "The overseer said he'd see the master this afternoon when he gets back. There wasn't time this morning. You won't speak to anyone till then, will you? Mama'll say I let her down. I promised to work hard and hold my tongue. She's mighty broken up."

"I promise. I know how you feel, a little. It is not so long since I lost my mother after all. I don't know when it will feel better; I wish I did. But your family will help you, Phebe. And you will help them."

"Thank you, miss. I'll be fine now." She stood and held the crumpled handkerchief out for a moment before shaking her head and cramming it into her apron pocket. "I'll see it's cleaned and returned."

"Keep it. Keep it and know I am thinking of you. You can hide in here any time you need to."

"I'm not sure Miss Judy would agree, miss. She'd say it's not proper. And she'd be right."

Phebe looked anxious all over again, but Nancy waved away her concerns. "Leave Miss Judy to me," she said. "Besides—she has other things on her mind these days."

Chapter Three

On New Year's Day, Nancy followed Judy and Father down the wide mahogany staircase at Tuckahoe. She took in Dick's upturned face and confident smile. His eyes were fixed on his bride, but Nancy's face warmed when she saw the younger Randolph brothers both looking her way. She stood straighter and concentrated on her sister's ivory-clad back. In the months since that summer day by the riverbank, Judy had told her nothing, but what else could have caused Mr. Tucker's change of heart? There were long conversations between Judy and Father in his study and a visit made to the Tuckers in Williamsburg. On their return, she loitered in the north hallway but heard nothing. It gnawed at her that Judy was so unconfiding. Did she fear Nancy would shame her? If she thought so, she was wrong. Nancy admired passion. She admired Dick and Judy for making their wedding happen. To her mind, the end more than justified the means.

The ceremony was mercifully short. With the Great Hall swollen with relatives come to witness Judy and Dick take their vows, the air was hot and close. Nancy didn't hear a word from *The Book of*

Common Prayer, wishing to rush the day forward to the dancing that would take place when the wedding feast was over.

"Mr. Tucker thinks it's too much," she whispered to Patsy Jefferson as they idled at the foot of the staircase, watching friends and family feast on venison, quail and oysters. "You can see it in his face, although he'd never say it. But I suppose it is nothing to what you knew in Paris."

"It wasn't all balls and social events. I was at school a great deal of the time."

"In a convent. I can barely imagine it! I think I'd be terrified!"

Patsy laughed. She was taller than Nancy, with enviable auburn hair. "It was far from exciting. You imagine too much, as usual. Paris was an education in many ways, but I'm glad to be back in Virginia."

"And being courted by Tom?"

"Hush!"

"What? He's my brother after all! You are practically my older sister. Or you could be."

"You're making me blush. I barely know him."

Nancy scooped a handful of sugared almonds from a tray. "Patsy, he visited with you again over Christmas. Anyone with eyes in their head can see he does nothing but look our way." She nodded to where Tom stood with a group of men, including Dick's brothers. All were deep in conversation, but their eyes repeatedly strayed to the two girls by the staircase.

"I could say the same to you about Theo and Jack Randolph. In a year or two, it will be your turn."

"By which time, you will already be married and giving me nieces and nephews to come and sing to."

"Nancy!"

They cut short their laughter as Tom approached.

23

"Miss Jefferson. I wondered if you might enjoy a little fresh air before the dancing commences. Your father spoke of our school-room on my recent visit. Might you like to visit it, while the light is still good?"

Patsy said nothing. Her lips parted as if to reply, but then she simply placed her hand on his arm, and they walked away. Nancy, abandoned at the staircase, chewed on her almonds, wished herself older and her hair any color other than its natural brown.

The dancing, at least, did not disappoint. In a house filled with cousins and uncles, there was no shortage of partners.

"You have a fine mastery of this art, Miss Randolph," said one of her father's friends, Mr. Morris. He danced impeccably, notwithstanding his wooden leg, a circumstance she speculated about furiously while he talked to her of an impending trip to Europe. In due course, he bowed and gave up his place to Theo Randolph, and she was happy with the exchange—at least until she discovered that Theo was a much less accomplished dancer, even with his advantage of two legs. Still, he gazed at her in open admiration, doing a great deal to make up for her displeasure at his clumsy feet.

"You will miss your sister, I imagine," he said.

"It will be strange without her. And quiet."

"But perhaps you'll visit? Stay with them at Matoax?"

"I certainly hope to! It's not far from Molly's plantation, and we have several cousins who live nearby."

"Indeed. I think Dick plans a merry life for himself and Judy. I hope to be there often." Theo's eyes glittered, and Nancy wondered if he'd been sampling the madeira. It wouldn't surprise her. Already, Cousin Archie had staggered into a side table and been sent outside for some fresh air.

"Monopolizing my new sister, Theo?" Dick appeared, smiling broadly. "Off with you. Go and see if you can make Jack do something other than lean against the doorframe as if he's holding the house up. Get a drink in him. It's my turn to dance with Nancy."

With a nod to Randy Harrison and Cousin Mary, the other couple in their set, Dick displaced his brother and took her hands.

"You look remarkably handsome, sister." Dick had no difficulty keeping his eyes on her and his steps neatly in time to the music.

"Thank you, sir. I might point out that you are the only one of my brothers to make such a kind remark."

He let out a crack of laughter. "Well, Tom is too busy pursuing Patsy Jefferson, and William is such a stuffed shirt, I doubt he's ever paid a young lady a compliment."

"Whereas you are quite the expert?"

"You wound me, Miss Randolph. I've seen a little of the world, it is true. And charm is never lost on the charming. I imagine you'll break a few hearts in a year or so."

"A year or so? I am fifteen years old, you know, not twelve."

"Don't worry, Nancy." Dick lowered his voice. "No one would ever think you were twelve."

She found Tuckahoe dull without Judy and the possibility of visits from Dick and his younger brothers. Archie Randolph visited on one vague pretext after another, but his interest, flattering though it was, didn't light any fires in her. With Mother gone, her father seemed less anchored to the house. She ate meals with her younger siblings and passed the winter reading books and sewing. She did her best to oversee the kitchen and the storehouse, and although she and Cilla both knew who was truly managing things, appearances were maintained, and the house functioned without a hitch. After months of begging, Father agreed to promote Phebe out of the nursery and allowed Nancy to train her as her maid. They spent hours together in front of the looking glass, torturing her hair into different styles and working on alterations to dresses and hats. Mostly, though, she was lonely. Snow blanketed the roads. Trees were sharply bare. Cold air pulsed from every windowpane. She yearned for something to lift her spirits.

Tom married Patsy Jefferson in the parlor at Monticello in late February. Patsy wore a bronze ball gown—brought back from Paris, the finest dress Nancy ever laid eyes on—and the couple were entirely enamored with one another. She watched the way they touched: his hand on her lower back, her fingers finding his, a touch to his cheek, the firmness of his hold on her waist as they danced.

Judy and Dick didn't attend, but Theo was there, and Nancy was thirsty for news. "Have you visited them at Matoax? I long to see the house. Judy's own household. It makes me smile to think on it."

"They're certainly busy. New furniture arrives daily. Carpets, pillows, and a great deal of other fripperies I can't even name. Dick has style, I'll give him that."

"And Judy? Is she well?"

"Yes, yes." She raised her eyebrows, compelling him to say more. "In truth, I barely caught sight of her. I expect she was busy with the storehouse and what-not. Not my province. Dick and I were out hunting every morning, you know. I look forward to more of the same when I return to Virginia. Just as soon as my studies are complete."

"My father told me Mr. Tucker hopes you'll take up medicine."

"Pshaw! Lord knows I respect my stepfather, but do you think he has any notion of the degree of work a man is expected to do to become a doctor? Consider all the traipsing across the countryside a medical man does. No. He's been a valued father to us, but he's not our blood. He cannot understand, as Dick, Jack and I do, that the land is our future, not some so-called profession. He's all about learning, is Tucker. That might suit Jack—or Dick at a push—but it's not for me, and he needs to recognize it."

"You're not a reader then?"

"Not a bit! Yet old man Tucker proses on and on. 'The boy who diligently attends his studies,' he's always saying, 'will always be attentive and diligent in the larger theater of the world.'"

"But you attend Columbia? What do you do in New York if not work on your studies?"

His grin made her blush. "I could curl your hair with some of my stories."

Happily, Aunt Page chose that moment to draw her away, although her chatter didn't please Nancy any better.

"Judy is quite the lady of the house, child though she is. The bills they've racked up already must be quite shocking. Furniture shipped across the oceans, Dick told my husband. I hope the plantation can support it."

"They have a great deal of land, do they not?"

"Lord, yes, but is it profitable? That's why Mr. Tucker wanted them to delay. But they forced his hand in the oldest and simplest of ways."

"Judy will have a child?"

"Yes. She's to go to Molly when her time nears. Judy will need her."

Nancy said nothing. Childbirth was a mystery. Only married women knew its secrets.

"But what your older sisters and I really want to know," said Aunt Page, "is how much time your father spends with the Harvies?"

"A fair amount, but then he and Colonel Harvie are good friends."

"And how friendly is he with Miss Gabriella?"

"What would Father want with Gabriella?" Her aunt's eyebrows rose. "Oh!"

"This won't be the last wedding we meet at this year, Nancy. Mark my words."

Chapter Four

Judy had thought to be a mother by the time her Cousin Mary's wedding to Randy took place. Instead, she spent most of it trying not to cry. It wasn't her first public outing since losing the baby, but the crowd and the prospect of so many familiar faces intimidated her. Father, for one. Would he mention their loss? Dick had written, and Father expressed condolences but sent no separate message for her. She supposed all her sisters knew. Molly was kind but pitying. David, Molly's husband, had made himself invisible in his own home. Dick had wept and held Judy close. His love poured strength into her bones, and she imagined them forever bound in tragedy. But it didn't last. In the time it took to travel back to Matoax, his grief evaporated. Dick picked up their life as if nothing of significance had happened. A dull, cold ache crept up her arms and had not left her. She thought she might never feel warm again.

"No oysters," murmured Dick into her ear. "A shame, but no surprise."

Mary and Randy's wedding wasn't as lavish as their own had

been. Clifton was a grand property, but it was an open secret that the Harrison family was selling land to pay off debts. They didn't try to impress their guests with oysters and venison, and Judy admired them for it, whatever Dick might say. She had learned a great deal about him in recent months. Only a few days ago, they'd endured harsh words from Mr. Tucker, words it clearly pained that amiable man to pronounce. Dick hung his head like a sulky child and threw a vase at the wall the moment Tucker's carriage rolled away.

"Judy!" A familiar voice brought her back to the present.

"Patsy Randolph! How are you, sister?" As the ceremony concluded, conversations broke out, and a band in the corner struck up a lively tune. Judy kissed her sister-in-law and held her by the shoulders. "Don't answer that. I see married life suits you."

Patsy's cheeks grew rosy. "Your brother is most affectionate."

"You are not … ?" Judy couldn't say the words.

Patsy tossed her curls. "No. Although I hope it will not be long. Tom tells me he plans to take his responsibilities seriously in that regard."

"Patsy!"

"Is my wife shocking you with some gossip, sister?" Tom kissed her on the cheek and placed his arm around Patsy's waist.

"Not in the least. I was merely complimenting her on her looks, but she dismisses all my words as flattery."

"Hmm. I wish I could say the same for you, Judy."

"Tom!"

"What? She looks a little pale, that's all I'm saying."

"You are saying too much. Ignore the brute, Judy. I think you look well. And your gown is most becoming."

30

"Thank you, Patsy." She couldn't look at Tom. "If you'll excuse me, I must congratulate Cousin Mary."

She moved away, but not quickly enough to avoid hearing her brother's voice once more. "What? She looks positively haggard. I hope that lazy dog Randolph is looking after her properly."

Every muscle in Judy's back tensed. In another setting, she would have given Tom a dressing-down for his insults. She scanned the crowd for her husband. He was talking to Nancy and laughing, as carefree as any young man in the room.

Nancy smiled up at Dick as he whispered about Gabriella Harvie. "She'll turn milk sour in a few years, I've seen that type of girl all too often."

"Surely, Father can see that if you can? I can't abide the thought of her in my mother's room. Tell me you don't think he'll do it. How can I share my home with her? She can't be a mother to me, and heaven knows, I've no shortage of sisters."

"True. But I don't see Gabriella getting the better of you, Miss Nancy, and besides, you'll be setting up your own household with some young dog soon."

"Will I though? Do you see suitors elbowing their way across the floor to pay homage and claim my hand then? For I see no one."

"Surely, Archie will be by your side any moment. I can't think what's keeping him."

"Can't you? He will feed his belly and quench his thirst first. He might imagine himself in love, but believe me, he thinks of nothing and no one until his stomach is satisfied."

"Do you see through us all, as you see through Archie? No," he raised both hands, "don't answer that."

31

Nancy dropped her gaze. "Your brothers Theo and Jack do not attend today?"

"Looking to enslave all the Randolph brothers are you now?"

"No!" She saw the amused sparkle in Dick's eye and laughed. "You are unkind to tease me so. I'm simply making proper conversation. Are your brothers busy with their studies?"

"Jack is, to a degree. But Theo?" Dick shook his head. "I enjoyed myself at his age and certainly kicked up the traces now and then. But let's just say Theo may be a little too wild for his own good."

Nancy and her father were silent in their carriage as it rolled and rattled through the darkness to Tuckahoe. She had much to think about. Judy didn't look well, and there was no sign she was carrying a child. Her sister was not happy and perhaps never had been, at least not in the way Patsy so evidently was. Dick, on the other hand, was as relaxed and charming as ever. His brother might not be her ideal suitor, but Theo's absence disappointed her, never mind Dick's commentary. He wasn't an accomplished dancer or conversationalist, but he was younger than General Henry Lee, a widower in his late thirties, recently introduced by her father in a suspiciously friendly manner. The general had become a frequent visitor at Tuckahoe. On his last visit, she'd been directed to show him their herb garden. He was vastly knowledgeable about horticulture, she'd learned. It was a shame he was not so well acquainted with the art of charming a young lady. He was old, boring and not dangerous in the least. Theo, on the other hand? He might be a bit of a blockhead, a little wild even, but was that the worst thing in the world? Mary's brother Archie paid his usual attentions at the wedding, but no one could consider him handsome, no matter how amiable he was. And he had warm, sweaty hands. Theo didn't dance terribly well, but she didn't flinch when he took her hand.

Did Gabriella Harvie flinch when asked to dance by Father? The consensus of the Randolph sisters present at Clifton was she did not. Concerns were expressed in whispers between bowed bonnets and the kissing of cheeks as the wedding party came to an end. Under the rumble of coach wheels and the stamp of hooves, they all agreed—his interest was fixed and likely reciprocated.

"I expect you to write and let me know of any developments," murmured Molly, her lips half-pressed to Nancy's cheek as she bade her farewell. "This concerns you most."

"I know it. But what can be done?"

"Very little, I imagine," whispered Lizzie. She pulled her into a close embrace. "You must be prepared."

"I don't know how you'll bear it." Judy's head was bowed. Nancy couldn't see her eyes and hadn't managed a single private word with her.

No wonder she spent the drive home fretting. She'd write to Aunt Page to try and learn what had happened to Judy. With that decided, she turned her thoughts to Gabriella Harvie. The idea of her moving into Tuckahoe as her stepmother sat like a rock in her stomach. Gabriella was pretty, certainly, but also waspish, her brittle smile often the prelude to a sting. In the darkness, Nancy shook her head. Their older brothers and sisters would help. There would need to be visits, long visits. Gabriella would not leave her to manage things with the slaves, and there was only one real path open if she wanted to leave Tuckahoe. She needed to marry. She bit her lip and glared at the shadowy outline of her father opposite her in the carriage. Was he dreaming of Gabriella Harvie? Worse, was he lusting after Gabriella Harvie? Nancy shifted uncomfortably. At sixteen, Judy had met Dick Randolph, a handsome, charming older son from one of the best branches of the family in all Virginia.

Where was Nancy's Dick Randolph? A loud sigh escaped her, stirring her father.

"Not sleeping yet? I should have asked the Harvies to travel with us."

She said nothing, thankful for the darkness of the coach, but Father was not satisfied.

"What do you say, Nancy? I only wish I'd thought of doing so earlier. A fine young woman, Miss Harvie. Wise for her years, too, don't you agree?"

She thought of the letter she would pen to Molly first thing in the morning. "Yes, Father. I hear nothing but good things about Miss Harvie."

"I am glad of it."

They settled back into silence for the remainder of the journey home.

Judy was more in command of her emotions by fall, when, after a short betrothal, her father married Gabriella Harvie. The Randolph sisters and brothers attended the wedding, feigning enthusiasm with varying degrees of success.

"Patsy hides it well," she said to Nancy, "but she must be as worried as Tom." They were huddled near the fireplace in the Harvie's home. The room was crushed and overheated, the air sticky with the scent of pine and roasted meats. She felt the heat of the fire on her legs and shifted her skirts before the delicate fabric was scorched.

"The thought of Gabriella Harvie having a child makes me nauseous." Nancy kept her voice low.

"Must you be so inelegant?"

"I'm speaking clearly and to the purpose. And to my own sister.

I'm not sure what's inelegant about it. That's what's worrying Tom and Patsy. Oh, Lord, here she comes."

"Mrs. Randolph. Miss Nancy." Gabriella put out a stiff little hand for her new stepdaughters to shake.

"Your gown is beautiful, Gab—" Judy's voice faltered, "Mrs. Randolph."

"Why, thank you. Your charming father certainly thinks so." Gabriella turned, and she followed her gaze across the room. Father had a fine face—a high intelligent forehead, a firm jawline, a wide nose—but gray hair sprang from his ears and hairline, and his cheeks sat heavy, almost pulling the corners of his eyes. His legs were thinner than Tom's, his shoulders hunched, his belly fuller than a younger man's might be. He was in his late forties, Gabriella still only eighteen. The thought of them lying together—no, Judy had no stomach for it. Her thoughts flitted to her own marriage, to her hasty commitment to Dick, to the problems they had encountered since that day on the riverbank, and she was stabbed by sudden concern for the girl. But Gabriella didn't look or sound like a bride in need of sympathy.

"I can barely wait until this is all over and Mr. Randolph and I can be at home with everyone. I have so many ideas and long to decorate."

"Decorate?" Judy heard the edge in Nancy's voice.

"Why, of course! Isn't that the first thing you did at Matoax, Mrs. Randolph? I heard you spent a small fortune. And yet, already, you have moved to Bizarre, Mr. Randolph says. How do you find the smaller house? And the isolation?"

"We are happy there, thank you. I hope you will visit us." Judy saw Gabriella kept her claws sharp, but she'd missed her mark for the moment. The change of location—forced upon them as part of an urgent need to economize—had done Judy good. Bizarre lay far west of Tuckahoe, in the southern tip of Cumberland County. Options for entertaining and spending money were limited—a relief, although she knew better than to say so to Dick. "Plantation management," she continued, "is hard work, mind you. A great deal of responsibility is now yours. Nancy will assist you, I'm sure."

Gabriella's chin sank into her neck. "I hardly think so. She's barely out of the schoolroom. A mere child. And you will agree, surely, Mrs. Randolph—if *you* can master the challenge of being a plantation mistress, it won't be beyond my powers?" She didn't take her eyes from Judy's face or acknowledge Nancy's existence. "I don't suppose you meant to be insulting, did you? I'd be sorry to have to tell my dear husband you hold such a low opinion of his new wife."

"That was far from my meaning!"

But Gabriella turned her back and walked away.

Within two weeks of the new Mrs. Randolph taking up residence, Nancy had written to each of her older sisters more than once, passionately detailing all of Gabriella's insults and snide remarks. She wrote at length to Tom and Patsy at Edgehill, a Jefferson property not far from Monticello, and while tempering her words somewhat to suit Tom's taste, she spared nothing in her stories of Gabriella's redecorating efforts, in particular her decision to paint the walnut paneling in the parlor white.

Her letter produced results. Tom paid a visit, and the fraying of his temper was clear. At the house, her brother sat on his views and opinions on his young stepmother's presumption, but he suggested Nancy return to Edgehill with him for a few weeks and waxed lyrical about the awfulness of Gabriella for their whole coach ride. Nancy lapped it up, agreeing with every word. Nothing suited her more than freedom from her stepmother's constant barbs about the number of children in the house and their utter dependence upon her kindness and good opinion for their future prosperity and happiness. She spent her days at Edgehill, curled up, re-reading *Clarissa* and *The Vicar of Wakefield* and trying to glean some poise from Patsy, who, when she wasn't wrapped up in household matters or scribbling letters to her father in Philadelphia, was happy to take walks and even share a few confidences.

"Tom and I are hopeful that your father will sell us some of the family land near here," she said, taking Nancy's arm and pulling her up a hill on the promise of a fine view of the orange and red of Albemarle County in the fall.

"You wish to be near your father?"

"Of course. We've been so close since Mother died. To be married is wonderful, but to leave one's family altogether?" She made a wry face.

"It makes sense when you say it. But my own case is different."

"Your father is not perhaps as openly affectionate as mine?"

"Definitely not! What does Tom say of him?"

"Very little. My father speaks so highly of yours, but he's not, I have come to learn, a warm man."

"No. And neither is the awful Gabriella. They are two cold fish, and I am sick of them."

"Enough! Your outspoken ways will get you in trouble one of these days!" Patsy's words admonished, but her eyes sparkled. "Here." She grabbed Nancy's shoulders and turned her to look down toward the house and the valley below. "This view will lift the lowest of spirits."

"If I were Tom, I would cleave to your father. In all seriousness, I would."

"You're a sweet girl to say so."

"You must be thankful he's never remarried. It's good to see not *all* old men seek to latch onto some poor girl with limited options."

Patsy stared for a moment and opened her mouth only to close it again. She shook her head and smiled. "You don't really think Gabriella is a 'poor girl' now, do you?"

Nancy snorted with laughter. "No, I certainly don't. But it's what *I* may be if things carry on the way they are! She and Father will marry me off to some prosy gentleman who snores after supper and grimaces whenever he stands up."

"Nancy!"

"He'll have tufty hair in his ears and his nostrils and crumbs on his waistcoat. I can see it all."

"You can see nothing, you pea-goose. There are many fine *young* men who would be far more suitable. Your sisters made good matches. Your father did right by them and will do right by you. I'm sure of it."

"That was my mother's doing. Or their own. That was before the new Mrs. Randolph installed herself in my mother's place. Everything has changed, now, Patsy. I used to dream of the future—of my own home, my husband, children. Now, I'm not so sure."

38

Chapter Five

"You're being ridiculous!"

"I most certainly am not." Nancy clutched the book in her lap.

"You are. Ridiculously childish, selfish and spoiled."

"Spoiled?"

Gabriella had found her in the parlor—the newly refurbished parlor with white-painted panels and a bright new carpet, shipped over from England. She should have known better than to read there. Gabriella saw the room as her territory and knew nothing of Nancy's fond memories of sitting in that space with her mother and sisters. As usual, only a few words set them at loggerheads. Gabriella had suggested she change for dinner, but Nancy refused. Informed that General Henry Lee would be joining them, she had burst out laughing.

"Yes, spoiled," said Gabriella. "Here is a perfectly decent and upstanding gentleman coming to our home and, who knows, perhaps take an interest in you. And you won't even change your attire?"

"Why should I? What is General Henry Lee to me? A friend of my father. Nothing more."

39

Gabriella put her hands on her hips. "Nothing more will be the truth of it if you don't make an effort."

"To what purpose?"

"What purpose do you suppose? Do you imagine yourself living here all your days with your father and me? You may disabuse your mind of that idea immediately. A daughter's duty is to marry well and give her husband a home and a family he can be proud of. Not to sit around reading sensational novels and daydreaming."

"I do not daydream."

"You do little else! Let me tell you, Nancy—you need to cut your coat according to your cloth. General Lee is a fine gentleman with a sizable property. He keeps his own stable and up to twenty slave-hands. He's taking an interest in you. I've neither the time nor inclination to be escorting you around Richmond looking for suitors when a perfectly good one has already presented himself."

"I wonder. Is that what Colonel Harvie told you, Gabriella?"

"What?" Gabriella shook her head. "Whatever do you mean? My father has nothing to do with this conversation. We are speaking of your situation and the choices before you."

"Are we? Are you certain of that?" Nancy relaxed her grip on her book. "Because it seems to me that your father is very much a part of this delightful conversation. You gave in to him, didn't you? You listened to the colonel when he said your options were limited, when he didn't have time to seek out a more suitable, younger husband for you. And because you were persuadable, you think I will be the same. I hope you are happy, truly I do, but let us speak plainly. You looked at the name and the house and the things that came with the man. You struck a bargain. Don't imagine I will do the same. I won't."

Gabriella stood rooted in the center of the room. Nancy opened her book before looking up and continuing, her voice steady and determined. "I won't be forced into a marriage like that. It is legal prostitution, nothing more."

Two bright red spots appeared on Gabriella's cheeks. "You will regret this moment. I promise you that. You will regret it, and I will never forgive it."

Regret it? As Gabriella stalked from the room, brushing past Phebe as if she were invisible, Nancy was certain she would not. She'd spoken nothing but the truth and would do so again in a heartbeat. She needed a route out of Tuckahoe. The obvious path, through marriage, was impossible given the current prospect being foisted upon her. Well, if she could not walk out a bride, she'd have to be pushed out by Gabriella. And if she knew anything about her stepmother, it was that Gabriella was across the hall in Father's study right now, pouring her hurt and disappointment into his ears and suggesting at first—but insisting if necessary—that Nancy and she could no longer reside under the same roof.

"Is everything all right, miss?" Phebe's soft voice surprised her. The girl had crossed the room and knelt beside her.

"Did you hear us?"

Phebe nodded. "But I won't tell no one."

"Thank you." She patted Phebe's narrow shoulder, and her thoughts drifted back to Gabriella and her father and what must surely happen next. Someone else in the family would have to take her in. It couldn't happen soon enough.

Judy woke and stretched a hand across the bed, only to find the quilt smooth and her husband absent again. It was so often this way when his brothers visited Bizarre. They were tolerable company over dinner, but when she retired to the parlor, the brothers remained in their seats, drinking and playing cards into the night. Sometimes, they stumbled upstairs, and sometimes, they slept where they sat. In the summer months, she'd several times found the three of them asleep outdoors, most often slumped on the porch but once, sprawled on the grass. She'd tried to fathom how it came about. Had they lain in the grass talking, like a gaggle of schoolboys, and grown drowsy with summer heat and strong wine? Their camaraderie surprised and excluded her, but the comings and goings of Dick's siblings was a constant feature of Judy's married life. That was clear the moment they halted the carriage at Matoax after their wedding tour to a bevy of relatives. Judy anticipated peace and quiet but was greeted by the sight of Dick's brothers' heads sticking out of a second-floor window. Queasy with morning sickness, she had blinked back tears.

After the move to Cumberland County, the brothers' visits were less frequent, and she was glad. Bizarre was smaller than Matoax and not built in the colonial style she was used to at Tuckahoe or any number of their friends' plantation homes. It was a sturdy, practical house, timber-built on a stone foundation with no pillars, only a timber-framed porch. It was never intended to be a permanent home, Dick said, although the family spent considerable time there during the war years, hiding out from the British.

Judy liked it at once. The rooms were small, but met their needs, with a parlor, dining room, a working sitting room for Judy and a study for Dick on the first floor and four bedrooms above. She saw the family home it could become and welcomed its relative remoteness even as Dick bemoaned it. Farmville was the nearest village, perched on the banks of the Appomattox River. They were twenty miles from the small town of Cumberland, over sixty from Richmond. Of their friends, Cousin Mary and Randy lived nearest, but it was still a four-hour coach journey to their home at Glentivar. Removed from the distractions of Matoax and nearby Petersburg with its racetrack and theaters, Dick focused on the land and the production of tobacco while Judy imagined the home and family she'd create.

Some days, she believed all would be well. But not today. She lay in bed, crushed by the weight of losing her child. Sorrow settled in the bones of her face. They were dense with it, pressing her head into the pillow. She closed her eyes and imagined her blood sinking in her veins, pinning her muscles to the bedsheets, making it impossible to ever get up. How could she face another day? People said grief was all emotion, all feeling, but it wasn't. It was physical. Every day, this weight upon her. Every day, this struggle.

Somewhere downstairs, a door slammed. Hooves clattered beneath her window. She heard a heavy tread in the passage passing her door. Judy sighed long and hard. And then she got up.

She discovered Theo in the parlor, lying on the floor with his cheek crushed against the floorboards. She took in the toppled armchair and her basket of small mending, strewn across the floor in a puddle of what she hoped was water.

"Get up!" She grabbed his shoulder and gave him a shake. "This room needs cleaned. Oh, why can't you take yourself upstairs?"

Theo rolled onto his back. "I'm on my way. Or I *was* on my way." He frowned and squinted at her through one eye. "Where's Dick? Where's Jack?"

"I've no idea, but I hope they're in a better state than you, Theo Randolph." Judy walked out, slamming the door behind her. He deserved that. And more.

She found Dick and Jack outside, saddling their horses and talking to Syphax, who'd been their father's most trusted slave. Judy thought better of asking Dick where he had slept. Syphax intimidated her, and Jack was an awkward young man. She didn't know what to make of him. One moment he was gauche, the next he sounded clever beyond his years, and his temper could turn in an instant. She'd seen him whip a slave at Matoax—a much stronger-looking man, but Jack set about the task as if born to it. She paused by the door to the kitchen house and bowed her head in prayer for a moment or two.

"Judy!" Dick joined her in the doorway, disregarding the women— tall Sarah at work kneading bread, her elder daughter, Lottie, heating water and mixing porridge on the stove, and her younger girl, Sally, sweeping the floor. "We're riding to Roanoke today and won't return until after dark. We'll need food and water."

She nodded. "For all three of you? Theo didn't look fit for much when I woke him."

"Where did you find him? He wandered off last night, right in the middle of a conversation. When he never returned, we thought he'd gone to bed."

"I found him sprawled on the parlor floor. The room was in disarray."

"I'm sure you'll put everything to rights. No harm done." His eyes moved to Sarah, and Judy saw his displeasure.

"I'm probably overstating things," she said. "I was surprised to see him there, that's all."

"Good girl." He ran his hand down her arm and bent to kiss her cheek. "Don't delay dinner for us, and if we don't appear, don't worry. If it gets too late, we'll find shelter for a few hours and be back in the morning."

As he spoke, Dick turned away from the kitchen and started down the path. Judy blinked back a sudden wash of tears. "Prepare a basket of food for your master," she said, keeping her face hidden from Sarah. "And bring me buckets of hot water to the parlor as soon as you can. That room is a disgrace. I'll need Sally for the rest of the morning. She needs to scrub every inch."

It was growing dark by six o'clock. When they were first married—*before*—when the loss of the baby was in an unimagined future, this was Judy's favorite part of the day. Now, she sat in her re-ordered parlor and stared at Dick's empty chair. The waves of visitors he'd encouraged in their months at Matoax had been oppressive, and the need to charm and amuse had exhausted her, partly because she had been in the family way but also because she was less naturally sociable than her husband. Judy's idea of a crowd was a group of six. Dick thought a small party meant twenty guests, singing, and the regular sound of glasses being filled and drained until well past midnight. She'd been so confident that the move to Bizarre would fix everything. The heaviness she'd banished in the morning crept back.

Dick was disappointed in her. His brothers' presence was proof of it. If he was content in her company, why drag them both here, halfway across Virginia, as often as he could? Her one hope was for another child. A child would fix her, fix him, fix them and lift the weight. A child would brighten everything, make their marriage what it promised to be that day on the bank of the James River, at Tuckahoe.

She needed to find such a moment with Dick again. There had been relations between them since that one fast coupling but without passion on her side—not because she didn't want to feel it, but because it simply wasn't there. In pregnancy, lovemaking was a challenge. Even sitting alone, she blushed to think of such matters. Their wedding night was a disappointment to him. She pushed away the memory of it—the nausea, her head turning from him, the tiredness, the words she said and his silence. Later, after the loss of the child, he didn't press her often. When he did, it was a fumbling thing with rumpled layers of cotton between them, a transaction, nothing more. In the early months at Bizarre, she was hopeful, but time ticked by. Dick was often tired.

The brothers didn't return home that night, and Judy dragged herself upstairs to her empty bed alone.

In the morning, dismal thoughts crowded in even before she opened her eyes. Tears flowed, running into her hair and ears as she lay still. Misery so consumed her that she didn't hear the men arrive back, or Dick's boots on the stairs.

"Whatever's the matter?"

He stood in the doorway, handsome in the half-light, and she crammed her hands in her mouth to stop herself from howling. He rushed to her and held her, stroking her hair and rubbing her heaving shoulders.

"Hush, hush," he murmured, dropping kisses down on her head.

Some of the weight lifted. He still cared. His voice and touch gave her hope. She squeezed her eyes closed and prayed he wouldn't let go. He did not. Her breathing steadied. She felt him shift and braced for disappointment, but instead, his fingers slid inside her nightgown. He touched her shoulder and reached for more, but the cotton restrained him. He ran his fingers down her face and teased away stray hairs stuck to her cheek by her tears. They stared into each other's eyes and Judy conjured the smallest of smiles of encouragement. He needed no more invitation.

When they lay still afterward, she stared at his profile on the pillow beside her. His long fingers were at his lips, she saw him frowning.

"What are you thinking, husband?"

"That I've neglected you." He shook his head when she tried to argue. "No, I've been selfish. You're alone a great deal. No wonder you dwell on our sorrows." He got to his feet, pulled his shirt from the floor and threw it over his head. "We should have your sister here with us!"

"Nancy? Here?"

"Why not! She despises Gabriella—who wouldn't? Damned snipe of a woman. Nancy needs a home, and you need company." Dick smacked the bedcovers. "Why should I be the only one who gets the benefit of the company of my siblings, Judy? I've not been fair to you, not a bit!"

She tried to remonstrate, but he waved her away. "It's the perfect solution," he said, pulling on his breeches. "I'll write to Tuckahoe today and propose it. We could use some cheer around here."

Nancy only saw Father once after her confrontation with Gabriella. The following morning, he ordered Thomas to drive her to Lizzie's house, and neither he nor Gabriella troubled themselves to say goodbye. While she was there, a letter arrived, informing her of Dick and Judy's offer of a permanent home with them at Bizarre. Lizzie sniffed and muttered about young girls mired up in the middle of nowhere, but Nancy radiated excitement. She'd be with people her own age. Judy wanted her. Dick was always good-humored. Bizarre might be miles from Richmond, but there was one young man she was sure would be visiting. Theo Randolph.

She returned to Tuckahoe for one night—enough time to box up the rest of her clothing and suffer through a short interview with Father. Gabriella wasn't present, and her name wasn't mentioned. Instead, his topic was Phebe.

"There." Father sat at his desk between the two tall windows overlooking the front of the property, holding a folded paper. "She belongs to you now. Make sure you look after her. With property comes responsibility."

"I—"

"Don't pamper her. She's not your friend. But until you find a husband to tame your wild tongue, she is yours to command." He tapped on the table and got to his feet.

"Thank you, Father. I—"

"Spare me," he said. "I'll be gone in the morning, before you depart. Travel safely, and be helpful to your sister. Take the paper. You may go. The girl must say her goodbyes tonight. She'll be on the road with you tomorrow."

Phebe

Mama said the words, but it was Cilla's stony face that told Phebe it was true. She was leaving Tuckahoe in the morning with Miss Nancy.

"You is still with the family." Mama cupped her cheeks. "You not lost. Could be worse. Could be a whole lot worse."

"Look after Miss Nancy real well," Cilla told her. "So's she'll look after you."

Sixty miles or more, someone said. She had no idea what that meant. Her stomach swayed with nerves. Sixty miles in a coach. She'd never seen the insides of one in her life. She didn't enjoy it. Found it hard to keep her seat. Every bounce rattled her jaw.

Miss Nancy surprised her. She leaned across the space between them and took her hand. "I'm so thankful you're with me, Phebe. You've no idea!"

The girl heard her grandmother's words roll and echo, as though her mind was an empty room. "Yes, Miss Nancy. I's very glad to be here."

49

Her mistress grinned. "It's going to be wonderful."

Not for Phebe it wasn't. Soon as they arrived, she was led to the kitchen house by a slip of a girl, name of Lottie. Her mother—Sarah Ellis—looked Phebe up and down and made it clear she found her wanting.

"You're alls I needs," she huffed. "Another mouth to feed. Sure hopes your Miss Nancy ain't gonna be no trouble. I've one fancy missus givin' me orders as it is. Don't need her sister too. Lottie, git her a roll-up bed so she can sleep near her mistress. We ain't making room in our cabin for no stranger."

When Miss Nancy didn't need her, Phebe was mostly alone. Oftentimes, she'd sit under the old wooden porch out front. It was cool in the summer months, with the stone foundation against her back. No better place for shade existed. Voices reached her down there. Oh, the things she heard!

Only Syphax took notice of Phebe. Called her out from under that porch. Took her to sit on a rocker outside his cabin. Poured her a tumbler of water. Asked about her family.

"Always wanting to be someplace else is no way to live," he said when she finished answering. Close up, he wasn't as old as she'd believed, the gray in his beard and at his temples belied by a smooth forehead and sharp brown eyes. She'd seen him around the plantation, walking with a stick, often talking to Mr. Randolph.

"Why don't you work? Like the rest of us?" She spoke without thinking. Was relieved when he smiled.

"Oh, I works, Miss Phebe. I works just like anyone. I'm Mr. Randolph's man, as I was his father's, from before the war and through it. I suppose since my leg got broken and didn't heal right, it might seem to a young'un like you that I'm not working. But I certainly am. Keeping an eye on those Ellis folks. Checking on Johnson and Rachel, the negro he keeps." Syphax nodded in the direction of the overseer's home, a wooden house set a little apart from the slave houses but with a clear view of every building.

"You watch Johnson? A White man?"

"I watch everyone. Mr. Randolph relies on me. When the time is right, he'll free me, mark my words. For now, I watch."

"Are you watching me?"

"Do I need to be?"

"No!"

He laughed then, and for the first time since leaving Tuckahoe, Phebe felt easy.

"But I will watch *out* for you," he said, patting the arm of her chair. "And if you is ever troubled or lonesome here, you just come to Syphax."

For the longest time, seemed he was the only person that saw her. Back at the house, the White folks, excepting Miss Nancy, ignored her like she didn't exist. And yet there she was, flesh and blood like them, with ears as sharp and eyes as keen. In time, she knew them better than they knowed themselves. Mrs. Randolph, fearful, lips always mouthing some prayer. Mr. Theo Randolph, all swagger and noise, not seeing how the reaper reeled him in with every breath. Mr. Jack Randolph, his eyes on her mistress like a fly on sugar. And Mr. Dick Randolph, who wanted to be a good man, but was as bad—no, worse—than any of them, for he was the master, and yet he couldn't even master hisself.

Chapter Six

From the moment the coach pulled up at Bizarre, Nancy felt free. She stood with her hands on her hips admiring the house as Dick and Judy rushed out to greet her.

"What do you think?" asked Judy. "It is not so fine as Matoax, but we like it."

"I love it already." Nancy turned in circles, taking everything in. The house was two-storied and rustic-looking, charming against a backdrop of tall poplar trees ranged protectively behind it. Beds of nodding daffodils and bright blue irises ran around the stone foundations, and her eyes followed a path to the side of the house where two dark-skinned girls in long aprons peered from behind a sprawling forsythia bush blossoming fiery yellow.

Judy drew her up the steps and inside, leaving Dick to holler for the boy to feed the horses and direct the driver to the kitchen house for a meal.

"Father let you bring Phebe?"

"He gave me her." She turned to remove her bonnet and saw Judy frown. "Why? You don't object, do you? She'll be no trouble. This way, my coming doesn't upset your household."

"True enough." Judy's shoulders relaxed. "That was generous of him."

"I'd say it was more a stab of conscience. He let me go without a backward glance, you know."

Judy's mouth opened, and Nancy braced for a lecture, but before she could begin, Dick was back.

"Our parlor is smaller than you will be used to at Tuckahoe, but what do you say to our fine view, eh, sister?"

"Dick, let the poor girl look around and get her breath before you start pointing out every prospect. I think Nancy might like a moment in her own room after her journey, don't you?"

"You're right, of course!" Dick swept a hand through his hair and laughed. "Ladies, march upstairs. I will attend to your trunk, Nancy, and Judy, I think we need to look to the furniture in this room."

"We do?"

"Certainly! We need better armchairs here by the fireplace, wouldn't you say?"

"Oh, please," Nancy said, "I don't want to put anyone to any trouble. I'm sensible of the kindness you—"

"Not a word about kindness." Dick threw an arm around her shoulders. "I won't hear of it. We're happy to have you here and expect great things from your company. We will have songs and conversation and all manner of good times, will we not?"

He wrapped his other arm around Judy and pulled her into him quickly before releasing them both. "But you're on your way upstairs. Don't let me hold you back."

She followed Judy up to a small but well-appointed bedroom with a canopied bed, a dresser and a slim wardrobe that filled one wall from floor to ceiling.

"It's not as grand as Tuckahoe. Lower ceilings, not as light—"

"But it is filled with people who want me, Judy. I can't tell you how relieved I am to be here." Her eyes filled, and she reached for her handkerchief. "I'm so grateful to you for rescuing me. I hope you'll let me help you and repay your kindness in some measure."

"I am so glad to see you, sister. You have no idea!" Judy gripped her by the shoulders. "But it is Dick you must thank. It was his idea. He is the best of husbands."

"I think he must be! I don't think I'll ever want to be anywhere else."

Her enthusiasm only increased as the days rolled into weeks. Plantation life was in Nancy's bones. She worked at Judy's command without a murmur, sewing hems, counting stores and tackling the vegetable garden needed to feed the household through the summer and beyond. She was cheerful with the slaves, learning names and relationships, and as Judy did, she treated Sarah with the respect she had been brought up to show Cilla back at Tuckahoe. But while the routine of the day might not be so different to her life before Bizarre, it was the evenings that made her spirits rise. A meal with Dick and Judy was nothing like eating under Father's watchful eye. At Bizarre she flew into dinner with her hands still damp from washing and her curls escaping her cap, but instead of being greeted with disapproval or disdain, Dick welcomed her, pulling out a chair while Judy chuckled or rolled her eyes.

After dinner, if Dick was absent, she read from his library. No more hiding out to read books for hours in the fields or behind the outbuildings. When Dick was home, they played cards or talked about his plans and ideas. As often as once a week, there were visits from friends—Randy and Cousin Mary, Anne and Brett Randolph, as well as Aunt Page and her husband, Carter. These evenings were full of singing and wine and good humor.

"Having her here seems to have done you good," murmured Cousin Mary to Judy as she said her goodbyes one morning after a long, noisy evening at Bizarre. "And Dick." She nodded to her carriage where Dick and Nancy stood laughing with Randy.

"He treats her like his own sister."

"And you are in good spirits?"

"Yes. Although Theo and Jack are due to arrive back next week. I suspect we'll see a lot less of him. You know how those three are when they get together."

But Theo took to his bed with a fever the moment he arrived, leaving Jack to follow Dick around the plantation all day like a waif. In the evenings, he talked over the women and sulked when the conversation was of no interest to him. Judy wasn't sorry when he returned to school in New York. In time, Theo recovered enough to sit downstairs and took a liking to Nancy's company. She fetched him drinks and read to him for hours—to the point where Judy suspected him of playing the invalid to prolong her sister's attention.

"I hope your brother will be on his feet again sooner rather than later," she grumbled to Dick when they retired to bed one night. "I've grown used to Nancy's help with the sewing. But now, she only has eyes for Theo."

"I'd hardly say that." Dick pulled his shirt over his head. "She's just being helpful."

"You're not watching closely. All the signs of flirtation are there. She hangs on every word he says and must have tested the heat in his forehead with her palm ten times this afternoon. I've never seen her so solicitous." Judy laughed lightly as she pulled a comb through her hair. "I think Theo is enjoying himself tremendously with a pretty girl running after him. He's in no rush to recover and—"

"I wish you'd stop being so ridiculous!"

Judy stiffened. Silence followed. She weighed some things she could say. She could defend her position. Or attempt to laugh off his rudeness. Mother came to mind. Ann Cary Randolph wouldn't have been addressed in such a way—she'd been afraid of no one, certainly not her husband. But Judy wasn't made from the same mold as her mother. Her eyes pricked with tears and her tongue stayed still. Dick said nothing more, but she heard him moving behind her, the sound of the bedclothes shifting, the creak of the floor and the bed frame, the soft *phut* as he blew out his candle. She finished combing her hair and climbed into bed. Words burned on her lips, but she wouldn't let them escape. He had silenced her. Let him explain himself. She'd done nothing wrong. The injustice was a lump in her ribs. She lay on her back and waited.

"Do you really think they like each other?" he asked.

He didn't sound angry, but he wasn't apologetic either. He was … measured. She chewed on her lip. "Yes, I do. I wouldn't say it was serious, necessarily. But they have been thrown together here. A flirtation is hardly surprising."

"You're right." The bed creaked as Dick rolled toward her. He brushed her arm with his fingertips, feather-light, up and down. "I'm sorry I snapped. I'm tired. It's been a long day."

She remained still as his fingers trailed across her nightgown.

He *was* tired. It *had* been a long day for him, out in the fields. His apology was a welcome surprise. Her body responded. And that was what she wanted most. His touch. The chance of a child. Nothing else mattered.

Chapter Seven

"Read another chapter. One more. Please?"

Nancy arched her brows. "Theo Randolph. Are you never to be satisfied? Judy expects me to oversee work in the garden. When I don't appear, she'll be full of sighs and silent reproach. You know how she is."

"Please?"

He was stretched out on the couch by the window while she sat in a nearby armchair with *Robinson Crusoe* open in her lap. His thick brown hair was damp with sweat, even though he hadn't moved for an hour. This bout of fever had proved worse than the last, and Theo had lost weight. His face was gaunt, the similarities between him and his older brother more pronounced. His chest heaved under a thick layer of blankets.

"You're not too warm? Can I fetch you something to drink?"

He pulled an arm out from his covers and twisted so that his hand found hers. His skin was hot but dry. She wrapped her other hand over the top of his, hoping to cool him.

"I just like the sound of your voice," he said. He had hazel eyes, flecked with gold. Handsome, but weary. He'd coughed all night again. "It might help me sleep."

She lifted the book once more. Judy would understand. And as soon as Theo was asleep, she would change her shoes and get to work on choosing seeds for planting. She read with her eyes on the words, but her mind wandered to a future where Theo was recovered and the garden she was supervising was not Dick and Judy's, but her own. And his.

But weeks turned to months, and Theo showed no sign of recovering. Shoots rose up in the vegetable garden. New scents filled the air at the brush of Nancy's skirts or the rub of her fingertips: tomatoes, rosemary, lavender. Dick helped Theo outside each morning, but any gust of cool air set off his cough, and the spasms grew longer, not shorter, even as the days grew warmer and the world grew green and lush. His spirits were good, but as they moved around him, the rest of the household frowned only more deeply. After some debate, Dick wrote to his stepfather expressing concern—enough to bring Mr. Tucker over one hundred miles from Williamsburg to examine the patient in person. He wasn't happy with what he saw.

Theo was removed from Bizarre the next day. Mr. Tucker had family in Bermuda and was sure the tropical climate would help overcome the congestion in Theo's chest. Nancy watched the carriage roll away, certain he'd return in a few short months, back on his feet and in good health.

Bizarre grew too quiet. She passed her days with Judy, but with her heart and mind busy with memories—the touch of Theo's hand, his grateful smile, his preference for her company. Would he feel the same when he was whole again? In the meantime, Jack Randolph was back, and Nancy found his presence less than charming. He'd a habit of staring at her. Theo could not return soon enough.

Summer came. Humid days sapped everyone's energy. She spent long night hours in her room, oppressed by heat and physically tired, yet with her mind restless. Sleep was hard to find. Bizarre was home, yes, but it was Judy's home, not hers, and in small ways, but consistently—and to Nancy's mind deliberately—Judy made that clear.

"Remind my woman, Sarah, to bring me the stock list for my smokehouse," she might say over breakfast. Or: "Tell Lottie that her master's boots were not properly shined yesterday, and her mistress has taken note of it." Or: "Dick and I feel our responsibilities keenly, Nancy. You're so fortunate. Able to contribute but without any responsibility."

"Disingenuous, that's my sister," she told Phebe. "Says one thing but means another." She didn't add that she felt Judy managed her, her own sister, not so differently than she did the slaves at Bizarre, which was to say not unkindly, but with distance. Over time, Nancy was happier out in the garden, working with Sarah's son, Billy Ellis, than she was stuck inside with Judy, always checking on her stitching and sniffing, much as their mother used to do.

With Jack's presence occupying Dick, Nancy looked to a visit from Aunt Page to ease the growing tension between herself and Judy. Their aunt was as frivolous as Mother had been serious, but her propensity for gossip became far less amusing to Nancy when she found she was her aunt's new target. She first realized it walking up to the front porch with a basket of lilies. Aunt Page and Judy were settled in wicker chairs, their heads together in cozy conversation, but as she reached the steps, they drew apart abruptly.

"Nancy, dearest," said Aunt Page, "how quickly you stride along. Almost mannish, swinging that heavy basket as if it were empty."

"It only holds flowers, Aunt."

"Ah, but a girl your age and in your situation cannot forget herself for a moment. Judy and I were just discussing your prospects. How I wish your poor mother were still with us."

"I don't see what there is to discuss."

"No?"

"Judy?" said Nancy.

"Our aunt is simply thinking of your future, sister."

"My future? Why? I am happy here. I work hard, I—"

"Yes, yes. Judy was just telling me what a help you are. And if that's how you see your future, well, then ..." When Nancy said nothing, her aunt shifted in her seat. "Sit down, girl. I told Judy that you needed some guidance. Don't look so stiff. Why, if that's the way you were around the new Mrs. Randolph, I can see why Gabriella sent you packing."

Nancy bit on her lip and sat down.

"Our aunt is only concerned for your welfare," said Judy.

"Really?"

Two pink spots appeared on Aunt Page's soft cheeks. "Indeed I am. Because unless you long to be a maiden aunt, running after another woman's children and never having a stick of furniture to call your own, you'd do well to stop looking so haughty and start realizing when someone is trying to do the right thing by you."

"You call this the right thing? Gossiping about me behind my back? Deciding my future without involving me?"

"You're overreacting." Judy threw their aunt a speaking glance. Nancy read it as clearly as if her sister had spoken. It said, *I told you so. I warned you she would not take this well.* Theo's name pressed on Nancy's lips as her eyes darted from one woman to the other, but she refused to dignify them with her confidences. They didn't deserve to hear of her hopes. Nor did she want them dashing those hopes with lies about his illness or his character. Aunt Page's opinion of Theo wasn't high. No need to give her an opening to disparage him.

"I am but seventeen years old, Aunt."

"By which age both your mother and I were married."

"Not Lizzie though. Or Molly."

Aunt Page waved Nancy's argument away and turned to Judy. "What about Cousin Archie? Is he still dangling after her?"

"I will not be marrying Archie!" Nancy jumped to her feet and grabbed the basket of lilies, dropping several blooms and sending up a cloud of yellow pollen in the process. She headed into the house with Aunt Page's answer ringing in her ears.

"You say that now, Nancy. But give it a year or so, and you may be begging for a man like Archie, foolish though he is, to take you and give you a home of your own."

For the remainder of the visit, Nancy was cool with her aunt. She put the confrontation out of her mind by indulging in daydreams. She pictured how Bizarre might be if she and Theo were in charge. While Theo might have some lessons to learn from the example of his excellent older brother, Dick, she was confident of being a better mistress than Judy, who was too thorough, too rigid with everyone and sadly lacking in any sense of humor. Marriage had changed Judy. And not for the better.

Nancy was glad, toward the end of August, to watch Jack Randolph ride away from Bizarre to return to his studies at Columbia. Dick spent his evenings with them again, and she enjoyed the change from long evenings spent reading or sewing with Judy. But Jack had not been gone a week before a lengthy letter arrived from him, addressed to her. What she read made her angry.

"Where's the master?" She went straight to the slave quarters and called over to Syphax. "Did you see his direction this morning?"

"North field, miss."

"Thank you."

The heat pricked her skin as she walked. Nancy thrust the letter into her apron pocket and wiped the sweat from her hands. A bead of moisture slid down her back between her shoulder blades. Beyond the line of trees behind the house, the sun baked the earth. She saw Dick astride his gelding, Cassie, and waved. She tried to flatten the curls escaping her hat in the heat as she strode toward him.

"I need you to speak with your brother, Jack, for me." She thrust the letter into Dick's hand as soon as he dismounted. "I've given him no encouragement. I hope you know that."

Dick looked over his brother's missive, his expression grave. "He is very young in some ways."

Nancy laid her hand on his arm. "I don't wish to hurt him, Dick. He's your brother. That's why I thought you might write to him. Tell him what he suggests can never be. Make it clear somehow. I don't know. Tell him I'm engaged to Theo."

"Are you?"

"Not formally, but—"

"You're in love with him?"

Was she? Nancy struggled for an answer, her mouth suddenly dry. The temper that had sent her traipsing across the fields to Dick deserted her. "I might be."

His eyes traveled from hers to the letter and back again. "I'll deal with Jack. You may be easy on that head. He will not embarrass you further."

She tried to read his face but could not. "Thank you." She held out Cassie's reins. His fingers grazed hers as he handed back Jack's letter. She turned to go but had only taken a step when he spoke again.

"Do you remember, Nancy, back at Randy and Mary's wedding, when I said you would enslave all the Randolph brothers?"

"You were teasing me."

"Was I?" The look in his eyes said something else entirely.

As fast as she had marched toward him, Nancy fled back to the house. She dared not look back.

Chapter Eight

In October, Judy suspected she was expecting again. She wanted to feel elated, but underlying dread teased away any joy. She didn't trust her own body, doubting her ability to carry this child to term. She could taste failure like a fur on her tongue every morning. She waited for blood to spill, her expectation of disappointment and disaster rising with every day that passed. With her condition came an overwhelming exhaustion. In the middle of the day, great waves of tiredness rolled over her. Her limbs ached. Tears rolled down her cheeks at odd times—it might be a smell, a jarring noise, a turn in the weather, Nancy's girl, Phebe, loitering in the hallway, Dick's clothes discarded without care—her nerves were taut, waiting for the pregnancy to fail. Dick seemed to understand. He was gentle and genuinely moved when she told him her news. He withdrew from their room to allow her to gain what little sleep she could. He encouraged her to let more of the household management fall to Nancy.

An argument broke out over Mr. Tucker's wedding. Dick's step-father was re-marrying. Lelia Skipwith was by all accounts a prettily behaved woman—a widow, with two young children of her own. The wedding would take place in Williamsburg. Dick approved the match and Theo, back from Bermuda, would be there. Nancy begged and implored, but Judy refused to make the journey. She couldn't risk the jolts and bumps of a long carriage drive. Voices were raised but Judy was immovable. Dick went alone, and the two sisters passed the days in tense silence.

Not for the first time, Judy wished Dick had never thought of bringing Nancy to Bizarre. Oh, she was helpful enough, but Aunt Page was right. What were Nancy's plans? What was her future? Father was unlikely to approve of Theo as a suitor, not with his poor health and prospects. Even Jack, odd as he was, lacked neither brains nor ambition. Theo, on the other hand? Judy shook her head. Alone in her room, she lay on her bed with her hands on her abdomen. The baby was her focus. Nancy's help would be invaluable in the coming months. She should stay for now. At least until the child was a few months old. Then, perhaps Aunt Page or Molly would take her on.

Judy muttered a prayer for the health of the life growing inside her. Please, God, let her have a healthy child. A son for Dick. An heir for Bizarre. Please, God, let that not be too much to ask for. Please.

Nancy's spirits lifted when Dick returned with Theo. Judy spent the evening downstairs, a rarity this last month or so, and Nancy's sulks over the missed wedding were forgotten. Theo was back. Although she'd tried not to think about it, every exchange between herself and Dick had taken on a different character since their meeting in the field. She'd developed a physical consciousness of him, as if the air was a tangible substance, pressing against her if he so much as moved her way. He didn't need to touch her. The air touched her, her skin vibrating in response to his nearness, her breath growing short the moment he entered the room. Now, with Theo's return and Judy's presence, that tension released. Now, she might believe she had imagined it. It had been nothing, or at least nothing serious—a form of brain fever or delusion.

Theo was louder than she remembered. "Our Uncle Tudor was a tremendous nag, let me tell you, Dick. I was better within a week of our arrival on the island, but would the old man believe me? Not a bit. There was no drinking, no parties, except long dinners with other prosy old men. Not a pretty woman in sight. I longed for Bizarre."

He stared across the room at her, and she managed a tight smile. He certainly looked and sounded healthier. His skin was a better color, and the journey from Williamsburg hadn't tired him. He was still thin, however, and dark shadows lingered under his eyes. She heard Dick's voice asking *are you in love with him?* and imagined everyone's eyes on her.

"Shall we have some music? Nancy could play," Judy said.

"Later, later. I need conversation. And cards! Dick, how about a hand or two? Perhaps in your study?" Theo tapped his empty glass, suggesting the allure of Dick's study lay in his whiskey collection as much as anything else. Within a minute, the brothers had quit the room, leaving the sisters alone.

"He appears much improved," said Judy.

"He does." She crossed the room and picked up a book. "How are you feeling?"

"Less sick, thank goodness. Did you watch Lottie churn the butter this morning?"

Her fingers curled around the spine of her book. "Yes. And stitched the wristbands on countless shirts and darned a hundred stockings."

She tried to read a few pages of her novel, but her mind wouldn't settle. "You think Theo looks well?"

"Yes. Do you not?"

"Yes. Although he seemed a little different."

Judy shrugged. "Naturally he is different. The man feels himself again. None of that hacking cough or rumbling with every breath. He wants to be with his brother." She got to her feet and shook her head. "Do you want him to be an invalid so you can nurse him and flatter yourself that he needs you? Are you so much of a fool? I'm going to bed. Make sure the candles are snuffed and the door locked, won't you?"

With a whirl of her skirts, Judy was gone. Nancy put her book to one side and closed her eyes. It would not do to compare Dick and Theo. She knew that.

For a week or two, all was well. Theo paid her a pleasing amount of attention, carrying her basket as they moved between the kitchen house, the dairy and the storehouse and even reading to her in the afternoon as she sewed. True, whenever Dick called him, Theo dropped her in a flash, but she was confident of his regard for her.

His mind was not on the future, however. After a visit from Randy and Mary, he was cross and chose Nancy as the audience for an airing of his grievances.

"Did you hear Randy over dinner?" he asked, catching her on the way into the house and patting a chair on the porch so she would join him.

"Not particularly. Did he say something out of the ordinary?"

"More of his typical prosing. He's worse than old man Tucker. What are your plans, Theo? When will you return to your studies, Theo? Or do you have other ideas? Damned busybody."

"But you do have plans, don't you?"

"What do you take me for? I have grand plans, I'll have you know. But when a man's been ill as I have been? When a man finds his life derailed by poor health? Don't you think I deserve a little time to enjoy myself before settling down? You of all people, Nancy, know how much I have suffered in the last year!"

"Of course I do."

"There! I knew you'd understand." He leaned back in his chair and stretched out his legs. "A man like Randy, you see, never knew how to be young. He was bailing out his father and talking like a grandparent before he was even twenty. He has no idea of fun or good humor. I don't know what Dick likes so much about him! There's a time for business, and I'll be a great success when I turn myself to such matters. But I deserve a little more fun before then, don't you agree?"

That evening, Dick and Theo disappeared early to Dick's study and stumbled up the stairs long past midnight. Several times during the night, she heard Theo coughing. He wasn't at breakfast.

A week later, she rose early to take a walk down to the river. She poked her head out of her door and gently tapped on Phebe's arm as she lay, tangled in blankets on her bedroll in the hallway. As the girl stirred, Nancy looked left and right. Theo's man's bed was empty. That concerned her. He didn't speak of the night sweats and the coughing, but she saw the evidence of his struggles in the laundry work that went on each day. She stifled a sigh and asked Phebe to fetch hot water, smiling as the young girl swung her legs to the floor, stood up and stretched.

Nancy went back to her room and opened her window. She watched a line of pink and orange creep up behind the snow-kissed tree line. To her left, the moon lingered while the sky around it slowly lightened. The cold air made her skin tingle, and she sucked in a deep breath, filled with the scent of pine and smoke, as someone lit a fire in the kitchen across the yard. Snow dampened the normal sounds of morning, or perhaps it was a little early for the animals to stir and the trample of workers and breakfast to begin. Behind her, she heard the door open.

"Shh." Dick stood in the doorway, his hair disheveled, his shirt half-buttoned.

"What are you doing? Is something wrong?"

"Nothing is wrong. No. Everything is wrong. I must speak with you." He closed the door and leaned back against it.

"Phebe is—"

"Gone for water. I heard. I was waiting. You must hear me out."

She stared into her brother-in-law's eyes. It was madness. Yet she took his hand and pulled him to perch beside her on her bed. "If you must speak, Dick, speak quickly. Phebe will not be long; she mustn't find you here."

"It's Judy." He still held her hand, his eyes fixed on it. "I'm in torment. She's not the woman I thought she was. It's not the marriage I believed it would be."

"She's expecting a child. She's anxious. The previous loss weighs on her."

"No. I should never have married her." He shook his head and stole a look at her.

The sadness she saw took her breath away.

"Men need passion, Nancy. You know that. I don't need to tell you it. You're so alive."

"Dick. No."

"Don't say no. Just listen. You must listen."

Her thoughts flew to Phebe warming the first water of the day in the kitchen. They had some time yet. "I'm listening."

70

"You know what kind of man I am, don't you?" She wanted to speak but he put his finger to her lips. "No. Don't answer that. Don't say anything. I need to be honest with you, you of all people. I've lived a little you know. Before I married your sister and was trapped in this miserable life without feeling, that is. Women wanted me. Betsey Talliaferra. Kitty Ludlow. But not Judith Randolph." He hung his head. "Do you know how she treated me on our wedding night? That first night? She denied me. She made me up a bed in the corner of the room and told me I'd never touch her but when she saw fit. And that's how it has been between us. Loveless. Without passion or feeling. I'm nothing more than a breeding animal, and now I've planted a pup in her, she turns from me all over again. How is a man to bear that, Nancy?" He grabbed both her hands. "I can please a woman. I would please you, Nancy, if you would let me."

"Dick, you cannot speak so!"

"But I must. I've been awake all night and think of nothing but you and what we could be together." He fell on his knees and laid his head in her lap. "We must be together!"

"No!" She thrust at Dick's shoulders and scrambled back across the bed. "No. Get control of yourself. Phebe will be back any moment. You can't talk in this way to me. It's wrong."

For a moment, Dick put his head in his hands. She thought he might begin again and gathered the bedclothes to her chest, but when he dropped his hands, his face was calmer. He crossed to the window and spoke in a quieter tone.

"It may seem wrong, Nancy. But love is not wrong. I'll never believe that."

"You don't love me."

71

"Don't I? Then why is it that the thought of you marrying Theo sends me almost insane? Judy says you want to marry him. She told me so again last night, and I've not slept since. I married the wrong sister. I should have waited. Waited until you were older, until I had *seen* you. You're everything I thought Judy was but isn't. When I think of Theo and I, and how we're similar but far from the same, I can't rid myself of this conviction that we are all mismatched. That you and I—"

He broke off as Phebe entered the room.

"Mr. Randolph." She stood with a steaming pitcher in each hand, her eyes darting between them.

"Good morning, Phebe." He turned and made a short bow to Nancy. "I'll take your sister your answer, then. And we can talk more on the other topic later." With that, he excused himself and left the room.

"Miss Nancy!" Phebe set the pitchers on the chest of drawers and rushed to her mistress. "What in heavens? What did he say to you? Did he make you cry?"

"No!"

Phebe raised her eyebrows. "No?"

"It's nothing. I can explain."

Phebe turned and busied herself pouring water in the basin and laying out a fresh towel while Nancy frowned. Her eyes felt hot and puffy, her thoughts jumbled. A longing for easier times overwhelmed her, and she had to bite her own lip to stop a fresh wave of tears.

"We will not speak of this again, Phebe. But I can tell you one thing," she said, breathing in deeply. "I have never missed my mother more than I do now. I need to write a letter to my father this morning."

"Yes, Miss Nancy."

Phebe slipped out of the room as Nancy cupped water in her hands and closed her eyes. She wondered if Phebe could have any idea of the real substance of Dick's visit, but surely not. No one must know.

She waited anxiously for Father's reply, but when a letter came, it was Gabriella's round sloping hand that she saw, and her stepmother's answer was brief and pointed. Return to Tuckahoe was not an option. The horses were lame and could not travel. *Lame*!

She scrunched up the paper and threw it across the room. Another letter had arrived at the same time, this one from Lizzie. She opened it with a burst of optimism. Might it be an invitation to visit?

It wasn't. Lizzie wrote at length about how busy her household was, with Jane and John staying, and of suffering through a recent visit from Gabriella. Nancy's hands tightened on the paper as she looked at the date.

"And she's telling me the horses are lame?"

Nancy stomped downstairs. She pulled on her boots, her bonnet and cloak and marched out of the house. If she could not escape Bizarre, then she would put some distance between herself and its inhabitants—at least for an hour or two.

Chapter Nine

Nancy welcomed Tom and Patsy's arrival in early December. The busier the household, the less opportunity for Dick to catch her eye or brush against her in the passageway. But it also meant that Theo was less attentive, as the men passed their evenings away from the women. She occupied herself with amusing her new niece, Annie, named for Tom's mother—a point Patsy made more than once as she wondered aloud about potential names for the child Judy carried.

"Would you choose Ann Frances, or Frances Ann, Judy? Or what if the baby is a boy? Dick's father's name was John, wasn't it? Almost as ubiquitous as Thomas."

"We've talked of John St. George for a boy," Judy said. "St. George after Mr. Tucker, of course. Then I thought we might call him Saint."

"I like it! Do you like it, Nance?"

"I think it's charming. Although Annie would love a girl cousin to play with, don't you think?"

The three women were gathered in the kitchen house, with Sarah banished from the building as the Randolph ladies set about candle-making. Nancy had spent hours the previous day washing and drying buckets of bayberries, plucked from the hedges by the field hands' children. She'd pinched out stems and rinsed and patted the firm, black berries until her fingers were purple-stained and wrinkled. Now, Judy stood over a vast old metal pot, heaped full of berries and water, while Patsy opened a parcel of beeswax from Monticello.

"We'll plant a bayberry hedge in the spring, I hope, so we may have a harvest of our own next year," Patsy said. "But in the meantime, my father will be grateful for this gift. If you have sufficient, that is."

"Dick insists," said Judy. "He is delighted to be able to send your father a token of our esteem. The candles will bless both our houses."

Nancy, tasked with cutting lengths of wick and soaking them in paraffin before tying each end with a small metal hoop for weight, sat at the kitchen table a little removed from the stove. From time to time, Patsy came her way—first to tie cheesecloth over the tall coffee cans they would set into pots of simmering water and strain the wax into, next to fit a layer of old newsprint under the wooden frame erected to hang the tapers while the wax set.

"And how is Dick? He must be excited for the child?" Patsy asked Judy.

Nancy looked up. The two women had their backs to her, Patsy setting up the coffee pots in water and melting beeswax in another basin while Judy waited, ladle poised, ready to skim the wax as it boiled out from the berries.

"He's been quiet. But I'm sure he's glad."

"He'll hope for a son. Has he said as much?"

"Not in so many words. We are both a little anxious. After our previous loss." Judy paused and bent over the pot, skimming the pale green wax as it rose to the surface and spread fragrance through the room. "At the time, he did not seem much affected. But he's so reserved this last month or so. We barely exchange words. I think it must be fear of another disappointment, keeping him so cool. Don't you think? What of Tom? Did he hope for a son? He could not be disappointed in Annie, though, could he?"

Nancy saw a smile on Patsy's lips. "If he was disappointed, he hid it well. Although he gave me fair warning that I should be ready to bring him more children, and soon."

"My goodness!" Judy lowered her voice, but Nancy still caught the question. "And how long after—after Annie—how long did he wait?"

She pushed back her chair and went to the window. She didn't understand her sister. The image of Dick and Judy beyond the button-bush at Tuckahoe swam across her vision, contrasting with Dick's whispered description of their wedding night. The tremor in Judy's voice sounded like fear. No wonder he …

She squeezed her eyes closed. It was wrong, all wrong. And yet she took pleasure in his preference for her. Pleasure in her secret knowledge.

"Nancy, are you finished already?"

"Yes. Might I skim the wax a little? You look a little flushed, sister."

Judy nodded and retreated to a chair, her hands on her stomach, while Nancy worked with Patsy, removing the last of the bayberry wax and straining it through layers of cheesecloth until they had two full jugs of the sweet-smelling green wax ready for dipping.

"Judy?" Patsy gestured for her to move away from the stove.

"Let Nancy do it," Judy said. "I'm so tired. She has always had the steadier hand."

With the last candle hung to set, Nancy took herself off to the porch. She wrapped herself in a blanket and stared at the treetops, idly picking slivers of wax from her fingers, drinking in the warm bayberry scent. She didn't expect him to find her there. The house was still. It was the hour of the day when Tom spent time with his daughter while Patsy read or wrote letters. Judy rested in her room around this time, and Nancy usually did likewise, but today, she wanted the cold air on her cheeks. The gray sky suited her bruised emotions. Dick ought to have been with Theo or his overseer or out on the plantation or visiting Syphax. He'd no business appearing on the porch.

"Nancy."

"Where's Theo?"

"Am I not good enough to bear you company? Must you always prefer my brother?"

"I didn't mean that, I—"

"You don't prefer him?" Dick laid hands on the wooden rocker next to her and took a seat, pulling it round and leaning forward so they almost touched. His smile made her catch her breath. She grabbed a handful of the blanket and held firm.

"I was merely going to say that it wasn't a matter of preference. I only wondered where he was. Nothing more."

"No? Nothing more?" He tilted his head, and his gaze moved to her lips. Her skin prickled.

Then he leaned back.

"Theo has been 'resting' these past hours." Dick squeezed the bridge of his nose. "I fear for him, Nancy. He's thinner these last months. His cough returns."

"You let him drink too much."

"It helps him sleep. He won't let me call in a physician. He insists he'll be well in the spring. He says it is only the colder air pulling him down."

"Perhaps he's right. Think how much better he was after Bermuda. He needs to keep his strength up."

"He does. And we will help him, together, won't we?" Dick took her hands in his. He was so changeable. Talk of Theo's health had taken the heat from him. He was her kind and thoughtful brother-in-law again. "Thank you, Nancy. Your kindness to him is immeasurable. To us all. I'm so grateful you're here."

After he left, she put her hands to her face, inhaling the bayberry scent once more. His love for his brother was her safeguard. Talk of Theo's health threw cold water on his passion. She had managed it now and would do so again. Even as tears dampened her fingertips, she swore that she would.

She had to.

Judy enjoyed celebrating New Year at Bizarre. Heavy rains and wild winds delayed Tom and Patsy's departure, but the bad weather didn't deter Aunt Page and her husband Carter, or Randy and Cousin Mary who drove down from Glentivar on the one dry day in the month. Judy brightened in the company of her closest friend.

She felt stronger and, encouraged by Mary and Patsy's confident talk of the child to come, allowed some of her misgivings to lessen. Dick was at his most charming, teasing awkward Jack and demanding participation in parlor games and charades that allowed Theo to join the festivities without taxing his obviously weakened body. She prayed the new year would be a turning point for Theo as well as for herself. He would gain strength, and she would have a child. In the company of family and friends, everything good seemed possible. Judy found herself in charity with everyone. Even Nancy.

As the clock ticked toward midnight on the last day of 1791, Dick called the party to attention. "Mrs. Randolph?" He extended a hand to Judy. It was time to light the bayberry candles. Her hands went to the arms of her chair, but then she changed her mind. The room was warm, she was comfortable where she was. She shook her head.

"Let Nancy do the honors. I'm content here watching." Dick rewarded her with a broad smile. He spun on his heels.

"Sister?"

Nancy sprang to his side, and each of the couples in the room stood together around the table by the window where Judy had set out four candles. Jack stood by Theo's chair to watch. With arms entwined, each couple picked up a candle and traded it for another.

Dick led the familiar chant:

These bayberry candles come from a friend,
So this New Year's Eve burn it down to the end.
For a bayberry candle, burned to the socket,
Will bring joy to the heart
And gold to the pocket!

As the flames flickered in the window and a woody scent filled the air, Judy thought she had rarely known such happiness.

The house grew quiet in January, but before Aunt Page went home to Richmond, she grabbed Nancy's arm and led her outside, speaking quickly as their breath smoked in the cold air.

"What are your plans now, niece?"

"Plans?"

"How much longer do you mean to stay at Bizarre?"

"How long?"

"Must you parrot my every word, child? No, never mind 'child'. You're a young woman. What future is there here for you?"

"I don't know what you mean."

"Then it's time you did. Let me lay out the future for you if you lack the wit to do so yourself."

"Aunt!"

"Listen to me. In a few months, your sister will have a child. God willing, it will be healthy, and Judy too. But after the child comes, you need to leave. Do you see nothing in your future but tending to Judy's children and running *her* errands, managing *her* household, instructing *her* slaves? It would be another story if you were older. But you're not yet eighteen, Nancy. I'm determined to write to Lizzie and Molly the moment I arrive home. Your father too. You need society. Young men to meet."

"But Aunt—"

"But me no buts." She rounded on Nancy and looked her squarely in the eye. "What can be your hopes of matrimony, here at Bizarre?"

Nancy's cheeks burned. "Theo Randolph—"

"Theo!" Her aunt threw her hands in the air. "Theo?" She paused for a moment. "There." She indicated the stone bench at the edge of the kitchen garden, and they both sat. The cold slid through the folds of Nancy's skirts.

"Theo," Aunt Page said, "is not well."

"I know that, but he is always worse in the winter. You will see. And when he recovers—"

"Nancy." Aunt Page compressed her lips so that two lines carved down, cutting between her plump cheeks and apple chin. "Nancy, Theo will not see another winter."

"I don't understand—"

"He is sick. He may rally in the spring, but consumption is an ugly illness. It doesn't let go. You mustn't carry false hope. Nancy, perhaps you are too close to see it, but Theo is far, far worse than he was this time last year."

"You're wrong," she said. But a small voice inside her head disagreed.

Chapter Ten

The winter days were long and somber. Nancy read anxiety in Judy's pale face, in the way she held herself and the way her hand went often to her back or side in reaction to some nagging pain. She retired early and rose late. At other times, her sister broke off mid-conversation and placed both hands on her growing waistline. She'd turn her head, like a small creature listening to the wind, and then resume their conversation as if nothing had happened. It was a source of mystery and fascination. Sometimes, at night, Nancy lay in the darkness with her hands on her own flat stomach and imagined something stirring inside her. But that brought other thoughts, vague and disturbing, for before there could be a child, there must be a man, and Aunt Page's words haunted her. Scenes played in her mind where she left Bizarre, and it wasn't Judy's eyes that filled with tears to see her go, but Dick's. Although she snuffed out such visions as sharply as she would her candle at night, the rush of feeling and longing she had whenever they crossed paths, the tightness in her chest, the heat on her skin—all these things and her own good sense were like hammers in her brain, insisting her aunt was right and she must not stay at Bizarre.

Theo kept more and more to his room. He refused offers of help and saw only Dick, his man, Paul, and Syphax. On the first day of February, he didn't come downstairs at all. Dick's face was gloomy when she enquired after his brother. She did not like to press and didn't linger, afraid to be alone with him. Nothing was said, but he stared at her mouth whenever they spoke. The coldest of rooms grew hot when they were together. And still, she hoped that Aunt Page was wrong about Theo.

Ten days later, Dick rode for the doctor. Nancy and Judy waited for news in the parlor. Soon enough, she heard the echo of boots down the hallway and the thud of the door. Later, came the crunch of gravel as the doctor's carriage rolled away, and still they waited. When Dick finally joined them in the parlor, his face was ashen.

"I must write to the family. I do not know if Jack or Tucker can get here in time, but the doctor says to try." Nancy rose, but he waved her away. "No. Theo will see no one. He doesn't want to be seen. He looks—"

Dick broke down. He leaned his forehead against the doorframe, and his shoulders heaved as he tried to regain his self-control. Judy went to stand by him, one hand on his back, gently circling. Tears spilled down Nancy's cheeks. The Lord knew she did not love Theo as she once imagined she might, but he was so young, only a couple of years older than she was herself. This was to be his life? The unfairness of it floored her.

Three days passed. The doctor came twice a day. The house fell into an uneasy silence, broken only by the sounds of footsteps and quiet murmurings as food was brought and removed. Phebe moved around her room like a ghost. Dick sent Sarah's husband, Ben, to collect their letters each day and grabbed what he brought back only to discard them all when he didn't find Jack or Tucker's handwriting amongst the folded pages.

On the fourteenth, in the morning, as she and Judy sewed nightcaps for the baby, Dick came slowly into the room and sat down. He looked hollowed out. Her heart wept in silence at the sight of his sorrow and pain.

"He's dead."

She sat frozen and cold as Judy went to embrace her forlorn husband. Then she followed them upstairs in silence to Theo's room.

All was tidy and light. Only a faint smell of sickness lingered under the heavier scents of lavender and cedar oil, indicating that the room had been cleaned and all the linens changed. Syphax and Paul would attend to everything, Dick muttered as he bade them say their farewells.

Theo's face was pinched and withered. Nancy remembered him at Tom and Patsy's wedding—his face ruddy with liquor, his breath warm and sweet and his eyes roving over her. It made no sense to see him so reduced. In turn, the sisters took up Theo's right hand and kissed it. His skin was thin, loose over his bones, and yet his hand was heavy in its lifelessness. A tear dropped from her lashes and settled on his wrist. She dashed it away and stepped back from the bed.

Dinner was a gloomy affair. Dick pushed the food around his plate, and Judy ate mechanically. Nancy chewed on a mouthful of chicken that tasted of nothing and lay in her stomach like a stone. She soon set down her fork. Comfort was needed. Affection. Expression of shared loss. Something. But Judy and Dick were silent, and she didn't dare reach her hand across the table to Dick, although she longed to. Just a touch. Just a token. Nothing more. Nothing wrong.

After Lottie removed their dishes, Dick declared he had letters to write and bade them goodnight. Unable to think of reading alone in the parlor, Nancy followed Judy upstairs. They parted in the hallway without a further word or touch between them. In her room, Phebe took her dress and brushed her hair. Her face was soft, concerned.

"Would you like me to sit with you a little, miss?" Nancy was about to answer yes, when they both turned at the sound of a light tap on the door.

"No. You may leave now." She opened the door as she spoke. Dick stood there, head bowed. Her heart hammered in her chest as he entered and walked to the window. "Leave us, Phebe. See if Sarah wants you in the kitchen house. Mr. Randolph will only stay a moment, and I won't need you again tonight." Blood drummed in her ears. Her lips were dry. She barely knew how she managed to speak and didn't look at Phebe's face. When the girl was gone and the door was closed, she turned.

Dick stood with his back to her, staring at the blackened windowpane.

She went to him.

Phebe

She pretended ignorance of what they'd done, even as her mind whirled with it. She imagined discovery, shock and screaming anger. But they were careful, and Mrs. Randolph saw nothing.

Not careful enough though. Phebe had seen it in her sister—the tiredness, the nausea and the sign that forced her to speak up.

Miss Nancy was at her window, rubbing sleep from her eyes. Phebe set down the clean linen she'd fetched. "May I speak?"

"You don't need to ask, Phebe. What concerns you?"

"It's the sheets, miss. I gave Sarah mine in place of yours. For washing."

Confusion rippled across her mistress's face. "Why? I don't understand."

Phebe swallowed. Her leg trembled. "You have not bled, Miss Nancy. Not for weeks." She watched her grow pale. "I didn't want Sarah knowing something before you know'd it yourself, miss."

Months passed. Visitors came and went. Mrs. Randolph gave birth to a healthy son, and Miss Nancy's condition remained hidden.

Phebe didn't speak of it again, but her mind rang with questions. She longed for her mama or Old Cilla to confide in. The temptation to whisper to Syphax, to tell him what she knew, was strong. Turned out, he knew it anyways.

August. Twilight. She was under the porch, leaning her back against the cold stone wall, listening to the cicadas whine, trying to put Miss Nancy's troubles out of mind. She heard the door open above, a heavy step and the creak of wood as someone sat down on the porch up to her left. Mr. Randolph, most likely, she'd have heard skirts swish if it were Miss Nancy or her sister. Whoever it was sat in darkness. No light filtered down between the boards above her head, but the smell of tobacco burning reached her, and soon, in the distance, she saw a lantern sway, heading toward the house. The tap of his stick told her it was carried by Syphax. He stopped before the steps of the porch and spoke softly.

"Mr. Randolph?"

The boards creaked. The master's feet must be only inches from her now. She pictured him leaning over toward Syphax. "Well?"

"I've found someone that will take it. But it must be a boy. A girl is no good to no one, but a boy? They'll take a boy."

"A good family?"

"Johnson will say it's Rachel's. She's carrying. Last chil' was pale. Twins they'll—"

"Spare me the details."

They were quiet for a moment. Then the master spoke again.

"And if it's not a boy?"

Phebe held her breath.

"I'll manage it, Mr. Randolph. Trust Syphax. Trust me."

Part Two

Part Two

Chapter Eleven

Bizarre, Virginia, late October, 1792

"What exactly are they saying?"

Judy looked at her husband, standing in the doorway of Bizarre with Randy Harrison. It was early in the day for a social call, and Randy must have risen well before dawn to arrive at their house at this hour. Dick's voice was strained. And Randy? Confident, competent Randy was red in the face, his eyes not meeting hers.

"Is something wrong?" Judy slid her arm through Dick's.

"It's nonsense. Slave chatter. Nothing for you to worry about."

"You're wrong, Dick. She has a right to know. Mary has written to her. Here." Randy pulled a letter from his pocket, but Dick snatched it, even as her fingers closed on the paper.

"Dick!"

"We should talk inside," said Randy. "Where's Nancy? She must hear this too."

"She's walking with our sister, Patsy." Judy turned to Dick. "What

91

is this, husband?" She read nothing in his face and flushed. "Well. I have no idea what ails you two, but this is no way to treat our friend and guest. Follow me, Randy." She led both men into the parlor and called for Lottie, watching the way Dick fiddled with the letter—her letter—in his hands. "Lottie will fetch Nancy and Patsy. I can't imagine what troubles you, but she is family too."

Randy stood in front of the fireplace, fooling with his hat, and Judy's patience snapped. "Sit down and gather yourself. At least tell me, is Mary in good health? The baby?" When he nodded, her shoulders relaxed. "And we are all well here. Surely, strong enough to bear whatever slave tale you may have to impart."

She sounded much calmer than she felt. They waited in silence for Nancy and Patsy, listening to the clock on the mantel tick and avoiding eye contact with one another.

Nancy blew into the room and stopped up short. "What is this?" she asked, looking at the three of them. Patsy, weighed down by pregnancy, entered more slowly.

"Randy has brought us some news. Unwelcome news, it appears. And insists we all hear it," said Judy.

"Well, how exciting!"

"Hardly that, Nancy." Dick snapped. "It's a piece of nonsense and should be treated as such."

"What is?" asked Nancy. "Randy?"

"It's not an easy thing to talk about. But I knew I had to come and tell you all. In person."

"Tell us *what*?"

"Nancy. Let him speak." Dick's voice had changed again, from anger to resignation almost. He stood by the window with his arms folded across his chest.

"It's about what happened at Glentivar, on your recent visit," Randy said.

"Nothing happened." Dick's voice was a low growl.

"Nancy was ill, nothing more," Judy said.

"That's not what people are saying."

"What people?" asked Patsy. Judy felt a burst of thankfulness she was present. Patsy didn't traffic in nonsense and gossip and would quickly settle this. Whatever *this* was.

"A rumor is circulating. It began with my slaves."

"I can't believe we're having this conversation." Dick looked ready to quit the room, but Patsy quickly moved to his side and laid a hand on his shoulder.

"Perhaps we should hear Randy out, brother."

Dick slumped into a chair. "Go ahead, then. Don't let me stop you."

"Not long after your last visit, I can't say for certain the date, one of the negro women spoke to Mary." Randy paused. "She told my wife that some of the slaves had found a body. The body of an infant."

"Impossible!" Judy said.

"I dismissed her. Ignored her story."

"But what had happened? Had one of the slaves given birth? Where was this body?" asked Patsy.

"She claimed the infant was found far from the house. She talked about a pile of shingles discarded between two logs. You know we've been building—" He paused again. "It was fair-skinned."

"There's not a word of truth in this." Dick shook his head. Judy wanted to catch his eye but could not.

"Very likely not," Randy agreed. "No one else saw it. And we all know how they talk. How things get blown up. Exaggerated."

"We know nothing of this," Judy said. "It has nothing to do with us." Pressure built in her chest.

"I thought nothing of it. I inspected the shingles and saw some marks, nothing more. At that point, I dismissed it out of hand. It was ludicrous to me. The idea that your sister ..." his voice died away.

"My *sister*?"

"Nancy?" Patsy knelt before her and lifted her chin.

Judy watched Nancy purse her lips and shake her head. "What does this have to do with Nancy?"

In the silence that followed, Patsy turned to Randy. "Some crazed slave woman told you a tall tale. You ignored her and rightly so. What has changed?"

"I thought nothing more would come of it, but I was wrong. The rumor has spread beyond Glentivar."

"Slave chatter, nothing more," muttered Judy.

"My neighbor's wife asked Mary about it two days ago."

"Who? Which neighbor? Dick, give me that letter." Judy snatched the paper from Dick's hand and scanned it quickly. "Jane Bland. A gossip. Listening to her negroes and spreading filthy lies about our family. Dick, you should return with Randy and visit the Blands. Demand they stop defaming us at once. It would be laughable if it wasn't so vile."

"No," said Patsy. "That won't answer."

"Patsy's right," said Dick. "I say we don't dignify this slave gossip with a response. You're overreacting, Randy. Who would believe a slave's tale, over us? Over the Randolph family? I don't know why we're even discussing it."

Judy got to her feet. Dick had recovered himself. She would do so too. But she couldn't look at Nancy.

"Although," Patsy's voice was slow and thoughtful, "it might be worth hearing the worst of it. My father often says we must be bold in our pursuit of knowledge. That we should never fear the truth. Exactly what story are they spreading? They're saying the child belonged to Nancy?"

Judy lingered by the door, wanting—and not wanting—to hear Randy's reply.

"Yes. They're saying that the child was Nancy's. And that Dick took it and abandoned it, hoping an animal would take it. They say—I'm sorry Dick—that the child was also yours. And you left it to die there."

"They're saying I'm a *murderer*? Of my own child?"

Judy turned and looked at her husband. His eyes were wide, his surprise genuine. She thought of their five-month-old son, Saint, lying upstairs in his crib and straightened her back.

"As if anyone in his right mind could suggest such a thing about Dick Randolph," she said. "I think we have heard enough. Dick dearest, I'm going to check on Saint. Please ensure the conversation has moved on by the time I return." She flashed a smile at their visitors and left the room.

Judy walked briskly, her heels clacking on the wooden floor, but at the top of the stairs, she paused. Her shoulders dropped. She leaned her forehead against the wall. It was cool. She focused on her breathing. Randy's story was too ugly. It hurt her stomach. She would not think of it. She turned her mind to caring for their son.

He didn't stir in his crib as she entered. Her first thought was to check his breathing. Would she always have this lump of panic in her chest until she saw the gentle rise and fall of his tiny frame? The room was in shadows. He lay on his back with both arms raised and bent at the elbow, his hands in fists, his dark-lashed eyelids closed. Her own breathing relaxed as she watched him. A light whistle came from his tiny mouth, and his lips peeled open a fraction. She felt a fierce love and moved to gather him up in her arms but stopped herself.

Instead, she turned and closed the door behind her. Then she stepped back to stand beside the crib. Biting on her lips, Judy raised her hands. She brought them together in a resounding clap. Saint didn't stir.

She left the room with the taste of blood on her tongue.

Naturally, Patsy didn't let it go. Nancy tried to avoid being private with her, but her flame-haired friend was tenacious. Cornered at last by the stables, she steeled herself for the inevitable barrage of questions.

"Nancy. You must tell me exactly what went on at Glentivar."

"Nothing." She imagined the word spiraling up into the air and disappearing.

"You were ill. In what way ill?"

"Colic. You know how I suffer from it."

"And nothing more?"

"Of course not."

"You didn't say much about Randy's news."

She forced herself to look Patsy in the eye and even managed to smile. "It was such nonsense."

But Patsy was frowning, and she disarmed her by grabbing her hands and pulling her close. A muscle twitched in her neck.

"Sister, life is complicated. Mistakes can be made. Things can happen against our will." She colored a little. For a moment, Nancy saw what this cost her. Patsy always wanted life to be ordered and honest, even though they all knew it was not. "But you can trust me. I can keep a secret. Even from Tom."

Tom. With his name, Patsy brought Tuckahoe, the family and

Father into Nancy's mind like a slap in the face. She blinked. "There is no secret, sister."

"You were never pregnant? When I was here in the summer, I did wonder ..." Her voice trailed away, and she dropped Nancy's hands.

"I was never pregnant. I suffer from the colic. How could I be pregnant, sister? Theo is dead."

She stared at Patsy, daring her sister-in-law to contradict her. She did not. Instead, Patsy said, "I've spoken to Judy about these rumors. I've told her I think you should leave here."

Nancy's stomach clenched. "And what did she reply?"

"She said it would do more harm than good. That it would be seen as evidence of guilt when no one is guilty of anything."

Relief washed through her, and she nodded. "Then there is nothing more to be said."

Nancy turned on her heel and walked away. She was colder than ever. She would be firmer than ice. She was stone.

It was slave gossip. Dick had dismissed it. Judy was reassured. And yet in the weeks that followed, she turned again and again to Mary's letter. The details haunted her.

Judy had been excited to visit Glentivar, looking forward to time with Mary, who was also nursing a child. She sensed Dick needed more company too. Jack was with them, and since Theo's death, his visits were uncomfortable. With both brothers elsewhere, perhaps Dick fancied they were both still alive, but when Jack was at Bizarre without Theo, that fiction was impossible to maintain. These were her suppositions at any rate. Nancy had claimed she was unwell, but Judy overrode her objections. It would be rude to Mary and Randy, and they'd promised to collect their sister, Jenny, who had shuttled from house to house since their father's remarriage. And now, with Gabriella expecting? Judy didn't want to think about it. There had been much said on that subject in her sisters' letters. She offered up a prayer for the child's safe delivery. As for what happened in the family afterward? She chose not to consider it.

Nancy was quiet on the drive to Glentivar, sitting next to her slave girl, Phebe. Judy cradled Saint on her lap. He was placid—an easy baby, Sarah had said, looking over his crib with a slight frown between her brows. Why would anyone look at a sleeping child and frown? Judy turned her thoughts to the view. The weather was fair, and the men rode on ahead—Dick, Jack and their cousin, Archie, still trying to woo Nancy, although with no success, as far as she could tell.

Glentivar was roughly thirty miles from Bizarre, and Judy's back ached, and her hips complained when the coach wheels finally rolled to a stop and Randy handed the ladies down. She was swept along by Mary, revived by a glass of water, and with Saint asleep, they toured around outdoors and in to witness and admire a range of alterations and innovations since their last visit. Nancy professed to feeling unwell and spent the afternoon and evening upstairs in her room, sipping tea for an upset stomach. Jenny had been fascinated by Mary's baby, a round-faced ball of spit and gurgles who sat up and clapped his hands with such fervor and enthusiasm that the tufts of brown hair on his head quivered like plumage, and his heels drummed the floor. Judy had thought to raise her worries about Saint, only to find herself unable or unwilling to put the thoughts into words. In the end, she'd returned to Bizarre with no real confidence being exchanged. Jenny's constant presence had been a barrier, and then the fiasco overnight pushed thoughts of Saint to the back of Judy's head for the first time in weeks.

Her recollection of what transpired was not the clearest.

Dick's footsteps. Blood on the stair and in Nancy's bed. A memory of Phebe's face, her eyes wide with alarm. The sound of Nancy crying out. But all these fragments swirled in the fog of a few drops of laudanum, her only escape from the exhaustion of feeding Saint. The next day, Nancy had been pale but composed. It had been the colic. Terrible cramps. None of this was unusual. It was only the timing—their being away from home—that made the situation uncomfortable. Mary was understanding. Judy forgot about it. Until Randy's visit.

No one spoke of it after Patsy left. It was possible, at Bizarre, to forget the rest of Virginia even existed. Besides, she had much to do in preparation for the long months of winter ahead, as well as Saint to think of. One morning in early December, she waited until Sally had lit the fire in the parlor and Nancy was busy at the table, stitching a new dress for Jenny. With her back to Nancy, Judy bent over the fire and drew Mary's letter from her pocket. It was the right thing to do. She threw it into the flames and watched it burn. Christmas passed quietly, with only Aunt Page and her husband visiting. Nancy spent most of her time shut up in her room on some pretext or another, leaving Judy to enjoy their aunt's company. Glentivar was never mentioned.

But in late January, a letter arrived from Jack.

"From your brother?" she said to Dick as he joined her in the parlor and broke the seal on the letter. "I'm surprised." Jack had left them only a week before, after a lengthy and difficult visit. He had been sick in December with scarlet fever, and although he mended, the illness changed him. Dick had made some veiled remarks, and Jack had been different, particularly around Nancy. Where before, he'd tended to follow her around like a mooncalf, now he avoided her entirely. Oh, she still caught him staring at her sister, but the look in his eyes had changed, grown dark. Judy, when she thought of it, wasn't sorry. It did neither Jack nor Nancy any good. The idea of Nancy transferring her affections from Theo to Jack had crossed her mind and didn't please her. Helpful though Nancy was, Aunt Page was right. Nancy should be looking for a husband, and that meant spending time away from Bizarre. She watched Dick unfold Jack's letter and thought she might write to Lizzie. Nancy should take a visit to Richmond. Then again, she was so useful at Bizarre. Judy frowned, in two minds about what would suit her best—Nancy there or Nancy gone—but startled when Dick suddenly screwed up the paper and threw it on the fire.

"Damned lies!" he said, and walked out of the room, slamming the door behind him. Later, when she asked what had upset him, he told her it was nothing. But the following day, there was another letter, this one from Mr. Tucker.

The story about Glentivar had spread far and wide. Jack had heard it in New York, Tucker in Williamsburg. Dick announced that they were going to stay with the Tuckers and decide what should be done. All of them. He would brook no delay.

Chapter Twelve

"It's worse than we thought," said Mr. Tucker.

They were assembled in the blue-paneled room Dick's stepfather used for formal business. He stood by the fireplace, as somber as Judy had seen him. Her husband had flung himself into an armchair opposite Mr. Tucker's new wife, Lelia, but now, he straightened up and folded his hands in his lap. This was difficult for Dick, Judy knew. But then it was hardly easy for any of them.

"You had best tell us what happened. Honestly now. In the knowledge that not a word will leave this room."

"Nothing happened," said Dick.

"Nothing? You have made a long day's journey for this 'nothing'."

"I didn't come to be hauled over the coals, sir. We want your help in scotching these damned rumors. Is that too much to ask?"

"Not at all. Nor is it too much to ask to be in possession of the facts. The best defense is based on knowledge and trust. Is it too much to ask my own son to tell me the truth of what happened at Glentivar?"

"I was unwell, sir," said Nancy.

Judy stiffened. "Nancy. It's not your place to speak."

But Mr. Tucker waved away her scruples. "We are family, my dear, and can be frank with each other. Go ahead, Nancy."

"I suffer from colic. The pain is extreme. Judy will vouch for it. I have suffered it for years. I had a bad bout. Randy and Mary were disturbed. They were sleeping downstairs with their child."

"Glentivar is a small home," said Dick. "Judy and I were to sleep in the room at the top of the stairs, with Nancy, little Jenny and Nancy's girl, Phebe, in the adjoining room." He turned to Lelia. "It was far from ideal, but with such distances between us all, we take what beds we can find. Jack and Archie laid up at the local inn. Judy slept heavily, but I was called by Jenny, upset to find her sister in so much pain."

"I took a sleeping draft," Judy said. "I haven't slept well since our son was born. My worries …" Lelia reached across and squeezed her hand.

Her touch warmed Judy. Lelia was such a contrast to Gabriella, who had recently been safely delivered of a son named Thomas Mann Randolph Jr.—their brother, Tom's exact name, even though Tom was still alive and well. Patsy's letter had been blunt on the point, and relations between Monticello and Tuckahoe had never been cooler. Judy envied the way Mr. Tucker's gaze brightened whenever he laid eyes on Lelia, but at least she could reassure herself that Dick's family was no less at odds than her own. Jack had made no secret of his disapproval of the new Mrs. Tucker. Dick dismissed it as immaturity and suggested there was still some aftershock over the loss of Theo. Everyone knew Jack to be temperamental. Judy released Lelia's hand and turned her attention back to Dick's stepfather.

"So, you have little to tell us," said Mr. Tucker. "Jenny is too young. What age is she now? Seven?" Judy nodded. "Explain what occurred then, Dick and Nancy. In as much detail as you can."

"Nancy fell ill early in the evening," Dick began. "She retired after dinner, taking Jenny with her. The girl, Phebe, was upstairs too. Judy followed soon after. Mary settled the baby while Randy and I smoked a pipe on their front porch. I'd no apprehension Nancy was anything more than under the weather until I said goodnight to Randy and went to retire myself. Phebe asked permission to go out to the kitchen and boil some water for fennel tea. While she was gone, Jenny took me in to see Nancy. I was mostly concerned that if Jenny started crying, the whole house would be disturbed. I sat with Nancy and tried to keep both her and Jenny calm. Phebe brought tea. It didn't help. In fact, Nancy vomited." He pulled a face. "At that point, I think I went down to find a basin, warm water and some towels. Phebe told me where to look. I ran back upstairs and gave the women what they needed. Judy woke up around then. I know Randy and Mary heard me on the stairs. The house is timber, and the stairs whine with every footfall. Mary was helpful. She gave Nancy some laudanum. That seemed to do the trick."

"The whole episode is embarrassing," said Nancy. "I wish I had stayed at Bizarre. I wanted to, but Judy said it would be rude—"

"It would have been. Randy and Mary expected us all. Although heaven knows, now, I wish you *had* stayed at home." Judy didn't glance in her sister's direction.

"And the blood on the stairs?" Mr. Tucker looked from Dick to Nancy. "We can't dismiss *that* as slave chatter. Randy Harrison confirmed it to me himself." He waved a hand at the desk behind him.

"You wrote to Randy?" asked Dick.

"I did." Mr. Tucker raised his eyebrows as Dick threw himself back in his chair. "The matter is serious."

"But it's nonsense! And insulting."

"Quite so, but we are family and must hold together, whatever the storm. I will ask you again, without emotion, and wish you to answer in kind. The Harrisons report there was blood on the stairs and in Nancy's bedclothes. It must be explained."

Dick turned to her sister. Judy tried to read his expression but could not.

"A nosebleed," Nancy said. "Brought on by the vomiting. Phebe tried to clear it up in the morning. We were afraid to make any further disturbance during the night." She bit her lips and looked down at her lap.

There was a moment's silence, and then Judy spoke up. "I wish I'd been more aware of what was happening. I saw nothing and heard little. But Nancy is certainly prone to nosebleeds. The story the slaves concocted is an outrage."

"Well, there we have it!" Lelia clapped her hands together and rose. "Mr. Tucker, dear, do you think I might take the ladies away for some refreshments? The children are keen for us to join them."

Her merry tone broke the tension. Judy smiled. She saw Nancy unclasp her hands and flex her fingers. Mr. Tucker extended a hand to Judy, and the ladies stood and shook out their skirts. They followed Lelia to the doorway with Mr. Tucker and Dick only a step behind. In the hallway, she heard the men talking.

"We will leave the matter for today, Dick," Mr. Tucker said. "But it is not enough to have your story straight, as I'm sure you know. We must work out what to do to stop the rumors."

"I know it, sir. That is why we are come, and I am grateful for your support."

"You have it. Rest assured. You, Judy, Nancy—all three. I will not fail you."

* * *

In early March, Judy and Dick were summoned from Williamsburg to Tuckahoe.

She was apprehensive. Dick said little, but he didn't need to—a Virginian's honor was as vital as his heartbeat. Jack wrote frequently, sparing no one's feelings and railing against the sly looks and jokes he claimed to be subjected to as the brother of the Randolphs of Bizarre. Even the name of their home was used against them, he declared, waxing lyrical about the aspersions being cast against Dick's character. Judy sensed Dick and Tucker's unease rise.

And now, this visit to Tuckahoe. Judy traveled alone in the coach while Dick rode ahead, thinking who knew what. She leaned her head against the doorframe and tried for optimism. Tuckahoe was her home. They were going to her father and her brothers. They must support them. Without Nancy there to antagonize, she would manage Gabriella. That left Dick to enlist the support of her father, Tom and William.

But the moment the carriage drew to a halt at the north door, it was evident that all was not well. No family stood on the steps to welcome them. Their arrival couldn't have gone unheard, and yet only James, her father's footman, was present, nodding to her driver and calling a boy to stable the horses. Judy looked at Dick, but his face was blank. She picked up her skirts and followed him into the house.

The Great Hall was empty and silent. Judy noted some changes—a new, bright carpet, matching sideboards at each window. She reached for Dick's hand, but he had turned to James.

"Is Mr. Randolph at home?" he asked, his voice tight.

"The family are in the dining room. They will receive you there."

The dining room. Judy sucked in her cheeks. Dick pulled off his hat and thrust it at James. "It appears we are all business today." He offered her his arm. "Come, Mrs. Randolph. Let us go and meet your family."

They were nearly all there. That was the next surprise. Father, Gabriella, Tom and William, along with Patsy and William's new wife, Lucy. Lizzie and her husband were absent, but Molly was there with her husband, David Meade Randolph, who Dick had never liked. Father was the only person to rise when they entered the room.

"Randolph. Judith," he said. "Please take a seat."

"What kind of greeting is this, Father?" She struggled to take in the implications of what she saw. No one looked at her. The table was bare of refreshments. They took their seats at the lower end of the table, with her father and Gabriella at the top and her siblings ranged down each side. She shrank inside her dress and tears pricked her eyes. Dick gripped the arms of his chair. Her father remained on his feet.

"You can be under no illusions as to why I required your presence here today," he said. "The family deserves answers. Do you dispute the facts of the case, Randolph?"

"There is no case, and there are no facts before me, sir. What would you have me say? What would you have me think of such a reception?" Dick stared down the table.

"I told you all how it would be!" William threw up his arms and leaned back in his chair. "To expect reasonable behavior from a man like this!"

"A man like me?" Dick was on his feet in an instant. "Sir, are you going to allow such rudeness to go unchecked?"

Her father threw a mild frown in William's direction. Judy saw it and quailed. It told her they were all ranged against them. Dick knew it too. She sensed his tension as clearly as if it were a hot ray of sun dancing across her skin.

"Let us remain civil and keep our emotions in check, shall we?" Father said. "William did not mean to offend, I am sure. And yet, you cannot have expected us to react to these rumors with anything other than great distress? Accusations of adultery? Murder? Come, Randolph, did you look for a warm welcome under such circumstances? I hardly think so."

"It's all lies."

Judy scanned the sea of grave faces. Light shining in from the west windows cast the figures on one side of the table in white light and buried those opposite in shadow. Lucy's mouth was downturned. Molly gazed at her hands. Patsy offered her a half-smile, but Tom had a bullish set to his jaw, and William glared at Dick in open disgust.

"There are many reputations at risk here," Tom said.

"Indeed, there are!" Dick placed his palms on the table. "Which is why I hope you will join me and my family in pushing back on the gossip wherever we hear it. This is a foul lie, conjured up in the foul minds of disgruntled slaves. Randy Harrison's slaves, not mine, you'll note. I hardly believed it could be possible for such mud to stick."

"What you *believe* is neither here nor there at this point," said David Meade Randolph. His meaty face was expressionless. Judy wanted to slap him.

"What matters to us most," said William, "is the damage done to our sister."

Judy's breath caught, and her heart expanded in her chest. She opened her mouth, but Tom chimed in before her.

"What is to become of Nancy, Randolph? That's what we are asking ourselves. You were trusted with the care of our sister. Our eighteen-year-old, unmarried sister. And yet here we are. It's not *your* reputation that concerns us, but hers. Nancy's. Nancy's reputation and Nancy's prospects. What can they be now?"

Judy put her hands to her cheeks. "Am I not your sister too, Tom?" She shook her head in confusion. "You bring me and my husband here to talk of Nancy?"

"Certainly. She is our primary concern," said Father. "A Virginian man is responsible for the safety and well-being for all who make their home with him—for his wife, his children, all his slaves, tenants and dependents. In offering my daughter, Nancy, a home, Dick, you became as a father to her. And now this!" Color rose in his cheeks for the first time. Gabriella reached out and touched his hand, but he waved her away. "We have discussed these events as a family—"

"What events? Father, there was no 'event'. It is a misunderstanding. Gossip. As if my husband and my sister would—" Judy broke off, unable to say more. Her head throbbed; tears spilled forth. Molly's hand was on her elbow, and she allowed herself to be led from the room.

Her older sister tried to persuade her to lie down upstairs, but Judy would have none of it.

"No. Only give me a moment to compose myself. It's so unexpected. I thought we would find support here. It is not true, sister. None of it." She looked at Molly, but nothing in her expression reassured. Moments later, her father's voice boomed out so loudly that she heard every word.

"Whether there is any truth in the story or not, Richard Randolph, my daughters were in your care. One as your wife and the other, her sister, as a dependent, a girl, a young woman, whose entire future prospects are now blasted. Blasted, by this base narrative. I find that you are the responsible party here. You are the party at fault. Whatever the tawdry truth may or may not be, I do not care. Do you hear me? Whether it's all lies or every word is true, it is too damned late. You are equally dishonored in either case.

Naturally, I would prefer that my son-in-law *not* be an adulterer, *not* be a child-murderer, *not* be a liar and a cheat. But even if you are as innocent as a babe against such charges, you are dishonored forever in this family. How could you let this happen? My daughters. In—I repeat—*your* care. And this is where we find ourselves? Our family, the subject of tavern gossip and street-corner laughter. The Randolph name become a source of merriment. Slaves whispering. Our friends, our fellow landowners whispering. This is where you have brought us, Richard Randolph. And all you can do is shrug your shoulders and tell me it's not true."

Judy opened the dining room door and watched. Dick was on his feet.

"You say it is too late, sir, that I have brought us here, but that is hardly fair or true. Can you seriously believe that slaves did this? That slave chatter could bring lies and gossip to such a fever and tumult that we are the talk of Virginia and beyond? No!" Dick's eyes glittered as he glared at them all. "This has been allowed to spread, has been perpetuated even by those who should stand our friends. By our own family. I have it on good authority that William here has been one of the worst. I'm told he has never defended my name. Worse, he's given the rumors credence, even spreading these foul slanders himself." He turned on William. "Do you deny it? Will you sit there and deny your part in this disaster?"

Judy saw William's eyes slide to his new wife, Lucy. She had not met the girl. Lucy was pretty, with large, dark eyes and a pert mouth. Her clothes looked costly. She read his expression—a mix of arrogance, coupled with a desire for approbation—and realized what had happened. William, lacking the optimism of Tom or the confident indifference of Father, had found his extended family plunged into scandal just as he tried to fix the interest of Lucy Bolling Randolph, daughter of Virginia's former governor. He'd repudiated his family at Bizarre, Judy was sure of it. How quickly he must have distanced himself from them, coward that he was.

"Try and spread the blame as you will, Randolph," replied William, "but there is no one here in doubt about who is at fault."

"Damn you, man! I tell you it is all talk, and yet you sneer at me? On my honor as a gentleman, I will not accept such treatment. I must have satisfaction."

"Here now, Dick." It was Tom's turn to intervene. "We can have no dueling in the family."

"What family? This is not how family are treated! My wife ignored. My honor insulted. Keep out of this, Tom. William? Give me your answer? Will you name your seconds?"

Again, Judy saw William glance at Lucy. Her eyes gave nothing away, but she certainly didn't look concerned that her new husband was being challenged to a pistol fight.

"Only gentlemen duel, Dick," came his slow reply. "Father, I don't intend to dignify this attack with a response. What say you?"

"I say that Richard Randolph needs to keep his temper in check and remember whose house he is in!" Judy's father thumped his right hand down on the dining table. "You are not here, young man, to force a fight on my son. I asked you here to discover how you intend to remove this scurrilous gossip from around my daughter Nancy's innocent head. And so far, you have failed."

Dick glowered at William, but something, perhaps the coldness in Father's tone, blunted his temper, and the high color faded from his cheeks. He sat down heavily. "If I might speak with you alone, sir?"

Father shrugged but nodded, and the family rose. Judy stepped into the room to return to Dick's side, but her husband shook his head. She was forced to funnel out with her siblings and their husbands and wives, none of whom—not even Patsy—acknowledged her, and who soon dispersed into the Great Hall, leaving her stranded in the hallway, a stranger in the home she grew up in.

She didn't have long to wait. In fewer than five minutes, Dick emerged. Judy looked past him, hoping her father would follow. But there was no sign of him, and when she went to the door, Dick blocked her path.

"Don't speak with him. It will make you no happier. We need to leave."

"Leave?" Her voice was a whisper. "How can we leave? This is my family. What about the horses?"

Dick put an arm around her and dug his fingers into her shoulder. "I will manage the horses, Judy. But I won't stay here a moment longer. Do you understand?"

She looked up. His handsome face was drawn. "Yes, husband," she said.

It was only later, miles from Tuckahoe, when they stopped at Providence Forge to change horses, that Judy found the courage to ask Dick what her father had said. They stood on a stone bridge, overlooking a gurgling stream, a short walk from the hostelry. Judy watched the water flow and churn.

"I asked him to help me sue anyone spreading these rumors for slander. He refused."

"What reason did he give?"

"The same as you heard him give when you were in the room. It is too late. The damage to my reputation is done. I—we—*our* cause is already lost. Your father wanted only to speak about Nancy. About what might be done to save Nancy."

Judy's hands curled into fists. "What did he suggest?"

"That she leave Bizarre and return to Tuckahoe. Which is, and believe me I pointed this out, the only certain way to damn us all to infamy for ever."

"Are you quite sure? Might it not be better for all of us if she were gone?"

"No! Nothing more surely indicates guilt. You said so yourself back in October. We have done nothing wrong. Nancy cannot leave Bizarre until the matter is put to rest. Then she can leave with her head held high, and we can get on with our lives."

"Promise me you won't do anything rash. When you called out William, I thought I might turn hysterical."

"Hysterical? I should be sorely disappointed if you did. No. I've had enough of this whole sorry saga."

"Please, Dick. Promise me you will let it go. We will wait. The gossip will fade. Surely it will." He didn't answer but stepped away from the bridge and stretched his back.

"Why don't you take a seat?" Earlier, he'd pointed out a stone bench on a patch of grass between the bridge and the hostelry. "I'll join you in a moment."

Nodding, Judy left his side and was almost out of sight when she thought of Lizzie. Lizzie had not been at Tuckahoe. Perhaps she might stand their friend still. She turned, thinking to share this hope with Dick, but he wasn't looking her way. She watched as he pulled some papers from his coat pocket, ripped them into pieces and flung the fragments out over the bridge wall. She took the last few steps to the bench and sat down. What had she seen?

Doubt gripped her. She had been queasy that morning, another sign, adding to her recently raised hope that she and Dick might have another child coming. She squeezed her eyes closed and breathed, slowly, deeply and deliberately. Their treatment at Tuckahoe had shaken her. Seeing Dick tear up that letter worried her. But she had her children to think about. There was no room for doubts.

Chapter Thirteen

No one told Nancy what went on at Tuckahoe, and she didn't ask. She felt removed from everything and everyone. In Williamsburg, she was almost happy. She could almost believe none of it had ever happened. Or that it had happened to someone else. Not to her. Not to them. Except, of course, it had. She saw it in Dick's eyes on the rare moments he looked at her. She saw it in the frown lines on her sister's face. She saw it in Phebe's eyes when she sat at her glass and watched as she curled her hair. She felt it in her body. How could she not? In the early days after Glentivar, she thought she'd never hold a child without tears streaming down her cheeks. But Saint's sweet innocence soothed her, and in Williamsburg, she could escape painful memories, spending time with the children of the house—Dick's youngest half-siblings, Lelia's children, and of course, Saint.

Her nephew, now eight months old, sat, smiled, laughed and sometimes cried like any other boy of his age might. He interrogated the world through his mouth, grabbing anything within his reach—a fistful of his fond aunt's hair, a brooch pinned to her dress, his rattle, the blanket he had grown so attached to—rubbing each with his lips and tongue in messy exploration. He was strong, they all said so, admiring the grip that clutched at their fingers or at his spoon as he took to solid food with hearty enthusiasm. He was a handsome fellow too, with fat, pink cheeks and a shock of brown curls that his mother, aunt and Lelia could not resist touching. Eyes softened when they saw him. Mr. Tucker sat with his little namesake in the garden, bouncing him on his knee and singing soft lullabies until the sun fell behind the rooftop and the cold chased them back indoors.

But what use were lullabies if the child could not hear them? Nancy saw the signs. He didn't turn his head when someone entered the room. His face lit up when his mother appeared in his line of sight, but he didn't stir at the sound of her voice. He didn't react to clapping, although he had learned to clap himself, copying Lelia's daughter, who spent hours with the baby, sitting on the floor with him, telling stories with her dolls and playing peekaboo with her hands. Loud noises rarely disturbed him. Once, a serving girl dropped an empty tin bucket on the hearth just feet from where Saint sat banging on a toy drum. The child was startled and dropped the drumstick in his fist. Hope fired in Judy's eyes, but Nancy didn't see it the same way. Saint's reaction was delayed, more likely a consequence of Judy's own sudden movement as she heard the noise. There was no evidence of Saint hearing anything that went on around him, and what the implications were—well, no one, as yet, was prepared to discuss it. Judy's plan, according to Nancy's observation, was to pray for a miracle. Much good that would do.

Daily life in Williamsburg was easier than at Bizarre, never mind that there were so many in the household. Nancy felt time slow. She slept better and grew stronger, at least in her body. In Williamsburg, she closed her mind to the past and resigned herself to a future that would take care of itself. She dreamed of her mother and sometimes was surprised to wake up, not at Tuckahoe, in her warm bed with her sister by her side, but in a small room in Mr. Tucker's house with wagons rolling along the cobbles beneath her window, the clatter of horse hooves and shouts and giggles from the nursery next door.

She saw next to nothing of Dick and Mr. Tucker. She asked no questions, but all three women knew the men were as concerned as ever. One day, Lelia reported that Mr. Tucker believed that more than a miracle was needed to drag the family out of the havoc wreaked by the October visit to Glentivar. Judy had broken down and cried. Nancy looked on, feeling wretched, saying nothing. Both Tucker and Dick were, by nature, drawn to action, rather than reaction, and after the visit to Tuckahoe, they spent long evenings huddled together in Mr. Tucker's study, leaving the women to read or sew in the parlor, each privately speculating, but saying nothing, about what their menfolk might be about to do.

Everything changed in the middle of March. Dick announced they would leave the Tuckers and travel to the family's house at Matoax. If a return to Bizarre was discussed, Nancy was not party to it, nor was her opinion on the matter sought. The feeling she had experienced in Williamsburg—that strange, dislocated sense of being suspended, as if by some unseen threads, between what had been and what would come—continued at Matoax.

And then, at the end of the month, Dick penned a public letter. It was time, he declared, to resolve the matter. Once and for all.

TO THE PUBLIC
March 29, 1793

My character has lately been the subject of much conversation, blackened with the imputation of crimes at which humanity revolts, and which the laws of society have pronounced worthy of condign punishment. The charge against me was spread far and wide before I received the smallest notice of it—and whilst I have been endeavoring to trace it to its origin, has daily acquired strength in the minds of my fellow citizens.

To refute the calumnies which have been circulated, by a legal prosecution of the authors of them, must require a length of time, during which the weight of public odium would rest on the party accused, however innocent—I have, therefore, resolved on this method of presenting myself before the bar of the public.

Calumny to be obviated must be confronted—If the crimes imputed to me are true, my life is the just forfeit to the laws of my country. To meet and not to shrink from such an inquiry as would put that life in hazard (were the charges against me supportable) is the object of which I am now in pursuit.

I do, therefore, give notice that I will, on the first day of the next April, Cumberland court appear there and render myself a prisoner—

Judy threw the paper on the table and covered her face with her hands. "Dick! You can't mean to publish this? It's insanity."

"Far from it."

She continued reading. "What do you mean here? '*Let not a pretended tenderness toward the supposed accomplice in the imputed guilt shelter me. That person will meet the accusation with a fortitude of which innocence alone is capable.*'"

117

"It means what it says. Your brother, William, will not meet me. Yet he and others let this slander spread, all the while pretending deep concern for Nancy. I'm not supposed to clear my name in case it further injures hers. That was your family's message to me. Well, Tucker and I have determined it will not serve. We must pull clear of this, Judy."

His voice cracked, and Dick threw himself into an armchair in their Matoax parlor.

The room was cold enough that Judy saw her breath on the air. "When will this become known?"

"It will appear in tomorrow's *Gazette*. Your sister will be protected if I stand forward to answer the rumors and prove them unfounded. Tucker and I have it all worked out. In a month, we'll be back at Bizarre where we belong. I hate this house."

Time and again, she had shown him in word and action that she supported him. She had never demeaned herself or him by asking Nancy about Glentivar. She had never questioned Nancy's girl, Phebe, who was as close with her mistress as any slave girl Judy had ever known. True, she'd thought of doing so, but the idea was as quickly dismissed as it was conceived. The girl's word meant nothing, would serve them no purpose and therefore was without value. Besides, even asking her admitted a level of doubt in Nancy and Dick that Judy's mind revolted against. She forced herself to stay in the moment and concentrate on her husband's words. Was she supposed to contradict him? Judy had no love for Matoax either.

"Why do you hate it here?"

"It's full of the dead, Judy. Can't you feel it? They are all here—Father, Mother, Theo."

His parents. His brother. Not their child. Dick's list of losses was incomplete. She swallowed the words that rose in her throat, tasting a disappointment in him that had grown so familiar she almost welcomed it. The death of the child had become something Judy understood as only hers. Returning to Matoax returned the loss she had experienced in full force. Even as she fussed and prayed over Saint, even as she prayed for the new child she hoped to deliver, always, she clung to that loss. Remembering the first child, when everyone around her seemed to have forgotten, that was her duty, the responsibility of parenting that Judy now relished. A little girl. Born still, but she had not always been still. Only Judy had experienced that. Dick didn't share her grief, and his failure to remember, or care, bitter though it was, proved she was right.

"As if the loss of my brother has not been enough for myself and Nancy to contend with," he said.

"Nancy? Why Nancy?" Judy drew in a breath, and the cold air stung her teeth.

"Weren't you the one that said Theo and she would marry?"

"Perhaps they should have. Then none of this mess—"

"*Mess?*" Dick pressed his fingers into his eyelids. "What kind of word is *mess* to describe this hell? Have you any idea of what I'm going through? My honor, my reputation, all at risk. What would my father think? Or my mother? Finding myself at the mercy of tattling slaves and malicious, jealous men like your sniveling brother. Forced to submit to your father's scorn. Accused of killing a newborn, Judy! An infant. I am sick to my stomach from dawn until dusk. This is not a mess! This is an open wound in my chest! And while you might lock up your feelings and pinch up your face and stopper your ears and eyes to what is happening to me, I am not so stiff. Not so cold and unfeeling. Good God, what kind of woman are you?"

He jumped to his feet and towered over her. When she shrank

back, it only seemed to anger him more. Disappointment, revulsion, scorn stormed across his face, and she panicked.

"Dick!" She reached for his hand. He pushed it away. He strode to the door but paused in the doorway. When he spoke, his voice was cooler.

"For better or worse, Judy. We are man and wife. And whatever our failings, we are all each other has, or can have in this life. Let us not make it any worse than it already is. Find it in yourself to understand what I am dealing with. Support me. You are my wife. I'd like you to act like it."

A short distance away, across the hall, Nancy rocked on the balls of her feet. She had been considering what tasks she might get done before dinner. It was how she made her way through each day—keeping busy, not thinking. Now, Dick's words hammered her ears like nails into wood. *We are all each other has, or can have, in this life … understand what I'm dealing with … support me … my wife … act like it.*

Saliva pooled on Nancy's tongue. She must swallow, or gag on it.

Phebe

Bizarre was quiet when the family was in Williamsburg.

Sarah barely tolerated Phebe at mealtimes. "Yo mistress found herself somewhere else to live yet? I knew she was trouble. Didn't I say it, girls?" Lottie and Sally nodded, neither glancing Phebe's way. Sarah's husband, Ben, and her son, Billy, were kinder, but it was only the kindness of wishing a fellow being a good day or sharing a smile at the sight of a cloudless sky. Phebe had been too fine for Sarah's liking, and now she was too low. Her mistress had brought scandal to their door, and Sarah, for all she'd complain about Mrs. Randolph's moods and inconsistencies, had taken her side.

"Imagine folks believing your own sister had a child with your own husband?" Sarah said, shaking her head. "Kind of thing that eats you up inside."

"It's not true!"

"Don't even matter what the truth is," Sarah told Phebe. "Don't matter one tiny bit. Damage is done. Damage is done."

Sarah wasn't wrong, but trouble was, Phebe didn't know what the truth was either. She knew what she'd seen and what she'd heard. Last time Phebe saw Miss Nancy's child, it was breathing. Small. Pale. Breathing. Mr. Randolph had taken it only to come back later and break her mistress's heart, saying the child had been weak, not strong enough to last the night. A tragic loss.

But then came talk of the overseer Johnson, and how Rachel, the woman he kept, had a new child, white enough to pass. How they'd moved to Mr. Randolph's lands south of the Appomattox River. How Rachel had gotten her papers and was free.

The story ate at her. Suppose her mistress was grieving a child that hadn't died but had been taken? Then again, the child had been a girl, and girls were a burden. Rachel had only agreed to take a boy.

Syphax would know.

But for all his seeming kindness, she was afraid to go to him and ask.

Chapter Fourteen

Dick insisted Nancy and Judy wait at Matoax while he returned to Bizarre with only Jack for company. His public statement had immediate impact. With the scandal the talk of the county, local justices ordered the sheriff to arrest both Dick and Nancy Randolph, but when he arrived at Bizarre, only the men were at home. Jack wrote that his brother sat in a cell for four days before being charged with "*feloniously murdering a child delivered of the body of Nancy Randolph, or being accessory to the same.*"

A week later, with Dick still in the jailhouse, Mr. Tucker took the sisters back to Bizarre.

"I wasn't sure I'd ever see this house again," Judy said, as he helped her out of the carriage.

"All will be well soon." Mr. Tucker held his hand out to Nancy while Judy walked ahead into the house.

"I'd welcome an opportunity to speak with you privately, sir," Nancy said. "Perhaps we might take a walk while my sister rests?" She led him down the familiar path to the kitchen garden and tobacco fields that fanned out behind the plantation buildings like long undulating rolls of cloth. "If I understand things correctly, you are shielding me."

"We are."

"I'm grateful. It strikes me that you are kinder to me than my own family."

"You *are* my family."

She smiled at him. "Am I?"

"How old are you, Nancy?"

"Eighteen."

"A mere child. No, hush." He squeezed on the cold fingers she had tucked in his arm. "I'm more than twice your age and have all the advantages of travel, experience and knowledge of the world. Let me tell you something, and then you may tell me anything you like and ask me anything you wish." When she nodded, he continued. "I first met Dick, Theo and Jack when they were only seven, six and four years old. I loved them, all three, without reserve. I loved their mother and saw her in them. I still do. I swore to protect them and to support them without reserve. When your sister married Dick, that oath extended to her. When you joined their household, that oath extended to you. And when you love someone, Nancy, truly love them, you don't love them less if they make mistakes or are at fault in some way. When someone you love stumbles, you help them recover. That is my belief, it was Frances, Dick's mother's belief, and it is Lelia's. There. Lesson over." Again, his hand pressed hers. "Enough from me. Now, you may talk."

She drew in a breath. "I will not speak of Glentivar. But I did write a letter for Dick. Did he tell you?"

"He did."

"He will not use it?"

"No."

She bit her lip. "It is my wish that he would."

"And it is mine—and his—that he will not. It was destroyed. And rightly so."

"Why?"

"For many reasons. But mainly because you're young and a woman."

"What will happen to Dick?"

"Nothing. He will be examined by the Cumberland County justices and exonerated."

"Are you sure?"

He smiled down at her. "I can't be truly sure, of course not. But on the balance of probabilities, I am confident. Let me see if I can set your mind at ease. Dick is accused of murder—a terrible crime, yes—but one where he is presumed innocent until proved otherwise. The burden of proof is on the court, not on the accused, and here we have a case with no body and no witnesses. Virginian law prohibits slaves being called to testify in a case where the defendant is white. And with Dick as the accused, his wife cannot be asked to testify against him as she might be if it were her sister on trial."

"Judy could say nothing that would harm me."

"No, but Dick and I both wish to shield her from the courtroom. It will not be pleasant listening. And now she's with child again, it's essential she's comfortable and at ease as much as possible."

Nancy pondered for a few moments. "It seems so risky."

"Believe me, it is sound strategy. When your family would not help, Dick and I talked through what would likely happen next. The rumors showed no indication of dying down. Once the story was the talk of Dick's peers, it was inevitable that there would be a call for his, and your, arrest. His letter in the *Gazette* provoked what was going to happen anyway, but it allowed us to at least control *when* things happened. By publishing as he did, Dick ensured that the scandal was the first point of order when the county authorities began their next session. He returned to Bizarre, you remained in Matoax beyond their reach. Dick ensured the judicial focus was on him, not you."

"But why not me? I—"

"Because the charge against you, my dear, would have been much harder to defend. You could be charged with infanticide, and Virginia law views that charge very differently to murder. Infanticide—the murder of a child conceived out of wedlock by its mother—requires the accused to provide a witness that the child was stillborn."

"There was no child born at Glentivar!" She threw him a defiant glance.

"When the case against Dick fails, we believe the justices will have no appetite or grounds to pursue a charge against you. We have the best lawyers working on Dick's behalf. Enough legal talent to convince a gaggle of rural Cumberland justices. We need to go through this process. And then we can talk about your future."

"I've considered that." Her voice sounded hollow. "My future is here, with Judy and Saint."

"We will see. After the examination, we can talk again."

"No."

Mr. Tucker stopped and turned to look at her. Nancy held his eyes. Nothing more was said, and they walked back to Bizarre.

The days until Dick's examination passed slowly. When Nancy wasn't needed in the house, answering the questions of Dick's much-lauded lawyers, Patrick Henry and John Marshall, she disappeared to the kitchen garden, pinning up her skirts and pulling on stout boots each morning. She left the house before Judy rose, leaving her sister to go through the day's tasks with Sarah and preferring silent hours of snipping, weeding and watering. Sarah's son, Billy, worked with her, taking on the hard work of digging, lifting and fetching. He had a habit of humming, and sometimes, she wondered if he longed to sing but could not when she was there. Would she like it if he did? Or would it be too familiar, embarrassing him, embarrassing them both? He was the same age as her, they worked side by side, but they could never be friends. Not like she and Phebe. She allowed a few flashes of memory from those terrible days, recalling Phebe's face, her eyes widening, her soft words, the squeeze of her hand. Phebe's eyes. They were the last thing Nancy saw every night, the first to greet her in the morning. Over Billy Ellis' muttered objections, she picked up a trowel and dug into damp soil. Think of nothing. Speak of nothing. Dig. Mr. Tucker had to be right. The trial must bring it to an end. Dick had to come home. She'd spend the rest of her days trying to make it up to Judy in any way she could. These terrible rumors had to be squashed. Dick had to come home to Bizarre.

Judy insisted they both attend the courthouse. She stood across the fireplace from Mr. Tucker with her arms crossed and refused to move or even sit until he had agreed to convey both her and Nancy there. She would walk otherwise. She made sure he knew she meant it.

"My presence will help, I'm certain," she told him, as the coach swayed away from Bizarre the following morning.

Mr. Tucker took her hands. "It will be a show of strength to the justices. To see you there will give Dick confidence also. Truly, I commend your bravery. But harsh things will be said of him. And of your sister."

Judy closed her eyes. The concern in his face was upsetting.

"How are you this morning, Nancy?" he asked. "Are you well? You've been quiet since your interview with John Marshall. He's a fine attorney."

Always this concern about Nancy.

"I'm sure she will be perfectly happy, as we all will, as soon as this charade of an investigation is over." Judy hoped he didn't catch the bitterness in her voice. "Let's worry about poor Dick for now, shall we?"

Still, she quailed when they arrived at Cumberland courthouse. It was a small but somber-looking stone building with tall pillars that towered over a crowd of curious onlookers.

"I didn't think ..." Judy saw Mr. Tucker had anticipated what she had not—the attraction of this spectacle, of this scandal. There were wagons crowded with men and women, jostling for a view through the courtroom windows, and boys perched in trees, loudly reporting on what they saw to groups of children gathered below. She shrank into her father-in-law's arm as he helped them down from the carriage and into the cold courtroom building.

The sea of familiar faces made her feel worse, not better. She recognized Father's narrow shoulders and tilted head as he leaned in to listen to her brother William. Beside William was his wife, Lucy, come to feign shock and disgust whilst enjoying every moment, no doubt. In front of them, Patsy and Tom sat quietly and beside them, David and Molly, Lizzie and John. There were noticeable absences for which she was thankful—no Gabriella, none of her younger siblings—she hated the thought of them even hearing of this—but there was Aunt Page with Carter, there was Jack, Dick's brother, sitting separate from everyone else, and there were Randy and Mary, looking as miserable as Judy felt. Mary managed a weak smile as Mr. Tucker steered Judy along a bench, far from her Tuckahoe relations.

She tried to focus her thoughts on Dick—on where he might be, whether he had slept, washed or eaten. He would be determined, she knew that, and imagined the thrust of his chin as he masked his fear and looked family and friends squarely in the eye. She'd send him what strength she had with her gaze. She was carrying another child. And if God was willing to give her this blessing, and if God would make this child live and be whole, then that child needed a father.

She was taken out of her thoughts by the light touch of fingers on her shoulder. Judy turned and found Jack's face close to her. He leaned forward from his seat on the bench behind. His eyes were wide and red-rimmed. He looked like he hadn't slept for days.

"All will soon be well, sister," he said, nodding in the direction of Mr. Tucker, who'd drawn a small volume from his greatcoat pocket and been reading with every appearance of calm since they sat down. "Tucker knows his business. And so do those two." Judy followed Jack's eyes as they swiveled to two men arriving on the courtroom floor, followed by two clerks. "Patrick Henry and John Marshall could have these rural justices believing their own mothers were harlots if they chose to."

"Enough, Jack." Clearly Mr. Tucker was not as absorbed by his reading as Judy had thought.

Judy studied the two men tasked with saving her husband's reputation. Marshall was the younger of the two, tall and slim. A younger version of Patsy's father, almost, with similar bearing and even features, although Marshall had a squarer jaw. Henry was older, barrel-shaped, like a man who lived well. He was altogether less hawkish-looking and softer than his colleague, with a high-domed forehead that suggested intellect and belied his famed showmanship and rhetorical flourish. They appeared relaxed, leaning back in their chairs, nodding at acquaintances, smiling, shuffling papers, rising as the sixteen justices entered and took their seats. She recognized several of them. Dick was going to hate this.

The jeers of the crowd as he was marched through the street from the jailhouse to the court chilled her. She prayed to God that they might all go home. Didn't they have work? Their own lives and concerns to deal with? Dick was horribly pale. The dark circles under his eyes told Judy he had barely slept. He looked both himself and not himself, as if his handsome face had slipped askew under the weight of his days in confinement. His eyes raked the benches of familiar faces before resting on hers. She caught her breath. This was why she had come, to send him this strength through her eyes. But he didn't hold her gaze. She saw him glance at Nancy, on Mr. Tucker's other side, before he turned to look at the justices. Disappointment washed over her. Tears pricked her eyes. When he needed her, she was determined to be there. That was what mattered. Not how hard it was. Not how unfair. How shameful. She pulled a handkerchief from her pocket and twisted it through her fingers, pulling it tight until she was numb.

Chapter Fifteen

Nancy had never been in a courtroom before. It was cold enough to see her own breath at first, but the sheer number of people in the room soon changed that. The place was austere, with whitewashed walls, hard benches and a dark wooden balustrade separating the general populace from the justices on their raised platform and their clerks and the attorneys ranged below. Soon enough, the court was called to order, and a clerk read the charges. Dick's face was immobile. She flexed her fingers, and for a moment, was tempted to reach for Mr. Tucker's hand beside her. Only for a moment. Instead, she let her eyes drop from Dick's profile to her lap. A snag of skin curled by her left thumbnail. She stroked it with her right index finger then pinched it with her nails and pulled. The sting made her eyes water. As the tiny wound throbbed, she looked again at Dick. This time, she caught his eye. He looked away.

"You are Richard Randolph? Owner and resident at Bizarre, a sizable property within Cumberland County?" The sheriff's face was unreadable, his voice toneless, as if he were reading lines from an unfamiliar book.

"I am."

"As such you submit to the jurisdiction of this court and these sixteen Gentlemen Justices?"

"I do."

"We are gathered today to examine the evidence against you, Richard Randolph. You are charged thusly: that you feloniously murdered a child said to be born of Ann Cary Randolph, known as Nancy. What say you?"

"I am not guilty."

The sheriff turned to the Gentlemen Justices. "Mr. Richard Randolph pleads not guilty to the charges. You will therefore examine witnesses and hear from Mr. Randolph's lawyers. Mr. Joseph Carrington will speak for the justices, Mr. Henry for the defendant." He nodded to the clerk. "Call the first witness."

"The court calls Mr. Randolph Harrison."

Nancy watched Randy rise and walk to the hinged gate in the wooden barrier that separated the court from the spectators. Time slowed. Nothing felt real. She forced herself to listen to Randy's account of their visit to Glentivar.

"They arrived on Monday, October first."

"At what hour?" The lead justice, Joseph Carrington, was a thin man with a surprisingly loud, piercing voice.

"Before dinner."

"Describe the scene."

"My wife, Mrs. Randolph Harrison, watched for their arrival. She and Mrs. Randolph are close friends. The coach appeared, and we greeted them as the horses pulled them to our door. Their visit was much anticipated. I handed the ladies from the carriage."

"Name them."

"Well, there was Mrs. Judith Randolph and her younger sister, Nancy. And a negro. Their maid. I don't know her name."

Carrington had his elbows on the table in front of him and his hands clasped. He leaned forward. "Describe Miss Nancy Randolph's appearance."

"She looked much as she always does," said Randy. He groped for words. "She wore a greatcoat, buttoned to the neck. I remember thinking she must have felt cold on the drive."

Nancy thought of the coat—dark red, warm. Rough wool. It had been their mother's.

"Could she have been pregnant? Did you notice her shape?"

Randy hesitated, and several people shifted on their benches. From outside came some muffled laughter as the question was relayed to the crowd in the street. "I neither remarked on her shape nor observed any change in her that made me suspect she was with child." Nancy felt her tension release, but Randy wasn't finished. "Although in that great coat, it would be impossible for me to be certain." He threw an apologetic glance over at Dick, who sat gazing at the table before him. "And she soon complained of being unwell."

"When was this?"

"Not long after they arrived. We were showing them some alterations we had made. My wife led the party upstairs. We showed them the outer room at the top of the stairs. It had no door at that point and was open from the staircase. Judy—Mrs. Randolph—said she and Dick would sleep there. There was an inner room on the other side of the staircase. Mrs. Randolph said that Nancy and their younger sister, Jenny—she had been staying with us already, and collecting her was part of the reason for the visit—could share the bed in there. Miss Nancy stayed upstairs for a time. She said she needed to lie down."

"And where were you to sleep? And the others in the party? Mr. Jack Randolph? And Mr. Archibald Randolph?"

"We had agreed that I, my wife and our son, would sleep downstairs in the sitting room during the visit," Randy replied. "And the two younger men put up at The White Hart Tavern. It's an easy ride between there and Glentivar."

"When did you next see Miss Nancy?"

"At dinner."

"And her demeanor?"

"She was quiet and soon retired back upstairs. I know my wife was concerned. She and Mrs. Randolph took her a drink. Essence of peppermint, for colic, you know." Randy ran a finger between his collar and his neck.

Justice Carrington leaned forward in his seat. "And what occurred overnight?"

"We were awakened by screams."

Nancy's cheeks grew hot. She heard the response of everyone watching. There was a rustle of skirts, the scrape of shoes, the creak of wood as if Randy's words were a sudden gust of air sending ripples across a still pond. She stared at the floor, forcing herself to remain still even though she longed to cover her ears, block it all out. Again, from outside, there were loud guffaws, the word "screams" being repeated. She leaned into Mr. Tucker.

"Please continue, Mr. Harrison."

"I thought it was Mrs. Randolph, but when I called up from the bottom of the stairs, Dick said Nancy was unwell. There was more crying from above. The noise woke our son, but after she settled him, my wife went up to Nancy. Mary fetched some laudanum. We were concerned a guest in our house had fallen ill. I dressed, thinking if a doctor were needed, I would go for him myself. But a little while later ..."

"How long?"

"Less than an hour. I can't say for certain."

Carrington waved a hand. "Continue."

"A little while later, Mrs. Harrison returned and told me Miss Nancy was much better. The laudanum had settled her. We lay down once again and did not leave the room until morning."

"Did you hear anything further?"

Had they, Nancy wondered? She had spent the last six months blotting out every memory of those terrible days. And now this.

Randy's face twisted a little, and he threw another brief glance at his wife across the courtroom. "I was dozing. It's hard to be exact. Several times we heard movement on the stairs, perhaps someone coming down and returning up a little later." He looked at the justice. "I can't say for how long or who. At the time—at one point—the steps sounded heavier. We both thought it was Dick—Mr. Randolph— coming to request a doctor."

"But no request was made?"

"No."

"And in the morning? What happened then?"

"Miss Nancy kept to her bed. Mrs. Randolph explained her sister had 'a hysterical fit'."

"What did you understand that to mean?"

Color rose up Randy's neck. "I—I'm not sure." He shot a helpless glance at his wife. "Perhaps women's troubles. Or a night terror, such as children have."

Judy bent her head and pinched the bridge of her nose. What a question to ask of a man like Randy. As if he could ever understand or imagine. Different emotions spiked and receded. Anger with Dick for taking this public stance. A wild urge to laugh at Randy's discomfort. A desire to take her sister by the shoulders and shake her for her behavior at Glentivar. If only Nancy had stayed home at Bizarre. But Judy had not let her, and now, they were here, to their eternal shame and misery. To *her* eternal shame and misery. She felt it in every muscle. Her blood was thick with it.

"When did you next see Miss Nancy Randolph?" Randy was asked.

"She kept to her bed all the next day, but I did go with Dick to see if she wanted a fire laid."

"And what did you observe?"

"Nancy was pale but composed."

"And the room?"

"All in order. There was no sign anything was amiss. Perhaps an unpleasant odor." Judy saw this catch the attention of several justices who straightened up and leaned forward. "But nothing that suggested childbirth. An illness. Sickness. That sort of thing."

"And did Miss Nancy recover fully during the course of the week?"

"On Wednesday, she kept to her room but was said to be recovering. Mr. and Mrs. Randolph rode out with my wife, to a local store I believe, but I remained at work at home. There was nothing else unusual about the visit, and they left us on the Saturday morning."

"You are familiar with the matter before us, are you not?"

"I am."

"When did you first hear it suggested that Miss Nancy had, in fact, given birth in your home?"

"Some time later. I don't know the exact date."

"Please describe what you were told and by whom."

"One of my negroes, a woman, she told me. She said Miss Nancy had suffered a miscarriage."

"Did she offer any evidence?"

"None."

A note was pushed along the table to Carrington. "None, you say. What of this talk of a pile of shingles? A body? Of bloodstains?"

"That was later."

"Please explain."

"There was much talk amongst the negroes. There always is. None told the same story. I didn't take it seriously. I thought it preposterous then, and I do so now."

"Did you examine the site?"

"I did. And there was nothing to see."

"Nothing at all?"

"A stain. Could have been anything. It proved nothing."

"And when did you undertake this examination? How long after October first?"

"I'm not sure. Some weeks."

Carrington sat back in his chair. "I find myself wondering why it took you so long."

"Because there was nothing to it! Slave chatter. Idle gossip and speculation, blown up out of an illness and stained sheets. If I were to run down every tall tale these people bring to me, my house would never have been built and my fields would yield no crops."

"So, you give no credence to any of this? This story of a birth? The rumors about the relationship between Richard and Nancy Randolph?"

"None at all."

137

Randy's firmness settled between Judy's shoulder blades. His calm voice strengthened her.

But Carrington wasn't finished. "You have been often in company with them both, yes? With Richard Randolph and Miss Nancy Randolph."

"Yes."

"Have you ever witnessed any impropriety between this man and his wife's sister?"

"No."

"You don't sound sure."

Randy's hand went to his necktie. "They were familiar. As families are."

"All families are different. Some affectionate, others less so. How would you characterize the household at Bizarre? Is Richard Randolph a demonstrative man? As a friend, as a husband, as a brother?"

"Yes, yes, but as you say, only as one would expect in a friend or brother. Nothing suspicious or untoward." Color crept up Randy's neck. "Dick and Nancy are close, it is true. Affectionate, certainly. But let me be clear, I've the highest opinion of them both."

Next to Judy, Mr. Tucker let out a sigh. Randy was excused.

Mary followed her husband into the witness box. For Judy, this was even worse: seeing her friend and confidante put in this position was painful. She felt another stab of anger at Dick, at Mr. Tucker, for putting them all through this. Thinking of her father, sitting only a few feet away, was like touching a hot stove, but she forced herself to breathe out and remain calm. She even looked at Mary and smiled. One day, she thought, we will sit with our babies in the sunshine. We will sit on your porch at Glentivar, or mine at Bizarre, and it will be as if this never happened to us. To me. One day.

Mary's evidence fell in line with Randy's until it came to the matter of the drink Nancy had taken when she retired upstairs after supper on the night of their arrival.

Carrington rifled through the papers before him. "You and Mrs. Randolph attended Miss Nancy, I believe."

"We did. Nancy complained of stomach pains. She is prone to such maladies."

"And your husband told us that you took her a peppermint drink. Is that correct?"

Mary glanced over at Randy and looked sheepish. "Yes. Although it was more than simply peppermint. Judy—Mrs. Randolph—asked me to prepare some tea so they could add a dose of gum guaiacum powder. They had a supply with them."

"Gum guaiacum? For colic."

"Indeed." A pink rash crept up Mary's neck. Her words were relayed to the crowd outside, and this news drew a few whistles and much murmuring. Judy pressed her nails into the back of her hands and stared at the lines they left behind. Even the most innocent actions sounded different in a courtroom. A sweat broke out on her forehead. She wished she had not come.

"And this seemed to help?"

"I can't really say. I returned downstairs and settled my boy. Hours later, as Mr. Harrison explained, we were woken by screams from upstairs. I found Judy sitting up in bed. I asked her what could be amiss, and she said that her sister was in hysterics. I heard another screech and tried the door. It was locked."

"Locked?"

"Bolted. But the door could be held shut in no other way. The spring-latch needed attention. Randy—Mr. Harrison—had not gotten around to fixing it. Anyway, Mr. Randolph opened the door as soon as I knocked."

"And what did you see inside the room?"

"Very little, to be honest. Mr. Randolph begged me to leave my candle in the outer room. He was afraid the light would set off her shrieking and said she was in great pain in her stomach. He feared the light might hurt her eyes. Nancy was lying in the bed, weeping. Her sister, Jenny, was there and refused to leave, although I tried to coax her out. Nancy's negro, a girl of about fifteen, had a bowl of water and a cloth. She was dabbing at Nancy's tears. I went for some laudanum, and that gave her some relief."

"And where was Mr. Richard Randolph?"

"In the doorway, I think. He may have left the room and then returned. I sat with Nancy and asked her about the pains. I offered to send Mr. Harrison for a doctor, but she begged me not to. She said she was embarrassed to have caused so much disruption already. After a time, I left her. I had my child to tend to. Nancy didn't wish to keep me from my own family."

"And you heard no more screaming?"

"None."

"But you did hear further movement? Heavy footfall up and down the staircase?"

"Yes. Exactly as Mr. Harrison described."

"And what about the following days? You are a meticulous house-keeper, I imagine."

"I should hope so."

Judy watched her friend's face closely. Mary's countenance was always open. Dick had been known to remark on it, not always kindly, laughing at her wide eyes and the way her jaw would fall slightly and her lower lip inch forward when she lost the thread of a conversation—which happened often, at least when Dick was about. Now, she had that same look.

"The sheets, madam. The bedclothes." Carrington's fingers drummed the table.

Mary's mouth formed a small "o". "There was some staining. On the pillows. Also on the stairs. I saw nothing amiss with her sheets and quilts while our visitors were with us, but after they departed, I had to have my women take the feathers from the bed and clean it properly. There were bloodstains. We thought a poor attempt had been made at a clean-up. That explained the mess on the staircase. But, if I may say, it is a hazard of womanhood, sirs. I saw nothing to give me any concern—not in the sheets, nor in the behavior of my friends. Miss Nancy was unwell, as women sometimes are. Nothing more, I'm certain."

Carrington looked left and right along the ranks of his fellow justices. When no one had further questions, he turned to Dick's lawyers, Henry and Marshall. Henry's chair scraped the wooden floor as he lumbered to his feet.

"Mrs. Harrison, you say you had no concerns about your friends' behavior?"

Mary thrust out her chin. "None. Judith is my closest friend. There is no disharmony between my friend and her husband."

"You observed no uneasiness of mind in Mrs. Randolph during this visit?"

"Nothing more than a natural concern for her younger sister."

"And in subsequent visits with the family. Any rupture between the sisters?"

"None."

141

"No change in atmosphere? No alteration between husband and wife."

"None."

"And when you first heard of this story of a birth or a miscarriage?"

"One of the slaves at Glentivar came to me with the tale. I dismissed it then, as I dismiss it now."

"Thank you, Mrs. Harrison. I believe you may return to your seat."

Mary didn't wait to be asked twice.

Chapter Sixteen

Judy tried to put herself in the justices' position. What did they think of all this? Of Dick? They gave nothing away. After Randy and Mary, the court moved through their witness list at a faster pace. Mary's housekeeper, Mrs. Wood, confirmed her mistress's assessment that the appearance of Nancy's bed, while not ruling out the possibility of a birth or miscarriage, was not beyond the ordinary.

Randy's mother was called. She described her visit to Glentivar on Tuesday, October second when she had not seen Miss Randolph, although she was told the young girl had been ill and required laudanum. She returned on the Friday and passed a couple of hours with her in her bedchamber. She observed no sign that Nancy had recently given birth.

"Women," she declared, "know these things." Randy's mother wore the air of a woman who had tolerated much from the menfolk in her life. She turned her eye on Justice Carrington as if daring him to ask her more, and he visibly quailed. Not so Patrick Henry. Again, his chair scraped the floor.

"You say you observed no sign that Miss Nancy had given birth, is that correct?"

"It is."

"And that a woman would know?"

"Certainly."

"But if you look before you, madam, you will note that our esteemed justices are all gentlemen."

"They are."

"And so, perhaps, you might be more explicit."

At the back of the room, someone laughed. Old Mrs. Harrison pursed her lips. Echoes of laughter filtered in from outside.

"No fever, no discomfort and no milk." She glared at him, and for a moment, Judy feared he would go further, but Henry merely nodded and returned to his chair by John Marshall. Mrs. Harrison was dispatched and replaced by Archie.

He looked ridiculous. Their cousin was overdressed in a coat that strained at the shoulders and had no hope of being fastened. His neckerchief was a comedy in itself, tied so high that Archie's head swiveled like a turkey at every turn. He radiated excitement but spoke in a solemn tone so different from his normal, casual way, she was certain he'd rehearsed every word over and over before his looking glass.

Yes, he confirmed, he'd had suspicions about Dick and Nancy's closeness. They were fond of each other, quite possibly too fond.

Judy bit down on the inside of her cheek and looked straight ahead. Damn Archie Randolph. How dare he?

But no, he had observed no sign that Miss Randolph was in an interesting condition. He wasn't present overnight during their visit to Glentivar but knew that Miss Randolph had been unwell. On the third day of the visit, he'd assisted Miss Randolph on the stairs. She'd been weak and in need of his support. There had been an unpleasant odor. He could not describe it, but it caused him no misgivings at the time. He had no concerns—it was not until some weeks later that he heard it said that Miss Nancy Randolph had either had a child or miscarried. He hadn't noticed anything amiss in the Bizarre household either before or since October last. Except that there had been some breach with the wider family. No one from Bizarre had attended William and Lucy Randolph's recent wedding. He'd remarked upon it but was given no explanation for the absence.

Judy couldn't help herself. She leaned forward and looked across the benches to where William and Lucy sat with her father. All three faced forward, their expressions fixed and unmoving.

Nancy saw the wisdom of Mr. Tucker's planning when Jack was the next of those present at Glentivar to give testimony. No one who had been in those two rooms at the Harrisons' home had so far been asked a single question. Jenny was too young, and the rest of them—Judy, Nancy herself and most especially, Phebe—were allowed to remain silent. Nancy thought of Phebe's wide eyes gleaming in her dark, quiet face. As for Dick? If there was one person whose evidence she did not fear, it was his.

Jack proved reliable. He was deathly pale, and his high voice caught the interest of the crowd outside, but he lifted his chin, nodded at his brother and voiced his support.

"Miss Nancy Randolph was close with my brother, yes, but not Mr. Richard Randolph. She was engaged to my other brother, Theo. She was devastated by his passing, as we all were. There was nothing improper between my older brother and Miss Randolph.

Miss Nancy and her sister are as close as sisters can be. There is a fondness between them far greater than I have ever witnessed in the rest of the Tuckahoe Randolphs." He turned an icy and deliberate gaze on her relatives, and Nancy longed to stand up and cheer. "The family at Bizarre was in perfect harmony. I challenge anyone to say otherwise."

Justice Carrington appeared unmoved by Jack's vehemence. "Did you observe any signs of pregnancy in Miss Nancy Randolph? Prior to your visit to Glentivar?"

"Absolutely not." There was a brief silence as Carrington read a note passed along by one of his fellow justices. It unsettled Jack. He frowned. "I mean to say that I am quite certain on the point. If she were expecting a baby, we must have all known of it. Yes, she wore dresses loosely. Nancy never wears stays—"

Across from him, Dick closed his eyes. She knew what he was thinking. Jack never knew when to stop speaking.

"We're an informal family at Bizarre," he continued. "Nancy is always busy, particularly in the garden. I have frequently sat closely with her; we have lain together reading ... I saw no change in dress or size. Nothing to make me suspect she could be pregnant. At Glentivar, she was plainly simply unwell. She was pale. I remember shadows under her eyes. That greenish-blue hue that indicates infection or obstruction. It was a digestive issue. Nothing extraordinary. I visited her in her room in Glentivar. Rode in the carriage with her for part of our return to Bizarre. The accusations made against my family are dishonorable slanders, invented by mischievous negroes and circulated by jealous gossips." He had worked himself up, his own words and rhetoric producing beads of spit on his lower lip. Such a strange creature, Jack, but he had done his part. If only the same could be said for those who spoke next.

* * *

After Jack Randolph, Aunt Page was called to testify.

Judy noted that she was dressed in dark green silk and wore a new bonnet, no doubt purchased for this unusual occasion. Like Archie, her aunt's excitement was palpable, her lips pursed, presumably to create an impression of seriousness, but she might equally have been struggling to suppress a smile. Judy thought of all her visits to Bizarre in the last year and their comfortable closeness. As much as she had shared her concerns about her son with anyone, she had shared them with Aunt Page. She ought to be able to rely on her aunt with as much confidence as she had Mary Harrison. But where her friend had met her eye as she took her place before the justices, Aunt Page's gaze and nods were all for the Tuckahoe family. Judy's mouth went dry.

Justice Carrington referred to a sheaf of notes before he began. "Mrs. Page. For the benefit of the court, can you please outline your connection to the defendant and your involvement with his family?"

"I am aunt to Mr. Randolph's wife, Judith, and her sister, Ann Cary Randolph, known as Nancy. Their mother—bless her memory—was my oldest sister. My nieces and I are close in age. I had come to look on Judith as a sister."

Had come? Judy glanced at Tucker. His expression was grim.

"And you have been a frequent visitor to Bizarre?"

"Most frequent. We were there these last two Christmases and have stayed with them on several occasions since then."

"On any of these visits, Mrs. Page, did you observe anything untoward in the relationship between Mr. Richard Randolph and his wife's sister?"

Aunt Page nodded. "I am sorry to say that I did. Not at first. At first, Nancy was happy to be there, and everything seemed proper. Nancy was helpful. I believe she was sweet on Mr. Randolph's brother, Theodore, although he was unwell and traveled to Bermuda to convalesce—"

"If you could return to the question?" Justice Carrington's fingers drummed the desk. Judy noticed Patrick Henry had leaned back in his chair with his arms folded over his ample girth.

"I think it was one Christmas that I first remarked upon it."

"In 'ninety-one? A year and a half ago?" the justice asked.

"Yes. You have it right. It was then that I noted it. 'It is almost as if Nancy is the mistress,' I said to my husband, Carter. Those were my exact words. I saw a boldness about her. Mrs. Randolph was expecting and quite pulled about. She spent many hours upstairs resting. Nancy relished the opportunity to play plantation mistress. I remember a specific incident at Christmas when Mr. Randolph and Miss Nancy lit the bayberry candles."

Judy tried to recall it. She had noticed nothing.

"I mentioned it to Mr. Page," Aunt Page continued. "They lit the candles together. Hand in hand. His other hand on her back. Low on her back. It took little imagination." She paused, her eyes sliding to the courtroom door. Cracks of laughter were heard again from outside as word of her testimony rippled through the crowd. She dabbed her neck with the handkerchief. "My dear, poor Judy even said to me one day how glad she was that her husband had her sister for company as she was brought so low by the pregnancy and feared she'd miscarry. She said her sister was a companion for Mr. Randolph, who was always the more sociable one in the marriage.

"But my concern deepened in March. Mr. Randolph's younger

brother, Theo had recently died. Mr. Page and I visited toward the end of the month. I frequently saw Mr. Randolph and Miss Nancy in close discussion. Very close discussion."

Next to Judy, Mr. Tucker uncrossed his legs and gripped his knees.

"Did you have any suspicion that Miss Nancy Randolph might be with child?" asked Carrington.

"It gives me no pleasure to say so—" A loud snort from Patrick Henry gave her only the smallest pause. "But my answer must be yes."

Judy stifled a gasp. She heard the rest of her aunt's testimony only distantly as if her voice floated through a low-hanging fog.

"On a visit in May last year, I observed an alteration in Miss Nancy's shape."

Noise from beyond the courtroom turned Judy's ears hot. Listeners at the window relayed every word as Aunt Page plunged on.

"Throughout the summer months, I visited on two further occasions. Nancy complained of ill health and was fretful. You could barely hold a civil conversation with her. When I asked her about her future, she snapped at me in the most disrespectful manner. One evening, as I retired, I heard voices in Miss Nancy's room. She was discussing her figure with her maid, asking the girl if she thought she looked smaller, but the maid said no. I caught a glimpse through a crack between door and frame. Again, I am sorry to say it, but I saw Miss Nancy in a state of undress and, yes, visibly pregnant."

Judy closed her eyes. It was impossible. Impossible. But still, her aunt was not finished.

"After the stories about my niece began to circulate, I was naturally alarmed. What kind of future might she expect, given her circumstance? I hoped I had been wrong. That my eyes had deceived me. I shrank from the conclusions my mind reached for when I considered what I had seen in that room and in my observations of my niece and Mr. Randolph.

"I visited Bizarre most recently at Christmas last year. These terrible rumors were swirling. Some in the family were turning away from my dear nieces. I could not be so callous."

Mr. Tucker turned to Judy, eyebrows raised. She had no idea what her aunt might be about to say. As far as she had been aware, the visit was uneventful.

"I talked candidly with Miss Nancy Randolph," Aunt Page declared. "I didn't shrink from telling her what was being said and how it harmed her. I offered to examine her. If she was innocent as she claimed, I'd support her and scotch the gossip at a stroke. She refused."

"She refused you?" asked Carrington.

"She did. She said that her denial was enough, and I ought to need nothing more. She's a haughty and proud creature. I have always said so."

Several of the justices scribbled notes. Others exchanged glances. Around her, Judy heard silk rustle and hot whispers. Dread crept up her spine. How much damage had been done? How much danger was Dick in now? Carrington signaled to Marshall and Henry that they might ask any questions they wished of Mrs. Page. Judy began to pray.

"Mrs. Page," said Patrick Henry, "I must commend you on your industry."

"My industry?"

"Indeed. You have been so busy in the matter of your nieces. A frequent visitor. An advisor. An observer."

"They are motherless girls. Women now, of course, but still young."

"And how would you describe your relationship with them? Maternal? Or more that of sisters?"

Aunt Page frowned, like a woman trying to read without her glasses. "A little of both?"

"Thank you. Very helpful. You see, I ask that for a particular reason. I listened to your testimony with great interest and was much struck by your telling us that you observed Miss Nancy Randolph and her maid through a crack in the doorway."

"I did." Aunt Page colored but held his gaze.

"Because I wondered as you said it, if you did so as a sister or as a mother to the young lady?"

"I—"

Patrick waved her into silence and turned to the crowd on the benches with his eyebrows raised, his lips quivering on the brink of either laughter or a sneer.

"I'm an old man, I know," he said, "but I cannot think of a single occasion where I discovered my mother or my sisters or my wife, for that matter, loitering in hallways and peeping through cracks. I'm having trouble picturing it, truth be told. I wonder, Mrs. Page, if you might demonstrate?" He leaned forward and raised first his right hand to cover his right eye and then his left, shaking his great head in between. "I'm wondering … which eye might you have peeped through? The left? Or the right?" Laughter broke out across the room and Aunt Page's face turned purple. She folded her arms and turned to Carrington for help, but the justices were struggling to keep their countenances, and Henry had the floor.

"Can't remember? No? A pity. But I do thank you for your time here, Mrs. Page. You have been so illuminating."

With a final roll of his eyes, Henry returned to his seat and in an audible whisper, declared to John Marshall, "Great God, deliver us from eavesdroppers."

As Aunt Page huffed her way back to her husband, Justice Carrington called for a break in proceedings.

Chapter Seventeen

"What a witch your Aunt Page is," muttered Dick as he leaned over the barrier to shake his stepfather's hand. None of her family came near them, Judy noted, but Jack was by their side, and Randy and Mary also. Nancy remained seated, her expression unreadable. Dick only had a moment before Marshall and Henry called him back to his place. Judy looked for signs in their faces—of confidence or dismay—but saw nothing. Then Jack's breath touched her ear.

"I thought that woman was your friend, Judy?" he said, his voice higher even than usual. "As if my brother does not have enough to endure without any more betrayals from your damned family."

Fury filled her throat. Was there no one—no one—who saw what *she* was going through? That her aunt's words were daggers, that this scandal was strangling her? She clutched at her chest, feeling for the silver cross that hung there. Jack cared only for Dick. Dick cared only for Dick. Mr. Tucker, perhaps, cared for more than just his stepson. He talked of Judy and Nancy as his own family, his own daughters. But her thoughts grew clamorous and loud, beating at her ears, when she came to her sister. Henry made Aunt Page a figure of fun with his eavesdropping pantomime, but he had not addressed her offer to examine Nancy and Nancy's refusal. Judy tried to recall the December visit, but she had shut out so much, her focus on Saint, even as her despair over him grew day by day.

Tucker's hand at her elbow brought Judy back into the room. He guided her back to the bench.

Nancy wasn't surprised that the final witness called by the justices caused a stir. The daughter of Thomas Jefferson, Washington's Secretary of State and Virginia's favorite statesman? Called to testify in this small rural courthouse? Within the family, Patsy was Patsy, but Nancy saw how the justices straightened their backs as she walked forward, and heard the shouts from outside as people climbed on shoulders trying to catch a glimpse inside.

Justice Carrington came straight to the point. "Is it correct that you were responsible for supplying Miss Nancy Randolph with the resin, gum guaiacum?"

Gum guaiacum. Nancy recalled the flavor. Woody. Dry. It had made her thirsty.

"It is," said Patsy.

"To what purpose?"

"Gum guaiacum is well known in the treatment of colic. Miss Nancy Randolph was suffering particularly keenly with colic when I visited my husband's family at Bizarre in mid-September."

"Are you aware of other uses for this medicine?"

"I am."

"You are aware that it is used to produce an abortion?"

"Yes."

Nancy went cold.

"Did you have any suspicion that Miss Nancy might be pregnant?"

"I did suspect that, yes."

"In September last year? Shortly before the family's visit to Glentivar?"

"Yes but——"

"That is all. Unless Mr. Henry has any questions?"

"I do indeed." Henry got to his feet and threw Patsy a kindly gaze. "You are uncomfortable, Mrs. Randolph, and I believe I see why. Let us probe a little deeper. You were asked to supply gum guaiacum for Miss Nancy, you say? When was this? Mid-September?"

"Yes."

"For the treatment of colic? Not as an abortifacient?"

"Certainly not."

"You discussed the medication with Miss Nancy?"

"With Mrs. Judith Randolph mainly. Although Miss Randolph was present."

Present? Nancy remembered staring out of the window at the rain while Judy and Patsy talked.

"Did you discuss the dangers of the medicine as well as its merits?"

"We did."

She had not been listening. She should have been listening.

"And you supplied it to them then? On that visit?"

"No. A few days later, I received word from Mrs. Page that her niece, Nancy's colic had worsened. She asked if I could supply some of the guaiacum resin to see if it would ease Nancy's discomfort. I sent only a small quantity."

"A small quantity? Enough to produce an abortion?"

Nancy felt a wave of nausea. How much had she taken? How much?

"I don't believe so. I have known of more being given to a pregnant woman with no mischief resulting."

"And you can bear witness that Miss Nancy Randolph had suffered
from colic and stomach pains for some years?"

"I can."

"One final thing. Did Miss Nancy appear in September to have a
change in shape that suggested advanced pregnancy?"

"Not really. I had a fleeting suspicion, nothing more." Patsy turned
her eyes on the justices, her chin held high. "I would never have
supplied the resin to a woman ready to be delivered. She needed it
to ease her colic. Nothing more."

"Thank you."

Judy tried to push Aunt Page and Patsy's words from her mind as
Marshall and Henry readied their defense. Tucker squeezed her hand
as Henry got to his feet, and panic fluttered in her chest at the thought
of Dick's stepfather growing anxious. She gazed at the blank faces of
the justices. They were well-fed, slightly self-important, but surely,
honorable men who should be fair to a man of Dick's family and
standing. She had to believe so, although the way her own family
had turned their back on them had shaken her faith in her own
judgment. At least now, finally, someone would speak up on Dick's
behalf. She squeezed Tucker's hand in return and tried to calm herself
with her breath.

"Gentlemen of Cumberland County," wheezed Henry. "We all
know why we are here. Gossip. Not facts, not evidence. Gossip. A
man's future, his happiness, his freedom, his reputation and honor
hang in the balance. He is in your hands. Let us hear from him."

She watched her husband walk to the witness stand and swear an oath to be truthful. Careworn as he was, Dick was still proud. He squared his shoulders and met the eyes of the justices seated on his left as their equal. He didn't so much as glance at the familiar faces ranged on the benches around Judy. She tried to remember the last time he'd touched her. She could not.

"Please tell us, Mr. Randolph," said Henry. "What manner of illness did Miss Nancy Randolph experience at Glentivar on October first of last year?"

"A bout of colic. It was extremely painful, causing her to cry out and clutch at her stomach. She has long been troubled by it, although this episode was particularly severe. I wondered if there was perhaps an obstruction of the bowel and offered to fetch a doctor."

"Did Miss Nancy Randolph call you to her room?"

"No. It was her younger sister, Jenny. She's a child. Nancy's maid couldn't calm her. We asked Mrs. Harrison for some laudanum."

His eyes strayed to Judy. Was there reproach in his gaze? She had taken the small quantity of laudanum they had brought from Bizarre. But she had needed it. She had been so tired from caring for Saint. It was hardly her fault that he'd had to call on Mary for more. Judy rubbed her lips on her teeth and wished she could remember the night more clearly.

"I determined that if the laudanum did not settle her pains, I would ride for a doctor. But before long, she was quiet, and a doctor was not required."

"And what can you tell us about the bloodstains on her pillows and mattress?"

"Nothing. I saw nothing. The room was dark. Nancy said the candlelight vexed her, so I sat with her in the dark. Her maid and younger sister were there also. I saw no blood."

"And you cannot account for it."

"Not through anything I observed. When I heard of it, I assumed it was caused by her monthly courses. Or a nosebleed. She has been troubled by those. I couldn't settle for some time after Nancy went to sleep. I heard her girl, Phebe, go up and down the stairs—I presumed for water or perhaps something to settle Jenny. The little girl was distressed to see her sister suffer so. In the morning, Nancy was much improved, although she kept to her room and seemed tired and off-color. I was busy with Mr. Harrison and left my wife and the maid to take care of matters. I think I only entered the room once more during our visit, and that was with Randy, to lay a fire. I was anxious she remain well and not disturb the household for another night. As my wife's sister and a member of my household, I take my responsibilities toward her seriously." He glared at the Tuckahoe family. "Nancy has not always been treated kindly by those whose place it is to do so. Since she came to Bizarre, she has been part of my family and treated as such. These accusations touch my honor." Dick's eyes ran from one end of the row of justices to the other, and Judy sensed his temper was high. "I thank you for the opportunity to end this gossip and calumny here today."

With that, Henry ushered Dick back to his seat and addressed the court.

"Gossip," the large lawyer said again, sticking his thumbs in his waistcoat and rocking ever so slightly back and forth. "Not facts, not evidence. Gossip. An upstanding member of the community, a man of family and breeding, with his reputation, with his *honor*, on the line. And yet, are there grounds for suspicion? I will be honest. The answer," he paused, looking around the sea of faces, "is yes." Dick pursed his lips and grew even paler. His shoulders slumped, whether in defeat or anticlimax, Judy could not say. He stared off into the distance, and she returned her focus to the lawyer.

"Yes, I say. There are grounds for suspicion about what happened on October first at Glentivar, and you have been presented with a range of circumstances that excite that suspicion. Let us examine these, then, without favor or prejudice. For we are not gossips. This is a place of justice, and we are men of the law. Let us examine each circumstance and apply the weight of reason and common sense for which Virginians are known and renowned in this great new country and beyond.

"First, the apparent fondness between Mr. Richard Randolph and Miss Nancy Randolph. How many of us live, or have lived, in a house with a younger lady in residence, a younger lady who is not our sister or wife? I believe most of us here have done so. We have wide family circles, we're generous hosts, we travel great distances to pass time together. This is Virginia. We are sociable men and women, are we not? Can we not now pay attention to a young lady in our household without falling suspect in the eyes of others? Is not the sister of a wife the very person a good husband should be paying attention to? More so, when the young lady is Miss Nancy Randolph, a person brought up in the lap of ease and indulgence, until suddenly her father's house is no longer home to her. More so, when the young lady has formed a sincere attachment to Mr. Richard Randolph's brother, young Theo, so tragically lost to the family only last year. Would not that serve to bring the husband and sister—the bereaved brother and the dead man's betrothed—even closer? What could be more natural? Consider. Had there been guilt here, would not their affection have been hidden? The public nature of their affection for each other pronounces their innocence.

Their openness, in the sight of friends and of Mrs. Randolph herself, speaks volumes in their defense."

Henry turned to Marshall and nodded, before licking his lips and returning to his task.

"While some increase in Miss Nancy's size—small, but observable—cannot be denied, it must be acknowledged that many reasons, other than pregnancy, may account for this alteration. Let us consider the math of the matter. For Miss Nancy to be visibly with child in May, she must by then have been advanced three or four months, for every person knows that there would be no observable sign in a young person before that point. By the first of October then, she must have been at eight or nine months, the size of a woman ready to be delivered. What do our witnesses tell us about her size in September? Mrs. Thomas Mann Randolph Jr. would never have sent gum guaiacum to a woman about to give birth. Mr. Harrison described Miss Nancy wearing a greatcoat: there is nothing suspicious in that. And for every witness who did observe an alteration in the lady's shape, we have another who did not. Mr. Richard Randolph's brother, Jack, for one. Mr. Archibald Randolph said the same. If pregnancy was the cause of the increase in size observed by Mrs. Page in May, some considerable further increase should have been visible by September. I put it to you, sirs, that there is no clear evidence pointing to Miss Nancy Randolph having ever been pregnant at all."

The old man bowed his head as if with the weight of disappointing his audience. This was his strategy, Judy saw, to charm, disarm and to disappoint everyone as politely, and yet as comprehensively, as possible. Hope flared as Henry moved on to the matter of the gum guaiacum.

"But let us imagine for a moment longer that she was, in fact, in the family way, remembering that she would have been in a late stage of pregnancy by September. The time for gum guaiacum had come and gone by then, to be sure. Had it been wanted for an underhand purpose, why acquire it in such an open manner? Mrs. Judith Randolph, Mrs. Thomas Mann Randolph Jr. and Mrs. Page were all party to its procurement. It was wanted only for colic. Surely, surely, if it had in any way been wanted for another reason, she would have taken it at home, and the whole episode concealed, not abroad, in another's home, where discovery would be inevitable.

"And let us not stop there, gentlemen. Follow me to Glentivar, where this supposed nefarious business was undertaken. There was an illness, that is certain. It was not concealed: Miss Nancy's screams are proof of that. Mr. Randolph was in the room at the request of his wife. Candlelight was forbidden—natural where a person is in pain and has taken laudanum. A range of reasons can account for the bloodstains described before the court. No untoward behavior was suspected at the time, none, until slaves whispered that there might have been a miscarriage. The story of the shingles has no weight. Had there been an infant's body found, the household must have been told at once. Such a claim has no merit. This is a fantasy spun from bloodied sheets left outside as the family tried to manage the upset overnight. Nothing more. There was no birth, no child, stillborn or living, nothing left on that pile of shingles but spoiled laundry. To imagine otherwise defies all reason and common sense."

Henry raised his arms and turned full circle, sharing his dismissal with the whole courtroom. A loud clatter broke the spell as the crowd outside reacted, and two men posted at the window slipped out of view for a moment. Henry smiled.

"We have not heard the testimony of Mrs. Judith Randolph," he continued, bowing in her direction. "By law, a wife's evidence cannot be presented. But here she sits. No one has reported seeing her in apprehension or misery. How could she sit there so dignified and calm if there were an iota of truth in this gossip against her husband and sister, her sister, who also sits and listens with Christian patience and humility? If you won't take my word on the matter, gentlemen, I beg you, take Mrs. Harrison's, Mr. Randolph Harrison's mother, who sat with Miss Nancy only days after her illness and saw no mark of delivery on her person. Why? Because no such thing had taken place."

Henry turned again to Marshall, a silent question implied in a slight lift of his eyebrows. Marshall nodded and Henry addressed the justices.

"There is, to my mind, only one minor question as yet unanswered. Mrs. Harrison observed no mark of delivery on Miss Nancy's person. But one other member of the family tells us she offered to make a more thorough examination and was refused. It is unfortunate, even imprudent, for Miss Nancy to have refused. She may well regret this now. But I think we can agree that the most innocent person in the world might have acted in the same manner. A heart, conscious of its own innocence, resents suspicion. Even more so when suspected by one who calls herself a friend."

Henry paused, turned to Aunt Page on the benches and slowly, oh so slowly, he winked. To Judy, it was the least her aunt deserved. Several younger men near the back of the room burst out laughing. Everything about this day was humiliating. Aunt Page deserved to be at least as conscious of that as Judy was.

"Miss Nancy may be deemed prideful in refusing this personal examination," he continued smoothly, "but it cannot make her guilty in the matter before this courtroom." He pulled back his shoulders and stood ramrod straight.

"Every circumstance that has brought Mr. Richard Randolph before you has now been accounted for. There is no evidence here for the court to consider. There is hearsay, there is gossip and there is a degree of suggestive circumstance—as unfortunate as it is unconvincing. I ask the court to find the defendant not guilty as charged."

Chapter Eighteen

The verdict came quickly. Nancy only heard snatches, but they were enough.

"… it is the opinion of the Court that the said Richard is not guilty of the felony wherewith he stands charged and that he is discharged out of custody …"

She wanted to throw her arms in the air. Her body was her enemy, swollen with a sudden energy and a sense of relief. Years fell from Dick's face. Lines flew from his brow, and he smiled broadly. He was young again, more a boy than a man, rising from his seat, grasping Marshall and Henry's hands in both of his, smiling and nodding at the Cumberland justices, once again, his equal as a Virginia gentleman. The great fear that had swept through her with all the talk of gum guaiacum receded, at least for now. In a moment, he was with them, crushing Judy against his woolen coat for a second before releasing her and embracing his brother. Nancy stepped away. Tucker's hand was on his shoulder, and Dick moved on in the direction of her family. She watched—hopeful, expectant—but Father wasn't smiling.

Instead, his lips were pursed. Two lines curved down to his jaw. He lifted one eyebrow at Dick and turned away. William and Lucy did the same. Somehow, Tom and Patsy had already managed to disappear. As they funneled out of the courtroom door, Dick turned to her.

"It doesn't matter what they think of us," he whispered.

Nancy wished that was true, but there was no time to dwell on the matter. The crowd that had heckled Dick on his way in, applauded him as he left. A few steps behind them, Aunt Page was not so well received. Nancy heard cracks of laughter and a man's voice shouting that he'd "let her examine me any time she liked!" Nancy had no sympathy.

The press of people on both sides was alarming, but Jack and Dick moved quickly, following Tucker, guiding her and Judy to the line of carriages. She scanned anxiously for their horses, keen to escape the commentary of the locals, who pointed and called out as they passed by.

"There's the wife!" A woman's voice rose out of the melee. "Not much of a looker. The sister's a better eyeful. The older one's face'd turn milk soon as look at it."

Judy heard it too. Her face shut like a fan. Nancy locked eyes with Dick. When he turned his gaze to Judy, his expression was empty. Nancy climbed into the carriage and closed her eyes. She didn't want to imagine what Judy was thinking.

If Tucker or Jack heard the insult, they ignored it. The carriage jolted as Dick slammed the door, and the men left them to mount their horses. The sisters were alone.

And silent.

* * *

165

Judy waited. The carriage rolled away from the courthouse. Houses disappeared. Trees lined the road, cutting out light. And Judy waited.

She was certain her sister could not sit in silence for all the long miles back to Bizarre. Nancy? Keep her thoughts to herself? She never showed restraint. Never thought before acting. Judy's lips curled in dark, silent laughter. Certainly, *she* did not intend to speak first. After all, what was there to say between them? An ugly laugh pressed up in her throat. Her mind raced. The verdict pleased her, but only because it meant their public exposure was over. Dick could come home, yes, but how could they continue together, after all that had been said and heard in the courthouse? Let's celebrate, Sister, she might say. Those respectable men chose not to see Dick as a murderer or you as his whore or the murderer of your own child, as a very devil on earth, in fact, if you thought about it. They decided you are not the lover of your own sister's husband, not a woman who carried a child in secret, who tried to get rid of it by drinking rotten tea, not someone who might let her child be taken out into the night and left exposed, whether already dead or still alive—

"Sister?"

And there it was. Nancy's voice. Judy covered her face. "Please," she said. "I can't."

"But, Sister, are you unwell?"

"I'm perfectly well." The coach lurched, its wheels jarring on a rut in the road. Judy lurched forward but was caught by Nancy's outstretched arms. She looked at her sister's hands. "Don't touch me," she said.

She turned her face and stared at the dark trees beyond the carriage. Rain was falling. Grim weather and evening gloom. The coachman would need a light. Dick and Jack were following, but she couldn't hear their horses over the creak of the wheels beneath her seat.

"I can't understand you. We should be giving thanks," said Nancy. "Aren't you pleased? Relieved? *Something*?"

Tiredness washed over Judy. It hugged at the bones in her face and the muscles in her arms. She longed to weep, but not with Nancy there. "Must you always expect me to act as you would?"

"Not just as *I* would. As anyone would! Poor dear Dick, did you see his expression—"

"Stop it!"

"Stop what? I'm being perfectly normal, while you—"

"While I what? While I sit quietly. While I'm tired. Distressed. After we've been snubbed by our own father. By our own brothers and sisters? When we have spent the day in a courtroom listening to people we have thought of as friends, people in our own family, talking about us, about you and Dick, about my life, my house, my marriage, as if, as if—"

Judy paused. And then she let out a scream. She slammed her fists on the seat beside her and glared at Nancy, who at least now was cowed and silent. She screamed again, so hard it scraped her throat.

"There!" she shouted. "There. Are you happy now? Are you?"

Nancy said nothing. Judy stared at her.

She was jolted by a sound at the carriage window. A hand banging on the panel. Jack's face in the glass.

"What's going on?" His voice was tossed on the wind. "Shall I ask the driver to halt?"

"No!" Judy waved him away and was glad to see him shrug and pull on his reins.

"Now look what you have caused," she muttered, before throwing back her head and closing her eyes. Her throat stung. She wanted to sleep. Nancy said nothing. But she made a racket, pulling blankets, patting her knees, a sniff or two, the scrape of her shoes, the creak of her seat as she shifted.

Then silence again.

Judy's scream had ripped through Nancy's chest. It echoed in her ears; her heart still pounded. Judy had screeched like a banshee, and now she was pretending to be asleep. *Look what you have caused*, she'd said. What? Did Judy think she was to blame for today? Did Judy doubt her? Now? Heat rushed to her cheeks. She bit down on her lip and used the pain to redirect her thoughts. What had been between herself and Dick was not to be thought of. She had placed all that in the dark. This was how it must be. Judy must be convinced. Nothing had happened at Glentivar. She had to believe there was nothing between Nancy and Dick. Otherwise, how could they live?

Memories threatened her. The months of concealment. The fear of discovery. The pain. The bleeding. The gum guaiacum. How much had she taken? This could only be borne so long as Judy believed them innocent. Damn Aunt Page.

Nancy passed several minutes ruminating on their aunt's many insults. Tears stung her eyes. She refused to submit to a wave of emotion, choosing to grit her teeth and picture her aunt at Bizarre, creeping along the hallway, sneaking, spying. She remembered the day her aunt offered to examine her. It was like touching a burning ember.

"I can help," she had said, standing in Nancy's bedroom doorway, her hands clasped in front of her. Phebe had been there, folding clothes, while Nancy flitted between reading a book and staring out her window. It was cold. Snow on the ground for days. The sky as white as the ground with only bare brown trees splitting them. Had Aunt Page even knocked? No.

"I mean with this trouble," she continued, crossing to the window. Nancy, curled on the window ledge, had met her aunt's gaze. Their eyes were level.

"What trouble?" She was aware of Phebe, no longer folding, but standing still, watching, listening.

"This Glentivar nonsense. At least, I call it nonsense, but if it is not put to rest, then your prospects are most certainly blasted."

"In your opinion."

"In everyone's opinion, young lady. Everyone's. No. The only answer is to deny it. Powerfully."

"I do deny it. I have denied it. I will always deny it. It's not true."

"Yes, yes, but you are only a girl. What use is your word? No. Here is my idea. I will examine you."

"You will *what*?"

"The briefest of things. We could do it this moment." She waved a hand toward the bed. Nancy struggled to comprehend her meaning. When she did, color flooded her face.

"No!" Book and blanket hit the floor. She stood inches away from her aunt, her whole body shaking. It was imperative that she refuse. "You will do nothing of the sort. To even suggest it!" Her voice rose. "Get out! Get out of my room. Now!"

Surprise, concern, a little fear, and then finally scorn settled on Aunt Page's face. "Ungrateful girl." Her lips curled, and she shook her head in a mixture of disappointment and disgust that had Nancy ready to strike her.

"Get out, Aunt Page," she said, each word a small, angry bite. "And do not speak to me of this again. Ever."

"Why didn't you let her examine you?"

Her sister spoke quietly, but Nancy was startled. It was as if Judy had read her thoughts.

"I don't want to talk about that woman."

"But I do."

"I thought you wanted to be silent." She felt Judy's eyes burning her and threw up her arms. "Talk away then. If you must."

"You could have proved the whole thing a lie? Why not?"

Nancy looked pointedly out of the carriage window.

"Of course, Patrick Henry argued the point well," continued Judy. There was an edge in her voice now. She sounded detached. Nancy stole a glance and saw Judy was staring off into space, head tilted, as if in a daydream. "You're a young lady, properly brought up. Private. Innocent. Insulted. But what if you were not innocent?"

They sat in silence. Nancy thought of the words she had written in the letter Dick had destroyed. Theo's child. Stillborn. Almost the truth. But no, he'd said. We deny it all. Always. Promise me. She hoped against hope that Judy was finished. She was not.

"You don't like our aunt, so I suppose there's that in your favor. I can imagine no one more likely to get your back up. I wonder if your answer would have been different if I or Patsy had proposed the examination?"

"It would not."

Judy ignored her. "Patsy saying she thought you might be expecting was a surprise, was it not?"

Nancy bit her lip. The rage had left Judy's voice, and this cold, quiet tone was more characteristic but no less disquieting.

"I could believe almost anything of Aunt Page," Judy said. "She likes nothing more than attention. I imagine she saw a choice between supporting us or ingratiating herself with our brothers and sisters. But Patsy?" Judy pressed her palms against the sides of her head.

"Sister." Nancy leaned forward, even though she knew Judy's fingers twitched, ready to slap her if she said the wrong thing. "Sister, after Theo died, I was terribly unhappy. I found comfort in sweet things. Ask Sarah. I spent the summer haunting the kitchen house or sending Phebe to bring me desserts and fruits to my room. Some days, I ate until my stomach was fit to burst. Ask her."

"I would have noticed."

"No, you wouldn't." She raised her hands defensively. "You had Saint. Your beautiful boy. You were busy. Patsy noticed the change in my figure. You know how I suffered all last year with colic and cramps. I didn't even see what I was doing to myself. Until Glentivar."

"You should not have gone."

Was there a softening in her voice? "No," said Nancy. "And I wish to God I had not! To have put you and Dick, the two people I love most in the world, apart from Saint, in this terrible situation? I brought this calamity upon you, upon us, through illness and my distress. All I want to do is make it up to you. Please, Judy, tell me how I can." She reached across the carriage and took her sister's hand. It was cold and limp, but Judy did not pull away. "Let me remain at Bizarre and help you with your children, Judy. Let me help you with Saint and the new child. Please! Let us be friends again like we were back at Tuckahoe. Before any of this. Before Mother died." She rubbed her fingers against Judy's, praying for a response. "You know I'll never marry now, don't you?"

Judy removed her hand.

"You don't know that."

"I do, Judy. And so do you. Mr. Tucker has invited me to Williamsburg to stay with him and Lelia. I will go if you want me to. But I'd rather stay at Bizarre. I love Bizarre. You have a new child coming. I can help you. If you'll let me."

It was dark now. She could see nothing of her sister's expression in the shadows. Perhaps that was a good thing. That meant Judy would not see her face either. She waited, hoping.

"I will think on it," Judy said at last. "But for the love of God, do not speak to me again until we are home."

Phebe

After the trial, everything was worse, not better. Miss Nancy was subdued. The brittle cheerfulness she'd maintained all winter disappeared. If anything, she was more lost than when it first happened, and she wouldn't say nothing about what had gone on at the courthouse. There was chatter in the kitchen house, of course, talk of the sisters' aunt causing trouble, of division in the Tuckahoe family, of the sisters going at it in the carriage on the way home.

All Phebe knew was that something had changed. Miss Nancy kept even more distance from Mr. Randolph. Spent long hours gazing out the window or with a book open on her lap but never turning a page. Her spirit seemed drained right out of her. A dozen times, Phebe went to speak up about the baby she'd lost. About the child growing up with Rachel, across the river. Fear that she was wrong stopped her tongue from wagging. Fear her words might hurt more than they'd heal.

Then Mrs. Randolph lost the child she was carrying. Miss Nancy took the news badly. Shut herself up in her room for three days, weeping, refusing to eat, unable to sleep. The house was quiet. In the kitchen house, Sarah shook her head and pursed her lips. Bizarre, so often full of overnight guests and the sound of Dick Randolph making merry, grew quiet. But there was still a child in the house, and when Phebe took him to Miss Nancy's room, it was Saint that brought her back to something like herself.

"At least we have you," Phebe heard her whisper as he snuggled in her arms and twisted his fingers in her unkempt curls. "I won't let you down, I promise. I have done terrible things, little one. But not to you. Never to you."

The next morning, Miss Nancy was already awake when Phebe arrived with warm water and fresh linens. She washed and dressed as if the past days had never happened.

"Here." She waved Phebe over to help pin her hair. "I am thinking about returning to Tuckahoe. But only when my sister is well enough to look after Saint. You would welcome that, I think?"

"Yes, miss."

"Good." She nodded. "But the boy comes first. I will never be a mother or a wife, Phebe, I know that now."

"But—"

"No. You don't even know the worst of it. Of me."

"I—"

"I said no." Her voice shook. "This is the last time I'll speak of what happened, Phebe. What I heard at the trial convinced me of my wrongs. I believed myself unfortunate, but I have been the author of my own woes in more ways than even you know. The moment I see Judy looking after Saint as she should, we will go to my father. I'll beg him for shelter if I must."

Later, Phebe thought, that was the moment. That quiet May

morning, with Miss Nancy calm and determined. With the light slanting in the window and the sound of the plantation stirring to work outside. Why didn't Phebe tell Miss Nancy her suspicions? What had stopped her? A lack of courage? The fear that it was not her place? Or the selfish hope that Miss Nancy's talk of Tuckahoe raised in her?

But before Miss Nancy was satisfied that Saint would be cared for, a lawyer's letter reached Bizarre. Thomas Mann Randolph Snr had died. His passing was sudden—his heart, the letter said. There would be further communication when the estate was settled, but Tuckahoe, the house, the land and its people were now the property of Gabriella and her son. The family at Bizarre was not invited to the funeral. The road back to Tuckahoe was closed.

Chapter Nineteen

Nancy knew most happiness when she was with Saint. He grew into a handsome boy with soft brown curls and wide-spaced eyes, but the somber cast to his expression had her forever trying to provoke a smile. She loved his deep, unusual laugh, although Judy stiffened whenever she heard it.

By the time he was three years old, Saint could ride a pony and throw a line to catch fish. He watched everyone around him intently, gathering from faces and gestures much of what he could not hear. He was far from stupid, she was sure, but he still did not speak a recognizable word, and it was clear that he could only hear the loudest of noises. Saint was deaf and dumb. That was the bald truth, and nothing in Dick, Judy or Nancy's experience had prepared them for it. Nancy was never alone with Dick if she could help it, but concern for her nephew finally prompted her to seek him out in the stable.

She found him in his shirtsleeves, brushing down Star, while the horse, Jack's favorite, chewed on hay and snorted, her long tail swishing back and forth. She stood in the shadows, watching Dick work. He dragged his arm across his face, wiping away a sheen of sweat. His cotton shirt was drenched, leached onto his back and shoulders. Memories brought heat to her face. When he straightened up, she cleared her throat.

"Nancy!"

He moved toward her, and she raised her hands. "I'm only here to talk about Saint."

"Ah." His expression was hard to read. He twisted the cloth he held in his hands, and his shoulders dropped. "Well, let's hear it then. What about the boy?"

"Perhaps you and Judy have already discussed it. But she won't speak to me on the subject." She drew a deep breath. "I'm worried about him."

Dick frowned. He turned and bolted Star in her stable and then led Nancy to a bench out in the open with a view down to the tobacco fields. She took a seat and was glad and sad at the same time when he sat down as far from her side as was possible.

"Saint does not hear well," she said. "I can't tell how bad it is, but I think very bad. I know little of such matters. I keep hoping for change. He doesn't speak. I fear he will not."

"He is only a babe. There's plenty of time for him to talk, surely?"

"But what if he doesn't?" Silence followed. Nancy thought of all she wanted to say. She watched a hawk swoop across the fields and the afternoon sun dapple the trees in a hundred shades of green. "It's time to call in a doctor and get some advice. I'll do anything in my power to help or teach him. He is a bright boy, I'm sure of it. I am worried, however, that he'll never be able to manage the plantation." She let that comment settle for a moment and then forced out the words she had come to say. "You and Judy need to have another child."

"What?" Dick sprang to his feet and turned on her. "My God, Nancy, what's this? The first time you speak to me alone in months, no, in a year or more, and this is your subject?" He stepped forward as if to grab at her, and she shrank back. He stopped and his eyebrows rose.

"Don't touch me," she said. Tears stung her ears and nose. His expression was so wounded. But they had come so far. His eyes bored into her, and a single tear slid down her cheek. "You and your wife need more children. It is your duty."

She couldn't bear his eyes. Dreaded what he might say.

"Duty." There was a hollowness in his voice that hurt her chest, but she forced herself to stay silent. In a moment, he resumed his place beside her on the bench. "You're right, of course."

She stole a sideways glance at him. His shoulders were slumped, his whole body defeated. "I heard you say to her once that she was your wife. That you were all each other had. You said that she was your wife and she needed to act like it."

"And now you come to tell me that I must act like a husband."

"I do."

"It is hard, Nance. Mighty hard."

"Yes."

"Do you find it hard too?" His voice was a whisper. She stole another glance, but he was looking straight ahead. Nancy forced herself to do the same.

"Every day." She sensed movement next to her, imagined him nodding, kept her eyes on the horizon.

"Wait here," he said. "I won't be long."

Her eyes followed him as he strode off. Unwelcome tears flooded her eyes and she fumbled for a handkerchief. He must agree to get advice about Saint. As for the rest? It was like cutting her heart out.

Within minutes, he was back. Her tears were under control and she hoped she looked calm enough. He sat down and fumbled in his pocket. "You are right in what you say. And I will do your bidding." She opened her mouth to speak, but he continued. "In both matters. I will write to Mr. Tucker, to Doctor Alves and to Benjamin Harvey, a fellow I knew at Columbia. I'm sure there was a similar case in his family. I pray you are wrong about the boy, but we will do as you wish."

"Thank you. I thought I might also write to Leslie Alexander in Edinburgh. He was our tutor at Tuckahoe for a time. He's a clever man. Might I ask his advice about Saint?"

Dick shrugged. "I suppose it won't hurt. But Nancy—"

She had to look at him again. His face was strained, his eyes dark, his mouth thin, all his customary brightness dimmed. "I want you to have this."

Dick reached into a pocket and pulled out a ring. "Don't say anything, I want you to have it. My mother gave me it after my father died. You don't need to wear it. Knowing you have it is enough."

With that, he left her again, disappearing back into the stable and calling for Billy to help him fill the water troughs.

Slowly, Nancy opened her hand and examined the ring. Black enamel. A small gemstone, shaped like a coffin. A mourning ring.

A few months later, she received a reply from Scotland. Leslie Alexander wrote extensively about methods used in Spain to teach deaf children not only to read and write but also to speak. There was a man from Edinburgh, a Dr. Braidwood, who'd recently opened a school in London. Hope flared as she read. Alexander planned to send her material and instructions. He wrote that there had been whole books published in Europe about teaching the deaf, and he would send her any he could get his hands on. For now, he proposed she begin working with Saint on the naming of household items and people. There was no reason why the boy could not read and write. She should start at once.

Nancy wasted no time. Saint loved horses, so she began in the stable. Horse. Saddle. Rope. Hay. Water. Tack. Hoof. Tail. Mane. With Saint watching her every move, she wrote each word on paper and pinned or placed it next to the object named. Then she made a duplicate of each and handed them to Saint. His eagerness and interest thrilled her. As Leslie Alexander had instructed, when she pointed to each word and the object it represented, she made sure to look Saint directly in the face and say each word clearly and repeatedly. It was easy to make a game of things. She put the word "hay" down on a bale by the stable door. She pointed to it and then to the pile of words spread out on the ground before the boy. She tried to look confused. Could he understand her? When Saint pointed to the word "hay" on the papers before him, she cried out and clapped. Saint clapped too and let out his low, gurgling laugh.

Teaching Saint to write, according to Alexander, was of prime importance, and she must begin with fingerspelling to make the connection between the whole words she was teaching and his handwriting practice. In a second letter, he provided a fingerspelling system for her to use, and she spent every spare moment with the boy watching him learn to mimic her gestures on his own chubby fingers. Dick and Judy showed little interest, but Nancy did not care. For the first time in years, she felt alive and useful. Leslie Alexander wrote again, sharing his correspondence with Dr. Braidwood. They had discussed the frustrations experienced by deaf children and the importance of using a language of signs to speed interaction. Writing would come, but progress was slow. If Nancy and Saint were to develop signs and gestures for specific activities or situations, their communication would be much enhanced. She read this with delight. They already had many such signs. When he wanted to ride, Saint held up imaginary reins and stamped his feet. When he wanted water, he drank from an imaginary glass. For milk, he drank from it in sips instead of gulps. Every morning, for months, Nancy had asked him how he was by tapping on his chest twice and tilting her head.

The kitchen house was a treasure trove of words. Sarah, Lottie and Sally all suffered having their names pinned to their dresses and their busy workplace littered with scraps of paper precisely naming everything from the Betty lamps to Sarah's favorite spider pans and kick toaster. Following Leslie Alexander's instructions, she began teaching him words in groups: pot, kettle, skillet, spit. Ladle, dish, basin, spoon. Door, latch, bolt, lock, key. Shirt, button, sleeve, cuff. She enjoyed it, seeing the world anew, and Jack became an unexpected ally.

On his first visit after Nancy began Saint's lessons, she sensed him watching them. This was nothing new and reminded her of a time when Jack's attention had caused distress, but she quickly realized that Saint was his focus now, not her. He asked no questions, but of all the family, Jack was the most consistent in his efforts to communicate with Saint, to talk to him face to face, to use gesture and facial expression to get his message across, and even to add a new word to Saint's written vocabulary—uncle.

On his next visit, Jack showed her several small bound leather notebooks he proposed giving to Saint.

"What do you think?" he asked, biting on his lip.

"They're perfect! Come!" She led him out to the kitchen garden where Saint was pulling weeds with Billy Ellis. Sarah's son was tall now and strong. A young man with firm muscles and bright eyes—eyes Nancy had seen falling more and more often on her maid, Phebe.

"What are they doing?" Jack stopped up short as Nancy closed the gate to the garden. She followed his gaze.

"Talking with their hands! Isn't it wonderful? Saint and I have taught Billy together. Syphax too." She sounded more confident than she was. It occurred to her that Jack might not approve of Billy being taught to sign, but if Syphax was involved and Dick allowed it, surely Jack could not object? She felt his eyes on her and lifted her chin. "I'll teach you if you like," she said.

"Boy!" Jack called out at Billy who looked up. Saint turned when he saw Billy react, and his face burst into smiles at the sight of his uncle. He ran to them, arms flailing and gurgles of laughter spilling from his lips. Jack opened the gate, and Saint barreled into his leg.

They turned to walk back to the house, but after a few steps, Saint tugged on her skirts. He stopped and gestured.

"What's he saying?" asked Jack.

"He wants to show you how he can ride. He asks if you will let him ride Star with you."

"He does?" Jack looked down at his nephew and then back to Nancy. "Why not!"

A few minutes later, Nancy's heart filled as she watched Jack ride off with Saint in front of him. They would find Dick, she was sure, and likely not be back until dinner time. Contentment, a rare feeling, settled around her shoulders. It was all she hoped for, and more than she deserved, but with the sun on her face and the scent of pollen in the air, she allowed herself to feel useful, and worthy, and perhaps even optimistic that things could change—and not always for the worse.

"Did you tell Sarah to slaughter the pig yet?"

Her sister stood ten feet away on the steps of Bizarre. She had one hand on her hip and the other on her midriff, holding herself and telling Nancy what Judy had not yet said in words: that she was pregnant again.

"You startled me."

"Always daydreaming." Judy rolled her eyes and her lips puckered in distaste. "There is work to be done. Where is the boy?"

Why must she call him *the boy*? The muscles in Nancy's jaw clenched, but she forced her face to relax. "He is gone riding with Jack. I expect they will be out for hours. What would you wish me to do first, Sister?"

"First? Did I not just speak to you? The pig, Nancy. Speak to Sarah about the pig. And tell her the parlor floor needs swept again."

She joined Judy on the steps. "How are you feeling?"

Judy glared. "When do I have time to stop and consider my feelings? You have enough feelings for us both, I'd say." She turned and walked back into the house, throwing a parting shot over her shoulder. "There are letters for you on the hallway table. But mind you see about that pig first!"

The letters explained at least some of Judy's sourness. One was from Mr. Tucker, now a regular correspondent, the other from Patsy. Their Tuckahoe relatives were a point of contention. None would visit, but not long after Father died, Patsy had written, making no reference to Dick's trial or her part in it. Instead, she wrote of the family, and if Patsy was not quite able to contain her bitterness over her husband's lost inheritance, Nancy didn't begrudge her that feeling and was glad to hear news of her siblings, particularly the younger ones. Any lingering resentment she held over Patsy's words in the Cumberland courtroom vanished. She offered the letter to Judy to read, but her sister recoiled. Every subsequent letter from their siblings brought on a storm of ill humor from Judy. Doors slammed, dishes were sent back to the kitchen, fault was found with everything. Dust billowed out from under the beds. Stains blossomed on bedclothes. Weeds sprouted in the flowerbeds. The slaves were rowdy, the women stared, the men were sly. Even Sarah, in the kitchen, knew the sharp edges of Judy's tongue. Lottie and Sally, if they weren't careful, suffered the force of Judy's hand. Dick simply disappeared for a few days. Nancy made sure to keep Saint out of reach.

She took the letters out onto the porch. Tucker's letters always brought her joy. Stories of Dick's extended family easily filled several pages, reminding her of past days at Tuckahoe with her own siblings and the watchful, busy eye of her mother—cherished memories. Patsy's letter was full of talk of renovations at Monticello, her beloved father's opinions and news of her growing family. Patsy and Tom had lost a daughter to a fever, but Patsy was expecting again and wrote of her optimism of being blessed with another girl to replace the lost child, Ellen. Thinking of the little girl, Nancy wanted to weep. Her hand went to the mourning ring, hanging around her neck on a chain, hidden by the cotton wrap she always wore and tucked firmly into her bodice. Its solidity steadied her. Still, this battle always to contain her emotions, to turn away from thoughts, to live braced against her own mind and feelings, was exhausting. She let the letters fall on the table beside her. Judy could pick them up and read or not as she chose. She closed her eyes and let the blackness of her eyelids swallow her up. The idea of dying came to her, and it seemed sweet. Then she heard her name called.

"Nancy!" Jack's voice broke the silence. "Come and take Saint from me." He rode up to the house and reined in Star as he spoke. "He's a capital fellow, but I promised to go back and look at the west field with Dick, and I can't keep my eye on him at the same time."

She jumped to her feet and flew down the steps. Saint's cheeks were pink, his hair windblown and curly. She was about to stretch out her arms to him when Judy appeared from nowhere and elbowed her aside.

"I'll take him," she said. "Come, boy."

Nancy took a step back as Jack lifted Saint from the saddle and handed him to his mother. She bit down on the jealousy that flashed into her mind. He was Judy's son, no one wanted his mother to love him more than she did. And yet, she resented being pushed away and enjoyed a flare of pleasure when Saint suddenly wriggled in Judy's arms and arched his back, stretching out for Nancy instead. Judy froze. For a moment, Nancy thought Saint would relax into his mother's arms, but no, he bucked again, his feet kicking, and Judy had little choice but to thrust him into Nancy's willing embrace. Saint threw his arms around her neck and buried his face under her chin.

"Good to see you, Sister." Jack smiled down at Judy as if nothing were amiss. "You look well." This seemed to mollify her. Some of the color in her cheeks faded, and Nancy hoped Saint would not suffer later for his rejection now.

Chapter Twenty

It was a difficult pregnancy, and later, Judy wondered if the fault in Tudor began there, before he was even born, in her bitterness, her unhappiness and her doubt.

But who would not be bitter, left in Judy's shoes? It was her fourth pregnancy and would likely be her last. Dick did not love her, that much was clear. This was her fault, not his. Physical love had seemed so important, so necessary, but the reality of it had proven uncomfortable and unpleasant. She'd even thought, years back, when she'd been pregnant with that first precious child, the one Dick had mourned and forgotten with such expediency, that if he took a mistress one day, she would tolerate it. Why should he be deprived of something he enjoyed simply because she did not? Judy believed herself a fair-minded person. She believed in marriage, in God and in her duty. There were other ways to love a husband. She was sure she'd fail him in no other way. And yet she had. She lacked his spontaneity. His love of society and chatter. His love of fine wine and splendid dishes. His joy in riding and in a life spent out of doors. But still, she had believed in their marriage. She'd believed in his loyalty. She'd believed him over the nonsense at Glentivar. She believed Dick had been maligned by slave chatter and the refusal of her family to speak up in his defense.

When had her doubts begun? She remembered the letter he had ripped to pieces on the way back to Williamsburg from their disastrous visit to Tuckahoe. What could it have said? And then there was the trial. Oh, Patrick Henry might have had the courtroom in convulsions, poking fun at Aunt Page, but her testimony weighed upon Judy. She could not set it aside. Aunt Page had said she had seen Nancy in a state of undress and believed she had been with child. Patsy had thought so too. If that was true, then who was its father? When was it conceived, and what had happened to it? It was torture to think about, but she couldn't stop herself.

She might force the truth from Phebe. She lost count of the number of times she resolved to do so, only to change her mind. Her dignity, her pride, her upbringing forbade it. Asking a slave for her sister's secrets was beneath the mistress of Bizarre, beneath a daughter of Ann Cary Randolph. She longed for her mother often, mostly at night, when the house was quiet and she tossed and turned alone.

Judy thought back to Theo's last months. He had been weak, feverish, barely able to rise from his bed. But if there was a child, surely Theo was the father? And it would be so like Nancy to involve Dick in her subterfuge afterward. Judy saw how it might have been. Theo dead. Nancy in trouble. A stillbirth. Or a live birth and the baby taken—where?—somewhere, not kept, but safe and healthy. Yes. She could see Dick shouldering his responsibilities toward the child of his dead brother, of his wife's sister. That much she could imagine. The rest? The rest was too dark, too distressing and involved too great a betrayal.

Yet there had been that letter. And those witnesses. Friends who talked of the closeness between her sister and her husband, who implied a relationship beyond what was appropriate. The refused examination. Her thoughts were slow poison.

What if the truth was as bad as she could imagine? What if it began with a man tired of his wife? He'd brought her younger sister into their home, not with the intention of betrayal perhaps, or at least not consciously, but still, bringing in someone younger, prettier, impressionable. Bringing in a girl who admired and flattered the tired husband. A girl who was jealous of her sister. Self-centered. Or lascivious. Or both. A girl who might be a little in love with her sister's man. Perhaps the wife bore some responsibility. She had pushed her husband away, been too cold, too lost in her own grief and disappointment. Certainly, she'd been naïve. She had been trusting. She had been betrayed. Was she a fool who sat in her parlor while her husband and sister laughed behind her back? A blighted woman, giving birth to a flawed son, a punishment from God for his father's waywardness? What if the younger girl had found herself pregnant? The guilty couple had no path forward but concealment. The child had either been born dead or sent elsewhere. Even in her worst imaginings, Judy couldn't countenance the suggestion there had been an infant's body on the shingle pile at Glentivar. No. No one had believed that for a moment. Blood perhaps. But not a body. The father of this new life inside her might be an adulterer. But not a murderer. No.

From the day they returned from the Cumberland courthouse to the day that Tudor was born, Judy watched them. Where was Dick, and where was Nancy? Were they together or apart? Did they glance at each other, touch or smile? If they were too distant, that was grounds for concern. Evidence that they were trying to cover their tracks. As Judy's waistline grew, she watched her sister. Nancy seemed devoted only to Saint and her ambitions of teaching him to read and write. Well, she might do as she wished there. Judy was determined to bring a new, healthy, perfect child to her home.

To achieve that goal, she needed rest and peace of mind. In the week that she felt that first flutter of movement inside her, Dick received a letter. Judy believed it was a godsend. His cousin, Anna Dudley, needed help. A widow with two small children, she hoped to pass a year or two lodging with family while leasing out her farm. Dick rubbed at his temples as he read her letter aloud to Judy and Nancy.

"Poor woman," he said. "But are we in a position to help?"

"Certainly we are, Dick," Judy spoke up at once. "Invite her to stay. It's the right thing to do."

"What do you say, Nancy?"

"I—"

"What she thinks is not the issue here, Husband."

"She lives here too, Judy. I'd wish my decision to be one we're all comfortable with." The look he gave her was far from friendly. "Nancy?"

"If Judy wishes it."

"I do."

"And it will not be too much trouble? Given everything?" Dick waved his hand in Judy's general direction, his eyes falling on her waist.

"No trouble at all. She will be company for us all. Perhaps, exactly what we all need."

Anna Dudley and her two children arrived a month later. She fell in with the household's routines easily, which pleased Judy, but wherever Nancy turned, there was Anna Dudley. She was a small woman, with smooth black hair, threaded with silver strands. Her skin was pale and freckled, and there was a hardened look about her, as if she had faced some troubles, which, considering the loss of her husband, was perhaps to be expected. She was loudly glad to be at Bizarre—outwardly pleased with everything and everyone and full of compliments and exclamations of her admiration—but from the first, Nancy knew herself appraised and measured. She'd hoped for companionship, believed an additional person might break up the tension in the household, but Anna Dudley wasn't the answer. She was sharp with her own children and barely acknowledged Saint. Several times, Anna Dudley picked up a book Nancy had been reading, examined it, and sniffed. When Nancy found herself repeatedly left alone with her in the parlor in the evenings—Judy claiming tiredness and Dick preferring to drink alone in his library— she braced herself for trouble. The silence between them was never comfortable. And then, within weeks of arriving, Anna Dudley set Nancy against her irrevocably.

"I wonder that you would stay on here," she began. "Given everything that has happened."

Nancy took a sip of wine and threw Anna Dudley a challenging look and said nothing. If the older woman noticed, she did not care.

"Indeed. Such a terrible scandal. The talk of Virginia and beyond, I heard. Of course, I discounted it. Those people are born liars."

"Those people?"

"The Harrisons should have more control over their slaves, I say. But still, I wonder that you have remained at Bizarre for so long."

"Where would you have me go, Cousin?"

Anna Dudley was silent, but not for long. "True. There is no good solution to your difficulties. Marriage is likely out of the question now."

Nancy gritted her teeth. "If you say so."

"You will soon learn I am not one to gild the lily, Nancy. I like plain speaking. No point in pretending otherwise. Your options are sadly limited."

There was a difference, Nancy found, of knowing something to be true in your head and hearing it confirmed out loud by someone else. "Which perhaps is why you find me still here," she said.

"Yes, yes. But for how much longer? Would you be your sister's unpaid maid? I suppose you are helpful with the boy."

The boy. Yet another person who treated Saint like less than a person. She'd indulged in a daydream of late. She pictured herself and Saint leaving Bizarre together. Judy, caught up with her new child, God willing, stood at the door, waving them away. The harder leave-taking took place later. In her imagining, Nancy and Saint stood at the railing of their ship waving farewell to Dick with the taste of salt tears on her lips. She was taking her nephew to Scotland, to a new country and new people. To help for Saint and for herself, who knew, but the face of Leslie Alexander, although smudged in feature and made hazy in the years since she had seen him, had a romantic appeal.

"The boy will grow up. And you will have no society. You're a good-looking girl, still. There might be a widower prepared to overlook your history. But you won't find such a one in Cumberland County."

Nancy remembered the old general Gabriella tried to foist on her. "I don't dream of marriage."

"Which shows some wisdom. I respect that. And realism. I'd like my children to be realists. When they are as disappointed in life as I have been, I hope they will, at least, be as resilient."

"You've been disappointed?"

"I lost my husband. I'm left with debts. My father hasn't given me so much as a horse these past four years. Your father—Lord rest his soul—at least settled some money upon you. In that, you have an advantage I lack. Of course, our positions are dissimilar in most aspects." She paused. "But we arc both dependent on the goodwill of others, are we not?" When Nancy only nodded, Anna Dudley prattled on. "Although the status of a widow will always be much better than a spinster. I know you won't mind my bald terms. I have my children. Such a blessing. Both healthy. And whole, unlike poor Saint ... well, least said, soonest mended I always say. I admire your effort with him. Although, likely, the afflicted child will never amount to much. How your sister must pray every night for a safe delivery! I'm glad to be here to help her. As a mother myself, I will know what to expect. Whereas you—" Anna Dudley broke off and her hand flew to her mouth. "Oh, now, what have I said?" Her eyes were wide, but there was something rehearsed about it.

Nancy managed to put her glass back down on the table, although her fingers trembled. "I am not sure what you have said, or what you meant by it, Cousin. But I think all topics have been exhausted between us, would you not agree? I will bid you goodnight. I trust you will put the guard on the fire?" As she rose, her heart thumped in her chest. Her eyes stung. She dared not blink in case tears came. She must not give Anna Dudley that satisfaction. She would not.

Somehow, she made it upstairs to her room, brushing past Phebe and burying her head in her pillow. What had the woman tried to insinuate? That Nancy would never have a child because she could never marry? Or was she implying she believed the gossip about

Glentivar was true? That Nancy had been a mother, even though it had ended in despair? In many ways, it didn't matter. The truth was as bad as the gossip, if not worse. She had harmed her unborn baby. Poisoned it with Patsy's colic remedies. Anna Dudley was right. There was no husband in Nancy's future. No infant sleeping in her lap. She'd always be alone. It was no more than she deserved.

Chapter Twenty-One

Tudor Randolph. From the first, Judy knew he was different from his brother. She knew it in the burst of wailing as the air met his lungs and skin, in the muddy blue of his eyes that turned brown so quickly, in his thirst for milk, in every jerk of his tiny, perfect limbs. She loved him instantly. With Saint, she had been unsure, awkward—an unnatural mother. She'd feared feeling so again. But no. When Anna Dudley first lifted him into her arms, Judy looked at his face, saw that Tudor looked nothing like Saint, and in a tumbled rush of relief, tears and gratitude, she fell in love.

Dick smiled at his new son but soon left him to the women. He'd been studying for the law, an admission, if silent, that the plantation was struggling financially and more income was needed. Matoax had been sold two years earlier—a blow to his ego, Judy was sure. He'd written a new will and made her promise she'd fulfill his commitment to free their slaves, beginning with Syphax, if he failed to do so in his lifetime. Hearing Tudor crying upstairs, she'd agreed fulsomely and left him to his books. This child, Judy thought. This child. She could bear almost anything, so long as he lived and thrived. Resolve settled in her as she stroked his cheek and tickled the palm of his tiny hand, watching his perfect fingers close around hers.

With both Anna Dudley and Nancy in the house, Judy was able to spend more time with Tudor than she ever had with Saint as an infant. He would grow to be a healthy, strong and capable man; she would make sure of it. Tudor would do what Saint could not. The intensity of her feelings for the child numbed her to the others around her. If Anna Dudley and Nancy couldn't abide to be in the same room as each other, that was their problem. So long as the work of the household was carried out properly, Anna and Nancy held no interest for her.

Concern for Dick and their relationship faded from her mind. It would be what it would be—she had other things to think about now. Tudor. Saint was learning to read and write, and she was glad. But Nancy's talk of a school in London, where he might learn speech flowed over Judy's head like the babble of a brook. Saint's future was uncertain, but it didn't concern her. Tudor was the future.

He was a fussy eater and didn't sleep well, but she didn't care as long as he was with her. They were connected, as if the cord had not been cut. His skin was her skin. His breath, her breath. His pain, her pain. When Anna Dudley offered to take the baby for a stretch, Judy bristled. She'd share him soon, she told herself. But not yet. Saint seemed more Nancy's child than hers. That wouldn't happen a second time. Tudor belonged with his mother. For the first time in years, she was happy.

But sudden illness changed everything. The rhythm and sounds of Bizarre altered the moment Dick came home sick. He had been caught in a storm, then stayed out in the stable, drying his horse before clattering through the door, shivering and unable to get warm. Deep into the night, Bizarre echoed with the consequences. The storm of feet carrying water for a bath. The thud of logs and the stoking of a fire to warm the master. The spicy scent of mustard, the beginnings of a cough, the chattering of teeth, his voice, plaintive, calling for wine, and more opening and closing of doors, feet running and a whispered debate outside her door. Then the knock.

Judy didn't get up at once. She was sitting with Tudor by the window, gently rocking him, enjoying the weight of his head on her shoulder. Putting him in his crib each night made her cold—she put off the moment for as long as she could. The knock came again. Clamping Tudor's small form to her shoulder, she went to the door and unlatched it. Nancy and Anna Dudley were there, their skin yellow in the candlelight.

"Mr. Randolph is unwell," hissed Anna Dudley.

"He probably needs to sleep. But how he can with all the racket everyone is making . . "

Nancy stepped into the room. "He needs a doctor."

Judy rolled her eyes. "Then send Ben." She was surprised to find Nancy's hand clutching hers.

"Thank you. I'll do that now." Nancy made for the stairs, leaving Judy and Anna Dudley still in the doorway.

"Was there anything else?" Judy asked.

"Will you come and attend to him?"

Judy smothered a desire to laugh. "Attend to him? When he has you, Nancy and Syphax and the doctor on his way? No. I will attend to my child. I'm sure Dick will be fine if he gets a good night's sleep. Now, goodnight."

The house was quiet when she woke the next day. She imagined Dick was as fast asleep as Tudor, who lay on his back with his mouth slightly open and his chest rising and falling steadily. It would only take a moment to check. Judy smiled at Tudor and tiptoed out of the room.

Phebe, asleep in a chair by Dick's bed, didn't stir as Judy leaned over him. He was horribly pale. A slick sheen of sweat coated his face, and yet salt lined his lip. He was asleep but unsettled. His limbs twitched, and his eyeballs squirmed beneath his thin eyelids. Always a slim man, he looked gaunt now, with a pool of sweat in the hollow of his throat and his dark hair wet against his pillow. She put a hand to his forehead. He burned.

She skirted the bed and shook Phebe's arm. "Wake up at once. The master is sick. Where is the doctor? Did he come last night?"

"Yes, ma'am." Phebe blinked rapidly. "He bled him and gave him a tonic. Master Randolph took more from Miss Nancy a few hours ago. Can't rightly say when. Miss Nancy said she come back in the morning, and we give him more then."

"Get my sister. Now."

She fixed her eyes on the window, watching the sky lighten while she waited. Her thoughts went to Tudor. She would take him outside today. It wouldn't be good for him to be in the house all day while his father lay ill. Sarah and the girls must wash down the hallway and scrub her bedroom. She bent over Dick and heard a light crackling sound in his breath—not good.

"Is he no better?" Nancy rushed in and fluttered around Dick's bed. Judy's temper rose, but she repressed the biting remarks that sprang to her lips.

"What do you think? He is certainly unwell. When did he last take any medicine? What did Dr. Alves give him? Show me."

Nancy handed her a glass bottle. Judy sniffed it. "Vinegar?"

"With molasses and butter. He should take another dose now." Nancy glanced at Dick and then at Judy. "Should I?"

"No." Judy moved to the bedside. "Fetch Ben and Syphax. They must get Mr. Randolph sitting up. And then I will look after him. You may go."

It was the correct thing to do, but Judy regretted her decision almost at once. The men got Dick bolstered up on a bank of pillows and awake enough to swallow the tonic, but once that was done, Judy was left in the room with him and nothing more to do than listen to the crackle of his breath and wait. Her thoughts returned to Tudor. She went to the door and called out Nancy's name.

Nancy was there in a moment. It wasn't lost on Judy, not Nancy's quick response, not her rapid breath, not the pink in her cheeks, not the concern in her eyes as she looked at Dick. Her eyes snagged on a chain at her sister's neck. At a ring hanging there. Where had she come by such a trinket? Nancy needed to leave Bizarre. The realization hit Judy with a certainty, but it could wait until Dick was well again.

"Sit with him," she said. "I have my new son to consider. I will send Anna Dudley to relieve you later."

"Don't."

"What?"

"I hate that woman. She mustn't come near. Phebe and I will manage."

Judy frowned. Questions sprang to mind, but a thin wail reached her ears. "Fine. Have it as you wish. Anna will be busy enough downstairs while you manage Dick. Whenever he wakes, try and get him to drink. If his breathing gets worse, send Ben back out for Dr. Alves. Let us pray this fever is of a short duration."

Left with Dick, Nancy sank into the chair by his pillows. Tiredness itched at her eyes, and she had a headache blooming. She hadn't slept.

Dr. Alves' eyes had dropped from hers when she had asked him how long he thought Dick might be laid up. The fever was the key. The fever must be broken.

Phebe brought soup for Nancy and brandy and milk for Dick, but she couldn't rouse him to take either. The hours dragged by. Phebe returned, and together, they changed his nightshirt. He was thin, Nancy thought. Thinner than he used to be. They rolled him one way and then back to change the sheets he lay on. This woke him, and he fixed his tired eyes on Nancy and smiled, but air hit his chest, and he was rocked by a frantic coughing fit. Dr Alves arrived as the sun began to dip, and a shaft of shadow cast its way across the bedchamber. He was a short man with a hooked nose and sharp eyes. His lips turned down when he looked at the patient.

"Calomel and tartar emetic." He snapped open his medicine bag and reached for a bottle. "Have the girl fetch some wine to bury the taste. Be quick."

She dispatched Phebe, but it was Anna Dudley who appeared in the doorway minutes later. Nancy grabbed the proffered jug of wine and glass and turned away.

"I see you are busy, but I'm sure Mrs. Randolph would like to know what the doctor has to say to Mr. Randolph's condition today."

"Not now. I must help Dr Alves. Tell Judy I will come to her when the doctor is gone home again." Before Anna Dudley could say another word, Nancy shut the door in her face.

"The doctor is here." Anna began in an ordinary fashion, knocking gently at Judy's open door, speaking softly with a nod to where Tudor lay in his cradle. But when Judy made no move to rise, her tone sharpened. "Won't you come and speak with him, Cousin?"

There was nothing so much in the words. With Anna Dudley, it was all in her manner, in her tone, in the muscles of her face that twitched and pinched.

"Not at this moment," Judy said. "Tudor has been fussing. I must be sure he's sleeping soundly." That should have been more than enough to get rid of the woman, but no, Anna Dudley pushed herself forward, coming fully into the room and closing the door behind her.

"I must speak."

A wave of irritation prickled Judy's skin. "Must you?"

"It is not seemly."

"What are you talking about?" Her neck ached, and she considered standing, but the last thing she wished for was a confrontation. Her eyes flicked to Tudor. He didn't stir.

"Nancy. In that room. Alone. With him."

"My husband is unwell, cousin. My sister is tending to him. Syphax or Ben is there. Dr. Alves is there. I struggle to share your concern."

"You will forgive me, Cousin, but you *should* share it! After all this family has been through. After what happened. When it is still talked of, still discussed. To let them be together. To be so intimate. In his bedroom."

"My husband and my sister are not intimate! How dare you speak in such a manner?" She was on her feet, Tudor forgotten.

Anna Dudley stepped back, her hand on her mouth. "Do I not have my own and my children's reputations to think of?" She threw Judy a glance so contemptuous, Judy knew she'd never forgive it, that she would never see the other woman without wanting to slap her.

"You are here, Cousin, in my house, as a result of my good husband's charity, and this is how you speak? While my husband lies ill? While I nurse a small infant?" Anna Dudley might be older than she, indignant and certainly rude, but she was nowhere near as angry. "Get out of my room. And stay away from my husband and sister."

She almost laid hands on the woman. Her palms itched to strike. Only a startled cry from Tudor prevented her. Anna Dudley scuttled away, and Judy burst into tears.

As soon as she composed herself, she went to talk to Alves. The doctor spoke in an undertone. The next few hours would be crucial.

"We will draw this fever out, Mrs. Randolph," he said, grimly. "Once the fever is broken and the body is purged, it can be bled. Then we will see what strength God gives him. Let us pray our Lord is generous."

Nancy remained in Dick's room for a second night. Purging was foul work, and she longed for a warm bath, for fresh clothes, for clean air to smell and an end to the retching that shook her heart, even as it shook Dick's shoulders. He grabbed at his stomach, twisted and moaned, pitiable in his illness. In the moments he recognized her and spoke, she heard a muddle of self-pity and gratitude, no different from Saint when suffering through a sickness.

She dozed for a while, upright in the chair by the bed with her cheek numb against the wood, until near dawn he woke her, putting his hand on hers. Still too hot—she thought of burning paper.

"Nancy." His voice was thin. She filled a cup of water and brought it to his lips.

"Thank you." He closed his eyes. "God, I feel wretched!"

She smiled. "You have been so unwell." He tried to move, perhaps to sit, but the effort was beyond him. "Lie still." She placed her hand on his forehead and bit her bottom lip to hide her disappointment. Too hot. Too dry.

"I'm feeling better."

"Hungry?"

"No."

Another flicker of optimism snuffed out. "I'll call Syphax in a moment. He won't be far away and will get you sitting up. You should drink. You must get better, Dick."

"I'll be better in a little. Stay with me for now."

Tears stung her eyes. The silence that fell between them gave her no comfort. His chest bubbled and wheezed with every breath. She thought back to his brother, Theo, and the space between her ribs contracted.

"Do you still have the ring?" His chest heaved with the effort of speaking.

She reached for her necklace, leaning down so he could touch it. "Here."

"I married the wrong girl." The coughing stopped, but his chest rose and fell like a ship in a storm. "When I am over this, I shall put it right. I shall—"

"Don't talk like this." She touched her fingers to his lips. "Don't talk at all. Get well. That's all I ask." He looked ready to say more, but she shook her head. "No. If you want me to stay with you, you must not speak of such things."

She was saved by a soft knock at the door. Phebe appeared, carrying a tray with a bowl of porridge and a tankard of beer.

"From Mrs. Dudley. For the master."

"Sit with him, please, Phebe. I need something from the garden." She slipped from the room and down the stairs. The early morning light was harsh on her eyes after two days in the sickroom. Her head throbbed. She went to a bushy clump of butterfly-weed growing behind the kitchen house. Its clusters of tiny orange flowers normally brought a smile to her lips, but Nancy was intent on its roots. She grasped two handfuls and tugged. The plants came away easily, and in moments, she had them in water in the kitchen, rinsing away the soil and requesting Sarah place a kettle of water over the fire to boil.

"What are you about, Cousin?"

Her shoulders sagged at the sound of Anna Dudley's voice. The woman was everywhere. "I'm making a tea for Mr. Randolph—not that it's any business of yours." Nancy grabbed a cloth and patted the roots dry. Sarah placed a board and knife on the table for her.

"I sent your girl up. He needs food and drink to fortify him."

"I know what you did." Weariness tugged at her eyes, and her head still throbbed. "And I am grateful. But I'm not sure he will take it."

"If I were to nurse him, you may be sure that he would."

Nancy stopped chopping. She stared across the table at Anna Dudley. The woman was almost quivering with anger. How ridiculous. Dick was ill, seriously ill, and here was his cousin trying to pick a fight. She couldn't stop it. She laughed.

A sea of emotion washed over Anna Dudley's face. Her mouth opened and closed. Then she shook her head and drew in a long breath through her nose. "Laugh all you like. But be careful you do not kill him with your ... your ... with whatever this is! I pray you know what you're about."

Chapter Twenty-Two

Judy woke with a feeling of dread. Tudor was well, sleeping soundly in his cot, and the house was quiet. Light rain drummed at her window. Dick had been sick for four days. She slipped out of bed and made her way down the hall to her husband's room.

The smell only increased the worry in the pit of her stomach. There was a rotten sweetness in the air and a stillness that made her rush to Dick's bed and lean over, listening for his breath. For a horrible moment, she heard nothing. But then he wheezed, and a bubble of breath, half air, half liquid, escaped from him. He was alive, but Judy feared for him. She put her hand to his head. Still hot, warming her palm and damp with sweat. His pillow was soaked. The room was dark. Nancy, curled on the chair by the bed, had not been disturbed by Judy's entrance. She was disheveled—hair escaping her cap, one sleeve rolled past her elbow and the other pulled up only a little above her thin wrist. Judy felt a spark of fondness, quickly extinguished by thoughts of Anna Dudley. Unhappiness weighed on her like a stone on her chest. She closed her eyes.

But a moment was all she could spare. She drew the curtains, letting light spill across the room. Nancy stirred, stretched her neck and got to her feet. Judy went to stand by her. In the light, Dick's face looked waxy. Unnatural.

"We must call in Alves again. Must we write to Jack?"

Nancy bent forward and laid her hand across Dick's forehead. He showed no sign of wakening. "Yes."

Judy took Nancy's hand in hers. She remembered waiting together at their mother's bedside. She needed her mother's strength now, but her mind swayed with strange thoughts—of her sons left fatherless, of herself alone on the porch downstairs, wrapped in a shawl but shivering with cold, of her sister weeping, of Dick as he had been when he had ridden up to Tuckahoe, of him lying on the grass, laughing with his two brothers, and of Mr. Tucker staring at his adopted son, sitting in a courtroom with his head bowed.

"Go and write to Jack and Mr. Tucker now, please. After sending Ben for Dr. Alves. Ask Lottie to mind Tudor. Sarah will spare her."

"And Anna Dudley?"

Judy's eyes remained fixed on Dick. "Tell her to stay out of my way."

Nancy squeezed her hand and then let go. Still, Judy stared at Dick, his features sharpened by illness, his hair damp and disordered, his face, even his lips, drained of color.

Slowly, she lowered herself into the chair by the bed. She leaned forward, propped her elbows on her knees and clasped her hands. "Please, God," she whispered. "Please do not take my husband. For my son's sake, if not for mine. For my boy. For both my boys. Please. Hear me. Help me. For I do not know how we can manage without him."

She was still praying a few hours later when Dr. Alves returned and bled Dick once again. Judy remained by Dick's side through the day and into the small hours of the night. Nancy had Ben bring in another chair and sat near the foot of Dick's bed. Syphax stood at the door. The sisters barely spoke. Whatever Judy requested, Nancy or Syphax supplied—more butterfly-weed tea, wet cloths, candles, a towel, a glass to hold above Dick's lips to check his breathing.

Somewhere in the night, long before dawn, she shifted in her chair and moved forward, lifting the candle at her elbow to shed more light on Dick. Shadows shifted and resettled as her hand trembled.

"The glass," she said, holding out her hand. Holding her breath, she held it over Dick's lips and then brought it to the candle. The glass was clear. She blew out the light and set the candle down on the floor. "He has gone," she said in the darkness. "It is over. My husband is dead. May God have mercy on his soul."

Nancy was upstairs when Jack arrived two days later. He leaped from his horse and strode directly into the parlor, calling over his shoulder for Ben to take his horse.

She ran down in time to watch in the parlor doorway as Jack stumbled across the room and knelt next to his older brother's coffin. The fog of Nancy's own distress shifted a little. Her heart hurt for him. Jack had lost both his older brothers in the space of a few years. She watched in silence as he bowed his head and wept. She understood his grief. For two days, she had been numb, barely able to sleep, her mind trying to accept a reality that it longed to reject.

"Jack," she stepped into the room and placed a hand on his shoulder, keeping her eyes on him, not daring to test her self-control by looking at Dick's ashen face.

He fumbled for a handkerchief and slowly got to his feet.

"What the hell happened? I should have been here." Emotion

unmade his features; his eyes were wide, his cheeks slack, his mouth trembling. He had never looked more like his nephew, Saint.

"Pneumonia."

"When?"

"He died on Monday. He came home soaked to the skin last Wednesday. At first, we thought little of it." She ran a hand over her forehead. "A week ago. It feels like a lifetime. He caught a chill that went straight to his chest. We called Dr. Alves and sat with him day and night."

"I should have been here. You should have written last Wednesday."

"I am sorry, Brother."

"Sorry?" Jack's face hardened. His lip curled, and his nostrils flared. "I race here. I walk into this. All the time he's already—" He half-nodded back at Dick's body. "And you are sorry?" Color rose in his face, and his voice rose. "Sorry?"

Jack grabbed Nancy by the shoulders. She almost thought he would crush her into his chest, but no, he pushed her from the room and slammed the door in her face. For a moment, she simply stood there, trying to take in what had happened. And then, she heard a movement to her left. Anna Dudley, standing in the doorway to the house with her hands on her hips, her daughter and son beside her.

"I expect that what Mr. Randolph needs now is his family. His kin." She patted her children's shoulders. "His blood. I will go to him. I suggest you go and tell Mrs. Randolph that her brother-in-law has arrived."

She opened the parlor door and ushered the children in. In the coolness and quiet of the hallway, Nancy waited. She expected Anna Dudley to receive no better treatment from Jack than she had. But all was quiet. She shook her head and went upstairs to find Judy.

Thankfully, Mr. Tucker arrived the next day and took Jack in hand. Nancy saw them disappear for long walks and ride over the plantation several times, as well as taking a day or two at the Roanoke property, some miles distant. The funeral was a quiet affair. Dick had never quite regained the status lost three years previously, despite his acquittal at the Cumberland courthouse. Friends came, of course: Randy and Mary, the Taylors, the Creeds, a few other plantation owners, Tom and Patsy. Dick's half-sister, Fanny, arrived with her friend, Maria Ward, both closer friends with Judy than with Nancy. Letters arrived from Lizzie and Molly. Nancy knew Judy had received a brief note of condolence from Gabriella, now remarried and become Mrs. John Brockenhurst, and William managed a bare two lines to her on the subject. One light in the darkness was that Judy told Anna Dudley to pack her bags the day after Dick was buried.

Her sister had barely spoken since it happened. She remained in her room, focusing on Tudor. Nancy watched Jack climb the stairs to see Judy, only to plod back down again within minutes. He didn't catch her eye but chose to sweep Saint up into his arms and take him for a ride. She was thankful Jack found solace in his nephew and grateful for time alone to compose herself.

Judy was Dick's widow—the loss was hers. But in her own room at night, Nancy took the ring from her neck chain, slid it on the finger of her left hand and cried herself to sleep. He was gone. The dream was gone. Only memories remained. She would protect those, protect him, protect her sister and protect their sons. It was the only way.

A few days after the funeral, Nancy found herself alone on the porch with Mr. Tucker for the first time since his arrival.

"I must tell you, my dearest Mr. Tucker, how valuable your correspondence has been to me these past three years." It was a glorious summer morning. The air was alive with the sound of birds calling, and a slight breeze stirred the leaves in the line of poplar trees that led to the river. No matter what happened, the seasons kept turning. The thought made her chest heavy.

"I told you I thought of you as a daughter, do you remember?"

She nodded. His voice was soft as always, but he'd aged since the trial. Deep lines fanned his cheeks. She saw his grief over Dick's death in the downturn of his mouth and the way he sank into his chair.

"Have you thought of the future, Nancy?"

"I will remain here with my sister."

"Is that for the best?"

"I believe so. She will need support. There is Saint to consider. And Tudor."

"She'll have Jack's help. And you are still so young."

She gave a half-smile. "Jack is only twenty-three. What burdens he must shoulder. He will rely upon you, I am sure."

"It will be hard on him. He has some ambitions that must be laid to one side, at least for now."

"Ambitions?"

"Politics."

"Really? I'd no idea. Although I know he has strong opinions."

"Which he is often willing to express." Tucker let out a soft chuckle. "Well, time will tell. He will finish his current studies and return to Bizarre to manage the family's interests. He has a great love for Saint and will feel the same for Tudor, I am sure."

"I still hope Saint may be able to go to school in England. In time, anyway."

"Perhaps, but not soon. There are the costs to be considered. And how certain can we be of the results? You believe he can be taught to speak?"

"I have high hopes for it. He makes great strides in his reading and writing, even at such a young age. I must continue to teach him. I cannot think of leaving Bizarre."

"But what about a family of your own, Nancy? Have you no thoughts of that?"

"None."

"You are young. That may change."

"But my situation will not." She bit her lip and looked down at her lap. "Believe me, sir, I have given it much consideration. Where would you have me go? You have a full household. I would never impose myself."

"You would be welcome, Nancy. Mrs. Tucker and I would welcome you."

"I know. But you would regret it. No—" she raised a hand to forestall his interruption. "My reputation is lost. We all know it. I might, perhaps, accept an offer from one of my brothers, should they be willing to take in such a cuckoo as I, but if my own family cannot stomach the humiliation of association with me, how can I ask yours to?"

"I say again, Nancy. You are a daughter to me."

Tears threatened. "You must care for those already under your roof, not add another, whose tawdry history might besmirch them by association." She shook her head and put a finger to her lips. More kind words might break her. "Anna Dudley made my position plain to me. I will not marry. I will not have my own children. I won't be independent. I won't run my own household. I'm beholden to Judy and will do my best to support her and Dick's children. There's nothing I won't do for them. Do you see?"

Tucker nodded but was silent.

Behind her, at the doorway to the house, Nancy heard the creak of wood under a light footstep. Then Judy's voice.

"I am glad to hear it, Sister. This is where you belong. Here. With me."

Nancy didn't turn, but she nodded her head.

Yes, she thought.

This is how it must be.

Phebe

Mr. Randolph's death shocked them all, but there was no warmth in the grieving, no shared tears, no talk of fond memories, no comforting. Mrs. Randolph only had eyes for her beloved Tudor, and Miss Nancy redoubled her efforts to teach Saint. The way Phebe saw it, those two sisters might've killed each other if it hadn't been for the boys. In countless ways, the children kept the pulse of life alive at Bizarre, and the women fell into rhythm with them, living in a fragile alliance that even had Sarah Ellis accepting that Phebe might be at Bizarre for good. Small changes eased her loneliness. An extra helping of cornbread. An offer to roll up her bed. A chuckle from Lottie, her plate cleared by Sally. Evenings spent sitting with Syphax, watching fireflies and listening to the old man talk. Forgetting the past. Minding her business. Accepting what was.

She knew Billy Ellis watched her—tall, strong Billy Ellis with his soft voice and the slightest gap between his two front teeth—but she gave no encouragement, none. Being with a man, having children of her own, those were things for other folks, not for her, with the things she'd seen. Phebe kept her eyes lowered when she saw him. Never spoke to him unless he spoke to her first. Until one day, the rain blew in from nowhere.

It hit the windows in great, fat, noisy splashes. It drummed the roof. Phebe ran outside and tried to bundle Miss Nancy's damp cotton sheets in her arms. Help arrived. Billy. Together, they kept the sheets clear of the ground and made for the porch. He shook the rain from his head like a half-drowned dog, and she found herself folding sheets with him, helpless with laughter. He left her with a neat pile of washing and a grin, but an hour or so later, the back door to the house banged open, and Sarah called her.

"Girl! You girl. I wants a word."

Phebe straightened her apron. Sarah led her to the kitchen garden, through the still damp grass, well out of earshot of the house. The sky was cloudless.

"I don't want you teasing my boy, you hear me?"

"I teased no one, and ain't done nothing! You leave me alone, Sarah Ellis."

"It's you needs to do the leaving folks alone. You's not the girl for him, even if he thinks you is."

The unfairness of it loosened her tongue. "After alls I've seen, I won't be tangling with any man, not your precious son, not no one. Never."

Sarah's brows flew up. "What you seen, girl, to make you speak like that?"

Phebe imagined telling her everything. Mae. Miss Nancy. But she saw Cilla's soft brown face as clear as if it had been yesterday, telling her to look after Miss Nancy real well. She held her tongue, and Sarah stomped back to the kitchen house. The possibility of

213

belonging disappeared. When Billy Ellis looked her way, she turned her back.

During the long years after the master's death, Mr. Jack was more and more at Bizarre, shaking up the quiet, bringing cross words and misunderstandings. None of them Randolph brothers were any good for Miss Nancy. But Mr. Jack? He proved worst of all.

Part Three

Chapter Twenty-Three

Tuckahoe, Virginia, 1806
Ten years later

Nancy woke to the heavy scent of pine and a pain in her left hip. She lifted her head and wiped a smear of sap from her cheek. The makeshift bed of branches she and Phebe had assembled in the dark last night felt like a blessing when she first lay down. Now she rubbed at aching limbs.

Light slid in, spreading a watery reflection of the bare window frame across the floorboards, not yet reaching the shadow by the door where Phebe lay wrapped in blankets.

This had been the room of her childhood. In the bustle of arrival at Tuckahoe, clutching the keys so reluctantly handed over by John Brockenhurst, and with the light of a single candle, she hadn't seen the sadness of the empty plantation house and this room, bare of furnishings. She had found familiarity in the archway leading to the Great Hall, trailed her fingers over the scrollwork, the daisies and

217

acanthus leaves carved in the newel post and climbed the twelve steps to the landing, turning right and up to reach the familiar bedchamber. In the light of day, that warm feeling disappeared. The bones of her childhood were here, but the change was stark. Nancy closed her eyes and filled the room with their belongings. She saw the heavy wooden bed with its pink and gray quilt, frayed at the corner where she'd picked and rubbed a comforting hole that helped her sleep at night. She saw the dressing table and chair and the soft green cushion Judy insisted must stay there, despite Nancy knocking it to the floor whenever she combed out her hair. She opened her eyes as Phebe stirred. The bookcase, the press for their dresses—all were long gone. Had Gabriella kept anything? Nancy doubted it. She had married John Brockenhurst and moved with her young son to Richmond. Tuckahoe would be his one day—should he want it.

"Did you sleep well, miss?" Phebe sat up and stretched.

"Surprisingly well."

"You will need something to eat, Miss Nancy. I should go and see who is still here."

"Thank you." Nancy rubbed her eyes. The house might be deserted, but the Tuckahoe Plantation was not abandoned. An overseer was in place, the land still worked and the slaves still here, including Phebe's family. "Go," she said, ashamed not to have thought of it earlier. "See your people. I'm not so hungry. Take your time. I must take better stock of things, now I can see my way."

She spent the morning wandering, reacquainting herself with places and sights that seemed to belong to someone else. She had left Tuckahoe an angry girl of seventeen. Now she was a woman in her thirties, unmarried and dependent on the goodwill of her siblings for her every need. She'd inherited six thousand dollars at her father's death, but that was long gone, handed over to Judy as part of the never-ending penance paid in the ten years since Dick's death.

Back in the house, Nancy went to the window in their old bedroom. She conjured up Dick as he was all those years ago, riding a tall chestnut up to the north door, leaping from the saddle, calling Judy's name. She leaned her head against the glass and welcomed the numbing cold on her brow.

Her brother, Tom, would arrive soon. What would his answer be? He had helped her so often these last years, taking her in at Monticello for months at a time when the situation at Bizarre grew too hard to bear. He must help her now. Surely? While she waited, she worked on a letter to Mr. Tucker. By the time Tom arrived, she was calm and ready to face him.

"My God, it's strange to see the house like this," he said, following her into the parlor. She could not disagree. The white paneled walls were marked with outlines of paintings and mirrors removed for storage. The mantel, another of her stepmother's additions, was bare of any familiar miniatures and fine china, the grate empty and swept clean. Only a small side table and two well-worn settles remained, presumably not to Gabriella's taste, placed on a threadbare carpet that had once been in her parents' bedroom.

"Indeed it is, brother. I'm sorry to drag you here."

"No matter, no matter." They embraced and sat opposite each other. Tom looked tired. As he set down his hat and ran his fingers through his hair, Nancy's optimism faltered.

"I won't beat about the bush, Nance. Monticello is not an option."

"But Tom—"

He held up a hand. "There's no use arguing about it. Patsy and I have gone back and forth."

"I have not upset her, I hope. I thought she had a fondness for me!"

"Never doubt it. She's most attached. But the truth, Nancy, is that none of us are doing well financially. Money is tight. Look at Molly and David."

"Yes, but Tom—" Nancy broke off, seeing the grim expression on his face. His point about Molly and David hit home. They had sold their plantation and were fixed for the future at Moldavia, their house in Richmond. Molly had written that she was considering taking boarders, and Nancy had been shocked to hear that things had come to such a pass. Jane and her husband were said to be struggling to hold onto their land at Dungeness, Harriet and Jenny were newly married, and her brother John? John was struggling to build a farm and in no position to help anyone, sister or not. She tried to marshal her arguments. "But wouldn't bringing me into your home allow me to be the least strain on your finances? I can help with the children. I can work, garden, sew, all manner of things. I don't eat much—"

"Don't labor it, Sister. Things are difficult and uncertain. We'll always welcome your visits but can go no further. A permanent arrangement is too much of a burden."

She winced, and Tom moved to sit by her, taking her hand. "I've already spoken with David. He's looking for suitable accommodation in Richmond. I'll pay your lodgings. Perhaps …" He hesitated. "Perhaps when you are settled, you might find some paid employment?"

Nancy forced herself to shut out a stab of anger toward Patsy. She could hear the word *burden* in Patsy's voice as clearly as if she was in the room. That one never forgot whose daughter she was. Her father's election to the presidency must have swollen Patsy's pride, but Nancy knew better than to say what she thought out loud. "Find employment? I'm sure I shall. That would be best. I see it now."

"Good girl!" Tom squeezed her hands and got to his feet. "Knew you'd understand. How was our sister when you left her? Things no better between you?"

"Would I be here if they were?"

"True, true. But you have been on the verge of leaving Bizarre upward of a dozen times in recent years and have always returned in the end."

She couldn't argue with him. Every word was true. There had been explosive moments. Harsh words exchanged. Long periods of silence. Lengthy absences—sometimes Nancy spending months at Monticello or with William and Lucy in Richmond. Sometimes Judy visiting Mr. Tucker's daughter, Fanny, or the ghastly Maria, along with regular trips to the Springs for her fragile constitution. Far worse than Judy, though, there had been Jack Randolph.

"The boys no longer need me, Tom. Tudor will go to Mr. King's School in Richmond and Saint is to travel to England, finally. You remember Leslie Alexander? He recommended a school for the deaf and dumb in London."

"I imagine it costs a pretty penny."

"His uncle bears the expense."

"Jack? He is good to his nephews. That is the best I can say though."

"Let's not speak of him. His latest insult to me will be his last." She got to her feet, and they stood at the window, looking out at Plantation Street. Two small boys were in view, struggling with a bundle of laundry so heavy, it bumped the ground between them.

"They'll be in trouble with Old Cilla," said Tom. "Lord, Nancy, it seems a long time since we were children here."

She laughed a little. "Because it was, Brother. You'll be forty soon."

"Don't remind me!"

"I'd like to stay here a few more days, I think," Nancy said. "I owe Phebe some time with her family. Then, perhaps Molly and David will take us in while he secures my new lodging. Will you arrange that?"

"Of course. I would wish to do more but—"

She patted his arm and shook her head. "Don't worry, Tom. There's no need."

His hand covered hers. "This will be a new beginning for you, Sister. A new start, away from Judy's martyrdom and Jack's lord-of-the-manor attitude. I can't abide to be half an hour in the same room as the man. Lord alone knows how you tolerated him at Bizarre all these years. Damned odd fellow."

"Didn't we agree not to speak of him?" Nancy twisted away and walked to the door. "Come. Let me find you something to eat and then send you on your way." She forced herself to affect a lightness of spirit she was far from feeling. "And while you eat, you must tell me how the children are. Is Cornelia still drawing so beautifully? And what of Virginia? Is it true she has lost her front teeth already? They grow so fast. I can barely keep up."

Chapter Twenty-Four

Judy stood in the doorway of her sister's room at Bizarre, empty of any sign of her years of occupation. Sarah scrubbed every inch while Judy supervised, tempted to order her to take bedclothes and hangings and burn them. But that would be foolish, impulsive, and the slaves would talk of it—a thought she couldn't tolerate. She mustn't be rash. Having Nancy gone was enough. Judy wanted only to enjoy the quiet. To enjoy her sister's absence from her house and her everyday life.

A noise at the bottom of the stairs disturbed her. Tudor, aged ten and rambunctious, was always clattering in and out, bringing in the stink of the stables and mud on his boots. It was all she could do to get him to wrap up warm. As a young child, he had been beset by coughs and fevers. His frame was slight, his chest his Achilles heel, as it was for his father and uncle. Judy had known days and nights of terror when she feared some flu or ague would take him. She left Sarah working and called to her son.

"Tudor? Come upstairs at once. Where have you been all morning?" She listened for his feet on the stair but only heard the slam of a door. Her lips compressed. Jack was right: Tudor needed to be at school. The thought lay heavy on her shoulders. For a moment, she hesitated outside her own room. The urge to cry was back, and she trembled with it, the desire to let out an ugly storm of tears and misery and spend the rest of the day in her bed. Tudor brought it out in her. Every time he snubbed her. Every time he disappeared. When he ignored her instructions. When he snatched food from the kitchen and ran. When he bolted his meals and left the table without permission. When he left his horse untended and shouted at Saint, laughing that his brother could not hear him, taunting Saint for his confused looks, his grunts and strange laughter. And yet, she loved him no less for it. In the evenings, when Tudor came to the parlor and laid his head in her lap or sat by her and leaned on her shoulder, she experienced a flood of maternal love. At those moments, the dark weights all disappeared. Only in prayer had she found a similar sense of peace. And even prayer did not always relieve her mind. Only Tudor.

She forced herself down the stairs. Saint had departed for England, and Judy tried to imagine him, her near-silent son, an awkward adolescent, standing on the deck of a ship, gazing out on nothing but ocean. As she reached the hallway, Jack threw open the door and marched in, waving a letter.

"Another bloody missive from Tucker about Nancy. Good God, you would think the man was her father, never mind he's only the stepfather of the woman's dead brother-in-law. I've had enough of his high-handed ways." Before Judy could say a word, Jack tore the letter into pieces. He shrugged off his coat and yelled for Ben to come and take it from him. "Why, if Tucker knew half the truth about your damned sister and her loose ways …"

224

"Enough, Jack! Tudor is near and the servants also. Think of Sarah. She mustn't hear you. Nancy's gone. That's enough for me and should be for you, too." She put her hand on his arm, and he looked down at it. His shoulders relaxed.

"You are right. And with Billy Ellis at Roanoke, there will be no reminders."

"Hush!" She pulled him into the parlor. "These were *your* suspicions, not mine, Jack Randolph, and I'll thank you not to mention them again in my house."

"All right, all right," he ran a hand through his hair. It was the only thing he did that reminded her of Dick. In all else, Jack was nothing like his brother, but with this one gesture, Judy conjured her husband in her mind's eye as clearly as if she had seen him only yesterday. She shook her head, and he disappeared.

"My beloved stepfather, Mr. Tucker, suggests I go to Richmond," said Jack. "To support your poor sister, if you can believe it. 'To help her find her feet in society.' That's a direct quote. I'm to assure her she can rely on him—and myself—as much as on your brothers."

"He has always taken her part."

Much of Judy's life after Dick's death was a blur, but one thing had always been clear—the divide between herself and Nancy. On Judy's side, there was Jack, Tudor, Cousin Mary, Dick's half-sister, Fanny and her friend Maria. On Nancy's, the Tuckers, their brothers and Saint.

When Jack first moved into Bizarre to manage the plantation, she'd been wary. His eyes had always followed Nancy. Judy had first seen his fascination with her sister a lifetime ago at Randy and Mary Harrison's wedding. But Jack was never the kind of man to attract her sister, and in the years after his tussle with scarlet fever and that disappointment with Maria, it became less and less likely that he would marry anyone. Little was said, but eyebrows were raised. Only Aunt Page had ever been indecorous enough to whisper her doubt about Jack's ability to father a child. Certainly his voice was not as deep as other men's, his beard was a sparse chaff, his boyish face never thickened the way other men's did. Besides, ever since Dick's trial, when his eyes followed Nancy, they glittered with something much darker than attraction. The love—if that's what it had been—was gone, but the fascination remained. He watched her for years. Only when Maria became fast friends with Judy had Jack seemed able to turn away from his preoccupation. But Nancy had spoiled that for him, gossiping about a letter he'd sent her years earlier. Judy felt a creak of conscience. Her friend had never been in love with Jack. Nancy's revelation that he'd made her some kind of proposal was enough for Maria to force a falling-out and end Jack's hopes. And Judy had been happy to let Jack heap all the blame for his disappointment on her sister's head. He hated her. It had only been a matter of time before he lost his self-control around her.

Judy understood how he felt. She felt it too. In the years after Dick's death, she waited and waited for Nancy to slip up in some way, but she'd been hard to fault. She cared for the boys as if they were her own, sewed clothes, tended the garden, ran errands, listened to all Judy's talk of her health and her boys. She was trustworthy enough to be left at Bizarre while Judy visited the Springs or stayed with friends and sensible enough to spend time away on her own account, so that there had been long periods where they were apart. Enough to keep Judy's anger at bay. Enough for her to find the convenience of Nancy outweighed the pain of having her there, reminding her.

But it wasn't so for Jack. Nancy's presence offered no benefit to him. She was a thorn under his skin, a stone in his shoe. For years after Maria broke with Jack, he and Nancy had circled Bizarre, and each other, never outwardly admitting that they avoided being there at the same time, and yet quietly checking on dates and plans, doing everything they could to avoid being on the property for too long together. Until last summer.

Jack, free for a time from congressional duties, had returned to Bizarre and spent more time on the plantation than he wanted to. Their overseer had left suddenly, and it took some weeks to find a suitable replacement. In the meantime, someone needed to manage the land and ensure the crops were flourishing. Nancy was home; it was the busiest season in the garden. From her window, every morning, Judy saw Nancy's straw hat moving about between rows of beans, green tomatoes and frilly lettuces. Usually, Billy Ellis was there too, working hard, fetching water, digging, following Nancy's directions. Jack saw it differently.

"I'm thinking of sending Billy to Roanoke," he announced one evening at the dinner table. The boys had already been excused.

"Billy?" Nancy said. "Don't we need him here? Judy?"

"I certainly think so. What would Sarah say?"

Jack pulled a face that made Judy want to snap at him. Why did men never understand how their mothers felt about them? Couldn't Jack see how important Sarah's contentment was to the smooth running of Bizarre?

"What Sarah thinks doesn't concern me, nor should it you. I have need of a laborer. He's a strong lad, is he not, Nancy?"

"Yes, but he is needed here, Jack. The garden—" She broke off as Jack sniggered.

"Oh, the *garden*."

"Yes, the garden. There is heavy work there. We have vegetables to harvest and store. We might lose half our winter supplies if the earth is not watered. Who will take his place?"

"Hmm. Who could take his place, I wonder?" Jack leaned back in his chair, wiping at his lips with his napkin. The sisters exchanged confused looks.

"What are you getting at, Jack?" Nancy crossed her arms. "If you have a point to make, why not make it? We're listening."

He made them wait—folding his napkin, taking a long sip of wine, letting the liquid pool in his mouth before swallowing. "You seem particularly *attached* to Billy Ellis, Nancy," he said at last.

"Attached? In what manner *attached*?"

"My very question."

"Billy Ellis is a good-tempered, pleasant man who works hard for us."

"In what way is he pleasant?"

"In what way do you imagine? He is polite. Knowledgeable." Nancy looked from Jack to Judy and back again. "He is one of our people. Sarah's son. You both know him. This conversation is absurd." She started to push back her chair and rise.

"I think he pleases you too much. I think he pleases you in ways a slave ought not to please his mistress. I think—"

"How dare you!"

Nancy's temper was up, but Jack remained unpleasantly calm. He shrugged as if indifferent. "He's a handsome devil, though. You must have noticed that."

"Certainly not!" Nancy sounded sincere but Judy saw a flicker of something in her sister's eye. Suspicion flared. What if Jack was correct? Billy Ellis was clear-eyed, smooth-skinned, strong. And Nancy? What really was she? What was she truly capable of? She thought of the ring on its chain around her neck. What was its story? But Nancy was staring. "You don't defend me, Sister?"

A familiar and unwelcome sense of weariness washed over Judy. She was so tired of it. So tired of Nancy. Everything, everything, always came back to her.

"You do spend a great many hours with him," Judy said.

Nancy was on the road to Tuckahoe within days.

Chapter Twenty-Five

She had never been alone with David Meade Randolph before, yet now, Nancy found herself in a closed carriage with him, being driven from Tuckahoe to a lodging in Richmond that he had found for her. Molly's husband was someone she knew, of course, someone whose home she had stayed in on many occasions, yet she couldn't recall a single conversation she'd had with him. He was heavy-set and not tall, with a broad chest and arms so short, his hands threatened to disappear up his coat sleeves. At least his distinctive, braying laugh was not in evidence. Instead, he was quiet, likely wishing himself otherwise occupied. He and Molly were both much older than Nancy. She imagined herself of as little interest to him as he was to her.

Phebe's presence was reassuring. Nancy had been afraid she'd ask to remain at Bizarre, tempted by the possibility of a marriage to Billy Ellis, or with her family at Tuckahoe, but she'd simply nodded when Nancy told her they were going to Richmond. Randolph raised his eyebrows a little when Nancy directed her maid to climb into the coach with them, but he didn't argue when she pointed to the dark rain clouds over their heads. As they rolled into Richmond, a heavy drum of rainfall assaulted their ears. At least it removed the need for conversation.

But once at the lodging, David Meade Randolph was in no rush to depart. He appeared to be on good terms with the lady of the house—Mrs. Booth, a wide-hipped woman in a low-cut muslin that needed a neckerchief to be properly modest, and blind to the clear deficiencies Nancy saw in her new accommodation. The room was almost bare of furniture. There was a bed, yes, but later, when she lay on it, the mattress proved to be no more than a pile of sacking, tucked in a rough blanket that scratched her skin. There was no press for her clothes, such as they were, and the basin in the washstand was cracked and stained. Worse was the damp. Nancy smelled it as soon as she entered, a musty odor that prompted her to run her hand along the wall and shiver at the moisture she touched there. But David Meade Randolph would have none of it, busying himself with laying a fire in the small hearth and promising she would be warm in a moment. After he took his leave, she noticed his carriage remained outside for some time, and an unkind suspicion crossed her mind about the nature of her brother-in-law's connection to her landlady.

The next morning, Nancy dressed, drank a cup of bitter coffee, nibbled on a stale slice of bread left at their door by a maid of work and prepared to visit her Richmond relations. The sight of Molly's familiar home on Cary Street brightened her hopes. Employment would be her answer—her route to independence and lodgings that, at the least, were warm and dry.

Molly was in the kitchen with her women, and the smell of meat roasting on the spit made Nancy's mouth water. But her imaginings of a comfortable cup of tea in the parlor with her sister, discussing what her first steps might be in finding employment, proved illusory. Molly was short with her, clearly shouldering difficulties of her own. She brushed off her hands on her apron and led Nancy out into the hallway.

"I've no time for you today, Sister, as you can see. Perhaps next week? I'm sure you are busy getting settled."

Nancy realized Molly was leading her to the door. "Wait. I need your advice, sister. Where am I to find work? How do I go about it? Might I not be of use to you? Perhaps I might lodge here and be of use to you?"

"Lodge here?" Molly's frown spoke volumes. "When my David has been to the trouble of securing you a place for the next three months?"

"Three months? Molly, I cannot stay there above three nights. The damp is shocking. I fear for my health!"

"Nonsense. You're being far too particular. I cannot have you here." She strained her neck, looking around. "Mr. Randolph's business ventures do not prosper, Nancy. The plantation is sold. We are much reduced here and have our children to think of. You must contrive to find employment."

"And I mean to, Sister, but where? What do you recommend?"

Molly shuddered. "As if I do not have enough to bear already. Try the schools. The Academy. You could teach, could you not? That would be respectable enough, I suppose."

But within a week of arriving in Richmond, Nancy knew she was in trouble. Her letters to educational establishments went unanswered. She could find no hint of any family who needed a genteel, unmarried lady to teach their children at home, and letters from her brothers, Tom and William, were full of their opinions on what work she certainly must *not* consider, without any suggestion of what she should do instead. No one bearing the name Randolph could consider work in any kind of shop or eating establishment. Setting herself up as a milliner or seamstress required supplies and materials she had no means of purchasing. Her sister, Lizzie, invited her to tea, but never, she noted, when other Richmond ladies were present. With an unwilling hand, Nancy wrote to Gabriella, thanking her for allowing her to visit Tuckahoe, before making it known that she was now in the city. Her stepmother sent a three-line reply and did not suggest a meeting.

When Phebe began coughing, Nancy knew they needed to move. She sent a note to Molly with an urgent request for David Meade Randolph to come to her aid. He'd been mistaken in the room he had found. He'd seen it only briefly and at night. She was sure in daylight, he would see it would not do. Black mold climbed the walls. Phebe was already ill, Nancy sure to join her. On his second visit, he was less conciliatory.

"The room is not the best." He studied the mold around the window and sniffed. "I thought you might have cleaned it up a little."

"And I thought you might have found me somewhere more suitable."

"You have little means, Nancy Randolph, and are reliant on the goodwill of your relations. You might remember that."

"There's no need to represent to me the difficulties of my position. Believe me, I am quite aware. But I cannot stay here. It's unhealthy."

For a moment, they stared at each other. He dropped his gaze first. "Very well. The younger Whiting daughter—you are familiar with the Whitings?" Nancy shook her head. "No matter. Their younger daughter is now a Mrs. Pryor. Her husband runs the Haymarket Pleasure Gardens. They have need of some help in the house. She will offer you a room at a low price if you will assist her in the kitchen and so on."

"They're respectable people? And their home is clean and dry?"

"Very respectable indeed. The pleasure garden is popular, but the house is away from all that—quite enclosed and separate. John Pryor is well-liked in Richmond. Fought in the war. Successful in business."

"I'll take it then. And I can take Phebe with me?"

"Indeed you may. Molly says you will have even less reputation if you do not keep your maid! If that were possible." He laughed his awful laugh and Nancy's stomach dropped.

"And you will deal with Mrs. Booth? Recover Tom's money? I'm so distressed she was given three months' rent in advance. Had anyone seen the place, they could not have thought it sensible."

Since they both knew David Meade Randolph had paid over the money himself, she was not surprised when he glared, but she didn't care. The less he liked her, the sooner he might leave her in peace.

But it was soon clear the last thing on David Meade Randolph's mind was leaving Nancy Randolph in peace. At first, he visited her in her new room on the pretext of his attempts on her behalf to secure a refund from Mrs. Booth. Instead of realizing how he had let Nancy down in that regard, he implied their troubles with Mrs. Booth had brought them together in adversity. He made himself at home in a way that made her uncomfortable. He filled the room to the point where she could barely breathe, and she made sure to keep Phebe with her whenever he stopped by. On the evening he finally admitted defeat over Mrs. Booth and the three months' rent, he arrived with a bottle of wine and looked disappointed when she refused to take any. After downing several glasses in quick succession, he began to talk.

"You will have heard, I suppose, that I had to sell the plantation?

Damnable state of affairs. My father is turning in his grave, I'm sure. And what do I get from Mrs. Randolph? A list of complaints."

"From Molly? She seemed happily busy when I saw her last."

"Busy? Yes, she is busy. Calls it 'making the best of things' and invokes her mother fifteen times a day."

Nancy smiled—a mistake—her brother-in-law took it for encouragement.

"Oh, she puts on a good show, I'll give her that. Never lets the side down in public. But, between us, she's been the devil to live with of late. Never a kind word. Little barbs here and there. When all a man wants of an evening is to sit peacefully with a pretty, restful woman to bear him some companionship."

Nancy had been thinking of Judy's little barbs, but his soft expression brought her focus keenly back to the present. He was about to pour more wine, but she forestalled him.

"I must bid you goodnight now, unfortunately, Mr. Randolph," she said, standing. "The family across the hallway are most particular that there should be no noise at this hour, and I have to be up and helping Mrs. Pryor early tomorrow morning. But thank you for visiting. Phebe, can you pass Mr. Randolph his hat?"

With the door closed behind him and his steps echoing down the stairs, Nancy turned to Phebe. "Whatever can I do to stop these visits?"

Every morning, Nancy rose early and oversaw the Pryors' servants in the making of breakfast, making the coffee herself and carrying the pot to the family dining room. Mr. Pryor said little, his face buried in the newspaper when he wasn't eating his bacon, but Mrs. Pryor was always cheerful, and Nancy enjoyed feeling useful. She thought of Saint often. It was hard to imagine him so far away from home.

A few days later, in the evening, David Meade Randolph returned, bearing another bottle of wine. Nancy had been ruminating all day on Mrs. Booth and the waste of Tom's money. She pressed him on the subject again.

"Let it go, will you," he said. "The woman is quite within her rights. You chose to leave."

"But I heard from Mrs. Pryor that Mrs. Booth has plans to rent the room to another person. If she has new income, she has no grounds for keeping what we paid her."

"I'm telling you the money is gone. Forget it. You are better situated here, are you not?" He waved his arm and smiled, as if the room they sat in was as pleasant as any he might see. She thought of all she could say. That the room had no fireplace. That the light was poor, and she'd no money to pay for extra candles. That her bed was behind a screen and had no hangings, such as she was used to, that her two chairs needed new cushions, and the little table by the window had such a wobble, she'd been forced to pull out the end pages of two of her favorite novels to prop up its one short leg. She pictured his comfortable home on Cary Street and her sister, with whom he should so clearly be, instead of with her.

"How is Molly? I thought I might call on her tomorrow. Might you take her a note from me?"

"Me? I hardly think so. She would find it most odd."

"But surely she knows you are visiting here?"

He leaned back further now and even laughed. "Not for a moment. Molly thinks I'm meeting with a prospective business partner. She is always on at me, don't you see? Money, money, money. No appreciation for how hard I work. No. This is our secret, yours and mine. A little oasis of peace for me. You don't begrudge it now, do you? I don't suppose you have many visitors, and don't they say a friendly face is always welcome?"

"You are my family, sir, and of course, welcome to visit," Nancy hesitated, and her cheeks grew warm. "But I would be happier if my sister knew of it. Your kindness is her kindness after all."

"*Her* kindness? My dear, do you *know* your sister? Kindness is not a word that springs to mind when one speaks of her. I could give you a few other words—but as a gentleman, I shall not."

"But your protection on the road from Tuckahoe. Your help with finding lodgings. I must be grateful to my sister, sir."

"I'm not sure you should. If you had seen her and Lizzie, all of a twitter when they heard your plan to come to Richmond, I doubt you'd be grateful at all. But then, it's often the way, isn't it? Women can be so hard on each other. And so careful of their own standing and reputations."

Nancy rubbed at her temples. "Are you telling me that my sisters didn't want me in Richmond?"

"Not a bit! But Tom was set on it, and William agreed. And simply because a woman makes a mistake, I'm certainly not one to judge her for it."

"Mr. Randolph! I don't know to what you refer but this conversation should end."

His face twisted then. He managed to look both incredulous and knowing at the same time. He turned to Phebe and tossed her a few coins. "Go down into the pleasure garden. I've a fancy for some hot chestnuts. Buy enough for yourself. No need to rush."

Nancy watched in near disbelief as Phebe drew her shawl about her shoulders and slipped from the room. Randolph poured himself another glass of wine.

"You're sure you won't join me?"

"No. And I must tell you that I am not comfortable with your manner of speaking. Perhaps I'm mistaken, but—"

"I doubt it. You're no fool, Nancy. No one could spend two minutes in your company without seeing it. And good looking. The prettiest Randolph girl, they always said. But sadly ruined." He talked like she was something left out in the rain. "I won't insult your intelligence by pretending otherwise. I was thinking of taking another one of the Pryor's rooms. Below here. A slightly bigger apartment, with no enquiring neighbors across the hall. What do you say?"

"I say you must not!"

"No? And yet the advantages to us both must be obvious."

His casual approach, his arrogance, his ugly, wide face—Nancy didn't know what angered her more.

"The advantage to you might be clear, but for me, I tell you plainly, there is none!"

"No?"

"What must you think of me to even make such a suggestion?"

"I think only what everyone must think. You're a single woman. Unmarriageable, but damned attractive. Someone will pluck you; why not me?"

"Perhaps because you are married to my sister!" Nancy strode to the window and laid her palms on the cold glass. There was silence for a beat.

"That didn't concern you in the past."

Nancy stared at her reflection in the windowpane. Was this how it would be for her? Was this what she deserved? Even now? After all those painful, long years at Bizarre?

She heard the door open. Phebe returning. She kept her gaze on the glass. "Don't close the door, Phebe. Mr. Randolph was about to leave."

He said nothing, but she heard the shrug of material as he drew on his coat, a rustle as he affixed his hat, the thud of the door closing and the rasp of the bolt as Phebe slid it into place. And still, she stared at herself in the window. The room smelled of roasted chestnuts. She had no appetite.

Chapter Twenty-Six

Judy watched Jack dismount his horse and lead it to the stables. She was used to seeing Tudor leaping around his uncle like a puppy, but her son had been gone for weeks now. She almost wished Jack had gone to Richmond to support Nancy as Mr. Tucker suggested. He could have visited and come back with word of him. Tudor's schoolboy letters told her nothing. Then there had been a letter to Jack, from the school, suggesting Tudor's behavior was not all it should be. She was afraid he was unhappy.

Perhaps Maria and Fanny would bring a letter from Tudor in Richmond. They were expected mid-afternoon, for a stay of at least a week. Some quiet days with good friends. Judy needed that. She wondered if Jack would stay for dinner or if he'd take himself off to Roanoke before Maria and his half-sister even arrived. She hoped so. She hoped he would leave them in peace. Jack was so hard to read these days, and although years had passed since all had come to nothing, who knew better than Judy that some scars never heal?

Maria had been married for several years now, but to her knowledge, Jack had never been involved with anyone else.

Judy shivered. It was impossible to think of those days without bringing Nancy to mind again. Must banishing her sister from her thoughts be so impossible? But in the case of Maria and Jack, Nancy had not been at fault. Not really. She'd been indiscreet, but then she'd had no idea how things lay between Maria and Jack.

Fanny and Maria arrived at Bizarre later than expected. There had been trouble with the horses and a long delay at a tavern. Fanny looked particularly pale.

"She has not been the same since Elizabeth was born," Maria confided. "She lost a great deal too much weight and told me she hasn't slept well in months. I think both she and John hope a week with us here—a break from the children and the plantation—will help her regain some strength."

"He travels too much," said Judy. "She is alone too much. Managing slaves? Children? A lazy overseer? All with an absent husband? It's almost worse than being a widow. I don't expect relief, but she suffers in his absence."

"I agree. She was talking in the carriage about her parents. In her memory, her mother never struggled, but managed everything with competence and good humor."

"Then we must contrive to distract her in these few days. We'll be quiet and restful, and we will eat well. Sarah can fetch cream from the dairy."

Their talk turned to kitchen matters and what meals might tempt their friend's appetite. For Judy, the visit was almost as good as a rest for herself. She knew none of the dragging heaviness that so often dogged her. Although not widowed as she was, these were women who understood her daily challenges. Their shared concerns about business and children, their faith, their belief in the central importance of family and all things domestic bonded them. Letters kept them connected, but visits fortified them through long, lonely months apart.

Maria, maintaining a young family and a lively household in Richmond, rather than a plantation, was applied to for information regarding a multitude of connections and extended family members. They passed many hours reviewing births, marriages and deaths, considering whose household was on the rise and whose social influence was on the wane. Who had hosted the most lavish events? Who had fallen out with whom? Who had been seen in the latest fashion, and what were the latest bargains acquired by their favored Richmond milliner? Names were thrown back and forth with easy familiarity, some of Judy's sisters among them. But not, she noted, Nancy.

At first, that pleased her. She had wanted Nancy gone from Bizarre and relished the chance *not* to think about her. But as the days of the visit passed without a single reference to her, it began to seem odd. Judy questioned herself. Was Maria waiting for her to ask about Nancy? Was Fanny? Might her friends find it peculiar that she had not enquired about her younger sister? Molly and Lizzie were both mentioned. William and Lucy also, even her younger sisters, Jenny and Jane. Why not Nancy? But how to ask now, when she had not done so earlier? She tussled with the question in her room at night and rose each morning resolved to bring the conversation around to Nancy, only to wait for one of them to mention her first—and being left dissatisfied.

It was Jack who asked about her in the end. His appearance at the table changed the mood. He was at odds with Mr. Tucker again, and Fanny, who had declared to Judy more times than she could count that she never felt better than when visiting her father and stepmother in

Williamsburg, was stiff with him, perhaps waiting for him to make some negative remark she would feel duty bound to contradict. If Maria was uncomfortable around Jack Randolph, she didn't show it. Most of the dinner conversation fell between the two of them, and just when Judy thought that he too had decided against asking about Nancy, he named her.

"And what of Judy's younger sister?" he asked. "Have you seen Nancy much around town?"

Maria paused, fork halfway to her mouth. Her eyes darted to Fanny and then back to Jack. A wave of foreboding swept over Judy.

"I have not."

Jack frowned. "Really? But you're a regular visitor to her sister, Molly, are you not? I thought you would be bound to cross paths with Nancy there, if nowhere else."

Judy watched Maria. Her discomfort was obvious. Why?

"I don't believe Molly and Nancy are on good terms," she said.

"I've heard nothing of this." Judy looked around the table. Jack looked amused, as if the idea of her sisters falling out pleased him, but Fanny's eyes were on her plate, and Maria's neck had gone red. "There's some mystery here," she said. "Please. What has happened between Molly and Nancy?"

"I don't think it's my place to say."

"Not your place? We are the best of friends, Maria. And if you have information about my relations, I'd be grateful if you would share it. Or must I leave the dinner table and write to them? And then imagine who knows what calamity while I wait for their reply?"

"Yes, come now," said Jack. "You can't leave us hanging like that. Out with it. What is up with them? Molly, of course, can be high-handed, but I'll wager that whatever has happened, it will be Nancy at fault."

"But I know nothing of the details. And it is the worst kind of gossip. I was quite determined not to tell you, for there may not be a word of truth in it."

"A word of truth in what?" Judy's temper rose. "I can plainly see you have already told Fanny, so you may as well let us hear the story too. What has Nancy done now?"

Maria spoke in a rush. "They say that Molly's husband is much enamored of his wife's sister. They say he haunts her lodgings. And when she was no more seen in Molly's company, many took that as proof that there is something inappropriate between Nancy and David Meade Randolph. But it could all be lies. I didn't want to upset you. It may be total nonsense."

"It can't be true." Judy's hand went to her mouth.

"Can't it?" Jack grabbed at the table, his face tight with fury. "Can't it? That damned woman. How I wish to God I'd never heard the name Nancy Randolph."

Chapter Twenty-Seven

Summer in Richmond was a hot, sultry affair. Soft brown earth baked dry. Grass yellowed. Dust flew. Mr. Pryor's Haymarket Pleasure Garden business thrived, especially busy in the evenings, when the heat of the day was blunted. Raucous voices battled with cicadas to dominate the night air. Pleasure seekers arrived with a thirst on them that only grew as they tried to slake it. It was no place for single women to wander, and Nancy kept to her room at night. During the day, when she wasn't busy working for Mrs. Pryor, she took long walks, seeking shady tree-lined pathways out of the harsh heat of the sun. She avoided the main shopping thoroughfares, having quickly found there were only so many snubs she could stomach. Richmond was full of familiar faces, and few were friendly. Gabriella for one. Judy's good friend, Maria, for another.

Her thoughts went inexorably to some challenging times at Bizarre. Judy had taken no small delight in telling Nancy she'd spoiled Jack's prospects with Maria, however unwittingly. She shook her head and sought happier memories. There was Tudor to think of. The boys at Mr. King's school were given free hours on Sundays after church service. Nancy had enticed Tudor to join her once or twice, with a promise of stained-glass candies in cherry and lemon. Every penny was precious to her, but that one hour a week with her nephew offered a different kind of sustenance. He was so much Dick's son. He had his father's thick dark hair, flopping over his forehead, and the same brown eyes with long lashes young girls might envy. He was quick to smile but also to frown, and his prattle was often of schoolboy quarrels, the unfairness of his masters and the trials he was put to, learning his Latin and mathematics.

"I'd rather be back at Bizarre, riding with Uncle Jack," he told her more than once. "But they won't have me back home. Jack said I was running wild and needed some polish—but if being a gentleman is all bookwork and sitting still, I'm not sure I want to be one. Jack says I will run the plantation one day, but he makes it seem like dull work, don't you think?"

"I think Uncle Jack is telling you what your own father would have said if he were here," she replied. "Although you sound much more like your uncle Theo at this moment, and I'm not sure that a good dose of hard work might not have helped him. Too much pleasure can be bad for a man's health, Tudor."

"Do you wish he had lived? Would you have married him? Mother said you might."

"I thought I might. But it wasn't to be."

"Will you marry someone else?"

"No." She looked down at his sharp face and experienced a twist of sadness. He was growing up, this boy she had nursed through fevers and agues, whose knees she had bandaged, whose hair she had cut and whose shirts she had made. What would he make of her story? And what version of its truth would he be told? He was thick as thieves with his Uncle Jack, hardly Nancy's friend.

Because of that, she had a sense that their Sunday meetings would not last, and when Jack Randolph arrived in Richmond to take his place on the jury for the trial of Aaron Burr, she was quickly proved correct.

The trial was held in the Hall of the House of Delegates, inside the State Capitol on Shockoe Hill, the white neo-classical building, designed by Patsy's father, that towered over Richmond's busy streets. Nancy thought little of it. Aaron Burr's alleged treason was of little interest to her. Feeding herself and Phebe, eking out her small stipend from Tom and keeping Mrs. Pryor happy and smiling were her daily concerns. And yet, she couldn't ignore it altogether. John Marshall, who with Patrick Henry had defended Dick at the Cumberland courthouse some fourteen years earlier, was now the nation's Supreme Justice, presiding over the trial. Jack and Gabriella's husband were both jurymen.

Her first intimation of trouble came in a note from Tudor. Mrs. Pryor gave it to her, along with a pile of mending, teasing that from the handwriting, she must have a new, and rather young, admirer. But its contents made Nancy frown. Tudor would no longer be able to meet with her later that day. He'd been advised that more time should be spent on his studies. Such a command could only have come from Jack. And sure enough, at the hour Nancy had planned to meet with Tudor, his uncle arrived at her lodgings.

In the years Nancy had known him, Jack had changed greatly. The thin, awkward youth she remembered had grown into a man with a keen sense of his own consequence. Nothing he did was unplanned or unstudied, and he carried himself with confidence, earned from his success in politics. He had been a member of the House of Representatives for eight years and proven himself—according to Tom and William at least—to be a politician through and through, condemning slavery but arguing that abolition would be ruinous for all and falling out with Patsy's father the moment it proved politically expedient to do so.

"Nancy." He stood in the doorway to her chamber, his eyes roaming the room and up and down her person. He didn't smile. "I see you're well."

"I am, sir, but a little disappointed that my nephew, Tudor, was unable to keep his appointment with me today."

Jack placed his hat on her writing desk and drew out the chair. "You don't mind if I sit, do you?" After he waved away her offers of refreshment, Nancy perched on the edge of her bed and waited.

"I'll be candid with you. I don't like this—" he pouted a little, "this situation."

"In what regard?"

"In every regard."

"The room was secured for me by my brother-in-law, Mr. David Meade Randolph. If he approved, why should you not?"

"I have no opinion of the man," said Jack. "Although I hear he is a great favorite of yours."

"You are misinformed."

"Am I?"

She thought he would say more, but he was silent, and she began to feel anxious. "I've had much pleasure in seeing Tudor these last months," she said. "I'm sure it does us both good to see a familiar face from home. Have you seen him since you arrived in town?"

"Naturally."

"And you are pleased with him?"

"Of course." They lapsed into another silence.

"Are you sure I can't bring you something to eat or drink?"

"Thank you, no."

"How was my sister when you saw her last?"

"Suffering with her stomach still. And perhaps finding life without her sons a little quiet for her taste."

"Does she go to the Springs at all?"

"I've no notion of her movements."

Something in his tone, the slowness of his drawl, his self-appointed superiority or the way he lounged in the chair while she perched stiff-backed, finally goaded Nancy. "Why are you here, Jack?"

His nose wrinkled. "Because you are the subject of gossip. Again."

"How so? How unjust!"

"Is it though? I wonder."

"Who speaks ill of me?"

"Your sister, Molly, for one."

"Molly? Why?"

"Because her husband's visits here are well known. Of course, she defends you publicly. But you may imagine my reaction. Yet another fool ensnared by you."

"Another? Are you keeping a list, perhaps?"

He disliked that—as she hoped he would.

"You deny there's anything between yourself and David Meade Randolph?"

"Certainly, I deny it! I will speak to Molly myself if I must. This is unjust, Jack." She waited, watching him run his teeth across his lower lip.

"There is a school of thought that you might be happier living elsewhere."

"I see."

"I'm not sure you do."

"Oh, I think I do. Let me see if I can populate this 'school' of thinkers you describe. I'd guess at Gabriella Brockenhurst for one. Then there is Maria Ward, as was. Remind me, who did she marry?" It was cruel, but he deserved it.

"I cannot speak for Mrs. Peyton," he didn't take his eyes off hers, "although yes, she is friendly with the Brockenhursts, as am I. John Brockenhurst has been on the Burr jury with me. And yes, we discussed your situation here."

"There's nothing wrong with my 'situation', as you call it. This is a proper household, quite separate from the pleasure garden. Mr. Pryor is respectable, is he not?"

"He is, and so is his wife. But then—" He paused and picked at an invisible speck on his coat. "Their lodger is not."

"In whose eyes, and according to whose word? My brothers support me. A woman's reputation depends on the support of her family. But have you supported me? Defended me? Jack?"

"I? Why should I?" He jumped to his feet, and she shrank a little. "A woman's reputation, you say? A man's is no less fragile! And yet my brother had to suffer his reputation being dragged through the mud. Dick was the talk of the state of Virginia and beyond! When I recall that sham of a trial in Cumberland County, when I think of what he went through, of how diminished he was, and with only three years left to him—"

Jack paced the room, visibly upset, even more than she had seen him at Bizarre in those last ugly days.

"And you blame me for that?" His back was to her, and she stood and tried to reach out a hand.

He spun around and pushed his face into hers. "Who else should I blame?"

Nancy dropped her eyes first. "No one."

Jack moved away abruptly and retook his seat by her desk. "I want you to leave Richmond." He was composed again, the sparkle of threatened tears gone from his eyes.

"Where would you have me go?"

"Out of Virginia. North. South. I don't care which. I thought having you out of Bizarre would be enough, but it is not."

"I see." She sat again on the edge of the bed and stared at her fingers. "And if I remain?"

"You will never see Tudor. You will not be accepted into society."

"Is that fair?"

"Fair? What is ever fair, Nancy? Is it fair that my brothers are dead? Is it fair that Saint is deaf?"

"Those things are not my fault."

"Are they not? I'm not so sure. Sometimes, I think the devil is in you."

He looked at her then, and she saw he was not lying, or even exaggerating, but speaking plainly.

"You hate me," she said.

"Have you not given me cause?"

For that, she had no answer, and in the silence that fell between them, Jack rose and picked up his hat and jacket. He paused at the door.

"Will you leave then?" His voice was calm, almost gentle.

"I will think on it."

"Please do. I hope never to hear your name or see your face again."

She said nothing. As the door closed behind him, Nancy curled on her bed with her face to the wall.

A little later, Phebe returned. Nancy heard her snuff the candles and unroll her blankets, but she didn't respond to her whispered inquiries, preferring to pretend to be asleep. She lay in the darkness with her eyes open and dry until, at length, sleep claimed her. Her dreams were unsettling, full of doors closing in houses she didn't recognize. In the morning, she went to see Molly.

Newport, Rhode Island. Not Virginia. Let that be enough for Jack Randolph. No one saw her leave. Lizzie had no time to spare, none of her brothers were in town, Tudor was forbidden to see her, and Molly made it clear that helping Nancy leave Richmond was the last support she was prepared to offer. It hadn't mattered that she believed Nancy had done nothing to encourage David Meade Randolph's visits. Molly's pride was wounded. Her marriage was the subject of gossip. She waved away Nancy's attempt to explain things but provided a letter of introduction to several families in Newport and arranged for a relation living there, a Richard Randolph, to find Nancy cheap lodgings. With that, Molly washed her hands of her.

The journey north was the most uncomfortable Nancy had ever known. She was unsure of her destination, nervous and jittery. Everyone but Phebe was a stranger. She didn't sleep for days. Men leered at her. Women ignored her. The press of people in the stage-coach made her hot. Sweat curled her hair. She itched for fresh air and fresh smells. Her back ached, and her legs cramped. She ate little and drank less, conscious of the small number of coins in her purse and how limited her methods were to replace them. If only the people of Newport would let her work. She pinned her hopes on this yet unseen relative, yet another Randolph. When they halted overnight near Philadelphia, she dreamed of Dick and Theo and of Bizarre.

In the morning, resuming her seat in the coach, she gazed out of the window, but it was Judy she saw, alone now, sitting in the parlor in Bizarre where they had once been so full of laughter, so young, so free and so entirely blind to the future that lay before them. She pictured the downturned lines at the corners of her sister's mouth, her thinning hair and the frown line that had burrowed between her brows. She pictured Judy's face when she heard the accusations about Nancy and David Meade Randolph.

Bitterness settled in her chest. Ten penitent years had brought her no forgiveness, only more allegations. Glentivar, Billy Ellis, now Molly's husband. She brooded from Richmond to Newport. Anger sat behind her modest smiles and thanks when old Richard Randolph handed her down from the stage and took her to a small boarding house, not far from the wharf. Outwardly, she was the same—taking tea with her newest landlady, enquiring about local teaching positions through which she might pad out her meager funds. But she returned to it all at night, in a cold room where she lay down, fully dressed, and wept into a threadbare blanket, feeling the cold bite at her fingers and numb the tip of her nose. Resentment was the heat that helped her raise her head from the pillow. It was the fuel that sent her out into the streets of an unknown town to find employment.

She'd never been allowed to defend herself. Not by Dick, who refused to use her letter. Not by Mr. Tucker, who always thought he knew what was best. Not by Judy, who never spoke of Dick's trial again after that terrible drive back to Bizarre. For years, Nancy had crushed any impulse to fight back, for how could she? How could she defend the indefensible? And yet now, out of Virginia, she felt differently. There was a truth that she and Dick had agreed on. A truth she was entitled to, all these years later. It was a good lie. A lie that deserved to be believed. A lie so nearly true. Phebe told her not to write, but Nancy refused to listen. She wrote to Judy. She wrote about what happened at Glentivar.

Phebe

Bizarre, Tuckahoe, Richmond and now Newport. Even back at Tuckahoe, Phebe struggled to feel at home. She had left as a girl and returned a woman, but the rush of disappointment at finding her mother gone had made her young again. Tears had flooded her eyes.

"Your mama's been sold." Cilla ran her hands down Phebe's face and arms like a blind woman trying to see. "Haven't had no word of her in years. But it does my old heart good to see you stayed safe."

"I missed you, Gramma."

"I missed you too, child. But what about them people at Bizarre? Name of Ellis? They a nice family? Treat you good?"

"Good enough."

"And there's no young man you gonna tell me about? You've no husband? No chillern?"

"I don't want no children, Gramma."

Cilla frowned, cupped Phebe's face in her hands, peered in close. "Why not?"

"And have them sold away from me? Like Mama from you? Or

255

die having them, like Mae?" She watched a tear slide down the old woman's face.

"When d'you get so sad, girl?" Phebe didn't reply, and Cilla sighed. "We thought going with Miss Nancy be the best thing for you. I was certain of it. But then we heard the stories. Want to tell your old Gramma what really happened? Sometimes talkin' helps."

"I promised her," Phebe whispered.

"I'm sure you did."

Cilla struggled to her feet, shuffled to the wide hearth and set more water on to boil. The smell of cornbread, the familiar grain of the table under her fingers, those same pots hanging on the wall and the comforting silence washed over Phebe. It was time. She told Cilla everything that happened at Bizarre. At Glentivar.

"She believes the child died?" Cilla said.

"And blames herself."

"What she doing? Pretending nothing happened? Does she talk to God? Pray?"

"I don't think so."

"That's a heavy burden."

"I've tried to look after her, Gramma. Like you told me. But the child? I never asked Syphax what really happened. And now I never will. Did I do wrong?"

Cilla rubbed at her forehead. "Sounds to me like you done nothing wrong. Past is past and best left there, I say. How's it going to be now, that's my question. You tied to her. You *hers*. And what she got but you? Nothing. No home. No husband. No prospects."

"She's strong, Gramma. And so am I. We gonna be fine. You'll see."

But that was before Richmond. Before they arrived at a cold, windy town called Newport and Miss Nancy lost her mind.

"Don't send it, miss. What good will it do?" She watched her mistress fold and unfold the letter, reading it time and again.

"You wouldn't understand."

"No? Ain't I been with you every step? Seen what you been through?"

"You don't have a sister."

Phebe stepped back as if she'd been slapped. She'd had a sister. Did Miss Nancy not remember? She reached for the door handle, her other hand dashing the hot tears that blurred her vision.

"Mae." Miss Nancy's voice was soft. "I'm sorry, Phebe. Forgive me."

Phebe stopped, and the door stayed closed. "It was a long time ago."

Nancy nodded. "I wronged my sister."

"And you done paid for that."

"I had thought so."

"So ..." Phebe's eyes dropped to the letter and then over to the small fire burning in the corner grate.

"No. It has been written, and it will be sent. She's my sister. These things need to be said."

Chapter Twenty-Eight

Whenever Judy's beloved Tudor returned from school, he ran wild. He took a gun and went out shooting rabbits, returning muddy and bloodied with a string of shattered carcasses hung over one shoulder. He took food from the kitchen from under Sarah's nose without a please or thank you. He missed meals, left his room in disarray and rolled his eyeballs through Judy's lectures. He pulled Lottie's daughter's hair and disturbed the animals. He slammed doors and upset piles of folded mending, pulling out a shirt he wanted from the bottom of the pile and leaving the rest scattered on the floor. He collected bugs in jars and released them in his mother's bedroom. He trailed muddy boots into the parlor, sending Judy into a cleaning frenzy. One afternoon, Tudor stole brandy from the study—now Jack's domain—and was found by Sarah Ellis being sick behind the smokehouse.

If that were not enough for her to contend with, Jack arrived unexpectedly, muttering about his congressional colleagues, his ambitions and some petty insult inflicted by her brother, Tom. Whatever Tom had done, it clearly rankled, despite all Jack's protestations to the contrary. For a few days, he barely seemed aware of Tudor's waywardness, but then a commotion arose in the henhouse. Tudor was discovered throwing corn at the hens instead of collecting eggs as instructed. Jack took him by the collar, manhandled the miscreant into the parlor and deposited him opposite Judy.

"Well?" Jack demanded.

"What?" Tudor thrust his chin at his uncle. A mistake. Jack cuffed him across the back of his head.

"Jack!"

"What? The boy deserves it and will have worse if he doesn't mind his manners. If you don't want to be treated like an animal, Tudor, stop acting like one. Tell your mother what I found you doing."

"It was nothing." Tudor's eyes were on Jack's hands, calculating the risk of another slap. "I was just teasing the chickens. They're so stupid and noisy—"

"And essential to the running of the household," said Judy. "Sarah needs those hens to put food on the table for us, for everyone. You know that." She threw Jack a despairing glance.

"Tudor?" Jack stared at his nephew.

"I'm sorry." Silence followed. Judy thought about resuming her sewing. But Tudor wasn't finished. Apparently deciding that the physical threat from his uncle had dissipated, he threw himself into the armchair opposite his mother and flung back his head. "At least, I'm sorry you caught me, but you must expect me to get up to some lark or other. It's so dull here, I don't know how either of you stand it."

"Tudor!"

"What? I'm only being honest! Richmond is much more entertaining. Here, there is nothing to do and no one to do it with. I even miss stupid Saint—if you can believe it."

"Tudor!"

"For goodness' sake, woman. If you can do no more than say the boy's name over and over again like a bleating sheep, it's no wonder he doesn't heed you."

Tudor's eyes danced, and so she surprised him by smiling. "Tudor. I see I have been mistaken. I thought you were tired from your studies in Richmond and in need of rest. There is always work to be done on a plantation, and no need for idle pranks. Your uncle and I will discuss how you might usefully spend your time. Come," she stood and reached a hand to him. He took it, his mouth a thin line, his brows lowered. "You will be a man before we know it. All at Bizarre will look to you as their master. Is that not a fine prospect?"

Tudor shifted from one foot to the other. "I suppose."

Jack clapped Tudor's shoulder, but in a friendly fashion now. "Go and brush down Star. We will take her and Thunder over to Roanoke tomorrow. Then fetch some firewood. No—"

Tudor had opened his mouth to object, but Jack forestalled him.

"Hush, boy. Fetch some firewood down to the clearing by the riverbank. We'll fish this afternoon, and what you catch, we'll cook. I'll show you how. And we will have a talk, man to man, about your future and what it means to be a Randolph."

Jack spoke to the air over Tudor's head, but Judy's eyes were fixed on her son's face. She saw the nod and the smile he gave his uncle. But as Tudor turned to leave the room he twisted, and his face found hers. His eyes were angry. *This is you*, he seemed to say to her. *This is all your fault.*

For as long as Jack remained at Bizarre, Tudor behaved well. He went about with his uncle and listened to all his lessons and strictures with every appearance of interest and respect. But he avoided his mother.

Judy was at a loss. She had a sense of scrabbling for time, of trying to hold onto her child even as he slipped through her fingers like sand. She was physically drawn to him, but when she reached for him, he leaned away, refusing to let her as much as ruffle his hair or button his coat. Every rejection made her long more for the past, particularly his earliest years when her only respite from mourning Dick was folding Tudor in her arms, knowing that he was the flesh of her flesh, their bond stronger than any other she had known. The dark moods that flowed through her, unpredictable, yet as inevitable as the seasons ever since the loss of that first child, re-emerged. Her bones weighed her down. She imagined her blood pooling in her fingertips, dragging at her shoulders, sucking her to the earth, giving way to a sense of emptiness that blanked out all other thoughts.

One evening, as she sat out on the porch alone, Judy heard singing coming through the trees from the slave houses. She had given permission for Billy Ellis to return from Roanake, bringing with him Ida Smith, one of Jack's slaves and a good needleworker. Sarah was happy to have Ida in her family, and tonight, they were celebrating their union.

She heard the scrape of the screen door behind her but said nothing as Jack lowered himself into a chair beside her. The glass of wine in his hand sparkled in the moonlight.

"You're surrounded by darkness, Sister. Should I fetch more candles?"

"No need. I will go upstairs soon. I like to hear them sing." She wanted to say more, and the words formed in her mind but only to be dismissed.

She listened to her slaves and saw their torches flash darts of orange through the line of trees. She tried to think of her son, Saint, far away, in a country she would never see, perhaps learning to talk—but probably not. Saint would never amount to anything. Jack and Nancy could dress things up as they wished, but Judy was no fool. Saint was her punishment. Tudor was her hope. If only she could find a way to bind him to her.

The answer came soon. It came in Nancy's letter from Newport.

She was surprised to see her sister's handwriting. Since Nancy's rushed, final departure from Bizarre, they had exchanged letters only twice, and it was Judy's turn to write, a task she'd delayed because it brought her no pleasure, and there was so little to say. While Sally cleared the table, Judy propped the letter up against her teacup and contemplated its thickness. Her writing was slightly altered. If Nancy had written while upset, Judy wasn't sure she wanted to read it. She got up and left the room.

This was a mistake.

After an hour of checking the stores in the smokehouse and dairy with Sarah, she was ready to tackle whatever her sister might wish to say. She walked wearily to the dining room but heard voices and was surprised to find Jack and Tudor in the room, in possession of her letter.

"What's going on?" She looked from one to the other. Tudor hung his head. Jack's expression was grave.

"The boy has opened your letter. And read it."

"No!" Judy snatched it and pressed it to her chest. "Tudor, how could you? What made you do such a thing?"

"His motivation is not the pertinent issue, Sister," said Jack. "You, boy, go to your room. I will consider what to do with you later." When the door closed, he sighed. "Judy, just read it. You may want to sit down."

She sank into the chair by the window. Her eyes narrowed as she read. Nancy had been feeling sorry for herself—that was quickly clear. She had left Virginia, never to return. Her tone was melodramatic, as it often was, and Judy had no patience for it. She quickly dismissed Nancy's pining for Tuckahoe and Bizarre, her love of plantation life and simple pleasures. Her fears, though, about a future alone up north did give Judy pause. She'd no envy for Nancy on that score, nor could she disagree with her sister's dismay at being at the mercy of their brothers' goodwill for any degree of comfort or security she might obtain. But then came strong words about Jack. And about David Meade Randolph and what Nancy termed his "attentions". Her handwriting grew erratic. Judy sensed worse was to follow. Her eyes scanned the next page, the word Glentivar leaping from the tangle of ink and causing the breath to catch in her throat. She closed her eyes to steady herself, and then she read it. Nancy's confession.

There had been a child. Stillborn, or too weak to survive, Nancy didn't make that clear. She was adamant, though, that it had been Theo's child, conceived in the firm belief that they were betrothed and would be married. He had been ill, yes, but she believed another trip to Bermuda would mend him, and she'd have the family she dreamed of. Dick had known. Helped her. Protected her. But she was ruined, nonetheless.

Judy threw the letter on the floor, her thoughts flying like sparks. A dead child. Months of lies. No. *Years* of lies. But not Dick. Not Dick. Disgust, relief, dismay, disbelief—she felt a rush of emotions, but relief most of all. She lifted her eyes to Jack. His expression was unreadable.

"She ruined us, do you see that? My brother was sick, and she tempted him. My other brother was honorable, and she disgraced him. I'm fortunate she only laughed at me, even though it cost me a wife. If she were here, I'd put my hands around her white throat and choke her."

"Jack!"

"She'll never enter this house again. I'll not be in the same room as the witch in this life. Is that clear? The boys must not be contaminated by her."

"My God. Tudor read this?" Judy's hand flew to her mouth. "What must I say to him? Should I lie? Perhaps say the letter is not hers?"

"Why do that? Why protect her?" Jack stooped to pick up the sheets from the floor. "She has damned herself in her own hand. She ruined the last years of Tudor's father's life. Who knows how different things might have been had she not ensnared him in her troubles and used him for protection? When I think of that trial, of Dick and Tucker forcing it, all to protect that whore's reputation, I could go mad!"

He flung himself into a chair and covered his face with his hands. Judy thought he might weep, and the idea of it brought sudden order to her thoughts. She must be calm. She must think of her son. She left the room and went upstairs to Tudor.

He didn't respond when she knocked, so Judy pushed open his bedroom door. He lay on his bed, curled on one side with his back to her. The sight of him, the tangle of dark hair, his long legs, his narrow hips and half-boy, half-man form, made her heart clench. She perched by his back and stretched out her hand to touch his shoulder.

"Mother!" Tudor twisted under her touch, but instead of shrinking from her he turned and threw himself into her arms, burying his face in the folds of her apron. "Mother, is this all true? What my aunt wrote? That she and my uncle Theo ... that there was a baby?"

"It seems so. I cannot think why she would write it if it were a lie."

He moved back, scrambling to sit upright with his arms wrapped around his knees. He looked both young and old at the same moment. "Uncle Jack hates her."

"He feels that your father was ill-used."

"Jack told me about the trial."

"He did?" Judy clenched her teeth. Jack had lost his head over the letter. Was this something else she'd have to explain, dredging up memories, feeling the old scars tingle, taking Tudor's knowledge of their family's disgrace as another set of weights on her shoulders? Before she could form any kind of coherent answer, Tudor moved again, swinging out his legs and shifting closer to her on the bed. His hand found hers. Her heart rose to her throat.

"It must have been terrible for you, Mother," he said.

Later, in her own bed with the hangings closed, with her prayers said and the house quiet, she acknowledged his sympathy had undone her. No one—not Dick, Jack, not the Tuckers, certainly not her own father or brothers—had ever expressed concern for how she lived with it all. And yet here was a boy, not yet twelve years old, a boy she loved and longed to be close to, holding her hand, speaking softly, showing her sympathy and concern. His opening of her letter was forgotten. Instead, she wept, and then, when the tears abated, she talked, and he drank in her words and begged for more. Judy had never told even her close friends—not even Cousin Mary—her story of it all. Never in her wildest imaginings would she have thought of telling it all to Tudor. But when she spoke, his hand stayed in hers. His head leaned on her shoulder. His gaze, locking with hers, was warm and encouraging. It was not ideal to have spoken of her sister in this way, Judy knew, but the bitterness danced on her tongue. The duplicity. To be pregnant and have kept it hidden. The lies she told. The deceit. Judy spared Dick, but not Nancy. All the family's trials and difficulties were laid at Nancy's door, all caused by her actions and the steps taken to protect her reputation. Dick became her victim, so too Jack, Judy and by extension, Saint and Tudor. With every grievance named, she felt her boy's fingers press on hers. She watched him frown at every mention of her sister's name.

In the days that followed, he asked her about it all again and again. God forgive her, she could not stop herself. It was a sweet release.

Jack took a different approach. With Judy and Tudor beside him, he sat down and wrote to friends in Newport. Nancy would not find safe harbor there.

"If we can't have peace, why the hell should she?"

Jack ruined Newport for Nancy. She knew it and wrote to Mr. Tucker in Williamsburg, begging him for advice. At first, she thought she was imagining it—the shoulders turning, a change in eye contact, sudden silences, groups fragmenting the moment she approached—but confirmation came with the loss of the teaching post she had so recently secured. That particular interview was too painful to dwell on. It lit a fire of anger in her, and she marched to the house of her relation, Richard Randolph, who at least had the decency to look embarrassed when he admitted he and many other leading families in the town had received letters from Jack, all warning of her "corrupting influence".

A few days after her dismissal, Nancy's landlord called at her door. When he told her he wished to negotiate a higher payment for her lodgings, Nancy begged for time. Without her teaching income, her ability to pay on the current terms was in doubt. She was no fool. It was an eviction, dressed up in false shrugs and excuses. Newport would not employ her, and Tom's money was not enough. After several hours shut up in her room with Phebe, Nancy ventured out alone.

She walked the length of Spring Street without seeing a soul she knew. It was October, and the pavements were wet with tawny leaves, the air thick with salt spray from the harbor and the cries of gulls wheeling and swooping overhead. She turned to the bridge. From the Long Wharf, she looked out toward Goat Island, listening to the waves crash, and trying to think.

It wasn't the first time she had come here. It wasn't even the first time she thought of dying here. Optimism was impossible, happiness unimaginable. Remaining at Bizarre with Judy had been her penance. She'd been occupied—with the gardening, with the sewing and mending, with Tudor and dear Saint. She contemplated the horizon, where gray water met the darkening sky, and tried to picture her nephew in a school in London, with other afflicted young men. Had he found peace? Had he learned to speak? If she were to fall into the water, she might never know. But even if she wearied on, she had little guarantee of seeing Saint again. Her rash letter to Bizarre had brought no response from Judy. And perhaps, when all was said and done, it was only what she deserved. It all seemed so impossibly long ago. And yet the echo of its consequences never faded. Where should she go if not into the sea? Where was the chance of improvement in her circumstance? She was tired, gnawed by constant hunger, sick with loneliness, weighted by despair. Her jaw and shoulders ached. The water invited her. How deep was it? How cold?

She shivered and rubbed hard at her arms, feeling the thin cotton of her old coat graze her skin and the press of her fingers on her bones. She wouldn't do it. Not today, and likely not any day. Thinking was not doing. Besides, it wasn't death that she longed for, it was a break in the road or a change of circumstance. She longed to escape her own life story, her own mistakes and her dependence on family members who bore the burden of her with patience and kindness but not with love or warmth—only duty and an eye to their own honor and dignity. She must find a way to be independent, for herself and for Phebe. She must escape from being Nancy Randolph—a grotesque figure, a byword for scandal and disgrace. She needed to leave Nancy Randolph in Newport and become someone else. The question was how?

A light cough startled her. She turned, and in the fading light, made out two figures: a maid and a young woman she knew, a Miss Pollock, recently Nancy's student in needlework at the Newport school that now found her too scandalous to employ.

"Miss Pollock! You have quite surprised me."

"Miss Randolph, it *is* you! I'm so glad. When I saw a figure standing so close to the fencing, I took the most horrid fancy that you might be about to leap!"

"Leap? Me?" Nancy forced out a laugh. "No, no, no. I am only here to clear a headache. The sea air is so restorative. But I'm surprised to find you still in Newport." Nancy searched the younger woman's face. Jane Pollock had left the school before Nancy's abrupt removal. Perhaps she was unaware of this new disgrace. Perhaps they might converse as if none of Nancy's woes existed, and perhaps, for those few moments, she could forget them herself.

"I'm happy to have this moment to speak with you," Miss Pollock said, stretching out a hand. "I hope I can speak frankly?"

"Of course."

"I'm leaving Newport tomorrow for Fairfield, Connecticut. My mother will meet me at the inn there. She's taken rooms for a few days—a break from the city for her. You will not be aware, but she runs a boarding house in New York City for gentlewomen seeking work and in need somewhere clean and safe to live. I wondered if you might like to come to Fairfield with me to meet her. You were the kindest teacher to me, Miss Randolph."

"I—" Nancy's mind was a storm of half-thoughts. "I fear if you knew—"

Miss Pollock's grip on Nancy's hand tightened. "I do know," she said.

"But I have no funds—"

"Nor do you need any. You would be our guest in Fairfield. You can meet my mother and talk with her. You have so many skills, and I can tell her myself how diligent you are. I'm sure that in a different place ..."

Her eyes were kind, soft and warm, but also mischievous and excited. It was infectious. Nancy found herself smiling.

"So you will come?"

She nodded.

The next morning, she and Phebe left Newport with Jane Pollock. She didn't think of the dark water that had pulled at her. She had made a different kind of leap. Only now, she had no idea of where she might land.

Chapter Twenty-Nine

Mrs. Pollock showed no surprise at the sight of an unknown woman and her maid emerging from the carriage with her daughter in front of The Sun Tavern in Fairfield. A tall, spare woman with a ready smile and intelligent eyes, she embraced her daughter warmly. Nancy knew just by looking at her that Mrs. Pollock's establishment in the city would not be damp or cold or infested with mice. She'd learned a great deal from Jane during the long coach journey. Her mother was a well-connected widow with a large establishment on Greenwich Street. Jane's father, a lawyer and keen Federalist, had served under Alexander Hamilton during the war, but the yellow fever had taken him from them. Mrs. Pollock was visiting Fairfield with friends, and there would be quite the party of important New York families there, but Jane knew Nancy's impeccable manners meant she'd fit in perfectly. Unused to compliments, Nancy struggled for composure, all the while hoping fervently that no one in the party would have a connection to the state of Virginia.

Loud voices and laughter flooded the tavern entrance. "The

gentlemen are in the taproom," said Mrs. Pollock with a wry smile. "They will join us in the parlor a little later. Please. Refresh yourselves upstairs and then join me for something to eat. The food here is excellent. Mrs. Penfield's reputation is well-deserved."

Nancy was swept up the stairs and given a narrow bed next to Jane's in a large chamber with room for past ten travelers. A serving girl followed them with a pitcher of steaming water and a dark-skinned boy with a limp carried both women's bags. Jane was so young and spirited, clearly happy to reunite with her mother, and as she had on the pier at Newport, Nancy found herself smiling. She resolved to forget the future—and the past—and simply enjoy an evening of good food and good company.

Downstairs, Mrs. Pollock and her friends proved affable and friendly without being inquisitive. She took a glass of wine and a chair near Mrs. Pollock, gradually finding the confidence to chime into the lively conversation and admitting she had, through her brother, a close connection to President Thomas Jefferson.

Mrs. Pollock and her friends were clearly well educated and comfortably settled in life. Nancy thought of her sister, Molly, who also talked of running a boarding house, and wondered if time and distance would soften her sister's attitude over the events that had pushed Nancy on the road north and her current state of near disaster. She took a deep mouthful of wine and scolded herself not to dwell on unhappiness, at least for this one evening. As she did so, the parlor door swung open. The men of the party joined them—among them, a man Nancy already knew.

Gouverneur Morris didn't recognize her. Why would he? His eyes scanned the room and rested on her, but only as they might on any stranger in a familiar throng, not with the light of recognition. Still, she noticed he looked at her more than once and guessed it would not be long before he made his way around the room and sought an introduction. For a wild moment, she thought of giving a false name. Most likely, he had been out of the country when it happened—hadn't he been about to depart for Europe when he danced with her at Tuckahoe all those years ago?—but he would still know her story, she was sure, and her spirits sank. The bubble of anonymity was about to burst. But perhaps he would be kind. He had been a friend of her father's, a lawyer, a man of principle, heavily involved in the writing of the Constitution. Perhaps he was too serious-minded for gossip and scandal. He had a merry, congenial look about him, however. He appeared light-hearted and sociable, smiling at all around him, unchanged from that meeting, twenty years earlier. How terribly old he'd seemed back then, at Dick and Judy's wedding. In all likelihood, he'd been little older than she was now.

Soon enough, he sought an introduction from Mrs. Pollock. She held her breath as her name was revealed to him, but his face, on realizing who she was, betrayed nothing but pleasure.

"But we are old acquaintances! Although Miss Randolph may not remember me, I believe we had the pleasure of dancing at her family home."

"You are right, sir, and I do remember, although I was young at the time. You were kind to a gawky girl."

"Not at all!" He waved away her compliment and turned to Mrs. Pollock. "She remembers me because of the leg, you know. When I first lost it, I thought it spelled the end for me with the ladies, but I discovered that for every ounce less handsome it made me, I gained as much by being memorable."

"Memorable you most certainly are, Mr. Morris." Mrs. Pollock laughed. "And do not pay any heed to his prattle, Miss Randolph. Mr. Morris is an accomplished flirt and will tell you fifty dramatic tales about how he lost his poor leg, none of them true. The real story remains a mystery."

She nodded and left room on the settle beside Nancy, a space Mr. Morris was pleased enough to occupy. There was no more nonsense about his wooden leg, which, as she had seen all those years ago, caused him no impediment. Instead, he asked after her family, particularly of Tom and William, before gently asking her what brought her to Fairfield. Nancy's face grew hot as she responded.

"I am here with Mrs. Pollock's daughter, Jane," she said. "I'm not sure for how long."

"You met in Newport?"

"I had the pleasure of teaching her."

"I see. And you plan to return to Rhode Island?"

"No!" said Nancy. "That is to say, I think not. But my plans are not settled."

"Then it is to be hoped a few enjoyable days in Fairfield will help you decide. And if I can be of any service—as an old friend of the family—it would be my pleasure to assist you." He smiled at her, his eyes kind and searching, but thankfully, he was far too much the gentleman to question her further. Instead, he suggested they examine the refreshment table.

"Tell Miss Pollock and Miss Randolph about the 'Saxon delicacy' that you encountered in Europe, Morris," someone said. He didn't need to be asked twice.

"Ah yes! The candied beetle, if you can imagine. They resemble, in some respects, what in America we call the locust but are not so large and have a hard cover to their wings, which are a bright, brick-colored brown. How it should enter into people's heads to eat them, unless driven to it by famine, is hard to imagine."

"No!" Jane's eyes were like saucers. "Tell me you didn't eat them?"

"How could I not? The reputation of our young country rested on my shoulders. I dared not have them think Americans unsophisticated."

"Or cowardly," said Nancy.

"Exactly so," said Mr. Morris. "I've been accused of many things in my long life, but cowardly, I'm happy to say, is not one of them. I hope anyone here would have done the same. For America, of course."

"Oh, I know I could not have," said Jane. "But Nancy, would you? Could you?" Her face was so contorted, Nancy had to laugh.

"I'm sure I should, my dear. Why not? There are many worse things to tolerate in this life than a locust or two. I imagine they might have an enjoyable crunch." She lifted her eyebrows as she spoke and was rewarded with a burst of laughter from all around.

Later, in the darkness of their upstairs dormitory, Nancy succumbed to temptation. "Mr. Morris, Jane. He is a close friend to your mother?"

"Oh, yes, although not in the way you might think. She says he is a terrible rake—or he was. Now, he's a confirmed bachelor, and surely too old to be marrying anyone now, least of all Mother. She's quite done with all of that. Mr. Morris is her loyal friend and advisor. How funny to think you met him when you were young."

"Yes. Although to be honest, that feels like a whole different life, like something that happened to someone else entirely. Does that make sense?"

"No. But then I am so sleepy and not to be relied upon for sense. Goodnight, dear Miss Randolph. I'm glad you came with me today."

In the darkness, Nancy smiled. "So am I, Jane. So am I."

She stayed three days at The Sun Tavern with the Pollocks. After breakfast on her first morning, Mrs. Pollock drew her aside and talked about her plans. The older woman offered to help her find respectable employment in the city, and when Nancy expressed a willingness to travel, Mrs. Pollock suggested a post as an attendant to a family or lady traveling to England might be possible to obtain, in time. They agreed she and Phebe would take a room in Mrs. Pollock's establishment in Greenwich Street. Although money was not discussed, and Nancy dreaded writing another begging letter to Tom, for the first time since she left Bizarre new possibilities were opening up before her. It felt good—and when Mr. Morris sought her out in the parlor or on a walk around town or at a musical recital held in the nearby Burr Mansion, she welcomed his company, responded to his conversation and found herself laughing more than she had done in years.

On her last morning in Fairfield, he met her at breakfast and suggested a stroll. She agreed, but not without misgivings. The behavior of David Meade Randolph came to mind. She was neither a green girl nor a fool. There was a light in Mr. Morris's eye when he looked at her. He admired her. And she was drawn to him. He was a tall man with a figure and presence that must always attract attention. His hair might be white, deep lines might cut his face—he was more attractive than classically handsome, with a high forehead and thick brows that arched almost comically over his eyes—but his eyes were soft and intelligent. He was charming, generous and thoughtful. He was interested in art, in literature, in their country and its future growth. He was political without being a show-pony, like Jack, or a partisan, like Tom. Above all, he was engaged in life without being angry with it. He enjoyed himself, taking pleasure in small and large things: from the taste of an orange to plans for a great canal. At Tuckahoe, she'd considered him one of Father's contemporaries, but he was nearly a decade younger than Thomas Mann Randolph Sr. would have been now. She liked that he was good-humored and self-deprecating—he waved away any talk of his part in writing the Constitution, and while many of the tales he recounted involved mention of great men like Washington and Hamilton, he did so humbly and naturally. For Nancy, who had been let down by Patsy—believing her sister-in-law put her illustrious father's reputation above any desire or duty to help a sister in need—Mr. Morris was a model of what a man could and should be. And yet, she feared what he planned to say now.

They strolled south from The Sun Tavern, past the old burying ground and toward the sand dunes. The view of Long Island Sound, he promised her, was not to be missed. As they walked, he talked of his home, north of New York City.

"It's called Morrisania. Not my choice of name, before you ask."

"I think it a sensible name. My sister's property is called Bizarre. No one seems to know why. Perhaps some idea of sounding French and romantic?" She shrugged. "Do you have much land?"

"Enough. My main interest has lain in the property of late. I've made some improvements, but I'm in need of a housekeeper. The last woman wrote to me that she could no longer tolerate the 'wild assortment' of staff I have in place."

"Whatever did she mean?"

"Oh, it's a fair appraisal. They're a motley crew. Two Irishwomen who speak so quickly, no one can comprehend them. A couple of lazy Frenchmen who fled here to evade Napoleon's conscription. Then there are two English immigrants running the stable. Rough types—she called them cutthroats, but to my knowledge, there are no dead bodies in my cellars. They may or may not still be there when I return. The rest are a family of Blacks—all free—and two quiet German girls, both maids."

"I think you would need someone with real gravitas to command such a tribe." She laughed. "I wish you good fortune in finding a suitable candidate."

They had walked beyond the houses of Fairfield, the road turning from mud brown to pale sandy beige. The wind lifted her skirts, and she smelled salt. She saw scrub and tall grass, the swell of a sand dune meeting the cloudless sky.

"I saw nothing like this in Virginia," she said.

"Wait till you see the Sound."

They continued, their path narrowing, growing sandier and softer until they crested the bank and could look down on the beach and out across the open water. Wind whipped her hair across her cheek and stung her eyes.

"Beautiful," she said.

"My home also has a prospect of the Long Island Sound." He pointed off into the distance. "Should you not find suitable employment in New York City—"

"Mr. Morris—"

"Hear me out. I mean you no insult or to suggest anything improper. I have need of a housekeeper. A woman with some strength of character who can command respect. You need employment. Security. Independence. I can offer you all three. That I enjoy your company, I cannot deny. But I don't ask for more. I live simply. I think of public affairs a little, read a little and sleep a great deal. I enjoy good air, the work of my good cook and some fine wine. I think you might be happy there."

She looked him in the eye. "I have been the subject of much gossip in my life, Mr. Morris." His expression didn't change. "What you offer me sounds like a dream. But how can I accept? What would people say?"

"They will say nothing. I am an old man. More than twenty years your senior."

His words were one thing, but the look he gave her said something else. There was feeling there, she saw it. When he spoke, his eyes were on her lips, and she found herself wondering.

"I—"

"Let us say nothing more." He stretched out a hand as if to touch her arm but then withdrew it. "Let us admire the view and the air and say nothing. You will go to the city with Mrs. Pollock. I will write to you. You will know no pressure from me. But I feel we have been friends here, Miss Randolph. May I call you my friend?"

She didn't turn her gaze from the water. So many shades of blue, so many shadows, so many sparkles of light. "Yes," she said. "I'd like us to be friends."

Once Nancy was established in Greenwich Street, Mrs. Pollock connected her with a family with six daughters who required training in all aspects of needlework and some respectable female conversation, as their mother had died, and their father, a lawyer, was much occupied with his business affairs. The work was undemanding and not unpleasant, but it didn't pay well, and Nancy suspected that Mrs. Pollock was charging her less than her normal room rate, perhaps because Mr. Morris was meeting the shortfall. He was a frequent visitor. She considered raising the matter with him. Every time they met, she intended to challenge him directly, but then his conduct was so exemplary, her suspicion seemed outrageous. Asking him might take their conversation down a path she feared to follow. She allowed herself to enjoy his company and a few months' respite from financial worries, hunger and anxious dependence on her brothers. Nancy was sure her best chance of independence would be to become a paid companion to some widow of means, preferably one who wanted to travel. Mr. Morris's stories of his European adventures—the horrors of the French Revolution notwithstanding—opened Nancy's eyes to all she had not seen or done, but Phebe was a sticking point. Paid companions did not travel with their own slaves, and Nancy smarted at a new appreciation of her own selfishness. She should never have taken Phebe with her when she left Bizarre. She might have been married to Billy Ellis by now, with a cabin and children of her own. With shame, she realized she'd never asked the other woman what she wanted, and she hesitated to do so, even now.

Uncertain of the future, Nancy found herself thinking more and more about the past. While she appreciated Mrs. Pollock's goodness, city life wasn't to her liking. She missed Virginia. She missed the trees and rolling hills, the long walks, the growing season, the rhythms of plantation life. In Greenwich Street, there was always noise: the rumble of carts, shouts and cries, the crash of boots on stairs, the clatter of boarders coming and going. City life did not offer nights on the porch, watching fireflies dance or the smell of tomatoes growing on the vine.

At night she wrote letters—to the Tuckers and her brothers and sisters, including Judy, who had never responded to Nancy's confessional letter. For a time, there was silence between them, but as her difficulties grew in Newport, Nancy had written again, acting as if her other letter had never been sent, and Judy had answered in kind. Regular correspondence had been reestablished, and although Judy's letters weren't of a confidential nature, they were precious to Nancy. Their connection was as important and necessary as the handrails on a bridge, and she reveled in any news of Saint and Tudor, or any aspect of life at Bizarre. Jack was often mentioned, and not always favorably, so that Nancy knew some moments of satisfaction, sensing she was not the only Randolph sister to ruffle Jack Randolph's easily disturbed feathers. Most recently, Judy was displeased that Jack was paying at least as much attention to his cousin, Anna Dudley's son, Theodore, as he was to Tudor. Theodore Dudley had been barely two years old when he'd lived at Bizarre, but Jack was close to the young man now, Judy wrote. She didn't need to explain it further to Nancy. Judy would not want anyone becoming more important to Jack than Tudor. And besides, disgust for Anna Dudley was the last thing Nancy and Judy had ever really agreed on. Nancy smiled, remembering how Judy sent her packing within hours of Dick's burial. No doubt, Jack delighted in needling Judy with praise of Theodore Dudley. Judy would hear every word as a criticism of her beloved Tudor, who, reading between the lines, was wilder than his doting mother wished him to be.

After she had been in New York for four months, Mr. Morris brought up his need for a housekeeper once again. He had driven her up to the library, and they had discussed books. She had picked up a copy of *The Power of Sympathy* on his recommendation. A tale of scandal and seduction, he said. Published anonymously. Everyone had read it. He looked forward to hearing her thoughts on the story. Now, they were on their way back to Greenwich Street, Nancy's protests that she could easily walk having been charmingly overridden.

Mr. Morris began with an amusing story about a fight between his French valet and an Irish laundry woman that had Nancy laughing, but there was nothing light-hearted in his tone when he asked if she remembered how he longed for a good woman to rescue him at Morrisania.

"Certainly, I remember it." They had stood so close to one another. They were close again now, in the privacy of his carriage.

"I still believe you're an excellent candidate for the position."

She thought he might take her hand, and her stomach lurched. She both wanted and did not want him to touch her, but instead of leaning nearer, he moved back and held up his hand in a gesture almost of surrender.

"You're concerned I mean something improper, I can tell, but nothing could be further from the truth. I have feelings for you, I won't deny it. But I've never taken an unwed woman to be my lover, and I'm not disposed to do so now."

This she believed. Nancy had learned a great deal about Mr. Morris since she first met him in Fairfield. He was well known to have had several lengthy love affairs—most notably, with a married Frenchwoman, who, according to Mrs. Pollock, had offered her favor to several gentlemen at a time, much to Mr. Morris's chagrin. Then there had been a married poetess in Boston, a well-known figure, although not familiar to Nancy.

"What more can I say to put your mind at ease? I've never had a housekeeper that I've approached with anything like desire, and while I admire you, I'm no rash youth. If you'll come to Morrisania, I will love you as little as I can." He leaned forward. "But I'll protect you from some of the storms of life you've suffered too much from already. I'll give you work you are fit for in a place where you will be respected and independent."

His words produced a flood of emotion. She saw herself at Morrisania, running his household. It was work she would do well and enjoy. He'd spoken often of his home, of his repairs and improvements, of his paintings and fine furniture collections, of his gardens, of the prospects and views. Had he done so with a salesman's calculated aim, he could not have been more successful—there was nowhere she could imagine enjoying living more.

"I'd be lying if I said I wasn't tempted," she said, with a shy smile. "You're so generous."

"Not a bit. You'd be rescuing me. We could be companionable. If I could only convince you that your virtue, your reputation, would be quite safe."

"You don't fear for your own reputation, Mr. Morris?"

"No."

He gazed at her with an expression so genuine, she found herself speaking frankly. "But you know my history. The name Nancy Randolph is not coupled with virtue."

"My dear." He took her hands in his. "I heard, it is true, of events which brought distress into your family. Don't dwell on it. If ever in the future you wish to speak of it, I will listen. Your tears will fall on my shoulder, and I will stand your friend. But don't tell me that Nancy Randolph is not virtuous. I know you. I don't talk of that tea-table sense of the word where a woman who has the malice of a dozen devils in her may be called virtuous. I'm talking about purity of heart, fortitude, grace and benevolence. I see all these things in you. I want to take you to Morrisania. Will you think it over?"

A single tear fell down her cheek. He stroked it away with his thumb.

"I will think about it," she said. "I promise."

A month later, with the best wishes of Mrs. Pollock and Jane, she and Phebe moved to Morrisania. It was March, with signs of spring visible in budding trees and brave bands of snowdrops and blue crocus. Nancy Randolph stepped out of his carriage and into a new and busy life.

Mr. Morris remained true to his word and did not take advantage of his attractive housekeeper. Instead, on Christmas Day, 1809, he married her.

"Did you ever think to see this day?" she asked Phebe, sitting at her dressing table and unfastening the chain and ring she had worn around her neck for over thirteen years. "He wanted to buy me a fine gown, but I choose to be married in my own dress. I can't forget what we've been through."

When Phebe left the room, Nancy remained still, gazing at her own reflection. She had been as honest with him as she knew how to be. Surely, *surely*, it was time to leave her past behind.

Phebe

At Morrisania, everything changed.

Here was safety. Here was dignity. Miss Nancy had a position within the household and her own pretty bedchamber. Phebe saw what it meant. First thing her mistress did was to run her hands up and down the splendid bed hangings. Second thing? Setting Phebe free.

"If you wish to leave, I'll help you in any way I can. But I'm hoping you'll stay at Morrisania with me, for as long as you are happy to." Phebe couldn't speak, only nodded. She would stay.

In her own room for the first time in her life, sleep was hard to find. She lay awake, watching the moon, welcoming the wind rattling the windowpane and the call of an owl. Her mind roved the past, from the slave cabins at Tuckahoe and her sister fading into nothingness in their mother's arms, to Mr. Randolph's face in the candlelight at Bizarre, to the blood and panic at Glentivar. She saw herself running down Mr. Harrison's staircase, so new, the smell of freshly cut wood still hung in the air. She remembered the fearful thud of her heart when she thought all would be lost. She scolded herself to forget what happened. It made no sense to be haunted by the past, and yet it came at her, night after night.

At first, she stayed distant from the other staff in the house. Those months in New York City were a jangle of new voices and accents, confusing enough to make her head spin, and it was no better here. Mr. Morris had a French valet who spoke English as though his mouth was crammed with cake. The two German maids, with broad foreheads and long blonde hair, whispered to each other in their own language. Those two were shy as mice with everyone but the cook, a free Black woman, as firm as she was frank.

"Call me Martha and make yourself useful," the woman said. "Your Miss Randolph says you work just for her, but in here, we pull together like family. And fight like family too, some days."

It was like no family Phebe ever knew, a muddle of Black and White, old and young, some wise-cracking, others quick-tempered, never quiet. They all heeded Miss Nancy, though—every inch her mother's daughter when she chose to be.

And then they were married.

"We've reached safe harbor," Miss Nancy declared one evening as Phebe combed her hair. "Mrs. Booth's damp bedroom and all the snubs and vicissitudes of Richmond and Newport were worth it, for they paved the road to Fairfield and my good husband."

"It does my heart good to see you so happy." They smiled at each other in the mirror. "Now, just imagine if you was to have a child."

Miss Nancy froze. Phebe could have bitten her own tongue out.

"You know that's impossible. God would not permit it."

Impossible? Not permitted? She opened her lips, but Miss Nancy was up on her feet and gone. Phebe was alone in front of the mirror, comb still in hand.

Impossible. The word buzzed in her head. It was unlikely, perhaps, but far from impossible. Something at that long-ago trial convinced her mistress she was to blame for the infant's death. But what if the child hadn't died at all?

It all came back. Syphax and Mr. Randolph talking. Them not knowing she was there under that porch at Bizarre. The child, taken alive from its mother's arms. The woman, Rachel, and the talk of her fair-skinned child. Questions Phebe might have asked, should have asked, but never did.

After all these years of silence? She saw no path to the truth of it now.

Part Four

Partfour

Chapter Thirty

Bizarre, Virginia, 1813

Judy's shoulders slumped as she sealed her latest letter to Fanny. Her dear friend was unwell, more than unwell. She squeezed her eyes so tightly, it pained her. Dick's half-sister was dying. Her loss would be immeasurable. Fanny was the one that kept the family together, who maintained contact with Jack, despite all his tempers and wild accusations. Fanny kept Judy bound to the Tucker family, softening the differences of the past. Fanny understood her. She knew the struggle Judy went through to clear their debts and keep Dick's promise to free his slaves in the face of Jack's opposition. Sarah and Ben had stayed at Bizarre, but Syphax, the Ellis children and many other former slaves now farmed their own parcels of land on the banks of the Appomattox River.

She forced her eyes back on the paper. She'd written to Fanny about Tudor's impending departure to Harvard, but as ever, there was much left unsaid. After a few wild years in Richmond, Judy had kept him close at home. It was yet another thing she and Jack had argued about—but she'd stood her ground and enrolled him in a nearby school run by the Reverend John Holt Rice. Naturally, Jack made a scene about it, arms flailing and his words running away with themselves. Because his quick rhetoric impressed some politicians, he assumed he could talk her into bringing up her child according to his own obsessive ideals of Virginian honor when it was as plain as day that Tudor needed good principles and faith to help him resist the temptations that brought down his uncle Theo. She had not been cowed by Jack's tempest of words, even when he invoked Dick's name and asserted that his brother would have nothing to do with the Reverend Rice's brand of evangelical fervor.

Jack might say what he liked. The reverend's sermons and writings offered great balm to Judy, something she would need if—*when*— Fanny left the world. Fanny understood her reliance on prayer and faith to push away the dark shadows that plagued her. It was only by believing in a more perfect place, a heaven where she might meet those she had lost, that Judy was able to quit her bed each day. Struggles a man like Jack Randolph would never comprehend.

Tudor going to Harvard caused another difficulty Judy chose not to share. Saint was furious. She turned her mind to him with reluctance. He was as broad and strong as any mother might hope her son to be. He towered over her and Tudor, inches taller than his younger brother, solid of feature, with a wide nose and forehead and thick black hair, making Tudor look almost girlish in comparison with his thin, pale face. Tudor had Dick's handsome eyes though. He didn't smile or laugh as his father had, perhaps, but then, he had grown up in different circumstances, and she didn't blame herself for that. No son was more loved. But Saint? He'd returned from England no better than when he left. At least it was

Jack's money wasted, not her own. Only now, Saint seemed to think he was entitled to the same opportunities as his younger brother.

She rubbed her eyebrows and stretched out her back. Little ailments assaulted her daily. Pains in her hips. A stiff shoulder. Some days, she couldn't lift her arm above chest height. In the spring and fall, she was afflicted with headaches and congestion in her nose and throat. In winter, she was plagued by every chill or fever that the farmhands seemed to breed and then look to her to cure, their stupid eyes bright in their dark and fearful faces. How she resented that fearfulness. Who did *she* ever have to look to for help when she was afraid?

A noise outside distracted her. Yells and thuds, clear sounds of a fight of some sort. She heard shoes scuffling on the dry dirt path at the side of the house and went to the window, but no one came into view. Her shoulders dropped. Was a little peace too much to hope for? As the noise grew in intensity, she bit on the inside of her lip and picked up her skirts, whisking down the hallway and out into the yard.

"Boys!" Anger spiked in her chest, hot and resentful at the sight of them. "Tudor! Stop it at once!" Her sons paid no attention. They carried on wrestling, fists flying, both grunting, their faces lit with fury as she called out, "Sarah! Ben! Fetch someone. Someone *stop* them!"

Three men came running. Her sons were pulled apart, chests heaving. Blood ran down Saint's face. Tudor struggled for breath. She rushed to him.

"Stay away from me, Mother," he snapped, trying to free his arms. "Get off me. It's over now. You can let us go."

She nodded to the man who held Tudor's arms and turned to her other son. "What were you thinking?" She tapped at her head, knowing he would understand her meaning. He scowled and dropped his eyes, only infuriating her more. She pulled a handkerchief from her pocket and crouched down beside Saint, waving away Ben who still knelt in the dust with him. Judy took her oldest son's chin in hers and forced him to look at her.

"You're twenty-one years old, Saint. Your brother is eighteen. You're men. What happened?" His eyes tracked her lips. She wiped the blood from a wound under his eye and gave him a corner of material to lick before pressing it against the cut to stop the bleeding. "Tell me."

"No!" His voice, as always, was low and guttural. She schooled her face to hide her pain when he struggled to speak. Judy didn't know what he'd gone through in England, whether he'd worked hard or found friends or missed his home. Clearly, he never missed his younger brother. They circled each other like resentful cats, rarely in the same room and often away, staying with Jack at Roanoke, but not together as normal brothers might. As Saint got to his feet and limped off to some quiet spot to nurse his injuries, she felt the eyes of Ben and the other men on her. Shame fueled her discontent.

"Tudor. Inside with me. Now." She marched to the house with what dignity she was able to muster and was rewarded by the sound of him following her into the parlor.

"What was that all about?"

Tudor walked to the sideboard and poured himself a generous glass of brandy. She settled down into the high-backed chair by the fireplace and folded her hands.

"He has no sense of humor."

Judy kept her face still and her mouth shut. Tudor hated silence.

"Well, it started with talk of Uncle Jack." He refilled his glass and settled into the chair opposite her. "He spoke frankly to me last night."

She waited.

"He's furious with Tucker in Williamsburg. Jack ranted for hours about the old man. About what a terrible stepfather he was to the three of them. How he knew nothing of the land—how should he, being born in Bermuda of all places? How he'd steered Jack and his brothers wrong at every turn."

"Was he drunk?"

"Only a little breezy." Tudor took another sip. "He has a catalog of crimes he lays at Tucker's door, but the greatest is the sale of the Matoax Plantation."

"Your father and I lived there when we were first married."

"Oh, I heard all about that. He gets quite sentimental when he talks about Theo and Father."

"They were very close. Unlike you and your brother." She threw him a pointed look, but his eyes were on the amber liquid in his glass.

"Jack says Tucker embezzled our money after my grandmother died. Says he took all the best male slaves and furnishings to Williamsburg. And—" he threw her another glance and his lips almost smirked, "—he said Tucker sent the female slaves he liked best to Roanoke."

"What?" Judy was confused. Jack had moved to the family property at Roanoke three years earlier, when their arguments over the management of Bizarre brought them to the point where they couldn't stand to be in the same room together. He'd said he couldn't eat a meal with her sour face watching him—that had stung—but at the same time, she'd known there was more to it. Jack was never a stable character. She believed his move to Roanoke would be a short-lived whim. The house was small and offered few creature comforts. His people there lived entirely off the land, working hard and maintaining traditions. In some way, she assumed, it satisfied his determination to be a Virginia gentleman. He retreated there when not caught up in politics or other civic duties and rarely set foot in Bizarre, preferring to do business with her by letter and have his nephews visit him in his rural retreat.

"Jack claims Tucker sent the women he had an eye for to Roanoke and would visit them. He said the younger slaves at Roanoke are all Tucker's children. Some are as pale as I am. Do you think it's true?"

"No! And this is not an appropriate subject for discussion."

"You asked me, Mother. And it's not as if Tucker's the first man to find those dark-skinned girls …"

"Enough." She straightened in her chair. "Your Uncle Jack is not himself. He's isolated at Roanoke and since he lost his seat in Congress, is too much alone and prone to wild imaginings. Anyway, what has this to do with you and your brother trying to kill each other? Tell me what you said to Saint."

"Just what I've told you now. And he was shocked, much as you are, but what's another lascivious story in our family? I thought you'd enjoy it. Something from the other side of the family to balance out the indiscretions of Aunt Nancy. The scandalous Tuckers. Makes a pleasant change."

"Tudor!" She heard the bitterness. The story of his father, of the trial and its lingering disgrace still held a fascination for Tudor. She pushed away the self-recrimination. "But why come to blows over it? What *else* did you say to your brother?"

"His reaction irritated me. He should have found it funny. I'd gone to such pains to speak slowly so he could read my lips and not go off only half understanding the story in his customary block-headed way."

"And?"

"It was only a jest. He has no sense of humor."

"Tudor?"

He rolled his eyes. "I merely said that since he'd no hope of finding a wife in this life, perhaps I should warn the negro girls that he might try to let off some of his oh-so-obvious frustration on them, as our father's stepfather had so prolifically done at Roanoke."

"Tudor!"

"What? It was a joke, Mother. A stupid joke. If he'd half a brain, he'd have known it. But he charged me like a bull! I'm glad I bloodied him. I'm sick of his miserable hangdog face. He's so bloody tiresome. I don't know how you stand him."

This was her moment to stand up for her firstborn. Time to correct Tudor and to insist upon kinder thoughts and words. Reverend Rice would know what to say.

She said nothing. Heavy weights slid over her bones. Her face ached, and her eyes burned. She was so tired. She didn't have the energy to argue. She never had. She longed to pack her bags and take herself off to Augusta County, to Fanny, to bring her, if not hope, then at least some comfort. She didn't have the energy to defend Saint or go looking for him. What could she even say to him if she did?

"I don't believe Jack's stories and neither should you. He's bitter, half mad I think sometimes. Perhaps you shouldn't visit for a time."

"And let Theodore Dudley worm his way into my uncle's good graces? Over me? You don't need to worry, Mother. I can enjoy Uncle Jack's tales and imaginings without believing every accusation he makes."

"Good. Because while I've no great fondness for Mr. Tucker, you know his daughter, Fanny, is one of my dearest friends." There was a catch in her voice, he must have heard it, but no, Tudor was still thinking about Jack Randolph.

"Are all his stories false then, Mother? I never thought there was much to that old one about Aunt Nancy and Billy Ellis."

"Nor me."

"Although, you didn't seem so certain at one time."

Judy couldn't look at him. He often did this, this son of hers. Turned conversations in ways that made her uncomfortable. Pressed on her bruises. Probed for weakness. Tested. Certain conversations she'd had with Tudor she wished could be left in the past. But he forgot none of it—particularly in relation to her sister, Nancy.

Fanny's funeral was acutely painful. Seeing Fanny's husband, John, and their three children, Mr. Tucker and Lelia and all the siblings and half-siblings circling her grave saddened Judy deeply. She remembered the loss of her own mother and had the same unwelcome feeling of her own individual grief lost amidst the swarm of relations staking louder claims to sorrow and sadness, of her own emotions shriveling in others' heat. Memories preoccupied her on the carriage ride back to the Tuckers' house in Williamsburg. It had taken years to truly understand what she had lost.

Mr. Tucker looked shaken by his daughter's death, but still had a kind word for Judy, thanking her for her friendship to Fanny. He took time to talk to Tudor and asked after Saint. Jack gave his stepfather a wide berth, but soon enough found his way through the crowd in the house to pick a fight with her.

"Where's my other nephew?"

"At Bizarre."

"He should be here."

"Saint's not well."

"*Actually* not well?"

Judy's jaw clenched. She nodded at a spot in the garden where they might not be overheard, and Jack followed her outside.

"Well?"

His impatience was one of many things she found annoying about Jack. Judy forced herself to speak calmly. "He's perfectly healthy in his body but has been emotional of late. He doesn't do well in crowds."

"He's a Randolph. The oldest son of my oldest brother."

"I'm aware of that."

"He should be here."

"He cannot be trusted to, to …" She hesitated, unable to put her fears into words.

"Ridiculous! You don't like to be seen with him. You never have. It's unnatural to watch how you are with him. What kind of mother—"

She struck him in the face.

Heat rushed to her cheeks, and she glanced toward the house. It appeared that no one had seen them. Jack's breath skimmed her face, his mouth inches from her ear. "Apparently, it's not my nephew who cannot be trusted to behave in public."

She turned back, unrepentant. "Your insults demanded a response, Jack Randolph. My son has barely slept in weeks. He and his brother do not look at each other, far less communicate. Saint's envy of Tudor's advantages, Tudor's lack of sympathy or compassion, Saint's struggles with the limits to his existence make him morose and destructive. Let me see you live with him before you question my motherhood again. Let me see you worry for his future when you're dead and gone. Let's see you watch your own flesh and blood tear at his hair and cut at his arms. He has pulled his own eyebrows out, hair by hair. He barely eats. He is miserable, abjectly so, and I'm forced to witness his distress with no answer to anything that ails him."

She had some satisfaction in watching Jack's response to all this ripple across his face in a wave of revulsion. She fell silent, tight in her chest and breathless. For a moment, his eyes softened. She thought he might reach out and embrace her. She didn't know if she would welcome that or not. How long had it been since anyone had held her? But his expression clouded.

"And meanwhile, that bitch is in New York, living in luxury," he said. "The rest of us all but forgotten." He turned on his heel and left. They didn't exchange another word.

Chapter Thirty-One

News of Fanny Coulter's death arrived at Morrisania in a series of letters. First, a stiff note from Jack to Mr. Morris, simply apprising them of the death in the family. Next, a tear-stained letter to Nancy from Judy.

"Her handwriting betrays her," Nancy said, leaning across the tea table to show Mr. Morris. "She talks of meeting Fanny again in the afterlife almost with longing. I wish we could persuade her to leave Bizarre and live in a more companionable setting. If I thought for a moment she would come to us—"

"Nothing you've told me about your sister makes me think that would be a good idea," he replied, his eyebrows lifting. "And besides. You will have no time for other people's woes and worries soon." His eyes fell to her stomach, where her other hand cradled the surprise blessing of their marriage, expected within a week or two.

"That's true." Nancy let thoughts of Fanny and Judy fade from her mind. They had not married with any hope or expectation of having children. God wouldn't bless a woman with her past with a child, she was certain, and when the first years of marriage slipped past, her belief was confirmed. She was thankful her marriage was happy, a strong partnership founded on friendship and attraction. She loved her husband, and he loved her. It was more, much more than she could have imagined, so that when she did fall pregnant, at the age of thirty-eight, she'd been shocked and afraid on many counts. She feared the child would not thrive. She doubted her own strength. She was undeserving. Mr. Morris was far from young—they had celebrated his sixtieth birthday over a year ago. She feared his reaction but should not have been concerned. He'd embraced her news and the prospect of fatherhood with his characteristic humor and vitality. If the child she carried had a fifth of its father's good-natured optimism and love for life, it would be blessed. But when it moved under her skin, she was crippled with anxiety. Memories rose up. Bizarre. Glentivar.

Another argument. Saint wanted her to find a new overseer—a man who might tolerate a deaf master—but Judy knew a fool's errand when she heard one. Such a person did not exist. Overseers were a rough class of men, and the few willing to run a small plantation in rural Virginia would never have the forbearance needed to work with Saint. Sending him overseas had been a mistake. He had come back thinking he was more than he was. It was past time he accepted the truth.

"It should be your Uncle Jack dealing with you, not me," she said when he paused his scribbling. This was how they argued now. Saint wrote down the words he could not say and read her lips for her reply. She was forced to look at him, but looking at him caused her distress. All she saw was the pink, damaged skin at his brows. It hurt to see it and pain sharpened her words. At Fanny's funeral, she'd come to a decision. Saint's future lay away from Bizarre. If she had to push him away, so be it. "I want you to go to Roanoke."

He wrote quickly, thrusting paper across the breakfast table. He wanted to work here. He had ideas. She stared at him blankly. What could she say that she hadn't said already?

He grabbed his notes, grunting, waving them in her face. Why couldn't he see that she was sick of it? Why couldn't he see that she had tried her best but found her best was not enough? He must leave. He must go to Roanoke and Jack, where at least they could fish and shoot and drink brandy—all things men seemed to be fond of doing with few words needed between them. But no, here he was, asking her to achieve impossible ends, to make miraculous changes and somehow overcome the fact that as a man and eldest son, he was a failure and always had been.

"I manage Bizarre," she said looking directly into his eyes. "I do. It is hard work, but I have done it, every day—every single day—since your father died. I don't need your help. I don't *want* your help. When Tudor is ready, he will run Bizarre." The pain in Saint's face was unmistakable, but this was a truth long overdue in the telling. "You're not fit for the life here. I don't know what life you are fit for. You're my son. You'll always have a roof over your head if you need one. But I won't pretend with you. You can't be the man you want to be. You can't inherit this land. The people who live and work here need a man—or woman—they can rely on and trust. You can't talk to them. You can't hear them. How can you understand them? Manage them? You know as well as I do that freed people are harder to manage than slaves." She shook her head, tears rising. "The best you can do is go and live at Roanoke with your uncle. Because this will be your brother's home, not yours, and I'm finished pretending otherwise."

The silence, when she finished, pulsed in her ears. She saw a range of emotions dance across his eyes—rage, hurt, anger, despair—but refused to react. It had to be done. It was a cruel kindness, the gift of the truth, unwanted but needed. She tried to see in his face and person that small, squalling being she had pushed from herself in the room upstairs with such desperate anxiety, such hopefulness and pride. But children were not who you made them. They were what they made of themselves. He had been dealt a terrible hand, it was true, but he should turn to the Reverend Rice and his teachings. That was where Saint's salvation lay.

"You must pray for strength."

"Pray?" The word sounded thick and ugly in his mouth. "Pray?" he asked again, louder now. He slapped his hands down on the table, rattling the cups in their saucers. For a moment, she thought he might grab her. He looked like he longed to shake her. Or worse.

Instead, he blundered from the room, slamming the door so hard, the whole house echoed with his rage.

The child was born in February. Nancy's labor was short, and the boy came squealing and twitching into the world, a mass of dark hair plastered to his head, his face red and his tiny tongue quivering as air rushed into his lungs. He announced his arrival with a shrill wail. Everything about the experience was so different than before. She had been terrified in the last days before the birth, but the moment she heard him, when she saw the beaming smile on his father's face, when she touched his soft, pink skin, ran her finger down his strong spine and pressed him to her chest, Nancy left the past behind.

From that day on, she reveled in the now. In her son. In her husband. In her own home and her own family. Everything about

Bizarre, all her regrets and sorrows receded, replaced by the living, breathing reality of her own healthy son, dressed in white linen and cradled in her husband's arms.

It was cold in the Reverend Rice's prayer room. A small fire burned in the grate, but it gave off more smoke than heat and caught the back of Judy's throat. She ought to leave. Services were over for the day. Tasks awaited her back at Bizarre. Saint had been packing when she left, preparing for his move to Roanoke, which Jack, for all his faults, had supported. It hurt to see him go, as it had hurt to send Tudor off to Harvard. She prayed for strength. She had to let them go, she had to trust them, but the Lord knew, it was a struggle.

Everything was a struggle. Dark clouds had descended on her again when she received the news of her nephew's birth. She wished neither the child nor her sister any harm. She wasn't envious. When she had first heard from Nancy that she and old Mr. Morris were to have a child, all Judy felt was concerned. They were too old to be starting a family, even assuming Nancy would be able to carry the baby to term. Her sister must have worried about that. Judy recalled her own trepidation leading up to both her boys' births. She still thought of the child that had been stillborn at Molly's home so many years earlier and the babe she lost after Dick's trial. The pain was an echo of its former self, but women did not forget these things, and Judy was certain Nancy's head was full of thoughts of her and Theo's child as this new birth grew closer. On that count, Judy admitted she was resentful. She had spent years trying to forget Glentivar, forget Dick's trial, forget Nancy's letter admitting that there had been a child, after Judy had spent years convincing herself that there never was one. With Nancy expecting, it had all come rushing back.

Perhaps that was why she'd reacted so badly. Perhaps she had expected something to go wrong. Not wished for, or hoped for it, but expected it. An unhappy outcome. When Nancy wrote of her beautiful boy, healthy, strong, named Gouverneur after his famous father, Judy had to reframe her thoughts. Perhaps she was a little envious after all. Babies held such promise. So much hope.

The fire died down, and the temperature dropped even lower. Shadows fell across the room. A glance at the window told her it was time she returned to Bizarre. She straightened her skirts and placed her bible on the table by the door. She would return tomorrow, return every day until the peace she could not find at home settled into her bones. Outside, Ben paced the small graveyard, his hands behind his back and his head bowed. When he heard her close the door, however, he moved swiftly to her horse and carriage and pulled the step for her to climb up before taking his seat and setting the horse in motion.

"I'm sorry I was so long, Ben."

"No apologies needed, Mrs. Randolph."

It was a cold night, and she pulled a blanket over her skirts, rubbing her hands in its soft wool. She would need to rub her hands and feet with liniment when she was home, or the stiffness in the morning would be hard to bear. She closed her eyes and swayed a little with the roll of the carriage. She thought of Saint leaving in the morning. She'd have Sarah spend the afternoon scrubbing out his room with vinegar.

"Something's burning!" Ben broke into her thoughts, twisting in his seat and tilting his head back. "Do you smell it, Mrs. Randolph?"

"Yes. What can it be? How far are we from home?" She peered out at the trees lining the road, trying to get her bearings in the semi-darkness.

"Not far now. I don't like it, missus."

Judy scanned the trees and sky for a trail of smoke, but the road was narrow and pine trees towered over them on both sides.

The smell grew stronger as they reached the turn for Bizarre. Now, she saw smoke. Her mind raced with the possibilities. The smokehouse. The kitchen house. A fire in the stables. They turned the last corner.

Bizarre was on fire.

Ben halted the horse and carriage well away from the fire, pulling off the track and into grass before leaping from his perch and running to the house. Judy gasped, trying to take in the scene. Orange and red flames lapped at every window. Smoke plumed and belched its way into the dark sky. Figures ran across the grass, crisscrossing and weaving. Someone ran into the house itself, and others emerged, carrying bundles, chairs, a painting. She watched as the strong boxes from the study were tossed from man to man, joining a pile of belongings out of the fire's reach. Other men and women passed buckets in a line from the well, trying to save the house. The noise was terrible, and at first, the sounds and smell of her life burning kept her frozen in the carriage, gaping and aghast, her mind struggling to grasp the enormity of the nightmare before her.

Her belongings, clothes and letters, her meager jewelry, her fine china plates. Her eyes told her it was all already gone. She slowly climbed down from the carriage and felt a rush of air as men from nearby Farmville rode in to help. Someone, not recognizing her in the darkness, ordered her to hold their horses, and she did so mechanically, unable to rip her eyes from the burning house. Shouts and hollers filled the air, fighting to be heard against the crackle of fire and the whine of burning timber. Judy scanned the men and women trying to save her home. Where was Saint?

The thought galvanized her. She called to Sarah, who had left the line of water and backed away from the house, her eyes streaming from the smoke and her chest heaving.

"Hold these horses. And do not go near the house again. It's too dangerous. Now, tell me, where is my son?"

She didn't answer. Instead, Sarah pressed her lips closed and shook her head a little, her eyes wide and darting.

"Not in the house?"

She shook her head.

Men had dropped their lanterns by the well, and Judy picked one up, holding it high near her face so that she could see and be recognized. Giving the fire a wide berth, she took the side path toward the kitchen house and the vegetable garden. Everywhere was cast in an orange glow, and the noise of the fire echoed out across the empty fields. Where was he? She lowered her lantern, looking for a sign of light. Surely, he wasn't out in this darkness alone? In such a crisis. She struggled to make sense of it, halfway between anxiety for his safety and fury at his disappearance. She called his name, screamed his name, knowing it was futile to do so, unable to stop herself.

"God damn you, Saint! Show yourself." She checked the stables, where the horses paced and snorted, upset by the smoke swirling through the air. Saint was not there. He wasn't in the kitchen house. She needed Ben. He must find Saint. She panicked, fearing that he was in the house after all, and quickened her step. The sight of her home from the rear was every bit as devastating, and she paused, realizing the building was lost. She thought she might fall and put out a hand, leaning on the gate of the kitchen garden for support. A tiny light caught her eye. The flicker of a lantern inside the garden.

She raced to the source of the light. There he was. Her son. He sat on the bare earth with his legs crossed and the lantern settled before him. He didn't turn as she approached. Saint's eyes were fixed on the house, but his hands moved. She watched as he scooped earth with each hand and then brought the fistfuls together, rubbing the soil between his fingers as if he held a cloth and was drying his hands. Dirt fell. His breeches were covered in it, but she watched as he repeated the same action, grabbing the earth, rubbing his hands, letting the dirt fall all over him, all the while staring at the burning house. She crept a little closer, letting her own light fall on him, illuminating his face. What she saw staggered her. He was smiling.

With the horror of understanding blooming in her chest, Judy turned and fled.

Chapter Thirty-Two

Nancy's heart was full on the morning he was due to arrive. Tudor Randolph, her nephew, was expected at Morrisania for a stay of at least a week. What would he look like? The last time Nancy had seen him was in Richmond, seven years ago. He was little more than a child then, gawky, mischievous, impulsive, fond of anything sweet. Might he look like Dick? Judy had written that the resemblance, so strong when Tudor was a boy, had lessened as he reached manhood. Nancy wasn't sure if she was glad about that, or sorry.

"Cousin Tudor should be here soon, Gouverneur. Isn't it exciting?" She turned from the window and smiled at her young son who came toddling over to her, leaning forward, like a ship's figurehead, as he strained to keep his balance.

"Ma-ma." His first words had come recently, emerging from a stream of babble, squeaks and gestures that had his parents enraptured. He pulled at her skirts, demanding to be lifted to her knee.

"What can you see outside, little man? Can you see the trees? And there, the path down to the lake where you like to run? Look how blue the sky is this morning. Shall we go down and walk until we hear your cousin come?"

Gouverneur was happy to be carried downstairs and patient as she buttoned his short coat and tied a cap over her curls. "Now, let me find a shawl, and we will be quite prepared." She beamed down at him and was rewarded with a broad smile. Her hand went to her chest. The wonder of him. Her delight in his company increased daily. With her son, she saw the world through new eyes. She talked to him constantly, narrating their activities, bringing words into his life, much as she had once done with his cousin, Saint.

Her nephews had been in her thoughts a great deal, and for the umpteenth time, she wondered whether to speak to Tudor about the fire at Bizarre or to confine their conversation to safer topics. Seven years was a long time. It was longer still since Nancy had seen Judy or Saint, and she and Mr. Morris had only met with Jack once since their marriage, nearly five years previously. They had been in Washington, Mr. Morris seeking support for a canal project linking New York and Lake Erie, and she'd traveled with him, thrilled to meet Dolley Madison at the White House and tour the new Capitol Building. Jack was speaking on the floor when Nancy and Mr. Morris joined the throng in the congressional galleries. She'd known a rush of pride. He was a powerful orator, no one who heard him could argue it, and when they crossed paths in the halls of the Capitol later that day, she offered genuine compliments. Jack, in turn, was polite and welcoming. She'd delighted afterward to write to Mr. Tucker, describing their meeting and her pleasure in it.

Truly, there was every reason to suppose this visit from Tudor would be successful. When she looked at her little boy, she could not doubt it. Tudor was family. Gouverneur's and her family. She could not wait to welcome him into her home.

"Oss!" Somehow, Gouverneur heard the horses before she did.

"Yes! He is here!" She scooped up her son and hurried across the grass to meet the phaeton as it pulled to a halt at the wide front door. As Tudor alighted, Nancy's hand flew to her mouth. Not look like Dick? Judy's memory must be failing her.

"Nephew!" She stepped forward as he bowed. "It is my greatest pleasure to welcome you. And to introduce you to my little boy." They both smiled. Gouverneur had succumbed to a sudden attack of shyness and buried his face in his mother's shoulder. No amount of twisting or turning would prompt him to raise his eyes to his cousin.

"Perhaps young Mr. Morris will be pleased to get to know me later," Tudor said. "Somewhere in my baggage, I believe there is a drum and sticks that he might like to play with."

"A drum?" Nancy laughed. "I'm not sure that is a gift a parent might thank you for, although I believe a little boy of my acquaintance will be enchanted."

She swung Gouverneur onto her hip and tucked her free arm into Tudor's. "Come. Welcome to Morrisania. I've been looking forward to this moment so much."

For the most part, Nancy was happy with her visitor. He was polite and quick to smile. He appeared pleased with everything, from his room to his dinner, to Mr. Morris's pistols and the opportunity to snag a brace of partridge before breakfast—at least on the one day he was up early enough to partake of the sport. But she sensed Mr. Morris did not quite warm to him. They were never long over their port after dinner, and her husband said little about her nephew beyond admitting that he had pretty manners and "seemed yet young".

Saint was not mentioned after her initial inquiry after his health and Tudor's response that his brother was "tolerably well". What that might mean, Nancy did not wish to think. After the fire, Saint was sent to a doctor in Philadelphia. Reading between the lines, Nancy believed he was not there of his own free will. But Tudor proved as tight-lipped as his mother had always been on matters of personal importance, and Nancy left the question of Saint alone, preferring to look for ways the young man resembled his father in character as well as in his looks.

Certainly, he was capable of being delightful company. Gouverneur was swiftly enchanted with the gift of the drum, and Tudor seemed equally enamored, encouraging his walking, sitting on the floor, building blocks and rolling balls to him with such good humor that no mother, and certainly not one as partial as herself, could have failed to be moved. In all this, she saw the Dick she remembered: charming, playful and light of spirit. Tudor also had his father's love of fine things. He wandered Morrisania, openly admiring every room, every painting, every object and every view. He was, though, quick to contrast the luxuries of Morrisania with his mother's reduced circumstances. Since the fire, she had taken rooms near the Reverend Rice's family in Farmville. Tudor also described Jack's Roanoke Plantation in unflattering terms and bemoaned the long-ago sale of Matoax.

At mealtimes, his wine glass was quickly emptied, reminding her of Theo. Like his uncle, he'd no more favored topic of conversation than himself and his splendid future plans. Tudor had been at Harvard for over a year, but he grumbled of perceived wrongs and injustices, much as he had done as a boy in Richmond, and although Nancy knew he'd hounded Judy, Jack and Mr. Tucker into supporting his studies at Harvard, now, all his talk was of a tour of Europe. This, at least, was something Mr. Morris could discuss, having traveled extensively through France, but Tudor, in a manner she supposed was not unusual, didn't have half as much interest in another man's actual travels as he did in the imagined travels he planned for himself.

Tudor had been with them for two weeks when she detected an edge in her husband's voice when he spoke of their guest. She chose the dark warmth of their private room to sound out Mr. Morris about her nephew. It was their habit to share their bed with their young son. Convention called for the boy to sleep in his nursery, but he was too precious to both his parents for them to part with him when they were at home, and he often slumbered between them while they talked.

"Tell me honestly, dearest. What do you think of my nephew?"

"He is well enough."

"Well enough? That doesn't sound too encouraging."

"He's young. And has been indulged." He held up his hands as she opened her mouth to object. "I know. Tudor lost his father at a young age. And his older brother's difficulties—"

"—led Judy to spoil him. You're right. I saw it happen. Although now we have our own child, I understand her better." She smiled as her husband stroked their son's soft curls. "But Tudor is still young. Not yet nineteen. Surely there's hope for him?"

"There's always hope."

"What is it? Has he said something amiss?"

"Perhaps I'm oversensitive. Old-fashioned."

"What has he said?" Mr. Morris was not oversensitive. He was as rational a man as any and far from old-fashioned. He had an openness to, and a joy in the new that made the age difference between them disappear. She reached for his hand.

"I find him too familiar."

"Familiar?"

"I have something of a reputation, you're aware of it. So is your nephew."

"What are you talking about?"

"Nothing we haven't discussed. I'm talking about Adélaïde de Flahaut. Tudor knows of her. And thought it a fit topic to discuss with me."

"No!"

"Yes."

Anxiety fluttered in Nancy's stomach. Adélaïde had been her husband's lover in France. She'd been a major part of his life, a woman he had even been prepared to share, not only with her husband but with two other gentlemen. Nancy doubted Mr. Morris had told her everything from his past—and, the Lord knew, she had been careful with what she shared of her own—but he had been open, telling her of the important women in his life, emphasizing his decision to remain single and only trifle with married women, until he had met her. She had loved him for it and spoken as truthfully as she was able to about her own past and those dark days at Bizarre and Glentivar.

"I imagine he wished to present himself as a man of the world," her husband continued. "He certainly did so—although perhaps not with the positive connotations he expected. But he also … I must ask … do you think he has any knowledge of your past history?"

"Mine?"

"It's a feeling more than anything he said directly. I can't pinpoint his exact words, but he intimated we're well-matched. And he said so in the context of prior romantic experience, rather than temperament or character or anything else."

"Surely not! Surely neither Judy nor Jack would have spoken of it. Might he have heard of his father's trial in some manner? From some gossip or troublemaker? Good God, is it never to be forgot?"

"Calm yourself, dearest." He ran his thumb down her cheek. "Tudor cannot harm you, or us. What happened between you and Theo Randolph, what happened at Glentivar—it was an age ago. We agreed the past would not touch us." His hand went to her shoulder, his grip firm and reassuring. "We know who we are and what we mean to each other. That's what matters. I just don't want this young man being rude to you. You have a fondness for the boy he once was, that's understandable. But I'll be glad when he is on his way back north. I've probably read too much into it. I only wish you to be on your guard, nothing more." He touched his fingers to his lips and then pressed them to hers, their shared signal that talking was over for the night. Mr. Morris rolled on his side, and soon, she heard his breathing slow.

Nancy lay awake long into the night. Tudor's visit wasn't what she hoped. She thought of the money he had borrowed from her, and the way his eyes glittered as he threw back glass after glass of Mr. Morris's French wine. He would be gone soon, and she looked forward to it. They would have peace again, and all would be as it had been.

But two days later, Tudor came in from a ride, gasping for breath and gripping his chest. He pushed away offers of help and charged to his room, only to falter in the doorway and bend double as a torrent of blood spewed from his mouth. He fell limply on his bed, his face white, his breath labored.

Nancy sent Phebe for Mr. Morris. They got Tudor undressed and into bed, then waited anxiously for their doctor to arrive.

Later that evening, she wrote to Judy, the sister she had not seen in years.

Chapter Thirty-Three

Judy bore the journey as well as she could. Nancy's letters had charted the story of Tudor's decline. They'd brought in the best doctor in New York City, but the situation was grave. Nancy also wrote to Mr. Tucker, and as a result, Judy was able to travel north in the Tucker family carriage, with Mr. Tucker paying for her horses and lodgings on the road. By the time she arrived at Morrisania, nearly a month had passed since Tudor's consumptive attack. She passed the hours of the long journey vacillating between hope and despair, longing and dreading to see him, praying for divine help to keep her precious son alive.

There was no time for any impressions of place or people when she arrived. The carriage drew up at a door. She climbed out. There was her sister. Hands were outstretched and clasped. She registered tremulous smiles and words of reassurance. Judy was swept through a hallway, up a flight of stairs, past many doors and then into the sight of her adored son—alive, in bed—upright, horribly thin, pale—but awake, happy to see her, ready to be embraced. Tears filled her eyes, and she saw them mirrored in her sister's. As if they sensed her need for privacy, she heard Nancy and Mr. Morris step away and the door close. She sat in the chair next to her son's bed and held his hand. Soon enough, he closed his eyes and slept.

The next morning, Judy was better able to take in her surroundings. She woke in a warm bed hung with blue and white cotton curtains, an elaborate and expensive canopy of swags of rich material that matched her bedspread and cushions. The room was decorated with blue wallpaper, thick rugs, a beautiful walnut desk and two newly upholstered armchairs arranged around the corner fireplace. A vase of white chrysanthemums sat on a small table by the window, next to a bowl and pitcher. Everything was clean and as neat as a pin—as fine as anything she had seen at Monticello or remembered from grander days in Tuckahoe and Matoax. If Tudor had to fall ill, Judy was truly thankful it had been here, at Morrisania, with family to look after him and every creature comfort available. The thought of him suffering in some miserable room in Harvard, with no one to look in on him or light him a fire, had tormented her since he left Bizarre. Now, she gave a prayer of thanks that in his lowest moment, his family was able to support him.

Family. Judy, with a good night's sleep under her belt and assured by her own eyes that Tudor was not at death's door, was ready, anxious even, to meet properly with Mr. Morris, Nancy and little Gouverneur. Just as she finished dressing, a maid knocked at her door, delivering hot water and returning a few minutes later to conduct her to the breakfast parlor.

Mr. Morris was at the table, tucking into a dish of eggs with the newspaper propped against the teapot and his chair set at an angle from the table that allowed him to straighten out his wooden leg. She was surprised at how nimbly he rose to his feet as she entered and smiled in response to his own beaming welcome. Seeing Nancy also start to rise, Judy put out her hands in protest.

"No. Pray do not disturb yourself." The small boy on Nancy's knee turned to gaze at her, a fistful of toasted bread and butter halfway between his mother's plate and his pink mouth. "Hello, young man," she said. A memory of Tudor at the same age flooded her mind. Perhaps it was the way his back curled into his mother so that they fit each other and were separate, yet not separate.

"I was with Tudor earlier," Nancy said. "He slept well and may be strong enough to leave his room for a few hours this afternoon. I think you might sit with him in the rose garden. The sun lasts longest there, and a line of trees keeps any wind out."

"I'll look forward to that." Judy allowed herself to be ushered to a chair by a manservant. "It is lovely to meet you, Mr. Morris. And your fine young son."

She had been nervous of meeting Nancy's husband, but quickly forgot all that. He was an affable and solicitous host who spoke warmly of his belief that Tudor was on the mend and waved away her profuse thanks for his kindness to her son. Later, she sat quietly in the rose garden with Tudor, enjoying the late summer sun warming her skin. For the next two weeks, she had nothing to do but concentrate on helping her son recover his strength. The sisters were comfortable together, conversing about Tudor's needs, reminiscing about his childhood exploits and entertaining Gouverneur.

And then Jack came.

Nancy wasn't worried. Jack had been friendly enough in Washington a few years previously, and anyone could see that his much-loved nephew was on the mend. Past days of bickering between herself,

Judy and Jack seemed like memories belonging to other people. She was pleasantly surprised at how comfortably she and Judy managed together and sorry she and Tudor would leave them in a few days' time. Difficult subjects—any mention of Dick, Saint or the burning of Bizarre—were avoided, and Mr. Morris had the happy knack of charming any visitor. She enjoyed watching Judy unbend in the face of his unremitting good manners and gentle optimism. A brief visit from Jack would seal the end to the breach in the family. As she picked up Gouverneur's toys from a rug in the garden and waited for Judy to join her for tea, she imagined she'd soon have the pleasure of thinking *her* family preferable to her husband's. His nephews and nieces were less than delighted with Mr. Morris's late marriage. After their son's birth, relationships had deteriorated markedly. Nancy's Randolph relations were starting to look a lot more palatable than the Morris clan. Would wonders never cease?

But within an hour of his arrival, Nancy knew herself mistaken. Jack swaggered into the house, filling first the hallway and later the dining room with his exaggerated presence. Of course, he looked as rustic as ever, deliberately disheveled and wearing a ridiculous planter's hat—pretending he spent his days on the tobacco field when the world knew he was the busiest of congressmen, ready to ally with anyone rather than risk losing his precious seat again, as he'd briefly done back in 1812. As soon as Jack was reassured about Tudor's health, he turned his attention to his surroundings. He admired anything and everything to the most uncomfortable degree and—worse—called upon Judy to agree with him. Nothing went unremarked, from their paintings and china to their silverware and table linen. He was certain he'd seen nothing so fine in all Virginia.

"Did you spend much time at your summer house this year?" Jack asked her the next day. They were outside. Tudor, for the first time fully dressed and seated without any blankets, had managed to walk out to the lawn on his uncle's arm looking considerably more like the fashionable young man who had arrived two months previously. Judy tried to fuss around him but subsided as her son glared, muttering that he wasn't an infant and could reach for his own teacup when he wanted it. Under Phebe's watchful eye, Gouverneur, busy with a butterfly net, happily stumbled around, offering no threat to the insect population but entertaining his mother a great deal with his enthusiasm. Mr. Morris had not joined them—a fact for which Nancy was shortly most thankful.

"Not so much as in previous years," she replied. "With Gouverneur starting to walk, we agreed staying home was safer. Besides, it's a long way in the north, and traveling with infants is not always easy." She threw Judy a speaking glance, mother to mother.

Jack sniffed loudly. "It must be pleasant, I suppose, to have such amenities at your disposal. Imagine, Tudor, how your mother might benefit from having a second property—oh, no, wait. To have a second property, one would be required to have a first."

"Jack!" said Judy.

"Because it does rather put it all into perspective, doesn't it?" he said.

"Does it?" Nancy glanced at her son, confirming he was out of earshot.

"Of course, I can only speak for myself," he continued. "But seeing you here, so comfortable and at your ease ... It's quite remarkable when you come to recall—"

"This is my home, Jack Randolph. Did you think to see me *un*comfortable?"

"Do you know, I suppose now that you say that, that I rather did. Was it difficult, I wonder, to move from housekeeper to wife?" He glared now, openly hostile. "Or perhaps not. Perhaps you came here with that end in mind. Eased your way into the old man's affections, teased him, tempted him. Used your experience."

"Jack!" She was on her feet, looking from Jack to Tudor and to Judy. "How dare you speak in such a manner? And in front of our nephew."

"Tudor? Oh, he's familiar with your history. He's an adult. Besides, there are lessons he can learn from you. You're a survivor, Nancy, I'll give you that. But I do feel pity for your poor sister, forced to sit here and take your charity."

"That's enough, Jack." Judy had been staring at her lap, but now, she whipped her head up and turned on him. "More than enough. Sister, I hope you'll ignore that unseemly outburst. You've been a nurse to my child and a generous host to us both. Jack Randolph does not speak for me." She rose, nodded at Nancy and walked across the grass to Gouverneur.

Nancy watched her sister and her son and knew a rush of gratitude, but Jack's insults could not be ignored. She felt a fool, suddenly, standing there with her fists clenched while Jack languished in his chair. She turned to her nephew. "Tudor?"

The young man's eyes flicked between her and his uncle. He seemed to be turning over a range of answers in his mind, perhaps weighing which one of them it suited him best to side with. She could make that calculation for him, and her heart sank.

"Enough men marry for money, Uncle Jack," he said. "Why shouldn't women?"

This had gone far enough. "I don't know what your uncle may have told you, Tudor, but I ask you to consider the time you have spent here and what you know of your host, Mr. Morris. He is not a fool. He is not an old man, hoodwinked by a young woman casting out lures in return for a fortune. He is intelligent, thoughtful, kind." Her voice wavered. "He has been a generous host to you. You should speak to me as you would speak if my husband were standing here by my side. Your father would not tolerate such disrespect."

"My brother!" Mention of Dick was a flame on dry paper. Jack jumped to his feet. "You don't speak his name. Do you hear me? You do not."

She remembered his cruelty in Richmond. Nothing had changed. Perhaps for Jack, it never would. "You will leave, Jack Randolph. You will pack your bags and go. I will tell my husband you were called away on business."

For a few moments, they stared at each other. She was aware of Tudor, eagerly drinking in the standoff. His ingratitude dismayed her.

Jack slowly nodded. He pressed his lips together. "Very well. I will call for my horse. It has been instructive to see you here, in this new setting." He sounded calm. The storm in his eyes when he spoke of Dick had passed and appeared forgotten, but she knew better than to judge Jack by his demeanor. "Tudor. Come and see me in the city with your mother before she returns to Virginia," Jack said. "We have much to discuss."

She watched him walk back to the house and fought to steady her breathing as she lowered herself back into her chair.

"Well, Aunt," said Tudor, after a few minutes. "You quite bested him there. I almost thought he'd strike you at one point."

"Did you, Tudor? And would you have found that as amusing as all the rest?"

"Oh, don't be upset with me! You know I mustn't cross Uncle Jack."

He stretched out a hand, and she let him pat hers while biting the inside of her cheek. He smiled, and she saw the boy he had been and, in many ways, still was. Her anger dissipated—replaced by gratitude that Jack was gone, that Mr. Morris had heard none of it and, for once, her sister, Judy, had sided with her. She was rattled, but not about to let her nephew see how badly.

"Let us not speak of it, Tudor. But I promise you, if I ever set eyes on that uncle of yours again, it will be too soon."

Judy closed her eyes in the coach, surprised by the strength of her emotions as she said farewell to Nancy. So much history lay between them, but in these past few weeks, they'd been something like friends. Nancy had cared for Tudor as well as if he were her own. It meant a great deal. And when Judy looked back on those years at Bizarre after Dick died, she saw how generous Nancy had been to her nephews with her time, her affection and her care. At the time, Nancy's efforts with Saint had rankled. Judy suspected her of what? Trying to impress Dick with her care for his damaged son? Trying to make her son love her, Nancy, more than his own mother? In the years after Dick's death, Judy viewed Nancy's closeness with Tom and William in the same light of competition. Now, she wondered if she had been wrong. From the few comments Nancy let drop, Judy understood life had been hard after she left Bizarre, much harder than Judy's own life now, never mind Jack's ridiculous harping. Nancy had been wholly dependent on Tom and William until Morris rescued her. Rescue was the term Nancy used, and although she said it lightly, Judy heard the undercurrent of seriousness in her voice.

Jack wanted Judy to be envious of Nancy's new life, that was clear. Well, Jack would be disappointed, and she'd tell him so when she and

Tudor met up with him in New York City in an hour or so. Because Judy was not envious of Nancy now.

She might have been, she knew. Jack's comparisons were valid. Nancy lived in comfort and luxury with a husband who adored her and a child with as sunny a temperament as any child Judy had met. But coveting what Nancy had served no one. Nancy having less wouldn't give Judy more. It was Nancy's good fortune that had saved Tudor, and there was nothing—*nothing*—more valuable than her son, for all his faults.

Was it possible to put aside those years before and after Dick's death? Years of disgrace, of suspicion and doubt. In her mind, she tried to hold up two images of Nancy, side by side. On the one side, the Nancy of today. A mother, kind-hearted and generous. Content. On the other side, the sister she remembered when she first came to Bizarre: lively, idealistic, flirtatious, bold. Falling in love with Theo Randolph, or so she had claimed. The rot of Glentivar had eaten at Judy. She remembered the letter, torn in two, fluttering in the air as Dick cast it from that bridge in Providence Forge. She remembered the ring swinging on a chain around her sister's neck, the one Judy never admitted noticing. Nancy didn't wear it now. At Morrisania, her sister wore little jewelry and nothing Judy recognized. For years, Judy had struggled to maintain her belief that there was nothing between her husband and her sister. Nancy's letter from the road to Newport had finally given her a level of peace. Theo, not Dick. Nothing else mattered.

Prayer gave her strength. She opened her eyes and looked at the motley cluster of houses as they passed. Roads narrowed, and the smells of the city assailed her—horse manure and wood burning, burned fat and coffee—as they stopped and started the last mile into the city. Tudor continued to sleep. He looked so innocent, not so different from his infant self, with his mouth relaxed instead of twisted in jest or cruelty. He didn't want to return to Farmville with her, but how could he manage at Harvard or travel abroad with his health so precarious? She thought of her small rooms at Farmville, leased through the Christian goodness of Reverend Rice. There wasn't much she could offer her son beyond care and affection. It was Jack he looked to for direction and funds. The most she could do for Tudor now, was to not be a burden. Thinking this way hurt more than a little. But as Reverend Rice said, prayer brought peace, and God was always with her. Prayer had sustained her through the loss of Bizarre and through the decision to send Saint to Philadelphia. It would help her now, to countenance returning to Virginia alone, leaving Tudor in his uncle's care.

Hopefully, Jack would be in a better frame of mind than when he left Morrisania. Nancy's expression when Jack accused her of marrying Morris for his money flashed across her mind. Judy had failed to support her sister in the face of Jack's accusations in the past, but not this time.

Chapter Thirty-Four

"Welcome, welcome. Accept my apologies for not standing to greet you, Sister, Nephew. Let the man show you to your rooms and then join me here."

It was hard, in such a dark cramped room, to see what ailed Jack, but after following his orders and leaving their hats and coats in the bedroom above the small parlor Jack had rented, Judy found her brother-in-law with one leg propped on a stool, heavily bandaged, and a tight look on his face, suggesting he was in a great deal of pain.

"Whatever happened?"

"Accident on the way from Morrisania the other day. Damned horse was startled by a deer. I landed awkwardly. The leg's fine, but my kneecap's smashed."

Tudor slid into the room behind her. "That's not like you, Uncle. Mind you, you didn't leave my aunt's house in the sweetest of tempers. Riding hard, were you?"

Judy blanched, not sure Jack would respond well to teasing, but it seemed her son knew him better than she.

"That damned woman! Of course I was riding too fast. Couldn't get away from her quickly enough. Oh, I dare say she took you two in with her teacups and napkins and her chubby young son, but it turned my stomach to be there."

"She's my sister! And her kindness to Tudor—"

"Kindness?" Jack's face rippled with scorn. "That woman has never done a kindness in her life that didn't have some self-serving motive. She was kind to Tudor to keep the old man sweet. There's no kindness in her. If your own recollection doesn't tell you so, you should talk to some of the visitors I've had in the last two days."

"Who?"

"David Ogden, for one."

"Whoever is he? Really, Jack, I think this pain in your leg—"

"It's my knee, damn you! And Ogden, for your information, is Morris's nephew. Had a lot to say on the subject of Nancy Randolph, none of it good. It's as clear to him as it is to me. She ensnared Gouverneur Morris and means to milk him dry. I heard she made much of her penury when she met him up north. She played him like a fiddle, according to Ogden, refusing to be his housekeeper for months with false plays of modesty and a feigned desire for independence. Then, when she finally agreed to take on the job, she refused any gifts, accepted only the most basic salary and even, wait for this, insisted on being married in her housekeeper's gown. She took nothing from him until the moment they were wed, but since then, it's been spend, spend, spend. The depth of his folly astounds me. But if there was ever a woman to make a fool of a man it was Nancy Randolph."

Judy didn't respond. She reached across the table and took an oatmeal biscuit to chew on while he raved.

"Ogden wanted to sound me out about the boy. The young 'un.

Ugly, fat little thing. I soon saw where he was going. When your aging uncle marries a harlot, and after three barren years, she suddenly produces an heir ... Well, he'd be a fool not to wonder. I wonder at it myself. What better way to secure herself? So, what do you say, Judy? Tudor? I barely looked at the infant. Does the boy look like his father? Or has she bred a cuckoo in the nest? Well, Tudor?"

"I—"

"How can you hesitate?" Judy said. "The child is the image of his father. To suggest otherwise is ludicrous, Jack. You dislike Nancy. Fine. You have your reasons. But to let this David Ogden talk you into suggesting the poor boy is not exactly who he should be is madness!"

"Is it?" Jack moved his bad leg and winced. The color left his face. She wondered what he was taking for the pain and if that explained his extreme behavior. Not that it really mattered. She had no power over him. All his attention was focused on Tudor. "You were there for months, boy. If anyone could see through her, it must be you. Think. Do you suspect her?"

Tudor looked to her and back to his uncle. Judy's mouth turned down, her lips pressing back her disappointment. His desire to please Jack was not new, and she could hardly fault him for it. She'd never hidden their dependence on Jack, she'd repeatedly told Tudor it was his duty to become a favorite. But at the expense of Nancy, the woman who had nursed him back to health? She held her breath.

"Tudor?" Jack flung his head back in frustration and yelped in pain as his own movement jarred his knee again. "You might answer me. If it was your cousin, Theo Dudley, I'd at least have a straight answer to a straight question."

"Dudley? What has Dudley to do with anything?"

Kate Braithwaite

"Theo Dudley was here this morning." Jack smiled and folded his arms across his chest.

"To what purpose? Other than the obvious." Tudor's tone was sulky.

"I asked him to come. I had some questions for his mother."

"For Anna Dudley?" It was Judy's turn to be surprised. "Whatever could you need to ask that woman about?"

Jack rubbed at his chin. He took a large mouthful of wine and nodded at Tudor to fill a glass for himself. Judy's fingers curled in annoyance.

"Well?" she demanded.

"If you must know, I asked her about Dick's death."

"What? Why?"

"Ogden believes that Nancy's simply biding her time, waiting for her chance to kill Morris and take his money for her son."

"No!"

"No? Would it be so extraordinary?"

"Of course it would! It's disgusting to even speak of such a thing. She may be many things, but Nancy is not a *murderer*." A desire to laugh wormed its way into Judy's stomach. The conversation was ridiculous. Jack had lost his mind. She tried to meet Tudor's eyes, to somehow send him a message that his uncle was perhaps drunk or befuddled by some pain medicine, not himself and not to be listened to, but Jack wasn't finished.

"I thought so at first. But only at first. Two things occurred to me. One, I thought of the child."

"What child? Gouverneur?" Her face creased in a frown.

"No. Nancy's other child. The first one."

It still didn't make sense. "Theo's child was stillborn. One of them must have buried it at Glentivar. And that was long before Anna Dudley ever came to Bizarre so—"

328

"Whose word do we have that it was stillborn?"

His accusation chilled her.

"No one ever spoke of what happened," she said slowly. "You know that. There was only her letter after she left Virginia."

"Exactly!" He smacked the table with the flat of his hand. Wine splashed from his glass. "Think about it. What would she have done if the baby had lived? She certainly wouldn't be Mrs. Morris today, would she? Who else knew the truth but Dick, my honorable, foolishly honorable, brother? And that made me think of Anna Dudley. She was at Bizarre when he died. If Nancy did kill her child and only Dick knew, then getting rid of my brother would be her next logical step. Theo Dudley brought me her answer this morning."

"Then I hope she told you the truth. Dick caught a fever. He battled it for several days. We did everything possible."

Judy found her hand was on her chest, as if to calm the beating of her heart beneath. Nearly twenty years had passed, but memories of the days of Dick's illness were as clear as if it had happened yesterday. It washed over her—the smell of sickness, the color of his skin, the damp bedsheets, the whites of his eyes as he fought the illness, the horrible silence when he took his last breath. She almost didn't hear what Jack said next. She had to repeat the words to herself before the string of sounds formed into meaning.

"Anna Dudley says Nancy gave herbal teas to Dick. She says Nancy could easily have poisoned him."

"No. Absolutely not."

"No? Are you sure, Sister? Really sure? After all, she'd already ruined him. Forcing him to hand himself over to the Cumberland justices and face trial in order to shield her from the charge of infant murder.

You can't say any different. Tucker and Dick planned it all out that way to protect her. She's a witch. A succubus. A—"

"That's enough!" Judy was on her feet. "Anna Dudley is a bitter, scheming harpy who wants nothing more than to tell you what you want to hear and taste a little bit of revenge on myself and Nancy for the way we showed her the door after Dick died. The woman is intolerable, and if you weren't crazed with pain, you wouldn't countenance her tall tales for a moment. Hate Nancy all you want, Jack, but don't make her what she's not. If you carry on in this fashion, we will have to leave. Tudor?"

She lifted her hand, indicating that he should stand. He did not.

Jack lifted the bottle of wine by his hand and poured a generous quantity into Tudor's glass.

"I want to stay here with my uncle," her son said, rubbing his teeth across his lower lip. "There is nothing for me in Virginia, Mother. If you will not take my uncle's comfort and health into account, then I will. Go if you choose. But I wish to remain."

"I don't want to leave you. Not with Jack run half mad."

"I am fully sane, Judy." Jack's tone was disdainful. "You and I both know it. The truth has always been there, but you never wished to see it. I know the truth now about Nancy, about Dick, about Glentivar—all of it. If you choose ignorance, that's not my concern."

Nothing more was said. Judy spent the evening in her room, and the next morning, she set out for Virginia alone. Prayer would be her solace. She thought of her children—Saint, ill, perhaps insane, in an asylum in Philadelphia, and Tudor, weak, influenced by Jack's bitterness, his health her constant concern. She thought of Jack and his accusations against Nancy. And she thought of his last accusation against herself—that she did not wish to see the truth and chose ignorance.

Did she? Judy found herself smiling, the muscles in her cheeks rising unbidden with a lightened sense of relief and realization. Jack's "truth" had nothing to offer her. What he did next—and she was certain he would do something next—did not concern her. She only cared that he would look out for Tudor's health, and surely, she could trust him on that head. As for Nancy? Well, Nancy had Mr. Morris now, and unless she had lied to him, she had nothing to fear from Jack. Judy looked ahead to the end of her journey, to her small rooms filled with the few sticks of furniture she still owned. It was little enough, but it was peaceful. Whatever storm was about to break between Nancy and Jack, she planned to ignore it. He was right about that at least. She'd live without the truth, whatever it was. What Nancy had done or not done. What had happened or not happened at Glentivar. None of it mattered to her anymore. As strongly as she believed in God, Judy chose to believe Nancy's letter, sent after she left Virginia. Theo and Nancy's child had been stillborn. Dick had done his best to rescue her sister's reputation, doing immeasurable damage to his own in the process but deserving the affection Nancy showed for him so obviously. He'd died tragically young, of a fever, and Judy's path in life had been set in hardship from that day. There was no other truth that mattered. Or if there was, she wanted no part of it.

Chapter Thirty-Five

Several days later, Jack arrived back at Morrisania with Tudor in tow. Nancy, busy writing to Mr. Tucker and Lelia, heard the commotion but assumed an unexpected visitor had called for her husband, and her presence was not required. It gave her pleasure to write to her friends and speak positively about her sister, Judy. Over the years, she had poured out her emotions to Mr. Tucker, the act of writing a release valve that saved her sanity. Her frustrations at her dependence on her brothers, her misery during those long years at Bizarre, her financial anxieties and all the snide remarks, barbs and disappointments she'd suffered in the years after Bizarre—Mr. Tucker and Lelia had heard it all. How many times had she promised to write to them of cheerful things, only to relapse into complaints of her loneliness, her fears for the future and the way the past kept its claws in her back? Meeting Mr. Morris had changed all that. Now, she wrote of her son and the new life she'd been blessed with. She wrote about Judy's visit, the good terms on which they had parted and her hopes for Tudor's improved health. She kept her reservations about her nephew's character to herself. Jack didn't merit a mention. Describing his rudeness would only make Mr. Tucker unhappy.

She was surprised, then, to hear a knock at her door and Phebe come to tell her that Mr. Morris requested she attend him and his guests in the parlor. More surprising was the expression of unease on her maid's face.

"What is it? Who called for Mr. Morris?"

"It's Mr. Jack and Mr. Tudor. I don't like their looks, miss."

"Oh?" Nancy found herself nodding. "Then I had better go and see what they want." Various possibilities crossed her mind as she descended the stairs. Money? Perhaps a loan for Tudor to return to his studies? It was clear Harvard was not the place for him. A letter of recommendation then? But why was her presence required? Or was this simply Jack acting as if nothing had happened? It wouldn't be the first time. The man was a chameleon. And shameless. She stiffened her spine at the door and walked inside. Silence greeted her.

The parlor was one of Nancy's favorite rooms at Morrisania. This was where she'd first imagined a future for herself and Mr. Morris, gaining confidence in his regard and trust that his intentions were honorable. He had kissed her first in this room, over by the fireplace when they had both leaped up from their books to catch a burning ember that had fallen on the rug. Nancy, more nimble, had reached it first, wetted her fingers and thrown the splinter of smoldering wood back onto the fire. She'd straightened and found him beside her. He took her hand, kissed her fingers then bent and found her lips. All her recent happiness began in that moment. It was here she told him they were to have a child and saw his eyes fill with happy tears. She remembered how his hand stroked her cheek, how she relaxed into the strength he offered.

Now, he sat by the same fireplace. He smiled as she entered, but his expression was grave. Tudor stood at the window and did not look her way. Jack sat opposite Mr. Morris, leaning back with his legs stretched out, looking for all the world as if this was his own armchair at Roanoke. He did not get up.

"My dear," Mr. Morris said. "Thank you for joining us. Tudor, please bring that chair across for your aunt. And one for yourself."

She watched as Tudor brought her a chair. He didn't raise his eyes to her face and retreated to the window without joining them. Mr. Morris's eyebrows twitched, but he said nothing.

"How are you, Jack?" Nancy asked.

"Limited in my mobility." He patted a stick by his side, and she saw one of his legs was padded above his boots. "Riding accident. On the mend now."

"I'm surprised to see you return to us so soon. I hope all is well. The family?"

"All well."

"Then?" She looked from Jack to her husband and back again.

"Mr. Randolph has had much to say to me this morning, my dear," said Mr. Morris. "To the point where I asked him if he was prepared to repeat his remarks to your face. To be honest, I'm surprised he agreed to do so, but I hope you'll hear him out, as I have. Although if you'd rather I just threw him out the door, I'd be happy to oblige."

She caught the brighter note in his voice and was strengthened by it. "If you would have me listen, husband, then I will do so."

"Very well then, Jack," he said. "If you might re-state your case?"

She waited as Jack rubbed his lips over his teeth and she knew his mind was busy calculating how best to proceed. "Jack?" she said. "It's not like you to be lost for words."

His eyes snapped to hers. Then he nodded, raised his hands and slowly clapped. "I am impressed, madam, as impressed as I have ever been with your contrivances."

"Contrivances?"

"You certainly have this fool fooled." He gestured at her husband.

"Mr. Morris?" she asked.

"A fool is nothing to what he calls you, my dear. Brace yourself."

She nodded. "Do go on, Jack."

"I shall, Mrs. Morris. I shall. Although your husband is too bewitched to realize it, I'm here for his benefit. I am come to impress upon your mind your duty to your husband, to rouse some dormant spark of virtue in you, if any ever existed. I come to wake your conscience or, failing that, Mr. Morris's consciousness of the danger posed to him by the woman he calls 'wife'."

"You consider me *dangerous*?"

"Are you not?" His tone sharpened, and he leaned forward. "Are. You. Not?"

"Of course I'm not! For goodness' sake, Jack, we've had our differences in the past, but this way of speaking is irresponsible. I hope you have not spoken in such a way of me in New York—"

She broke off as Jack's eyes flicked across to Tudor at the window. "Oh. I see you have."

"Not a bit," said Jack. "They came to me."

"They?" Mr. Morris's eyebrows were raised. "I imagine you mean some relative of mine. They're a disgruntled lot. Let me guess. David Ogden? My nephew has a love for my money and blames my wife for his diminishing expectations. No one takes him seriously."

"No?" Jack's lips puckered. He was annoyed, Nancy saw, and she wasn't sure Jack losing his temper was something she wanted her husband to experience. Mr. Morris appeared relaxed, but appearances could be deceiving.

"Why don't you tell me what you think I've done?" she said.

"It's what you have not yet done that concerns me and ought to concern your husband. I came to give him fair warning."

"Of what?"

"I believe it my duty to ensure that he knows what kind of woman he has married. And at what peril he continues living here with you."

She started laughing. "Are you sure you didn't hurt your head rather than your knee in your recent accident? Mr. Morris in peril? You've lost your wits, Jack Randolph. I love my husband and have never been happier in my life. Tudor must surely bear witness to that."

"Tudor has had much to say about his stay here, madam, and none of it favorable."

"Really?" She turned to her nephew, laughter forgotten, but Tudor kept his back to them, staring out of the window. In shame, she hoped.

"But first, let us consider your character and history. Mr. Morris tells me he wrote to Chief Justice John Marshall before he married you."

"I'm well aware of it."

"I'm sure you are. For a woman with your inveterate disregard for the truth, it was an obvious step. You told Mr. Morris of your innocence and knew Marshall, having presided over the proceedings against Dick and knowing nothing of your life before or since, would give the only response open to him—that Dick had been found innocent of all charges."

"Which he was!"

"Only because of your lies!"

"Jack! Your brother was the finest—"

"Do not speak of him! I have your own letter to Judy, written after you left Virginia, describing your disgusting manipulation of both of my brothers." Jack's face was pale, his nostrils pinched. "In October 'ninety-two you were delivered of a child. You imposed upon Dick, told him the secret of your pregnancy, put into his hands its dead body and begged him to consign it to an unmarked grave. His own dead brother's child. My dead brother Theo's child. The child of a man reduced to a mere skeleton by the time you must have lain with him. Do you ever think how close you and Dick were to the gibbet? Believe me, I do. Had Randy Harrison looked at that pile of shingles earlier, what evidence might he have found? Might we have seen my nephews' father and their aunt found guilty of murder?"

"I have nothing to say to you."

"You don't defend yourself? What must your husband make of that?"

"My husband knows what happened."

"Does he though? What is the truth to a woman like you?"

She felt her face redden and her muscles tense. She longed to look at Mr. Morris but feared showing weakness.

"You lied to everyone," Jack continued. "Your own sister had no idea of your pregnancy. As soon as you admitted the truth in your letter, we all knew what you were. Saint, Tudor, Judy and I—"

"You showed the boys that letter?" She counted back rapidly. "When Tudor was what? Eleven years old? You talked to him of this?"

Jack ignored her. "Your lies won you the support of my stepfather. He and my poor brother protected you. Only Dick knew what really happened to the child you claim was stillborn."

Claim? Images flashed across Nancy's mind. Dick's face contorted by sorrow. Phebe's eyes. Patsy, at the trial, talking of gum guaiacum. A tiny bundle whisked away.

"What are you saying, Jack?"

"I'm saying he was the only person that knew the truth. My brother, Dick. Dick, who three years later was dead, suddenly dead, when I was far from home."

"You can't possibly think—"

"I can and do think it! I have been in correspondence with Anna Dudley. She tells me you dosed my brother with something. How quickly was Anna driven from the house after Dick died? Why might that be? Because she knew what you had done!"

"No!" She jumped to her feet, fists clenched, but nothing was going to stop Jack now.

"You poisoned my brother to stop him revealing the truth. Then you tormented your sister and me with your presence for ten miserable years! You liaised with that slave boy—your dear Billy Ellis. I uncovered your intimacy, demanded you leave, and you thereafter lived the life of a common drab. Where did I find you in Richmond? Living in the pleasure garden, no less. Oh, you found your level there."

"Are you done, sir?" she asked.

"Nearly so. I came back here to lay out the truth to your husband. When I first heard he had taken you on as his housekeeper, I was glad of it. I thought him a man of the world, beyond the snare of female blandishments. I never dreamed he would *marry* you. How could I leave him here, in ignorance, a prisoner under your command?"

"You think he's my prisoner?"

"Why not? You, madam, are a vampire. You sucked the best blood of my family, only to flit off to the north and sink your teeth into an infirm old man. When you find yourself with cramps in your stomach, Mr. Morris, I hope you'll acknowledge that, if nothing else, you were

338

warned." He turned his gaze back to Nancy. "What is to stop you finishing him off as you did my brother?"

"I did nothing of the kind! But you ask what's to stop me now? Well, sir, beyond the love I have for my husband, there is the small matter of our son."

"Tudor says you care nothing for the boy."

She shook her head. "The only poison in our family, Jack, has been dripped in the ear of my nephew. To accuse me of neglect of my son is to court ridicule. My love and indulgence of the child are well known. If anything, I am said to love the boy too much, not too little."

"As well you might. He's your guarantee of future comfort, is he not? But given your reputation, I hardly wonder at the suspicions held by some in Mr. Morris's family."

"You have said more than enough on that head, Jack Randolph," said Mr. Morris. "I will not entertain such foul talk in my house. Indeed, I think it long past time you took your leave."

Jack pursed his lips. "I knew how it would be. You are bewitched, sir."

"You knew how it would be, and yet you came here anyway? Well, you have said your piece. I would like to say mine. What say you, sir?" Nancy asked her husband. "Shall I answer these charges?"

"Only if you wish to do so, my dear."

"I do. How many days ago was it that you first arrived here, Jack Randolph?" When he didn't reply she answered for him. "Less than a week. I think we can all recall the scene. It was heart-warming. You embraced me. Kissed me. Called me family. What has changed between then and now?"

"Your lewdness, madam—"

"What *lewdness*? This last week? Here? At Morrisania? One

moment you accuse me of keeping my husband a prisoner, the next of conducting lewd amours. Who with? When? For months I have been here, in my home, caring for our nephew. Ask him. That he stands at the window now, unable, you will note, to look me in the eye, is a testament to my nursing. What have you offered him, Jack, to come here and support your lies and accusations? Money, I'd imagine. Funds for a trip abroad?" She caught Jack's eyes sliding to the window and knew she was right. "And you, Tudor, accused me of self-advancement and selling myself for my husband's wealth. So easy, isn't it, to imagine one's own faults in other people." She fixed her gaze on Jack, a sense of calm washing over her. "It seems to me that your care of your nephew over there is somewhat haphazard. What possessed you?"

"What do you mean?"

"I mean leaving him in the care of a woman such as myself. Think how you have characterized me, here in this room today and to heaven knows who else in New York City. And yet you permitted your precious Tudor to be fed from my bounty and nursed by me for months. A woman you now call a common prostitute, the murderess of her own child and of your brother?

"You should be ashamed, Jack Randolph. Think of the ways you have spoken of your brothers today, brothers you profess to love, while slandering them by implication. You knew I loved your brother, Theo. You knew it because Dick told you himself of our engagement when I complained to him of the letter you wrote me. Did you tell Tudor *that* when you chose to share with him—with a child—the honest words I wrote to Judy after I left Virginia? Did you tell him that had your family's land been less hampered by debt, I would have been Theo's wife long before his death? My father wouldn't let me marry him, but he left me there, aged seventeen, at Bizarre with the man I loved. Dick understood. He was a man of honor. Your accusations against me are an insult to his memory. By charging me with these crimes, you charge him as my accomplice. What do you do to your brother's reputation when you talk of crimes and gibbets?

"In the presence of John Marshall, your brother and I were subject to the severest scrutiny. Dick was acquitted, and rightly so. But now, you revive events from over twenty years ago. You spread the story of your family's descent into scandal for what—to please David Ogden? Or because you cannot tolerate the knowledge of my happiness? You repay our kindness to Tudor by trying to divide us and blast the prospects of my innocent boy. Your conduct is shameful. Dick would be ashamed to hear you. I thank God Judy is not here to witness her son's poor conduct. Why, I received a letter from her only this morning …" Nancy broke off, recalling the letter and reappraising its contents, in the light of Jack and Tudor's visit. "My God, she knew what you were up to, didn't she?"

Jack shrugged, but Nancy was on her feet. "I will fetch the letter at once." She flew to her room and back to the parlor, brushing past Phebe in the doorway. It appeared no one had moved or spoken. Good.

"Here." She ran her finger down the page of Judy's tight script. "She says she cannot accept our invitation to spend the winter here with us but insists that she is proud of the honor we confer on her with the invitation. She writes, '*let nothing persuade you I am less than fully grateful for your kindness to myself and my son.*' I know my sister, Jack. She means she will not stand behind you in this slander. Her confidence in me betrays your lies. What kind of woman would be proud of the honor of being invited to spend a winter with the concubine of one of her slaves, after all?" She glared at him. "You are a fool, Jack Randolph. Billy Ellis wanted to marry my woman, Phebe. But you, wrapped up in your madness and envy or whatever it is that drives you, only saw what you wanted to see—a way to shame me and cast me from my home of fifteen years. Does it torment you that in doing so, you set me on the path that brought me here? I suspect it does."

Jack said nothing. Had she bested him? Finally silenced him? It seemed Mr. Morris thought so.

He rose and stared down at their guest. "You have been heard, Mr. Randolph, and treated more civilly than you deserve. I think now, however, it is past time you took your leave."

"Very well." Jack struggled to his feet. She was glad to see him wince in pain. He didn't look at her again but smiled ruefully at Mr. Morris. "I am sorry to see another man in her power, but not surprised."

It was a weak jibe, but she expected nothing less. He might be beaten, but Jack wasn't one to admit defeat. As Mr. Morris moved toward him, Nancy had the pleasure of seeing the younger man flinch. He had ridden here in a temper, determined to have his say. And now, so had she.

She turned to her nephew. Jack's hatred wasn't new. It was Tudor whose part in this hurt. Hearing he had lied about her was a fresh wound. His mother would burn with shame. His father would have whipped him, she thought. Her hand went to her neck where Dick's ring had hung for so many years. Tudor's face was expressionless as he stalked past her. She couldn't hold her tongue.

"I am sorry neither your father nor older brother are here today, Tudor. They might have shamed you into better conduct."

"My brother?" Tudor turned, frowning. "My brother is in an asylum, suspected of burning down our mother's house. If we are to talk of shame, then Saint outstrips me easily."

"You may choose to think so, nephew, but he is twice the man you are, or will ever be."

His mouth formed an ugly smile, but she saw doubt flicker in his eyes. It was a small victory, yet she relished it. As for Jack? Nancy watched him hobble from the room and stifled a desire to hook a foot around his good leg and watch him crash upon the floor. John Randolph of Roanoke they called him now. Beneath all his success and notoriety, he was still the same strange, unhappy boy he had always been.

When the doors of Morrisania closed on Tudor and Jack, Nancy reached for her husband, laid her head on his chest and sobbed. His hand on her back was a comfort, his solid chest a rock of reassurance.

"Will they spread this talk of me throughout New York City?"

"I rather think they have already done so."

"I'm so sorry," she whispered. "And we have been so happy."

He pulled back at that, gripping her shoulders. "We still are."

"Are you sure?"

"Certainly. There's nothing they can say or do to touch us, Nancy. They have words and accusations, but we have the truth. Do we not?"

Was there an edge to his voice? Did he doubt her honesty? Was it impossible, ever, to be free of her past? His face was full of nothing but love and kindness. She stared into his eyes. With the practice of years of concealment, of promises made and promises kept, she answered him. "Yes. You are right. I told you the truth of it long ago, and no one can come between us."

He held her gaze, and she returned it with intensity, fearing he saw right through her, had always seen through her, and knew, or suspected, the truth she would not speak.

But he only pulled her to his chest again and kissed her forehead. "All will be well," he murmured. "Come what may."

Phebe

She heard it all, standing, invisible, by the parlor door. The master took it well enough, watching Jack Randolph like a child studying a firefly trapped in glass, curious, but nothing more. Tudor, as sly a boy as ever lived, fairly jangled with discomfort, and so he should, the ungrateful dog. But mostly, Phebe watched her mistress and pitied her, forced to listen to Jack's torrent of words and be dragged back to their dark days at Bizarre and Glentivar.

When Jack finally saw his poison darts failing to land and took his leave with Tudor, Phebe slipped away to her own room.

She had remained with her mistress because she wanted to. When Miss Nancy bore a healthy child, she knew she'd been right in staying. The horrors of Mae's death, of Bizarre and Glentivar, receded. And then there was the surprising truth—Morrisania felt like it might be home. There was no way back to Tuckahoe and the remains of her family. Whereas here? Here was the cook, Martha's, tall son, Isaac, returned home after losing his wife to the fever in Philadelphia. Isaac never said much, always a quiet boy his mama said, but something in his rare smiles drew Phebe toward him—no, she'd no wish to leave Morrisania.

And so she hesitated. It was never her place to interfere. But Miss Nancy's face when Jack Randolph said she'd killed his brother because Dick knew what she done to her child? She couldn't unsee it. What had Miss Nancy said about having a child with Mr. Morris? That God would not permit it? And yet he had. For years, Phebe watched her mistress struggle with her guilt. It was time, past time, for a proper talk about what happened, and if Miss Nancy didn't like her speaking up, well, then Phebe would live with the consequences somehow. She might be on the road by nightfall. Maids were easily dismissed. Miss Nancy wouldn't even have the trouble of trying to sell her. Old Cilla, rest her soul, might have had some words to say about that. But it was Cilla who told her to look after Miss Nancy. Whatever the risks, Phebe knew what she had to go and say.

She found her deadheading roses. Some things never changed. Hadn't they both always sought peace of mind in fresh air and hard work?

"I heard Mr. Jack," Phebe said. "Heard every word. And what he said, it was alls wrong. Dead wrong." Miss Nancy didn't stop cutting. "He was wrong years back about Billy Ellis, and he's wrong about how Mr. Randolph died." The only sound was the scrape of the knife against the rose stems. "He was wrong about that baby too, Miss Nancy. You didn't do nothing bad. It weren't your fault. I knows it. I was there."

Now, the mistress put down her tools, wiped her brow. "You were not at the trial."

"What do you mean?"

"I wished the child away, Phebe. You know I did. I prayed to lose it. Imagine. Praying to lose a child. What kind of a woman was I? Am I?"

"Wishing is not doing, Miss Nancy. Ain't nothing like doing. You was a young girl. Afraid."

"I thought so too at first. Felt sorry for myself. Pitied myself. But at the trial, I understood it. What I'd done."

"You is making no sense. What they say at that trial?"

"The gum guaiacum. Do you remember it?"

"Course I do. Sent by Miss Patsy. Never helped none, far as I could see."

Miss Nancy gave a strangled laugh. "How old were you, Phebe? Fifteen? How old was I? Young, it's true, but not so young I couldn't have listened. Patsy and Judy talked about how gum guaiacum could harm a baby and make a woman's courses come. I was right there. Why didn't I listen? Instead, I took it. I took it, Phebe, and I killed my own child."

"No!" She took hold of Miss Nancy by her shoulders and looked her right in the eye. "No." She saw hesitation in her mistress's eyes and spoke quickly. "I remember it all, Miss Nancy. I can see you and the child you bore, clear as I see you now. Your baby was born alive."

"But the blood, Phebe." Miss Nancy's voice was a whisper. "I remember the blood."

"The blood was after. Not before. Only after, I'm telling you. I swear it. It wasn't your fault. The girl was alive and healthy looking. Mr. Randolph took her from your arms and said you needed to rest."

"What happened to her then?"

"I—I don't know."

Two weeks later, Phebe was on the road to Virginia. People might think little of it in New York, but as the Morrises' carriage rolled south, Phebe wondered how many folks seeing a Black woman riding in such comfort would think they'd dreamed her. She lifted her chin. She was a free woman, traveling to see a free man living near Farmville, Virginia, there on her mistress's business. Knowing it didn't fully settle the nerves a-jangling in her middle, but the papers in her purse surely helped. When Phebe offered to seek out Syphax and see if he'd answer her questions, she never imagined traveling in such comfort and style. Mr. Morris believed Phebe was needed by family. It didn't seem right, lying, in order to go searching for the truth, but what Miss Nancy said to her husband weren't no one's business. Phebe thought of nothing but finding the old man alive and persuading him to talk.

During her recent visit, Mrs. Randolph told the Morrises about her efforts to fulfill her husband's wishes and free the slaved men and women at Bizarre. Phebe only heard the bones of it from Miss Nancy, but it was clear their best hope lay south of the Appomattox, on a tract of land Mrs. Randolph leased to freed families in separate plots from twenty to fifty acres in size. Surely, Syphax, steadfastly loyal to the man who had promised his freedom, would be found there, if he was to be found at all?

And so it proved. Syphax was well known in the area. Her driver obtained directions to his home on his first inquiry. To Phebe's amazement, they drove through ordered parcels of land, worked and maintained by free Black men and women. No overseer in sight.

Syphax, resting in his familiar rocking chair on the porch of a wooden home—modest, but solid and nothing like his slave cabin on the plantation across the river—lifted her heart to gladness. He was older, of course. His hair was full white; he was slow out of his chair. More dependent on his cane than she remembered, but he knew her. His smile was wide, his welcome generous. Family spilled from the home behind him. A wife—a surprise—and three children who peppered Phebe with questions about her carriage, her horse and fine clothes.

"We heard Miss Nancy was married now," Syphax said when the children disappeared back inside and Phebe was settled in the chair next to him. "You lives in a fancy house now, I'm thinking."

"You might say so. I has my own room. A feather mattress."

He whistled. "Mighty fine. Mighty fine. Has me wondering what brings you back to these parts, looking for Syphax. Surprised you even remember me, in this fine new life of yours."

"You were kind to me. When no one else was. I remember that."

"I'd soon as been unkind to a kitten. You were little more than a child. Timid. Not so timid now, I'm thinking."

"No reason now, Syphax. I'm as free as you, but still loyal to Miss Nancy. As loyal as you ever were to Mr. Randolph, I'd say."

He nodded. "And not here for no reason either, I's guessing. Let's hear it, Miss Phebe. What you need to visit Syphax for? Hmm?"

She had thought to come at it slowly, to get him talking about the old days and set him at ease. How foolish. Syphax always spoke plain. She needed to do the same.

"Miss Nancy and Mr. Randolph's baby. I came to ask you about it."

His eyebrows rose. "That's more than twenty years ago." He scratched his head. "You wants to know about the child? But you knows already. That child died."

"Did it? Came out alive and well. I saw that with my own eyes. Only your word and Mr. Randolph's the baby died. Mr. Randolph had that child out of the room and out of sight in a minute. I never set eyes on it one moment more. My mistress blames herself."

Syphax stared, his eyes clouding with displeasure. Her mouth went dry, but she held his gaze.

"What you saying, Phebe? Think careful 'fore you answer."

When she was younger, his heavy tone would have silenced her. But she was a grown woman now. "I heard you and Mr. Randolph talking. Heard you say you'd a place for the child, but only if it were a boy. And then there was the overseer, Johnson, and Rachel, his woman. They left Bizarre around that time. Heard she had a child so pale, it looked full White. And so I'm asking. Was that Miss Nancy's child?"

A slow smile spread across Syphax's face. "You *has* grown bold, I'll give you that." He tilted his head and considered her. Then lifted his cane and twisted around till he could knock on the door behind him with it. The oldest of his children appeared in seconds.

"Hercules," he said. "Bring me a fresh tumbler of water and some for my visitor. Seems we got some talking to do."

Chapter Thirty-Six

Philadelphia, one year later

"Your brother is dead."

Judy enunciated carefully, feeling the push of her tongue against her teeth, the air slip and slide between her lips.

How?

He wrote the question down, a scrawl with a stick of graphite he was only allowed to use when someone was in the room with him. She tried not to think about that.

"Consumption. In England."

England had brought her boys no good. Saint returned thinking he could run a plantation. He'd been expectant, hopeful. He should never have left Virginia. Tudor begged to go overseas, and Jack let him. Now, Tudor had died there, leaving Judy with no body to bury or funeral to plan. She had received a letter describing his illness, a box containing his clothes and a sheaf of debtors' notes.

Sorry.

351

Saint scribbled the word and stretched out his hands. His room was small and dark. A puddle of blankets lay on the pallet bed under the window. She suspected the chairs and the small table they sat at had been brought in for the occasion. It was as austere as a monk's cell. As he walked her to Saint's door, the warden said her son was quiet, and she had stifled a sarcastic retort. Peaceful was another word he used to describe him. She liked that more.

She leaned across the table to touch his hands but hesitated and pulled back.

"How are you?"

Well.

"What do you do here?" She hadn't meant to ask such a question, but the thought of him spending hours alone, lying on that bed with only the ceiling to stare at tormented her. He scribbled.

I walk. I talk with the doctor. I taught him to sign.

She glimpsed a ripple of pride in his face at that. Something of his younger self. He wrote some more.

I read.

Saint gestured at his bed, and she saw that underneath, there were stacks of volumes.

"They give you books?"

He wrote again. *Nancy.*

"My sister sends you these?"

He nodded.

She looked down at her hands for a moment, contemplating what she had come to suggest. "I could learn to sign. If you came home with me." She watched his expression as he read her lips. He didn't write his reply.

"No."

She hadn't heard his voice in so long, but it still shocked her with its deep, guttural intensity. He snatched up the pencil again.

Have no home.

Judy bit her lip, disappointment and anger jostling her thoughts. "Think about it. If you change your mind, write to me."

He nodded, but she knew he never would.

The journey back to Virginia sapped her strength. She replayed the visit time and again, thinking of other things she might have said, wondering if she could have changed his mind. She wanted her son to come home. From the moment the letter telling her of Tudor's death fell from her fingers, she longed for her older child. His "treatment" in Philadelphia had been arranged by Jack. That thought had consumed her. Jack arranged for Tudor to go to England and now he was dead. He had come between her and her children—it could not continue. But when she saw Saint, older, thinner, calmer and yes, more peaceful, than he had been in years, her hope wilted. She had lost him long ago. A deep well of despair opened in her chest.

At length, she arrived back in Farmville and her rented rooms, only a mile or so from where Bizarre had stood. She closed the door to the second bedroom, the room she had planned for her sons to stay in, sons who could not, or would not, come. Tudor would have no wife. There would be no grandchildren. She'd never feel the strength of his fingers on her shoulder again, never hear his voice.

Her days drifted. The weights that throughout her life had kept her hair pinned to the pillow and her bones too heavy to lift from the mattress in the morning returned with a vengeance. She spent hours praying and often forgot to eat. Misery was the only dish she needed, and she feasted on it without remission. She prayed for death.

On a dull day in October, Judy took a walk out to Bizarre in the pouring rain. Water saturated her bonnet, plastered her hair to her head, clamped her clothes to her skin. She stared at the ruin and tried to bring Dick's face to mind, but she couldn't see him. Happy memories, if she had any, were too deeply hidden, or she was too lost to find them. She walked home, let herself in and sat in her wet clothes by an unlit fire until the sun set. At some point, she roused herself, lit a candle and wrote a letter to her sister Nancy. She asked to be buried at Tuckahoe.

And then she prayed.

Nancy had not been to Tuckahoe in years, had not set foot in Virginia since she left Richmond, and it was only with written assurance from Tom and Patsy that Jack Randolph would not be present that Nancy agreed to attend her sister's funeral. He'd done his damnedest to smear her after their confrontation the year before. This would be a test of his success.

Tuckahoe was much as she remembered it from her youth, more than in those strange days she and Phebe had spent there when she first left Bizarre. Every room was crowded. There were Randolphs everywhere, familiar faces, changed by age, and new, lively voices, the next generation, milling around from room to room and up and down the great mahogany staircases as she had done so light-heartedly as a child.

"We should bring Gouverneur here when he is older," her husband said. Her arm was firmly tucked in his, an acknowledgment of her nervousness at meeting with so many of her family at once. After hearing the news of Judy's death, Nancy visited Saint in Philadelphia. They shed tears together. But he refused to come with her and Mr. Morris to Tuckahoe, and now, Nancy was glad of it. Saint did not need to be a spectacle for anyone; he was safe where he was and had the sense to know it. Just at this moment, she thought a small, quiet room with enough light to read a book by had a great deal of appeal, but her sister's last request was a burial here, with her family in attendance. Nancy had spent ten years at Bizarre, doing Judy's bidding in a desperate, silent effort at restitution. She did not stop now.

Introductions were the order of the day. Since her marriage, Nancy had corresponded with most of the family now gathered at their old family home, but she and Mr. Morris had avoided the ritual post-wedding tour of relations, choosing to center their lives in New York and Washington. At least he knew Tom and Patsy.

Tom, nowadays, looked strangely like their father, with the same fine hair, the same coloring, the same elongated face that suggested a somber cast of mind. Patsy had aged, as they all had, but still held her head high, a woman confident of her place and importance. They greeted Nancy and her husband with great cordiality and friendliness. Those cold days after Dick's trial were a distant memory, and she was glad that Jack's attempts to raise the ghosts of the past appeared to have fallen on stony ground. Any resentment she'd harbored after they refused to take her in when she left Bizarre was long forgotten. Richmond and Newport were the trials that had led her to Fairfield and Morrisania, after all.

William was there, suffering from a bad back and much thinner on top than he had been the last time they met. How strange to observe all these signs of aging in family she once knew so well. Molly nodded but kept her distance with her odious husband standing stiffly at her side. Lizzie embraced her, smelling of lavender and oranges, her face plump and hearty, rather at odds with the sad nature of the occasion. Gabriella made a great fuss of Mr. Morris, thrusting forward her son for his approval. Nancy was glad to see the second Thomas Mann Randolph favored his mother rather than their father. She smiled at him, though, for he was only young, and the fault of his birth in her siblings' eyes was something she viewed rather less harshly since the birth of her own son.

Randy and Mary Harrison had barely changed, and Mary, one of Judy's closest friends, struggled to keep her emotions in check. Her cheeks and eyes were pink, and she twisted a handkerchief in her hands. Maria Peyton saw Nancy and moved swiftly in a different direction. As she talked with her younger siblings, Nancy wondered who the portly, red-faced man standing with Mary Harrison might be until, in the tip of his head to empty his glass, Nancy recognized Archie Randolph. Her hand tightened on Mr. Morris's arm. She'd been right not to take Archie, although her life might have been far easier had she done so.

One person she was happy not to find in attendance was Aunt Page. A quiet inquiry with Lizzie confirmed that their mother's sister was unwell and had sent her regrets at missing seeing her niece put to rest. Nancy was glad. A forgiving nature was all well and good, but it would take a better woman than she to forgive her aunt's damning testimony at the Cumberland courthouse. That she had told the truth, that Nancy *had* been pregnant, although so vehement in her denials that she had almost convinced herself of her own lie, did not change her sense of betrayal.

Nancy saw Mr. Tucker, alone by a window in Tuckahoe's Great Hall, and made her way over.

"I saw you stand like this at my mother's funeral. And never forgot the words of comfort you gave me."

His face, thinner, more lined but essentially the same, glowed with pleasure. "What did I say to you, Nancy? Might my wisdom have some value again today?"

"You said the pain would blunt in time. And it did. Although, when I look back now, I see that we lost a great deal when we lost our mother."

"You all did. Perhaps you and Judy particularly."

"Is that why you have always been so good to me? Writing cheerful letters, listening to my woes and concerns?"

"I treated you for what you were—one of my family. Although I fear I did a better job for you than for your poor sister. You both have borne unhappiness. I wish I might have seen a way to ease hers better than I did."

"At least you were not the cause of it. I wish I could say the same." He took her hands and squeezed them. Tears threatened. "Losing someone who has always been there is hard," she said quietly. "Even when we loathed each other, we were always *there*. I can't believe she's gone. I imagine I'll go home, and then one day, perhaps in a month or so, Judy will write that you've forced your carriage upon her, and she's packing to come to Morrisania again so she can see how Gouverneur is grown. But she will not. She is gone, and Tudor is gone, and Saint is happier away from family than with us. She and I will never talk again, and I'll never know if she forgave me, really forgave me, for what happened to us."

"Now, now." Mr. Tucker's voice was low, and his warm, fatherly hands still cradled hers. "Judy made peace with what happened long ago, don't you think? You wrote me so yourself after her visit and Tudor's illness. You don't want to believe me, but listen to your own words. What happened to *us*, that's what you just said. What happened at Bizarre and Glentivar happened to you too, Nancy. You were always a victim, to my understanding, and my son, Dick—"

"Theo," she whispered. "It was Theo."

He looked sadly into her eyes. "Dick or Theo," he said with slow deliberation, "it is all one to me. The person that needs to forgive you, Nancy, is not Judy. It is yourself."

"But how can I?"

"Talk to your husband, Nancy. *Really* talk to him. Morris is a sensible man, and he'll listen."

"I'm not sure I can."

"Find a way."

Chapter Thirty-Seven

In truth, she had resolved on it as soon as she'd read her sister's last letter. It was what she must do. Nancy insisted Phebe accompany her and Mr. Morris to Tuckahoe. They would continue across Virginia and go to Bizarre.

Mr. Morris, apprised of this new plan following Judy's interment, cast his wife a quizzical glance but complied with typical grace and good humor. They said their farewells to the family at Tuckahoe and drove off in silence. The weather was fine, and Phebe sat up with the driver. Mr. Morris claimed tiredness and closed his eyes, leaving Nancy to stare out at the familiar Virginia landscape, trying to reconcile her memories of her life there with the person she'd become.

The hours passed. As they drove through the familiar close line of trees that led to the house, Nancy visualized Bizarre as it had been, a mistake it turned out, as the contrast with the reality of what she found there took her breath away.

The house was gone. Where walls had stood, now there was nothing but air and a view of the other plantation buildings—kitchen, smokehouse and stables—all dilapidated and disused. The foundations of Bizarre remained, a blackened mess of charred wood and rubble, although nature was at work, and green shoots gathered where the parlor had once stood. She and Mr. Morris circled the ruin. She pointed out where the porch had been, the back door, her bedroom window, and he nodded, letting her take her time and absorb the changes. The kitchen garden brought her close to tears. The fence had fallen in, battered by weather or weighted down by the rampant weeds and tall grasses overrunning the old pathways between her lovingly tended vegetable beds.

Mr. Morris came and stood beside her. "Dearest. Why are we here?"

"I need to see one more thing. I'd like you to be there when I do. Only Phebe knows where." She saw him frown a little and touched her hand to his face. "It won't take long."

She beckoned to Phebe, who had wandered toward the old slave quarters, also now abandoned. "Can you show us now?"

Phebe nodded. "It's this way."

Nancy stretched out her hand to Mr. Morris, and they followed Phebe away from the ruined house and toward a line of trees to the south.

"This was a tobacco field," Nancy said, pointing to her left. "I'm surprised John Randolph of Roanoke has not maintained the land. Or am I?" She rolled her eyes and enjoyed her husband's smile.

"I thought we agreed never to speak of that infernal creature."

"We did. But it's hard not to think of him when I'm here. And not all my memories of Bizarre are unhappy."

"Where is Phebe taking us?"

"To my first child's grave. I've never seen it."

He stopped and stared. "I thought the child died at Glentivar."

360

She shook her head. "No. It happened here. Come. Let me pay my respects, and then I will explain."

They did not have far to walk. At a break in the trees, Phebe turned into a wooded area and stopped before a large white pine. She bent to examine its bark and with one finger, traced the outline of a cross.

"She's here."

She. "The baby" was how Nancy thought of her, never as *she* or *her*, afraid to open the door to thoughts of the little girl she never became. Her first child. Her lost daughter. Having Gouverneur sharpened her grief.

"Thank you." Nancy bowed her head. She had lost a child. Blamed herself. Known a late hope for her survival. Now this. A sense of ending. She took a minute to let some of the sadness unfurl and then turned to her husband.

"There are things I must tell you."

He nodded.

"She was born here in 1792, on September thirtieth. We were due to travel to Glentivar the next day. Judy knew nothing of it." Nancy sighed deeply. "She was only alive for a few minutes. I believed ... for the longest time, I thought I'd killed her. I'd wished her away so often, you see, that terrible summer. Taken gum guaiacum so carelessly. But Phebe learned it was an accident. Dick's slave, Syphax, brought her body here. I had never asked what happened. I was so certain it was my fault. It's only thanks to Phebe that we stand here now."

"But at Glentivar?"

"Judy insisted we all went. We'd sworn she would not find out. I had been carrying on for months that I was sick. I thought if I didn't go to Glentivar, she might suspect me. I thought if I could just tolerate the journey, then I'd claim an attack of the colic and retire to my bed. That's what I did. But then I bled. The afterbirth, Phebe said, it had not all come away. She was only young. We were both little more than children." Nancy put her hands to her face. "I nearly died at Glentivar. Phebe saved me. She found herbs to stop the bleeding. Begged one of Randy's slave women for new sheets. Dick took the bloody ones out and left them for the woman to clean them or burn them. He left them on a shingle pile—evidence enough to almost ruin us both. My God, we tried so hard to hide it all. And yet it followed me. It haunts me."

"It's over, Nancy. No one of real importance has listened to Jack. He hasn't come between us. We have our own son now—"

"But I haven't told you everything. I've never been entirely honest." She stared at the hollow in the tree, trying to find the courage to continue. Judy would have prayed for strength. Nancy could not.

"I think I already know," he said softly. "Do you remember the book? *The Power of Sympathy*?"

She turned her eyes up to him. "You *know*?"

"I told you about my Boston poet, Sarah Morton, did I not? It was her sister and husband's story you read in the novel. Sarah's husband seduced her sister. It was years later, when she and I were lovers, but Sarah talked of her sister often. She didn't blame her. Her suicide was the greatest sorrow of Sarah's life. I wanted you to know that nothing you could tell me would shock me. I have never sought to judge you."

"Judy would have judged me most harshly."

"She may not have."

Somehow, Nancy found a smile. "Oh, I think we can be fairly certain. It was a terrible betrayal."

"Did you love him?"

362

"Dick? Yes. Very much."

"And Theo?"

"Never. I suppose there were moments I thought I might have married him. We were thrown together. Children playing as adults. Far away from anxious eyes." She frowned. "No. It sounds like I'm making excuses. There are none. What I did to my sister was unforgivable. I spent years trying to make it up to her." Her voice cracked on a sudden wave of grief. "Do you—do you think she knew it?"

"No." His voice was solid, dependable, full of certainty.

"We promised each other she would never know, Dick and I. There was only unkindness in the truth. Only more pain and sorrow. I wanted to admit it was Theo from the first. I wrote a letter confessing to carrying Theo's child, but Dick tore it up. He said it was better to deny it all. He said Judy and the boys must never know the truth. I even lied to you about it. I'm sorry for that."

"You've told me now," he said, pulling her to his chest. "For what it is worth, I think telling Judy the truth would have done no good and much harm. The truth is overrated, Nancy dear, if it hurts and cannot heal."

"She did suspect us. There was a ring he gave me. I wore it on a chain. I'm sure she saw it. She must have wondered."

"I've not seen this. Do you have it still?"

"I removed it before I married you."

"Good."

They spent a final quiet moment at the grave. She knelt and put her palm to the earth, feeling its warmth and thinking of Gouverneur.

"Do you honestly believe the truth is overrated, husband?" she asked as he helped her back into the carriage. "Doesn't the Bible teach that the truth will set you free?"

"It does." His hand covered hers on his arm, and she welcomed the warm confidence that had drawn her to him in the first place. "But when it comes to the past histories of men and women, adults, who have found happiness together later—as we have done—I believe that the only truth we need is how we feel about each other today and tomorrow. Come, my love. Let us go home to our son."

Phebe

Was the truth overrated? Phebe felt his words shift and settle even as her mind's eye still pictured the tiny skeleton sheltering amongst the roots of that old pine tree. She thought it was. It was time to make peace with all of it. With what was known and what was not. With what she'd said, and not said, on her return to Morissania a year earlier.

Syphax had been blunt.

"Rachel's child you heard of? It was Johnson's. Pale, yes. But her child all the same."

His words crushed her. For years, she'd hugged onto hope that Miss Nancy's child still lived. Worse, she'd encouraged the mistress to think it too, been dispatched to Virginia to find her.

Syphax's story was this. Rachel was in the master's study, called the moment Miss Nancy's labor began. Mr. Randolph brought down the child and placed her in a basket of linens. "Rachel was gonna take her out that way, hidden, see, case Sarah Ellis saw her, or one of her girls." He rubbed his chin. "We turned our backs. Rachel starts causing trouble. Miss Nancy's child was early. Rachel was still carrying her own baby. Said where she suppose to hide this child till her time came? Twins suppose to come together. Lord knows what she'd been thinking, that they'd miraculously deliver on the same day?" He rolled his eyes. "We was whispering, hissing, not looking at the little one. Going round in circles. Mr. Randolph sayin' she must take her. Rachel asking where. Me promising to deal with Johnson. Her asking how." His hand went to his mouth. "I have children of my own now. Would do things different. We weren't thinking of the child. I swear, when I turns around and saw those sheets had tumbled on her, had done smothered her? I pulls them off, pulls her out, tries to help her. But she was gone, that little one." His voice sank to a whisper. "She was gone."

"But Mr. Randolph freed Rachel." Phebe heard her own hopelessness. The answer was clear. Rachel's freedom wasn't the price of caring for a child that was not her own. It was the price of her silence that the child had ever been born. Later that day, Syphax drove with Phebe to Bizarre. Showed her the pine tree so she could tell Miss Nancy. Disappointment made the road back to Morrisania long and wearisome.

All she could do was try to mix good news with the bad. No, her child wasn't living, but not cause of no gum guaiacum, not the mistress's fault. An accident. A costly mistake. Nothing she had done. All in the distant past. Miss Nancy's sorrow was real, but the guilt, at least, was gone.

Was it true though, Syphax's story? Was it? Phebe was upstairs that night with Miss Nancy, seeing nothing that Syphax described. She pictured it though. The master's study. The baby, placed in a basket with a weight of linen falling on her tiny face while the adults argued. Sometimes, she pictured it different. Johnson and Rachel had agreed to take a boy. Not an unwanted girl. It wasn't hard to imagine a hand. Sometimes white. Sometimes black. A hand covering a baby's face with soft, white linen. Fingers pressing as Rachel, with her back turned arguing, saw nothing amiss.

Trust Syphax. Trust me, he had said to Mr. Randolph.

Or perhaps not. Perhaps what mattered in the end wasn't what was really true. Perhaps it was only what folks chose to believe that counted. Mr. Morris and Miss Nancy believing in each other. Mr. Dick Randolph believing he'd chosen the wrong wife. Mrs. Randolph believing Mr. Theo the father of her sister's child. Mr. Jack believing the worst of everyone he knew. Cilla believing Mama was doing fine on another plantation, not able to send word. Mama believing Mae and her child had gone to a better place. Miss Nancy believing the child died by accident.

As for Phebe? For the girl who believed she'd never leave Tuckahoe? She believed she was at peace with it. She believed she was ready. Ready to go home—to Morrisania and Isaac.

The journey from Virginia was smoother this time. None of them looked back.

THE END

Historical Afterword

Nancy Randolph was born in 1774 and grew up on the Tuckahoe Plantation, not far from Richmond. After her mother's death and her father's remarriage to Gabriella Harvie, Nancy went to live on the Bizarre Plantation with her older sister, Judy, and Judy's husband, Dick Randolph. In October 1792, there was a disturbance overnight when the family was visiting friends at Glentivar. Enslaved workers reported finding the body of a White infant — or at the very least, signs of a birth and blood — on a pile of shingles near the house. Gossip quickly spread across Virginian society. The Tuckahoe family turned their backs on Dick Randolph, and he and his stepfather, St George Tucker, decided to force a hearing at the Cumberland County courthouse to clear his name. He was represented by two luminaries — John Marshall and Patrick Henry — and acquitted. I have kept as close to the remaining records of this event as possible, including the evidence given by Patsy Jefferson, Nancy's Aunt Page and the Harrisons.

The family returned to Bizarre. Dick died only a few years later, and Nancy remained on the plantation with her sister until 1806. From then until her marriage to Gouverneur Morris in 1809, Nancy's life was full of hardship. In 1815, the illness of her nephew, Tudor, allowed for some thawing of the often very difficult relationship between the sisters, but Jack (better known in American history as John Randolph of Roanoke), Dick's younger brother, bore a strong grudge against Nancy. His wild accusations and her rebuttal really happened, although they took place over an exchange of lengthy letters, rather than the in-person confrontation I've presented here. All the evidence suggests Nancy and Gouverneur Morris had a happy marriage, and his connection to Sarah Morton, whose sister's relationship and suicide was recounted in William Hill Brown's 1789 novel, *The Power of Sympathy*, encouraged me to believe he would be sympathetic to Nancy about the scandalous rumors in her past.

What really happened at Glentivar remains a mystery. In an oblique letter written in 1815, Nancy admitted to having had a child in 1792. And while she claimed the child was Theo's, his illness and death in February 1792, coupled with her steadfast insistence on Dick's perfections and her care for his reputation, suggest otherwise. In other letters, she describes Dick's visit to her room and his disappointment in his marriage to her sister. The more I considered Nancy's pregnancy, the more I imagined the pressure building over what would happen when the child was born.

John Marshall's notes on Richard Randolph's court appearance include two references to Nancy having a maid with her, both at Bizarre and Glentivar. In Cynthia Kleiner's excellent book, *Scandal at Bizarre*, she makes three mentions of Nancy having a maid named Phebe who was with her during her difficult days in Richmond and Newport, Rhode Island. In a letter to St George Tucker, one of many held in a collection at the College of William and Mary, Nancy talks of a cold she and "old Phebe's granddaughter" are suffering. In another, she talks about a maid called Polly who was with her at Tuckahoe and then Bizarre. It's my invention that Phebe is the granddaughter of Old Cilla at Tuckahoe and that Thomas Mann Randolph gave Nancy ownership of the young girl when she left the family home. While Phebe's part in the story is fictional, I hope her struggles are representative of the challenges faced by enslaved people during this time in history. Being able to fill in the gaps and give voice to those whose stories were not heard or recorded is one of the great pleasures of writing a novel, rather than a history book.

Judy Randolph did free many of the enslaved people at Bizarre, as directed in Dick's will, although it took some years for her to do so. The settlement where Phebe visits Syphax is talked about in detail in Melvin Patrick Bly's book *Israel on the Appomattox*. There's no doubt Judy's life was difficult. I picked up on hints that she may have been pregnant when she and Dick were married and found it easy to imagine that the loss of a child and her isolation at Bizarre might cause her to struggle with depression. Her son, Saint, was profoundly deaf. Nancy's work with him is based on the historical treatment of hearing-impaired people at that time, and Saint did attend a specialist school in England. There's no evidence he was responsible for the fire that destroyed Bizarre in 1813, but he spent some time after that in an asylum in Philadelphia. Tudor was as feckless as his uncle Theo had been. During his illness at Morrisania, he borrowed money that was never repaid and he died in England not long afterward. Judy died in 1816 and was buried at Tuckahoe, although the manner of her death, the funeral and the resolution of the mystery about Nancy's child are all fictional.

There are many famous men in this story, and the historical marker in Farmville, where Bizarre once stood, only mentions the Randolph men and none of the women who lived there. In writing this novel, I have endeavored to keep to the known facts as far as possible, while hoping to do justice to three resilient women and how they might have lived.

Acknowledgements

In terms of the research for this novel, I'd like to thank the staff at all the wonderful properties I was able to visit, particularly at Historic Tuckahoe and the St. George Tucker House in Colonial Williamsburg. I'm grateful for the assistance of staff at the Virginia Museum of History & Culture in tracking down primary sources, as well as at Winterthur Museum, Garden and Library where I was able to read John Randolph of Roanoke's letters to his nephew. Thanks also to Debbie Kellar at my local Chester County library for helping me access some great material about the education of deaf people in the early nineteenth century. Chandlee Offerman, who is working on her own novel set in a similar time/place, has been a wonderful sensitivity reader. Jean Taylor, Zoe Bell, and Jen Blab all helped me enormously as I worked on the drafts of this story. For bringing the book to readers, I'm so grateful to all the team at Lume and Joffe books, and particularly Becky Slorach, Miranda Summers-Pritchard, and Aubrie Artiano. Thanks also to my lovely family. Kids, Chris — you're the best.

Printed in the USA
CPSIA information can be obtained
at www.ICGtesting.com
LVHW030348150524
780341LV00003B/123